The
Real
Deal

The
Real
Deal

CAITLIN DEVLIN

LAKE UNION
PUBLISHING

Text copyright © 2024 by Caitlin Devlin
All rights reserved.

No part of this book may be reproduced, or stored in a retrieval system, or transmitted in any form or by any means, electronic, mechanical, photocopying, recording, or otherwise, without express written permission of the publisher.

Published by Lake Union Publishing, Seattle

www.apub.com

Amazon, the Amazon logo, and Lake Union Publishing are trademarks of Amazon.com, Inc., or its affiliates.

ISBN-13: 9781662520198
eISBN: 9781662518249

Cover design by Heike Schüssler
Cover image: © Brandon Colbert Photography / Getty Images

Printed in the United States of America

For Ella, who has always listened to my stories, and who made me sign a contract at thirteen to secure this dedication.

Most people don't know that Donna was the one who taught me to smoke. It was Howie that first put a spliff to my lips and told me to inhale, but he didn't teach me how. He laughed when I coughed, which I did, every time, and when I complained about the burning feeling he said, 'I'm not baking you brownies, Belle. Sorry.' And took another drag, smoke drifting easily over his knuckles.

Once, in LA, I had an audition for some indie film. I don't remember what it was called – *Knife's Point* or something similar – but they wanted an edgy girl, someone with a bit of grit. Actually, the casting call said 'damaged', which Donna and I interpreted as heavy eyeliner and tights with a ladder in them. The damaged girl was called Velma, like in *Scooby Doo*, and she had a twelve-line monologue about jacking off her teacher. And she was a smoker.

'Have you ever smoked?' asked Donna, lighting the cigarette on her deck and handing it out to me.

'No,' I lied. 'Never.'

At around eight every evening on Donna's deck it became vibrantly orange, the light hovering low and close to us, so that the orange was hazy and a little dusty. A perfect tangerine of a sun rippled in the centre of the pool. There wasn't much of a view of anything from her back garden, tall trees blocking our line of sight at every angle. I liked this because it meant that nobody had much of a view of us. At that moment, it really did feel like nobody. I knew this wouldn't make the edit.

'Hold it between two of your fingers,' said Donna. She moved them for me, one over, one under. Red eyes winked at us from the patio table and the roof of the pool house. 'That's good.' Her voice, crackling like an old radio, took on a note of laughter. 'You don't need to look scared of it.'

I made myself laugh with her. 'Do I look scared?'

'Like cancer's going to jump up out of it and bite you. It's just for the part.'

'They won't make me smoke in an audition, will they?'

'No,' she said, 'but when you get it, and you will, you don't want to have a coughing fit on set. Besides,' she added, 'you can always tell by looking at a young girl whether or not she knows how to smoke.'

The house was a little way out from the centre of LA but it wasn't far from a main road, so that beeps and honks and the shouts of taxi drivers became as much a part of my waking and sleeping hours as they had in London. They buzzed like cicadas in the background as Donna gently cupped my small hand in her slender one and raised the cigarette, still held between my two fingers, to my bottom lip.

'Gently inhale,' she said. 'Hold it for a second. Exhale.' I inhaled as gently as I could. 'No,' she said, 'not enough. Try again. Slowly, but be sure of yourself.'

It burned, but not necessarily in a bad way. I coughed, but only a little.

'Not bad!' said Donna. She gave me a little round of applause, nodding her head so that her earrings jangled. 'Not bad at all. We'll make damaged goods of you yet.'

Through the burnt-orange dusk, the red eyes sparkled.

Reunion special

Everyone always wants to know what I'm doing now. The nicer voices say it like that – 'What is Belle from *The Real Deal* doing now?' in loopy font, sometimes over an out-of-date photo of me shyly waving. The other voices ask it differently. 'What happened to Belle from *The Real Deal*?' There's always a photo of me on these ones. I am always crying.

Whoever asks it, however it is phrased, the answer is always the same. Nothing. I am doing nothing now. Nothing happened to me. They conclude it sadly, or gleefully, and then they ask you to subscribe.

'You don't understand the appetite for it,' Rupert says on the phone. 'I mean, Belle, you do this, and who knows? All the world needs is a little reminder of you.'

'Is that what you told Donna the first time around?'

He laughs. Rupert has always been remarkably good at laughing through his discomfort. 'Yes, more or less.'

'Well then.'

'Well, it was true, wasn't it? We put her back on the map.' A pause. 'It's hardly our fault she sort of . . . dropped off it again.'

I want to ask if this is the kind of sensitivity I can expect throughout the experience, but I already know the answer. Besides, Jane is already watching me closely from the kitchen table, Biology homework forgotten and a cheese sandwich held halfway to her mouth. I stick my tongue out at her and she reciprocates, but she still looks concerned. A small piece of grated cheese falls onto the front of her PE top.

'I just don't really want to drag it all up,' I say into the phone, gesturing to Jane to brush off the front of her top. She looks down, surprised. Her messiness definitely comes from Cameron's side. Mum and I were always neat to a fault.

'That's understandable,' says Rupert, and his voice dips lower, into the register he uses to show faux concern. It's so familiar that if Jane hadn't been watching, I might have shivered. 'But we can proceed gently.'

'So we don't have to talk about it.'

Another pause. 'Belle, I'm going to be straight with you,' says Rupert. 'We can't do this special and not talk about it. But we *can* be delicate.'

'Do *I* have to talk about it?'

'We can negotiate on that. *We* have to cover it, certainly, but that could be done with witnesses and news stories. No one has to ask you about it directly, if that's what it takes.' He waits. 'Belle? How does that sound?'

'What's the money like?'

He laughs. 'That's what I always liked about you. You're all business.'

'Well?' I know the number I'm expecting him to say. It's double.

'That's what the other girls are getting, at least,' he says. 'But I won't bullshit you. We'd pay what we needed to. You're our most valuable player. And like I said, this is going to be huge.' He quietens. 'Belle, I was so sorry to hear about Sofie.'

'Thanks.' It's not as if he could say anything different, of course, but it's still strange to hear. He never liked her.

'I keep thinking about that little baby she went home to have. It'd be what, ten now? Your little brother or sister?'

'Eleven. She just started Year Seven.' Jane is surprised to hear herself referenced. She drops another bit of cheese.

'And what does Sofie's partner do?'

'He runs a bookshop.'

'In London?'

'Bethnal Green.'

'Lovely,' said Rupert. 'Sounds idyllic. You'll think about it, won't you? Like I said, we'd pay what you want. And all the other girls are going to be involved.'

'Even Paget?'

'Well, the other four. I know they'd love to see you again.' He knows no such thing. He adds, because he's probably aware I don't believe him: 'Faye said as much when we spoke.'

I still don't say anything. There is a commotion behind me as Jane's pen rolls off the table and under the fridge. She scrambles for it. I hear the sandwich hit the floor. '*Belle*,' she hisses. I am very still, frozen in the half-light of the kitchen.

'Please think about it,' says Rupert. 'The world deserves to have Belle back on their screens. Have your people call my people and they can negotiate to your heart's content.' He hangs up before I have a chance to tell him that I don't have any people, any more. It's just me.

I tell Cameron that the money isn't what sways me.

'Then why?' Cameron asks me as the three of us sit outside on our camping chairs, Jane eating the chocolate off a Magnum.

'Closure,' I say. 'I suppose.'

This isn't a lie, not entirely. Closure sounds nice. And Faye wants to see me. That sounds nice too.

But it is the money, really. Mum's life insurance and Cameron's savings from his years in law have so far been enough to sustain a bookshop that struggles month on month to keep afloat, but they won't be enough forever. I don't want Cameron to give up the bookshop. And I don't want Jane to notice.

Jane is very small and slight, like I was at her age. She has Cameron's tanned skin and Mum's sharp nose and big eyes. She's a very pretty child. My throat seizes every time someone's head turns to look at her in the street. She thinks that this is because I am scared of paedophiles, which is the kind of thing that is hilarious when you're eleven and feel invincible.

She plays netball and hockey and shows no interest in acting or singing, but she loves to dance. I try to be happy for her when I watch her, sat in the audience with my hands curled in a claw shape under the chair and Cameron periodically whispering, 'You okay, Belle?' into my ear. I can't always manage it. She doesn't like me to come to her shows any more because sometimes I cry and it unsettles and embarrasses her.

Jane hates her name. 'Yours is so pretty. Mine's so flat and nothing.' I tell her again how carefully Mum chose her name, but it's hard to make her understand why.

She's never watched the show, even though she's asked me many times if I'll show her an episode. I'm not stupid – I know that any day now she could look it up online and watch it all in secret under her duvet. I'm just waiting for her to figure it out. I hope it takes her a while.

Before Mum died, she made us promise to be there for each other. I am there for Jane by being hypervigilant, conscious of any and all possible threats to her person, to her mind, to her innocence. Jane is there for me by letting me hold her hand through her wonderfully normal eleven-year-old life. I'm not always sure which of us is raising the other.

Rupert tells me that the special is going to be called *The Real Deal: Ten Years On*, to mark the anniversary of the final episode. I ask Rupert if we'll all be meeting up before filming starts, but of course he says no.

'And obviously I can't stop you, but I'd rather you didn't reach out ahead of time. We want to see all the electricity of that first reunion!'

I sit on my bed for half an hour after receiving this email and stare at the wall, until Jane knocks on my door and offers me a pouch of chocolate raisins. We eat them together in silence. After a while she says, 'Do you want me to come with you next week?'

'You've got school.'

'You seem scared,' she says.

'You seem like you're trying to get out of school.'

She grins. 'Belle, more than one thing can be true at the same time.'

She's much funnier than I was at eleven. She's sharply observational and very quick with her words, and she has far more confidence. In some ways she reminds me of Kendra, or at least, the parts of Kendra that I always secretly admired. But sometimes I imagine her being observed like that, the weight of all those eyes on her, trying to stay one step ahead of the adults around her, ducking and weaving to avoid their disappointment, and the image leaves me shaken. I can't see how her small frame could stand it.

The week before, Roni is on an American talk show. She wears a floor-length purple dress with a long slit and her hair is in lots of small braids with purple flowers scattered amongst them. She looks like a princess. She and the host talk about the second season of her show, and the film she's just finished making where she and an ex-pro-wrestler rob an art gallery, and then he tells her, 'Now, you actually started in the world of reality TV!' as if she doesn't know.

'I did!' she laughs. If there's any weariness in it, I'm probably imagining it. The host pulls out a picture of her in her black leotard, her arm around Kendra's waist. An *aw* from the audience.

'So that's you and Kendra Hale,' says the host, 'who was also on the show.'

'Yes, there we are. We were babies.'

'How old are you there?'

'Twelve,' she says, with another white smile.

'Just twelve. And now it's almost been ten years since the show ended. How do you feel about that?'

'I feel old,' she laughs, her hand on his arm.

'Oh, stop it,' he says.

'I do!' She laughs again. She has a perfect laugh: controlled, cheerful, a little throaty. You can tell she's worked on it. 'But, no, it was a complicated time. It was a baptism of fire, really, but it gave me a platform, and it gave me the girls . . .'

'You're all still friends?'

'Yes,' she lies, smiling.

'So,' says the host, 'I guess what we're all wondering is, hypothetically, if there were to be a reunion—' Whistles from the crowd. Roni smiles demurely. The host holds his hand up. '*If.* If. I'm not trying to get sued.' The studio laughs. 'Would that be something you'd be up for?'

'I mean,' she says, 'never say never.' More whistles. 'It's a complex one,' she says. 'Anyone who's seen the show, you know that's true. We all had a hard time at points. Some of us more than others.' She's not even looking into the camera but it's like I can feel her eyes on me, suddenly. The host rearranges his features, appropriately sombre. 'It's a complex one,' she repeats. 'But no matter what else there was on that set, there was so much love. We had so much love for each other.'

It's almost like I can see Rupert standing just off camera, mouthing the words.

She's been asked about it before. They both have, her and Kendra. Kendra especially, because her PR team is worse – Roni's seem to mostly axe the questions ahead of time. *What really happened in that final episode?* Whenever Roni is asked a variation of this question, she'll say, 'I mean, I think we all saw what happened. My heart really goes out to Belle. I really just wish healing for her.'

'I don't know,' Kendra will say. 'I wasn't there. You'd have to ask Belle.'

They have asked me. In the weeks after the final episode aired, press would call my home phone number and wait outside my door sometimes, asking me. *What happened? How are you doing now? Do the two of you still speak?* My social media comments became so repetitive that I eventually shut down all of my accounts. Into my silence, they spoke. I'm sure some of them spoke with nuance, but the voices I saw screamed with deafening certainty. *ABUSE ON THE SET OF THE REAL DEAL* read the tabloids. It wasn't phrased like a question. A Twitter account popped up – @therealdealtruth – supposedly to share 'evidence', but all they posted were compilations of clips from the show set to sad music, my micro-expressions slowed to a fifth of their original speed. There was much debate in the comment sections of these compilations as to whether this was proof of anything or not. Nonetheless, they inspired copycats.

Then the think pieces rolled in. First online blogs run by individual freelancers, and then *Variety, Cosmopolitan, The Washington Post*. Our phone rang so much that Mum redid our answering machine message with an additional warning: 'Journalists will be hung up on or sworn at, depending on what kind of day I'm having.' The few times I did pick up and heard an unfamiliar voice say, 'Hi, is that Belle Simon?' I would stay silent on the phone until they gave up. 'Hello?' they would say. 'I'd just love to talk, if you had a moment.' One man persisted for so long that I sat the phone down on the sofa beside me and painted my nails, listening as his polite frustration become steadily less polite.

When I wouldn't talk, they talked without me. The conversation closed with me on the outside of it. Like the rest of the world, I was a spectator. 'What *The Real Deal* can teach us about the warning signs of abuse,' they wrote. 'Why Belle Simon from *The Real Deal* has never been a villain,' they wrote. 'How Belle Simon's story on *The Real Deal* is helping Gen Z learn about power dynamics,' they wrote. It was scary, to let go of the reins and let them all run with it, but it was better than trying to explain it all myself. The details didn't matter so much to me. Not whilst everyone was speaking about me with so much warmth.

Within a year, it was no longer a matter of speculation. Nothing was up for debate. Which suited me fine because no one felt the need to ask me anything, any more.

We're shooting at a studio in Soho, which I'm grateful for. I know we'll be heading back to the Southbank at some point but perhaps even Rupert and Fred recognise that we all need that chance to acclimatise. To slowly lower ourselves into the water.

Jane helps me lay out my outfit the night before. We've been told to keep it casual but I can't help thinking that maybe this is a trick, a way to make me look like I'm doing worse than the others when they show up in cocktail dresses. With Jane's help I find the perfect compromise – a slightly slouchy but still tailored jumpsuit and low heels which Jane, with all the authority of an eleven-year-old social media addict, calls 'day to night'.

We stand at the foot of my bed and stare down at the jumpsuit like we're examining a body.

'I think it's good,' says Jane.

I don't say anything. I feel her skinny arms go around my waist, head pressed into the crook of my elbow. She doesn't know why I'm scared but I can feel that she doesn't like it. It must be hard for her, not knowing and feeling like she can't ask.

'Hey,' I say, squeezing my fingers into her side. She wriggles. 'Come here.' We sit beside each other on the bed, careful to avoid the jumpsuit. 'What do you know about what's happening tomorrow?' I ask.

She tilts her head at me. 'Um,' she says, with emphasis, to let me know that she thinks I'm being weird, 'I know you're going to film a TV show.'

'Do you know what the show is?'

'The one you used to be on.'

'Do you know what it's called?'

'*The Real Deal*,' she says, biting the skin around her thumbnail.

I've never actually heard her say the name of the show before, but of course she knows it. Even if she's never looked it up, friends will have told her. Maybe they've even shown her a clip or two – although the show is not as easy to access as it used to be. A journalist who I've never met started a conversation online a while ago about the ethics of having *The Real Deal* available on streaming services.

Anyone who knows anything about what went on behind the scenes on this show recognises that this is not entertainment, she wrote. *This is people's childhood trauma you are consuming whilst you make your lunch or brush your teeth. Imagine being one of these girls and having these clips come up on your social media feed day after day.*

She'd avoided naming any of us, but I was the one that got tagged, over and over, as the post circulated on social media. The result of it was that the official YouTube page for the show was taken down (*We hear you and we're sorry,* wrote some PR rep) and most channels stopped airing reruns. But it isn't as if the show is gone. A quick search can turn up any scene you want, and in many ways the censorship has only made *The Real Deal* more salacious viewing. It's more than possible that Jane has come across it, especially now that she has her own laptop and phone.

But when I ask her if she's ever seen it, she shakes her head. 'Do you know what it's about?' I ask.

'It's like, a dancing school, right? And you're taught by that woman—'

'Donna.'

'—and she wanted to make you all famous.'

She looks at me, like it's a question. I pull up the Wikipedia page on my phone. 'Here.'

She takes the phone cautiously, but I can see the eagerness in her face as she starts to read.

> The Real Deal *is a British docuseries that aired from 2009 to 2014. It follows six children placed in an elite performing arts programme under the mentorship and tutelage of actress, singer and dancer Donna Mayfair. Set first in London, England and later in Los Angeles, USA, the show follows the girls as they attend their first auditions, book their first jobs, and build their careers.*

The show is often credited with reviving Mayfair's career as well as breaking out performers such as Veronica Owayale and Kendra Hale. Due to backlash online, particularly surrounding the fifth and final season, reruns of the show now air post-watershed only.

I see Jane's fingers lingering over the 'Controversy' link in the menu and I take my phone back from her, gently but firmly. 'There you go.'

'So all six of you are . . . what? Going back to school?'

'Five of us. We're just talking. Remembering stuff.'

'Can I watch it?'

'I don't think it'll be very interesting for you.'

'Are you nervous?'

'Probably a bit,' I say. 'I haven't seen most of these girls in for ever.' I'd run into Hannah in King's Cross a few years ago. We'd had a brief, awkward hug and a promise to stay in touch before she ran to catch a train. She still had trouble meeting my eyes. She'd been doing her masters at UCL and she was heading north again for the holidays, to see her sister, she said.

How is your sister? I asked.

Oh, she said, *she's making pottery now. You know Faye.* I looked it up online later, half disbelieving, but she'd been telling the truth – she had an online storefront full of dishes and ceramics. I almost bought a glazed turquoise mug, before I thought better of it. It wouldn't have gone with anything else in the house.

Cameron makes me pancakes in the morning and sits with me whilst Jane gets ready for school. Before she leaves, she runs into the kitchen, hockey stick slung over her shoulder, and kisses me on the same cheek three times in short, sharp pecks. I squeeze her ribs on the third time and she wriggles away, brandishing the hockey stick at me.

'Good luck,' she says.

'I could have sworn I sent her to a state school,' says Cameron, as Jane rushes off to get her rucksack.

'You did.'

'That hockey stick makes her look like she's off to Malory Towers.'

'They play hockey at state schools too,' I say.

'I wish they'd stop.'

She turns back again at the door, to wave at me. Behind her, through the open doorway, I see a dark shadow pull up behind her.

'Car's here,' says Cameron, who is watching too.

He waits for me to gather my things, to collect myself, and then he hugs me tightly, a bone-splintering, tear-stinging kind of hug, and I know he's hugging for two.

Drivers sometimes tell me that they recognise me from TV. They mostly aren't in the show's target demographic, but occasionally one will take me by surprise. Then I'll have to keep the conversation on track for the length of the drive, distracting them with the celebrities I've met and the TV shows I've been on, so that no one asks what they all really want to ask.

This one looks at me in the mirror and opens his mouth.

'Do you want the radio on?' he asks instead. I tell him no, thank you, and then regret it. 'Soho?' he asks. 'Doing anything fun?'

'No,' I say.

He leaves me be after that. Silently, I watch the familiar silhouettes of buildings grow and gather over the river. It's rush hour and movement on the roads is steady but ominously slow. I said I'd never complain about London traffic again after LA. Now I find myself wishing I'd just taken the tube.

My finger moves over the hills and dips of my knuckles, back and forth, like waves coming and going. I make myself remember what I did on each of my birthdays from five to twenty-five, and then on Jane's from one to eleven. I count up all the countries I have visited. I recite the entirety of *The Sound of Music* in my head (safe, because I never got cast in that one).

'Here we are then,' says the driver.

The Soho studio is a large, square building, much squatter than the place on the Southbank with all its many stairs. No part of it is familiar to me. This is comforting. An assistant with a clipboard is hovering on the pavement. I don't know her either. She smiles at me. I smile back, my hand on the handle, taking a deep breath in through my nose.

We drive past, the assistant following us with her eyes. Alarmed, I look up at the driver in the mirror. He's glancing down at his phone.

'Sorry,' he says. 'We're just going to do another couple of loops.'

'Is something wrong?'

'It's all good,' he says. 'They're finishing up another shot.'

Someone else is arriving first. I turn back, staring through the back window. A black car, much larger than this one, with tinted windows, has pulled up on the pavement. A security guard exits from the front seat to open the door. We turn the corner before I get a chance to see who steps out.

'Was that Roni?' I ask the driver. 'Veronica, I mean?'

'I'm not sure,' he says. 'Sorry. I only know what I've told you.'

'Am I supposed to be the last one in there?'

'I don't know the order. I just know that you're next.'

He's probably lying. They've probably told him not to tell me. Shakily, I settle myself in my seat and start on Act Two of *The Sound of Music*.

We do another two laps before we finally pull up on the pavement outside the studio, now empty again save for the unfamiliar assistant in her black headset.

'Hi, Belle,' she says, shaking my hand. She looks younger than me by at least a couple of years. This is briefly disorientating. 'Sorry about all the faff. We're so pleased to have you.'

'Pleased to be here.'

'Just give me one minute.' She turns away from me. 'She's here,' she says, into the headset.

No name. I'm last.

There's Rupert, suddenly appearing from seemingly nowhere. I'm disassociating. *Focus.*

'Belle!' He gives me an unasked-for hug. I'm stiff in his arms. 'Goodness,' he says, grasping my hand and stepping back to take a good look at me. 'Aren't you grown up? Fred won't believe his eyes.'

'Hi, Rupe. You look well.' He looks old.

'We're ready for you in there,' he says. 'Everyone's so excited.'

To see each other, I think, sure. Then I force myself to remember what Rupert said on the phone: Faye's looking forward to it. Faye wants to see me.

I've never been brave enough to call her. I suppose I was always waiting for some external force to place us in a room together. And this is it.

'You okay?' asks Rupert, hand on my arm. 'You want some water?'

'So I just . . . walk in? That's it?'

'Just walk in and say hello. We've got a nice set up, there's some drinks . . .' He waves a hand. 'Just catch up! It's a chill one today.'

'Okay.' I brush him off and flex my fingers. He leads me to a small red door at the side of the building, his hand firm in the small of my back as he opens it and pushes me forward. 'Go on!'

And there it is.

It's a shoulder-operated Canon held by a grip in black who I don't recognise. The sound guy beside him looks vaguely familiar, holding his boom aloft. My eyes dart over them both for only a second before the muscle memory kicks in and I carry myself as if I'm alone, as if I'm not being watched, looking anywhere except at that dark shape just in the corner of my eye.

We move down a short corridor, turning the corner. Two double doors stand open at the end of it. The space inside is big and bright. I can see the edge of a pot plant, fairy lights. A velvet sofa comes into view, a glass of prosecco on a small wooden table beside it. A hand reaches out to pick it up. A thin hand, pale and small, with silver jewellery tinkling against the glass. It rings like a doorbell.

In my head, I am still singing *The Sound of Music.* I'm midway through 'The Lonely Goatherd', which is funny, although I can't show it. The camera can't see my lips turn up. The camera can't see my eyes crinkle.

I don't think I can do this.

Kendra notices me first. She's settled in an armchair, legs crossed, drink in hand. She looks at home. She doesn't change position when her eyes land on me, but she stiffens just for a second, cold like stone. It takes her a second to take me in – the shorter, darker hair, the wider face. Then she smiles, slowly, and her other hand comes to the base of her champagne glass.

'Belle,' she says.

'Hi, everyone.'

The sisters, their backs to me, turn to stare. I can't look at them. Roni is sat on Kendra's right, impossibly beautiful in a lavender suit. She's openly frowning.

They didn't know I was coming. That's why I was last. Not Roni, arguably the show's biggest success, but me.

I'm the twist.

'Oh my god,' says Kendra. She laughs.

I don't want to be the twist. I can't do this.

But there are two cameras in the room with me now, one very still, one circling, moving round to capture the sisters' faces with the boom stalking just behind. Somewhere else in this building, down the corridor or on the floor below, there is a room of people watching us on monitors or sketching plans for upcoming scenes based on an energy, a hint of tension, an interesting look at the wrong moment. In the doorway at the far end of the room, two dark shapes in suits stand side by side and watch us with a cool, passive interest.

I force myself to look at the sisters. Hannah is still wide-eyed in her disbelief, hair tucked behind her ears and an expression of surprise so genuine I can suddenly see the nine-year-old in her again. Faye is calm. Gentle, silvery, unflappable Faye. Very slightly, she nods at the empty armchair.

My eyes on her, I take my seat.

The audition

One of the things Donna told me that she liked about me very early on is that I always said yes. When she sent me into auditions and they asked if I could speak French or ride a horse, I would say yes. When she asked me if I wanted to do this guest appearance or take that meeting, I would say yes. The other girls would dither sometimes, or object, or complain, but I would always agree. Verbally. With a clear 's' on the end of the word.

When other people started to notice it – 'You're so game, Belle. That's what I like about you,' a director told me once – they would credit Donna's training. And while it's true that Donna taught me a lot, that's one thing she didn't give me, that want to please. I was just made like that. I think I came into the world nodding.

I said yes to everything that everyone asked me that whole morning. To an assistant running round with bottles of water – 'Thirsty?' she asked, and I nodded, unscrewing the top of the bottle. When one of the girls asked everyone if they'd worked professionally before, I said yes, even though it wasn't true. We all did. Only one of us, a willowy thing with silvery-blonde hair and big green eyes, shook her head. She looked surprised.

'I've only sung in talent shows,' she said in a gentle northern accent.

She'd been just a few girls ahead of me in the queue, carrying a stripy crochet bag that looked homemade. I'd seen her as we joined at the back, chatting softly to her mum and the small girl next to her, her hand reaching intermittently into her crochet bag and reappearing with a chocolate mini egg between its fingers. I wanted to communicate to her now, somehow, that she didn't have to be so honest, that it was probably better not to be. *Just say yes.* She looked at me, as if she'd heard me. I looked away.

We were stood in a circle, the kind that young girls will always organise themselves into when left alone in a group. A loud red-headed girl had assumed the position of leader and hadn't come up against any resistance. She was busy interrogating us all, pointing at each of us when it was our turn to answer a question. She'd started on where we were from (I'd nodded along to the sounds of unfamiliar London boroughs) and moved onto our résumés. Now it was about how well we danced. Did we all dance? What kind of dance did we do? Were we the best at our respective studios?

Oh, we all said, well, we were very good. Probably the best, yes. We did everything – tap, modern, ballet, even gymnastics.

The red-headed girl pointed at the silver-haired one. 'You?'

She grimaced. 'I'm alright. Good at ballet. Rubbish at tap. Can't do any gymnastics other than a cartwheel.'

'Why are you here then?' asked the red-headed girl.

Outside the window, girls and their mothers were still joining the queue, impossibly long now, snaking down the south bank of the Thames. They were queuing in the hall as well, and up the stairs – we could hear their chatter, although we couldn't see them. We were held between two sets of double doors, in a bright, high-ceilinged dressing room with wooden benches that ran along the walls. Our mothers sat and made conversation as we stood in our circle at the end of the room. I stared out of the window at the endless line and waited for the silver-haired girl to redeem herself.

'I can sing,' I heard her say. 'And I act alright. And I've got a face for TV.'

A surprised laugh rang around the circle. It didn't faze her. In fact, she smiled.

'That's what people tell me,' she said.

'Who? Your mum?'

She shrugged. 'Everyone.'

The red-headed girl looked at her for a second, deciding what to make of this self-assurance. Then she said, 'Well, I can't dance. I'm rubbish. I'll probably get cut in the dancing part.'

The double doors opened. We turned as one to see girls pouring out, each talking softly to their mothers. Some of them were smiling, some trembling. Some were crying their eyes out. One clung to her mother's arm and wept with an effort that bent her double, like a sapling battling a storm. Her mother's fingertips were black with her daughter's mascara. There was a funny feeling in my knees. I looked for Mum on her wooden bench, and she gave me a thumbs up. I could see that her hands were shaking.

'Group C?' said the producer, holding open the door. 'We're ready for you.'

We surged en masse towards the double doors, passing by the huge Georgian windows. Eight stories below, the enormous queue was still snaking down the riverbank. I'll remember that sight for ever. The shiny tops of hundreds of heads of hair pulled back into tight ballet buns. Girl after girl after girl, holding tightly to her mother's hand.

In the first twelve years of my life, my dad turned up exactly four times. Twice drunk, once with a birthday present, and once at my

21

school, which caused quite a stir and kept me in good supply of attention for about a fortnight. This was lucky timing as it was just before my eighth birthday party and, since I was the celebrity of the moment, every kid in my class wanted to come. I got twice the birthday presents I usually did. Good ones too, since all the mums felt sorry for me. Later in my life, social media would speculate that my dad's impact on me had been damaging, that it had created in me some kind of bottomless appetite for adult validation. The truth is that after that birthday party I hardly ever thought about him, except for just before my ninth birthday party when I hoped he would do it again. He didn't. My presents that year were okay.

These were the only four exciting things that happened to me in twelve years. Mum and I lived in the Cotswolds. We had a small farm, which was really just a field, slanted up the side of a hill so that we couldn't really use it as a garden other than for sledging when it snowed or the occasional lopsided picnic. My best friend at school, Freja, had a house in the middle of town with a neat little postage stamp garden – three times smaller than ours, but I envied it because it was flat enough for a trampoline.

'Champagne problems, Belle,' said Mum, which confused me. Freja's family went to Disneyland for their holidays. We went to Lyme Regis.

We lived next door to a much larger farm, not passed down like ours was from Grandad and Grandma but bought and done up, because Dave and Rebecca Malone wanted Stella to experience country living. It had a trellis in the front yard and a water feature in the garden, and a paddock in which Stella rode her horse. Stella was a year older than me and could just about remember what it had been like to live in London. She would talk about Christmas shopping on Oxford Street and shows in the West End with a languid air that verged on boredom, as if these were the most mundane, commonplace experiences a person could have.

Stella had been in Group A.

'I want Stella to be one of the first ones she sees,' Rebecca had told Mum at the kitchen table last week.

'Is that better, do you think?'

'Oh, sure. This way, every girl that comes after her has to measure up. She's the standard.'

'Ah,' said Mum. 'Clever.'

'So, we'll be going up the night before to stay with my niece in Hyde Park Mansions, and then it's up at five am and on the tube to Embankment—'

When Mum closed the door behind Rebecca Malone, she stood very still with her hand on the handle for a few seconds and her head lowered. Then she turned back to me and said: 'Belle, that woman is insane.'

'I know,' I said.

'I must be insane too.'

She said it again when she saw the price of the train tickets, and again when we joined the queue behind already at least a hundred girls, even though we were still there two hours before the call had told us to be. 'I must be insane.' Twisting her watch around her knobbly wrist.

'Sofie,' my drama teacher had told her a couple of weeks before. 'You'd be crazy not to send her.'

I was tidying up the prop cupboard, trying to pretend I wasn't listening as they stood by Ms Winnow's desk, staring at her phone screen. Even over the clatter of props I could hear the sound of Mum twisting her watch under her sleeve. The swoosh of cotton sleeve on suede strap made me shudder like I did when I raked my fingernails through carpet.

'She's perfect for it,' said Ms Winnow.

'What is it they want?'

'Girls like her.'

'I mean exactly.'

Ms Winnow had already printed out the article. There was a rustle of paper as she handed it to Mum. 'They're looking for girls aged between ten and thirteen who can act, sing and dance.'

'Oh, well,' said Mum, sounding relieved. 'Belle can't sing.'

'She's not bad. With a little training she could probably be okay.'

'You can't train someone to sing. You can either sing or you can't.'

I dropped a retractable knife down the back of one of the drawers and jammed it closed anyway. No one was paying attention to me.

'She really isn't bad,' said Ms Winnow. 'And she's been dancing since she was four—'

'She's stopping that,' said Mum sharply. 'I can't be doing it any more – so much money, and they expect you to be at every show to do their hair and you have to help find all their costumes . . .' I'd heard this rant before. It was full of empty threats.

'But that's the thing – they'd do all of that for you, and she'd get the best training. And it might mean an acting career for her.'

'I don't know if I want her to have an acting career,' said Mum.

'She's really very good. Look how good she was in *The Secret Garden*.'

'That was local theatre.'

'Still, lots of other kids auditioned. They didn't get chosen.'

'I don't want her to be an actress. Name a stable actress. Actually . . .' She was getting louder. Laughter entered her voice, to offset the volume. 'Name a stable reality TV star!'

'It's a docuseries.'

'It's all the same shit.'

I leant further into the props cupboard, scrabbling around among the Grecian masks. I could still hear her.

'I've always supported her interests. But local theatre is as far as it goes.'

'Sofie, you aren't realising what this could mean for Belle.'

'I'm realising. And I'm not turning my twelve-year-old into a junkie over a hobby she's reasonably good at.'

'You're jumping to a lot of conclusions—'

'I'm not jumping to shit. There's a pattern in that industry.'

'There's no guarantee that she'd even get cast.'

'Then why bother? BELLE!' I jumped. My head bumped against the top shelf. A Grecian mask fell onto my foot. 'Are you digging to fucking Narnia?'

'Sorry.' I could see Ms Winnow flinch at the swear word.

Mum looked at me for a second, fingers very still on either side of her watch strap. I set the Grecian mask back on its shelf, lining the others up beside it. Behind me, I felt her sigh.

'We'll talk about it,' she said. 'But—'

'Please do.' Ms Winnow lowered her voice again. 'Sofie, she's such a cute little personality. She'd be killer on TV.'

We drove back home down winding roads, fields of rapeseed passing like flashes of yellow light. I wound my window down and watched my face in the wing mirror. It was nice to be thought of as someone impressive enough to be on TV.

'Well?' asked Mum.

'Well?'

'We both know you were listening. You cute little personality you.' She reached out to tickle me under the chin, the car swerving slightly. I batted her off. 'Are you mad at me?'

I pulled at my tights between my thumb and forefinger and released, like firing an arrow. A cloud of dust mushroomed in the low sunlight.

'Christ,' said Mum, glancing over again. 'Those need a wash.' She drummed her fingers on the steering wheel. 'Is this about the swearing? Ms Winnow doesn't mind.'

'I mind.'

'Really?' She glanced at me. 'Alright, I'm sorry.'

'I think I want to do it.'

'Shocker. My twelve-year-old wants to go on TV and be famous.'

'It's just an audition. I think it would be kind of cool, doing a proper audition.'

'Belle, you get stressed going down an escalator.'

I sunk down in my seat, arms crossed.

'You know I'm right.'

'I still want to do it.'

'It's not about whether you want to do it. It's about whether I want you to do it.' A raindrop hit my cheek, and then her hand as it clutched the steering wheel. 'Put your window up. Do you even know who Donna Mayfair is?'

'Sure,' I said, winding my window up. 'She was on *Strictly*.'

'Oh, she *was*. With the Italian guy, right? The one I like?'

'He's old.'

'She made it quite far, I think. Guess she is basically a pro herself.' She tapped my knee. 'Belle, I don't know if it's worth it. Going all the way down to London just so some almost famous woman can tell you that she doesn't think you're very talented. Don't you think that'll hurt your feelings, having someone tell you that?'

'You just told me that.'

'Right. And it hurt your feelings.'

I picked at my tights again, releasing another pretty cloud of dust.

'Stop that,' said Mum. 'Disgusting child.'

'I could handle it. Anyway, Stella Malone's going. I'm better than her.'

'It's a low bar.'

Still sat low in my seat, I smirked.

'Don't be mean,' she said.

'I didn't say anything. *You* said something.'

'See, that's the other possibility,' said Mum. 'Donna Mayfair tells you she thinks you're pretty good and you turn into an arrogant little prick. It's a lose-lose.'

'It's not a lose-lose. If they tell me I'm bad then you'll be there to make me feel better, and if they tell me I'm good then you'll be there to make me feel worse.'

She laughed at that. 'I love your faith in me.'

'Come on, please. It's just an audition.'

'You promise it's not all going to end with you addicted to heroin?' She reconsidered. 'I suppose no one can ever really promise that they're never going to be addicted to heroin.' She reconsidered again. 'Don't do heroin.'

'Wasn't planning on it.'

'No one *plans* on it. That's the whole thing with heroin.'

'*The Secret Garden* was my favourite thing I've ever done.'

'And you were wonderful. Worlds away though.'

'I *really* want to do it.'

She looked across at me. 'You're getting surer by the second.'

I'm sure it wasn't how I remember it. Remembering these things is hard. I really try. I've tried all sorts of things – hypnosis, therapy, now this – but there are still gaps. I think there always will be. And there are changes. Tones that have shifted, faces that have warped. I remember myself as very small, very light, very easily blown in one direction or the other, and I'm sure that isn't true, I'm sure there was more of myself in my actions and my choices than my memory is willing to admit.

And I'm sure that Mum wasn't sad, when she said this: *'You're getting surer by the second.'* I'm sure she didn't grip the wheel and glance over at me, dry-eyed but hoarse-throated, her lips pale. But in my memory, she knows it all, and her entire body is heavy with it. She looks at me. She takes in my small face. She senses that it can't be fought.

'Fuck it,' said Mum. 'Alright. Childhood alcoholism here we come.'

One of the things she would tell me later, over and over, was to remember that none of it really mattered. The things I worried about and cried myself to sleep about and made myself sick over were all trivial, where it counted, and nothing compared to the rewards of a life like mine. She wasn't like Paget's mum Charlene, who spent the first season telling us all that we were the luckiest little girls in the world, and it wasn't that she didn't believe me that it was tough sometimes, because it was tough on her too.

'But it doesn't really matter,' she said. 'Remember that. Any of it. You're going to look back on it one day and remember it all as the most petty, privileged, inconsequential shit.'

She stopped saying it, after a point, after both of us stopped believing that it was true.

The studio was just down the road from the Globe, a fact that was whispered up and down the queue enough times that 'globe' started not to sound like a real word any more. I had never been inside the Globe, but when we walked past it, a round wooden structure by the river, it looked far less impressive than our local theatre. I wasn't the sort of twelve-year-old that knew Shakespeare. I didn't even know any twelve-year-olds like that. I was about to be surrounded by them.

They wore matching dance bras and tiny shorts, even though it was a cold March, and they held shiny plastic wallets that showed their résumé on one side and their smiling headshots on the other. Their mothers carried pink dance bags with their daughters' names stitched in loopy font across the front. Mum placed our plastic Sainsbury's bag between her feet and, whenever the queue made an excited push forward, she shuffled it along without picking it up, like a penguin balancing an egg.

We waited for three hours, inching gradually closer. I could see Mum searching for restaurants on her phone and I was deathly afraid that she'd say, 'Sorry, Belle, but it's not worth it, is it?' and take us to Pizza Express. Every time she started scrolling I stiffened, the sore soles of my feet cramping, but each time she slipped her phone back into her pocket with a sigh and stared straight ahead.

After some time, there was a faint hum of excitement further up the line, crackling down to meet us like a current. A breeze drifted along the riverbank. 'What's happening?' Mum asked, craning her neck. It was a camera. Someone dressed all in black had it mounted on their shoulder and they were moving in a strange little crouched run right down the length of the queue, lens pointed at the waiting girls. They shrieked, beamed, waved their arms. A girl ahead of me even winked. Her mother was pointing to her, mouthing something unintelligible, her arm with its jabbing finger moving back and forth like an animatronic.

Mum's nose wrinkled, but when the camera moved past us she gave my shoulder a little punch.

'What?'

'You didn't do anything.'

I hadn't known what to do. 'It's cringey.'

'Belle,' said Mum, 'what are we even doing here, then?'

And so the next time the camera came bobbing down the line towards us, I smiled, and waved my arms, and tried to look like someone who desperately, desperately wanted to be on TV. It wasn't too hard. Despite how embarrassing it was to admit, or to display, I *desperately* wanted to be on TV.

I wasn't sure where the desire had even come from, but ever since we had first spoken about the audition it had become all-consuming, the only thing I thought about before I went to bed, the thing I daydreamed about as I brushed my teeth and did my hair, and I realised it might actually be the only thing I had ever wanted in my entire life. I wanted to be on TV even more than I wanted to be beautiful.

A girl in a stripy t-shirt and jeans held one of the double doors open. 'We're ready for you,' she said.

Most of us moved cautiously at first, but the red-headed girl sauntered towards the doors as if she was here every other week-end. I imagined threads running between the red-headed girl and me and walked directly behind her, straightening the threads so that my shoulders were pressed down like hers, my neck elongated, my frank gaze on the table in the centre of the dim, wood-panelled room.

A line of white masking tape separated us from them. We stood behind it in rows. The red-headed girl had made her way to the front and the silvery one had drifted up there too. She didn't need to muscle through the other girls – they parted like the sea as she moved. Somewhere at the back, behind rows of girls, I held my chin up and did my best to be seen.

At the front of the room, a man in a black t-shirt and joggers pulled his left arm across his chest, and then his right. He bent down to stretch his thigh and waved at us. Behind him, at a table, sat two men in white shirts and the most beautiful woman I had ever seen in real life. She had deep dimples in her cheeks as she smiled at us, and a cloud of nut-brown hair clipped back at one side with a gold butterfly. Her eyes ran over the lines of girls, singling each of us out in turn with a reassuring nod. When they landed on me, I could only stare back at her, immobile. They were a very light green. I wasn't in the habit of noticing the colour of people's eyes, but hers were so unusual that you couldn't help it. You noticed them darting around; you felt it when they landed on you. It gave the impression that she was seeing more than anyone else in the room, or at least taking more in.

Even if I hadn't recognised her from TV and magazine stands, the excited whispers running round the room would have tipped me off. *That's Donna Mayfair.*

'Okay, Group C,' said the man in joggers, still stretching. 'How's everyone doing? Have you all had something to eat?'

There was a chorus of 'yes' – no mumbling, all with the 's' crisply on the end.

'I haven't,' said the red-headed girl, raising her hand.

The man, now jogging a little on the spot, crinkled his brow in a show of concern. 'Did you want to grab something, sweetie?'

'Oh no, I've got a packed lunch. I just didn't want to dance full out and then barf it up.'

A nervous titter ran through the group. I could see the two men in white shirts exchange an amused glance. Donna Mayfair smiled. It wasn't a half-hearted smile, either – her top lip pulled gently back to reveal a line of perfectly straight, blindingly white teeth. Her dimples deepened even further. She had a beauty spot on her right cheek – it moved as she smiled, rising higher along her cheekbone.

'Good call,' said the man in joggers, with a laugh. 'Okay. Girls, we're going to learn some super simple choreo, and then you'll have eight counts at the end for improv. If you have tricks, we want to see them.'

The mothers were lined up against the back wall on wooden chairs, legs tightly crossed, hands clutching dance bags. The room was dim, the lights trained on the makeshift stage, and I couldn't see Mum's face. Instead, I looked for a splash of orange tucked between two sensible shoes. I breathed out.

The music they played sounded like something you'd hear in a lift or on hold with the bank. I tried to find some kind of centre to it. When we danced, the lines shifted, and I found a space between two girls where I knew they could see me even all the way at the back. I stared at the Sainsbury's bag, just past the gold butterfly above Donna Mayfair's ear. I tried to remember to smile. Cameras passed in front of us, carried on shoulders back and forth, occasionally blocking the splash of orange, but I always found it again.

We took five. Girls walked over to their mothers for water. I stayed behind the masking tape, running the steps, muttering the counts under my breath.

'Okay, girls,' said the choreographer. 'Now without me.'

We went on. I could hear heavy breathing next to me, even over the music. Someone stumbled, knocking into the girl beside her. The hitch of a voice signalled that tears were imminent. I blocked them out. I danced to the orange.

'Good!' said the choreographer. 'That was great, girls! Let's take a break.'

Eager conversation was happening at the table. We were reorganised into one line, sweaty and breathless. The girl on my right was very small, at least two years younger than me, and beside her I felt awkward and gangly. The girl on my left was also shorter than me, and already crying, although she was trying to mask it with tiny, hiccuppy breaths. The woman in the stripy t-shirt gave me a laminated number to hold. *14.* I clutched the edges of it, the plastic cutting into my palms, and tried to breathe normally.

One of the men behind the table pointed at the small girl on my right. 'How old are you?' he asked.

She stiffened. 'Nine.' Her voice was little more than a squeak.

'That's a little younger than we said.'

'She's my sister,' said the silvery girl from somewhere further down the line. I recognised the cool brightness of her voice. 'Mum said if I was doing this then we might as well both come.'

'That's fair enough from Mum. What's your name?'

'Faye. And she's Hannah.'

'Well, Hannah,' said the man, turning back to the small girl. She went stiff again as soon as his eyes landed on her. 'You kept up very well for nine. Wouldn't you say, Donna?'

'Oh, absolutely.'

Her first words. Every spine straightened.

Donna dimpled at the small girl. 'Girls with big sisters are very lucky. You've got an expert to learn from, and you'll just get better and better trying to keep up.'

The small girl said nothing. I guessed from Donna's smiling face that she had nodded.

'You need to speak up, sweetie,' said the man. 'That's important.'

'Sorry,' came the squeaky voice. A pause. She realised they were waiting. 'I'm very lucky.' She sounded like a woodland creature, not like a real little girl at all.

'Right then,' said the first man, peering down the table at the second. 'Fred?'

The second man paused, holding his pen out like a conductor's baton and running it down the line of girls. He scribbled something down on his paper. Then he rattled off a list of numbers. We all peered forward over our laminated signs, to see if it was us.

'If I said your number,' he said, 'then thank you very much, you were great, but we're going to let you go for now. Go sit with your mothers.'

A few girls burst into tears. Most nodded bravely, with wobbly smiles. I stood there for a second. The way he'd said *fourteen,'* so coolly and easily, had knocked me back slightly. I took a step over the masking tape.

'Wait,' said Donna.

The men both turned to her.

'*Not* fourteen,' she said.

'Ah, sorry,' grinned the man with the list. 'You did say.'

'I think you're both mad.'

She smiled, beckoning me over. I bolted from my spot like a nervous pony. 'Hello,' I said, when I was stood in front of her. I'd thought it would make me seem more confident, to speak up, but my voice wavered and I could see a few of the mothers smirking.

Donna laughed. 'Hi! I think you're just gorgeous.'

No one had ever called me gorgeous before. I stared at her.

'Truly. With those big eyes? You see if you don't grow into your features just beautifully in the next few years. And you're a great little dancer. You really projected to the back of the room.' My focus on the Sainsbury's bag had unwittingly paid off. 'What's your name?'

'Belle,' I said.

'Ah. A princess name.'

At twelve, I would have considered myself too old for a compliment like this, but there was something about the way that Donna said it that made me feel delicate and finely worked, like something made of porcelain. I smiled, not because I thought I should, but because I couldn't help it, and she nudged the man next to her.

'You can't tell me she isn't adorable,' she said. 'Belle, Rupe here thinks you're too shy.'

'Oh,' I said. 'I'm not shy.' There wasn't much else that could be said to that.

'I'm just wondering why you stood in the back,' said the man. 'You're one of the best kids here, genuinely, but we're looking for personality just as much as we are talent.'

There was a camera very close to my face.

'Ignore it,' said Rupe. 'Focus on the chat we're having.'

'I guess other people got there first, and I didn't want to push them out of the way.'

'Well, that's very nice. I can tell that you're a very nice little girl. But you know that's a part of this industry, don't you, Belle? Being able to push other nice little girls out of the way?'

The Sainsbury's bag rustled.

'I'm pretty new to this industry,' I said.

There was another titter behind me. I flushed, but for some reason the three people behind the table looked pleased with this response.

'I like that you're not pushy,' said Donna. 'I think that's lovely. But occasionally, in show business, we have to learn to turn that on.' She grimaced. 'I know, I don't like it any more than you do. But it's still something we have to learn. Do you think you can learn it?'

I nodded. Rupe looked unconvinced. Donna smiled at me, but her dimples didn't deepen like they had before. 'Okay,' she said. 'Thanks, Belle.'

She was turning away.

'I can learn it,' I said, 'but I think I'm talented enough that I don't have to push other people out of the way.'

She looked back at me. The other man, the silent one, put down his pen. I heard a snigger from behind me.

'Are you?' said Rupe.

My heart was beating so hard that I felt motion sick. 'I was today.'

A pause. Then Donna laughed again – a louder laugh; a silvery, tinkly laugh that filled the space right up to the high ceiling.

'Thank you, Belle,' she said. 'You can go stand back in line.'

I turned back to face the other girls, who were a mix of jealous and unimpressed. I wasn't sure if that was a good sign or a bad one.

Then Donna's whisper floated over the wooden floor to me, as clear as if she'd breathed it into my ear.

Cast that one.

Reunion special

It's hard not to want to make more money. And sure, I should know better than anyone that the money isn't always worth it, except it is. It's the only thing that moves you forward when you're standing a few feet away from your mark with a thumping heart. And it lets you take things that were hard to do, that challenged you or pushed you or even just made you miserable, and turn them into good.

We've always needed more money. By fourteen I was a fairly overpaid child but there were enough people taking their cut that the money didn't actually go as far as I'd hoped it might, and I always seemed to be just around the corner from the huge cheques that people were forecasting for me. Now, the only money I make is whatever I feel able to accept from Cameron that month for working in the bookshop. God knows that the bookshop itself doesn't bring anything in, and I know that Cameron would give it up and go back to law, if he needed to, except it would break his heart. I don't want that.

And I don't want Jane's university years to be all tins of beans and five-pound club dresses. I want her to be able to study wherever she wants, in a nice flat near a park that she shares with two or three other girls. I want her to be able to stand at a large window sipping tea in silk pyjamas, with nothing to worry about except her essay deadlines and when next to visit home. Later, when she wants a house of her own, I want her to be able to go and choose any that she likes without stressing about how difficult it might be to meet the payments.

I tell Cameron all of this as we sit in our camping chairs, after Jane has gone up to bed.

'That'll ruin her,' he says. 'You spoil her enough as it is.'

I know that Jane won't stay eleven and undented for ever. Life ruins everyone, a little. I want to tell Cameron that in the grand scheme of things, this is a far better way to be ruined.

I don't because I know he'll say, 'Belle, you're not ruined. You're only twenty-six.' And then he'll go upstairs and lie awake and wish that Mum was still here, because he is the nicest man in the world and even he isn't sure what to do with this adult woman who lives in his house and does nothing and wants nothing except to spoil his perfect daughter beyond repair.

But I don't care what Cameron says, at least in this instance. I want Jane to have everything. That's why the only thought that makes me pick my feet up and move towards the velvet armchair between Kendra and Roni is this: *Just think how much they're paying you.*

'Wow,' says Kendra as I sit, in a tone that lets me know what she really wants to say is 'Fuck' only she isn't quite ready yet to start swearing on camera. She'll work up to it. 'We thought you weren't coming.'

'I wanted to see you guys,' I say.

'Clearly.'

I bet they all stood up to hug each other. I bet they brought fluttering hands to their mouths and dabbed at their eyes as they took each other in. The music will change, when I enter. There will be a lingering shot of each of them as they stay glued to their seats, mouths open. It wasn't supposed to go like this. Kendra was always supposed to be the villain.

She's still smiling at me. 'You look different,' she says.

'You guys look great. All of you.' They'll cut this awkwardness out. It's still painful.

'We were wondering,' says Kendra, after a beat, 'before you walked in, if you were still out in LA. You know, if that was why you weren't coming.'

'You know I'm not,' I say.

'Well, yeah, we do now.'

'I mean, you know I left.' Obviously she knows that.

'I think that's the last time I ever spoke to you,' says Kendra, after a quick glance down to her left. 'The night before you left for LA.'

'Yeah. Probably.'

And then it breaks through the silence, that low, gentle voice, slightly deeper now but still the magnetic something that pulls it all back into place.

'It's good to have you back,' says Faye. 'Look at us all. So old now!'

And we laugh, as if we don't feel old at all.

The assistant from the pavement comes to top up our drinks as we start to talk about Roni. 'To think we were all there for your very first opening night,' says Kendra, and I take a big sip of my drink as she reaches forward to squeeze Roni's hand. 'God, Donna couldn't have been more wrong. You really outdid us all in the end.'

So then of course we have to talk about Kendra and her soaps and then her far more legitimate TV and film roles (gently glossing over her very embarrassing EP). I'm doing so much smiling and nodding that I'm feeling a little lightheaded. Faye leads the conversation, so good at asking others about themselves that I start to think there would have been a career in this for her, if her relationship with TV hadn't been spoilt by the time she was fifteen.

'I almost bought one of your pots the other day,' I tell her, when drinks are being topped up for a fourth time. This is the first time any of us have drunk on set together – at least in front of the camera – and there's an air of giddy excitement.

'Almost?' asks Faye.

'I just couldn't decide which.'

'Still hard for you then?' asks Kendra. 'Making your own decisions?'

She's even better than she was when we were younger. It's like she's reading from cue cards. I can feel the excitement at the back of the room. When I was younger, I could tell if Fred and Rupert were getting what they wanted by the minutest sounds, or changes in expression, or shifts in atmosphere. By Season Three I could do it with my eyes closed and my back turned. Funny how it all clicks back into place.

'Belle?'

Her tone is still softly stinging, but when I look at her I can see annoyance on her face. It's not aimed at me. Her hand slips her phone back down the side of the chair, and I realise that I wasn't far off with the cue cards. They're texting her. She repeats the question.

'Yeah,' I say. 'Kind of.'

She's not sure what to do with that, glancing sideways at her phone again for guidance. When nothing happens, she looks back at me. We pause there for a minute, like we're waiting for a battery change.

Then, almost imperceivably, she shrugs, and I smile.

I don't know if Fred and Rupert saw what just happened, or understood it, but I know the girls did.

That's why Hannah starts talking about how she just got her masters and is looking for a job in an auction house. I tell everyone how I'm working part time in my stepdad's bookshop and Faye waxes lyrical about her pottery. We spent all of five minutes on

Roni's career but that small moment shared between Kendra and I, our brief acknowledgement that this is all farce, has given us all the encouragement we need to tank this scene. Here's their reunion. I hope Rupert and Fred are eating their own hair watching it. I'm getting paid either way.

'And what kind of glaze should you use if it's a really warm day?' Roni asks Faye.

Hannah conceals a snort of laughter in her champagne flute.

'Okay!' calls Rupert. He makes his way through the lights and over to us, clapping his hands. His smile is strained. 'We'll call time on today, girls, and give it another go tomorrow.'

'The same scene?' asks Kendra.

'Same scene, which means same clothes, same hair, same everything. There's still a lot of catching up to do!' We're all going to receive instructions later, I think, lists of things we'll have to ask each other. Today was a very small and very temporary victory. Tomorrow we'll do the whole tedious thing again and they won't be stupid enough to let us control the conversation this time.

The lights go out, one by one. The booms come down. Suddenly, it's just the five of us, in dim, cold overhead lighting. We stand there and stare at each other, unsure what happens now.

'Pub?' asks Faye.

It's not as if people in Soho usually dress down, but here's the five of us looking like we just walked off the set of *Loose Women*, and people know that they know us from somewhere, even with my hair chopped short and Hannah's braces gone. Faye leads us to a table right at the back and I watch the others go through their rituals – Hannah lets her hair fall over her face, Kendra glares, Roni slips on her sunglasses. In their hands and the set of their jaws I see teenagers who don't want to be looked at exactly, but who are perversely glad they aren't people who don't get looked at all.

We move towards a table. Roni guides us away from it and towards one in the back corner of the room.

'Shall I flag a waiter?' asks Roni.

'It's a Wetherspoons,' says Faye. 'We can order on an app.'

'Right.' Roni has probably never been in a Wetherspoons. She hasn't risked touching the table yet. There's a ripped salt packet in front of me. I take a pinch and throw it over my shoulder. Kendra watches me, eyes bright.

People are still looking. Roni pushes her sunglasses up her nose and shifts her chair so that the rest of the pub is staring at the back of her head. She and Kendra were neck and neck for a while after the show ended, both popping up sporadically in long-running TV shows and the occasional action movie, but last year Roni pulled ahead. She was cast in some gritty high school drama as part of an ensemble cast of newcomers, standing sullen on the poster between a gorgeous blonde and a man who looks about thirty-five, despite the school blazer. They've all gone nuclear, Roni included. She's just bought a house in Kensington. Maybe that's why she needed the money. Meanwhile, here's Kendra, having just signed on to a gameshow where the celebrity contestants hang out with their biggest fans in disguise. It has to sting.

Faye doesn't ask any of us what we want to drink. She closes her phone and places it face down on the table. 'Why did you guys do it?' she asks. Her face hovering over her folded hands is very pale, her chin very pointed. It's eerie how little she's changed.

'To see you guys,' says Roni, wiping the table with one cautious finger.

'Bollocks,' says Kendra. She points at each of us in turn. 'Money. Money. Money. A *shitload* of money.' She doesn't direct this last at me, but at Roni.

'Roni doesn't need the money,' says Faye.

'That's why I said a shitload.'

Kendra waits, eyes on Roni in her lavender suit. Roni looks back at her for a second, unsure, and then she rolls her eyes. 'I can't say.'

'Bollocks. Why not?'

'I said I wouldn't.'

'Who did you say that to? Fred?'

'I don't really feel like it's in good taste.' She tells us anyway, after a pause. It's far more than me. I was naïve to think I was really the one they were willing to dig deep into their pockets for. And I'd felt like such hot shit when Rupert agreed to up my fee.

'*Shit.*' Kendra sits back. 'Okay, so it really was the money.'

'And you guys. For real.'

'Call us then,' says Kendra. 'Calling's free. Seeing each other is a bonus and we all know it. The one I'm really surprised about is—' She points at me, her gaze level. 'I didn't think there was enough money in the world.'

'You guys were never the problem,' I say. 'Not from my end.'

'And I'm assuming Rupert made promises?' she asks. I nod. 'And you think he'll keep them?'

'Lay off,' says Faye.

'Ah, it's suddenly ten years ago.'

She's as poised as ever, red hair swept up on top of her head, her scuttling eyes faster and brighter. Even after ten years of radio silence, I know her best like this, at this age and at this point in her life. Edging into her late twenties, headed for the lucrative and slightly embarrassing world of TV personality fame, and realising that she has a mind that may never get to do anything it actually deserves to be doing. So much displaced energy and misplaced anger. Kendra could ruin me, if she set her mind to it. There's nothing she couldn't figure out. It's lucky that I don't have a life large enough for that kind of ruining to be worth it.

She applies her lip balm, watching me. 'I don't love that you're here,' she says. 'I don't think any of us do. But I also don't think we love that we're here. And we all know the game.'

'I think this was the last good day,' says Hannah. A rare contribution.

'Yeah,' says Roni. 'Probably.'

'For god's sake,' laughs Kendra. 'We're all so dramatic. It's just TV.'

A member of staff arrives, with a crowded tray. Faye ordered pints. 'I thought we'd all be sick of champagne,' she grins.

We're just raising them when I catch sight of the assistant from the pavement, scurrying through tables with her phone to her ear. She waves at me. The others turn to see what I'm staring at.

'Crap,' mutters Kendra.

'Hi, girls,' says the assistant, breathless, when she reaches our table. 'Hi. Sorry. I don't know if you know, but this . . .' She waves a hand. 'This whole *thing* hasn't been announced yet.'

'So?' asks Kendra.

'So, that means we can't really – I mean *you* can't really all be out and about together. I mean, it only takes one person to realise that it's the five of you all back together again and then there's a photo on social media and the jig is up, you know. People will start speculating.'

We're all looking at each other rather than her. It's: *Are we going to let them do this?* And: *We have to let them do this.*

No one moves.

'It's embargoed,' says the assistant, plaintively.

Faye rises first. The rest of us follow.

'Cars are waiting outside,' breathes the assistant, by way of a 'Jesus fucking Christ *thank you*'. Poor girl. I can only imagine what it's like working for Fred and being considered disposable.

No one says anything to each other as we walk outside and head for our respective cars. Roni steps into her tinted monstrosity. Kendra doesn't even shoot a glance backwards as she's driven off. Hannah steps down off the pavement with a small wave, and as Faye turns away, I think – *it's now or never.* I catch her by the elbow.

She turns back to me like I'm a customer in her shop, like she's wondering mildly and vacantly how she can help me. My heart squeezes.

'I just—'

'It's good to see me?' asks Faye.

That's exactly the lame line I was going to use and there's no point pretending otherwise. 'Yes,' I say, with an embarrassed smile.

With her other hand, Faye reaches out to hold three of my fingers between hers. She squeezes them, briefly, and lets them go.

Season One

I hated London for two weeks. I hated how it felt too big to properly know, like trying to make a hometown out of thirty towns all smushed together, and how the noise outside of our hotel never dulled and it was impossible to sleep. The tube was suffocating and I had to carry hand sanitiser with me everywhere I went, even though it tasted horrible when I bit my nails and Mum said I was wrong in the head.

'Understand this,' she said. 'Superbugs are real and you are breeding them. And do you know how many times you begged me for a trip to London when you were younger?'

But I knew she hated it too, despite the free hotel. She was working remotely, which she didn't like. She'd left her job in recruitment the previous year to work for herself and we both felt a little like I was jeopardising everything she'd built now that she was less present for her clients. She overcompensated by upping her hours, always on her laptop if she had a spare second. She tried keeping me in the hotel with her whilst she worked, or making me sit with a book across from her in a coffee shop, but we both agreed quickly that it wasn't really fair.

'You are *not* to get on the tube,' she said, and she confiscated my hand sanitiser and sent me out into the terrifying bowels of the city (or Westminster, as it's more commonly known). I think she hoped that I would do something interesting, come back to the hotel with some stories to tell at least, but there's only so much you can do in London with no Oyster card and no money. I spent a lot of time sat in Trafalgar Square with a book, staring at the bronze lions and trying to feel grateful.

A couple of days before shooting began, we showed up at a studio in Soho to have some pictures taken. I sat in a room with white walls and a wooden floor, Mum on her laptop beside me, and took a chocolate or two at intervals from the giant bowl by the door until Mum noticed and told me to stop. 'You're going to make yourself sick.'

'They're *free*.'

The red-headed girl was the first to arrive. She had been at the call-back, the first one up, and she'd once again got a big laugh from the table, this time because when they had asked her how she was she'd said, 'I'm sweating out of my *eyeballs*. The Circle line is a *nightmare*.' She sang like a West End kid and acted like a CBBC regular. I saw Rupe, Fred and Donna – still sat behind that all-important table – nod at each other. It wasn't said aloud, but even before everyone else had taken their turn we knew she was booked.

This was Kendra – outspoken, dazzling, with the brightest-red hair I had ever seen and a perfect pattern of freckles. She was thirteen, a year older than I was, and a real teenager which made her very intimidating. She wore a cropped t-shirt to the photoshoot with a sliver of pale stomach showing between her waist and hips and a silver heart locket resting between her collarbones. I was still straight up and down, but Kendra had a figure. I tried not to stare.

'Oh,' she said, when she saw me. 'Fourteen, right? I thought they'd go for you.'

'I'm twelve,' I said, before I realised that she was calling me by my audition number.

She raised an eyebrow. 'Okay. It was a princess name, wasn't it? Belle?'

It didn't feel so much like a compliment when Kendra said it.

We were two of six. Next came the sisters. Hannah stared at me with her wide, woodland creature eyes but Faye glided nonchalantly into the room, silvery hair draped across her shoulders.

'Hey,' she said, hands in her pockets. Kendra and I nodded at her. 'I've never had my picture taken professionally before.' Her need to admit her own inexperience was apparently chronic. 'Have you?'

Kendra nodded – I believed her – but I shook my head firmly.

'Okay,' said Faye, tucking her arm under mine in a decided motion, 'then we'll stick together. And Kendra can tell us what to expect.'

It was a skill she had that I have never found in anyone else, that ability to make everyone feel included whilst at the same time letting each one of us think that she was singling us out.

The last two girls had not been in our original audition group, but I remembered them from the call-backs. Roni I had noticed because she had been one of the few girls there who wasn't white. She had braided hair and the sweet, round face of someone who could easily have her feelings hurt. Paget I had noticed because she was the tallest and the quietest. She was only just thirteen and yet she was a whole head taller than Kendra, and very skinny. When she bent her elbows and knees, the bones looked as if they might jut through her skin.

We each had our headshots taken – Kendra first, the rest of us trying to copy the way she had posed on the stool and smiled like she was laughing, head slightly tilted – and then we took group shots. We shuffled awkwardly into the positions we were led to. Faye guided Hannah with two hands on her shoulders. When she went too fast and Hannah's heel came out of her shoe, she waited with folded arms for Hannah to redo the strap.

'Smile!' came the command. 'Beautiful!'

We crowded around the computer to see the shots. I'd expected to be stood in the middle of five Kendras, surrounded by dazzling teeth and jutting hips, but we were just a group of girls. All different heights, in all different outfits. Smiling our own individual smiles.

The first day on set, we all brought our headshots to Fred, at Donna's request.

'Oh,' he said, shuffling through them. 'Oh dear. These have to go.' We didn't get them back. When we next went to a studio to get our pictures taken, it was with a full hair and make-up team and a shoot director to organise us into strict formation. I never found out what happened to that original group picture, but if it's out there somewhere, I hope it never finds its way back to me. I think it would make me bawl.

Donna wore a long black dress to our first day of filming, so tight that it looked like a sleeve. She had to cross one leg all the way in front of the other in order to walk, but somehow she managed to make it look like the most natural thing in the world, like we were all wrong for walking any other way. Her shiny brown hair was in a ponytail so high that you could see it looming over the back of her head when she stood straight on. It bounced on her shoulders as she moved. All six of us, lined up in front of the big silver mirror, couldn't stop watching her.

She walked in smiling, opening and closing her hands to us. We smiled back, unsure if we were supposed to remove our hands from behind our backs, where we had been told to place them. ('Hands clasped behind your backs girls, shoulders down. Smile!') She stood between us and the mirror, still dimpling at us, beauty spot resting high on her cheekbone.

'I can't believe this day is finally here,' she said.

Rupert had told us to wait very quietly in a line and to look professional. 'Imagine,' he had said, 'that you're soldiers, about to meet your commanding officer. There's your first acting prompt!'

We were all steely-eyed in our determination, so stone-faced that he had to pause on Donna's cue and get us to do it again.

'Meeting your commanding officer, girls, not facing the firing squad.' Already we were doing it wrong. Paget was turning red in the mirror. Rupert came closer to micromanage, tapping us on the chin or shoulder to indicate that something needed to be adjusted. 'Don't worry,' he said. 'It won't usually be like this. This is just a very important shot, that's all. We want to really reel people in.'

'And we're hoping you girls will sort of pick these things up after a while,' added Fred from his position at the side of the room.

Eventually they had us where they wanted us. Still focused, still probably a little too intense, we waited for Donna. We tried hard to keep our narrow shoulders still and our small toes from twitching.

Rupert walked over to stand beside Fred. The two of them were never seated on set, always standing, hands in their pockets like strange mirror images of each other. Rupert wore t-shirts sometimes, left stubble on his chin for a few days at a time, but Fred was always in a pressed white shirt, facial hair always groomed. Never smiling. He must have done, at least once, but I can't ever remember seeing it.

'Let's have Donna,' called Rupert.

And there she came, heels clicking like a metronome. One leg crossing straight in front of the other, hair flowing down her back, beaming at us. Opening and closing her hands like small, perfect flowers.

We were going to be stars. That was the first thing she told us. All six of us had been handpicked from the most talented little girls in the nation to follow in Donna Mayfair's footsteps and become outstanding triple threats. We were going to be in movies like her, on TV like her, on stage like her, signing record deals like her. Modelling contracts, clothing lines, TV hosting gigs . . . There was no limit to what we could achieve.

This was confusing because none of us had known that Donna really did anything.

'She wasn't just on *Strictly,*' said Mum as we walked towards the tube station. 'She was huge when you were little. She started in the soaps, did *Corrie* and *EastEnders,* and then she went to LA and shot a bunch of films – some decent, some terrible – and made some pretty average music.'

'Her voice is amazing,' I said. She'd sung for us, gathering us all around the piano in the music room. We'd been spellbound. It wasn't just her voice – it was the way she looked when she sang, and the confidence with which she did it, just gathered us all in the room and said, essentially, *Now you're all going to look at me.*

'Sure, she can sing, but her songwriters weren't doing her any favours. I'll play you something when we get back if you like. Very girl-band member goes solo.' She hitched her bag higher on her shoulder – a real dance bag, by this point. She'd bought it for the call-backs. 'Anyway, she dropped off quite quickly when nothing she did blew up. Don't know what happened to her after that.'

'Maybe she just decided she'd rather be a teacher.'

'Those who can't,' murmured Mum.

But Donna could. Before she asked us all to sing for her, she demonstrated at the piano, sailing through *Maybe* from *Annie* like she was on a West End stage. Later we broke for school, and when we returned, she had changed out of her black dress and into dance-wear, ready to take us through a simple combination. She was tall in her leotard and legwarmers, statuesque, but impossibly fluid.

'Follow me, girls,' she called. We scrambled to keep up.

Our mothers sat on chairs at the edge of the room. Mum sat on the end of the row, the tap of her laptop keys always in the background of whatever else we were doing. Sometimes she would step outside to take phone calls, pushing past crew members and ignoring their requests to stay in the room. The other mothers watched us eagerly. Sometimes they communed in a whisper – never louder because Fred or Rupert or one of the sound guys would tell them not to interfere with the audio.

I got told off three times that first day for staring directly into the lens. There were only a couple of cameras in the room with us but somehow they managed to be everywhere. Every time Donna spoke to us, there was a camera trained on our faces, sometimes held inches away by a grip all in black. It almost felt rude not to acknowledge them. My eyes would dart over to them, and Fred would sigh and say, 'Belle, come on.' And I would look over to my mum, typing away. She wouldn't raise her head.

We weren't meant to talk to them outside of filming, either. 'If you have any issues,' Rupert had told us and our mothers, 'then you should come straight to me or Fred. Don't bother the crew.'

The producers and assistants and runners and grips and boom operators would move past us to the food and drink table (craft services, or 'crafty', as we quickly learnt to call it) as if we didn't exist, reaching around us to grab sandwiches and pieces of fruit. When I found myself in the bathroom at the same time as one of them, or a figure in black brushed past me in the corridor, I would get a strange kind of awed feeling like I was in the presence of someone famous. Over time we became aware of some of their names through eavesdropping. These became valuable pieces of gossip.

'You know the girl who brings Fred and Rupert their coffee in the morning and writes our schedule on the whiteboard? Her name is Tiffany.'

'Tiffany,' we repeated, in awed tones, and stared at her from the safety of our small circle.

We started to play dares. Kendra dared Faye to bump into a producer in the corridor. Faye dared Kendra to say, 'Good morning,' to one of the grips, which she did, in the smallest voice that we had ever heard Kendra use. Roni was dared to look into the camera during a pep talk with Donna – 'How many times, girls?' barked Fred – and Paget, the only one who had started her period, had to go up to one of the female assistants and ask to borrow a tampon.

'I'm going to *die*,' she pleaded, crimson up to her ears.

Kendra gave her a small shove in the right direction. 'You know the forfeit.'

The forfeit was something that Kendra had invented and it quickly became the blanket punishment for failing to fully participate in any of our games. It involved walking into the production room – the mysterious space into which the crew and producers periodically disappeared, to talk about us, we imagined – and stealing something. It could be a pen, or sheet of paper, or a pound coin, but it had to be a worthy offering. Once Hannah took a tissue and Kendra sent her straight back in.

'I dare Belle to forget her lines later,' said Kendra.

We were a week in and working on our very first audition: Alice in *Alice in Wonderland,* a six-month run in an Off-West End theatre. It had us all salivating.

'I've actually played Alice before,' said Kendra when Donna told us.

'*Have* you?' said Donna. 'Well, you should get it.'

We broke for school midway through the morning. This legally mandated time with a tutor had taken us a little by surprise when the concept had first been introduced, but we quickly learnt that we could crawl through the worksheets provided by our respective schools and spend the majority of our time talking, and the consequences would be slim to none.

Kendra was oddly quiet, pushing through the doors and marching up the stairs to the classroom ahead of the rest of us. Faye caught up with her and said, 'Kendra's basically cast, of course.'

Kendra just said, 'Ha!' with a wry smile, and nothing else. But later, when we were sat at our desks working from our individual textbooks and our tutor took the opportunity to rush downstairs and have a smoke, she laid her pen down and looked around the room, to let us all know she was about to say something of significance.

'Belle will get it.'

The other girls looked confused. I couldn't blame them. Paget was the best dancer, despite her gangly arms and legs. 'There's so much maturity in your dancing, Paget,' Donna had said on our first day. 'You don't dance like a little girl at all. I think the others here could learn from you.'

Kendra left the dance studio red-faced, thumping a flat palm against the door so that it opened loudly into the wall. Donna's pale-green eyes narrowed after her.

Faye was the best singer by far. Everyone else was good, and my thin voice wobbled through vocal lessons as best it could, but Faye shone. Her 'Maybe' had Donna misty-eyed. 'She's got quite a future ahead of her,' she told Faye's mum, Alex, who nodded without an ounce of surprise in her face.

I wasn't the best at anything. I did well when we read scenes in class, but the rest of the time I was flagging behind Paget and Faye and Kendra. I didn't mind this. I was surprised that I had even been cast at all.

'It's not going to be me,' I said. 'Obviously not.'

'Of course it will,' said Kendra, picking up her pen again. 'You're the favourite.' She went back to her worksheet.

To this day I don't know what it was that she saw, how she put it together far before the rest of us and possibly even before Rupert and Fred. Maybe it was just a guess. But it was a good one because, that afternoon, Donna asked me to lunch.

They asked Mum to come in the car with me but told her that she wasn't in the scene and no one was going to pay for her lunch.

'Okay,' she said. 'No, then.' She was behind on work and not in the mood to play along.

There was a bit of dithering over this – technically sending me in the back of a production van with a small group of non-DBS-checked crew members was, as Rupert put it, 'a safeguarding grey area', and putting me alone in a cab was vetoed by Mum. Donna was already on her way there as I stood awkwardly a little way off from the decision-making committee. In the corner of the dance studio, the other girls watched quietly.

'Here's a thought,' said Fred, who quickly grew impatient with any conversation that lasted longer than three minutes. 'How about Belle drives with Kay and Kay doesn't molest her?'

The meeting was broken up with a bout of uncomfortable laughter.

So, I was driven to a hotel restaurant in Tower Bridge by Kay, a twenty-something production assistant who made polite conversation with me for about five minutes of the journey and switched the radio on for the remaining ten. The production van arrived just ahead of us and I dithered awkwardly outside the hotel doors as they ran in to get filming permissions and set up. Donna was already there, sat at a table and chatting to one of the cameramen. She was using her phone camera to fix her hair, fiddling with her rings as she waited. Her elbow knocked the salt and she took a pinch and threw it over her shoulder. It felt wrong to watch her in this moment when she clearly felt unobserved. I looked at Kay instead.

'You okay?' asked Kay, without glancing up from her phone. 'We'll get you in there in just a sec. You hungry?'

'Not really,' I said. She wasn't listening anyway.

A gesture from one of the cameramen. Kay nudged me towards the door. They were already filming as I walked inside the restaurant and I did my best not to look at the cameras and focus on Donna instead, trying to smile as if we were old friends catching up for a coffee. Donna smiled back. She was sat at a table by the window, Tower Bridge in the background, a green velvet chair pulled out opposite her just for me. She had ordered herself a salad, and I had a panini and a side of chips. ('Don't eat while we're filming,' Kay had told me in the car. 'We'll just bag it up to go afterwards.' I didn't realise at the time that this was so that they could splice the conversation together however they liked in the editing room. I thought they were just worried that I was a messy eater.)

Donna had on large earrings shaped like two smiling suns; they caught the light as I approached her and I saw spots of white in my vision.

'Hi, Belle,' she said.

'Hello.'

'It's so nice to be able to sit down and have this chat, isn't it?'

I adjusted myself on the seat of the chair and nodded. I had started getting used to being filmed in the studio, but it was unnerving to have the lens still hovering close to me when I was out in the real world.

'Are you glad to be here?'

'Oh, yes.' I eyed the panini and sat on my hands.

'Good! We've got so many exciting things ahead of us.' Donna looked at me, and then very deliberately folded her hands into her lap. I copied her. 'This is the first time you and I have been able to talk one on one,' she said, 'isn't it?'

'Yes, I think so.'

'I just want to let you know how impressed I am with everything I've seen so far. I knew you were special from the very first moment I saw you at the audition. I think you're going to prove me right.'

'Thank you.' I couldn't believe that she was saying this to me and not Kendra. I was trying very hard only to focus on her and not the small team of men in black holding cameras and grips. Mum would have laughed at Donna's speech. The stream of compliments felt over the top.

'Can you talk to me about why you're excited to be here?'

'Sure.' I tried to match her sunshiny tone. 'It's just a great opportunity, I guess. And everyone's so nice.'

Donna nodded, still smiling.

'I'm really grateful,' I tried.

In the corner of my eye, I saw it – a small, quick glance exchanged between two grips.

'I think I've got what it takes to be a star,' I said. 'And I think this is my best shot at getting there.'

It could have been my imagination, but Donna appeared instantly happier. 'Do you think you'd be able to make it on your own, if you needed to?' she asked, raising her glass to her lips.

This felt like a trick question. 'Maybe. I think I could. But it would be a lot harder to do it on my own.'

Donna nodded, the kind of nod that made me relax a little. She took over again, and I brushed the sweat on my palms against the sides of the chair. 'You're right. I did it all on my own, and it was much harder. That's what this is all about – taking talented little girls and giving them all the advantages I didn't have.'

'So, I guess you're kind of like our fairy godmother.'

It felt awful to say. I didn't have a whole lot of self-awareness at twelve and even then it made me want to punch myself in the face. They had filmed me saying that. They were going to put it on

56

TV. My friends at school were going to make fun of me, even Mum was going to roll her eyes – but Donna was laughing, delightedly.

'I love that!' she said, clapping her hands together. 'Yes, that's exactly it. And what would you wish for, if I was your fairy godmother?'

Hotly embarrassed, I rattled off some wishes in the hope she would drop the subject – I wanted to play Alice, of course, and I wanted to be famous and be in films and on the West End.

'Do you want to be a dancer too?'

'Definitely.' I loved to dance, even though I didn't consider myself exceptional.

'And a pop star?'

This was more doubtful. 'Yes.'

'Who would you like to be as famous as?'

I skipped over the answers I would like to have given and went straight to the right one. 'You.' Laughter from the crew, which made me feel like Kendra. Donna laughed too.

'Belle,' she said, 'in my professional opinion, I think we could make you much more famous than me.'

We sat there for about half an hour, talking about the films that I liked, what it had been like for me growing up in the Cotswolds, what subjects I was good at in school. The effort of trying to predict what they all wanted from me was exhausting. When Donna finally turned around to the crew and said, 'Okay, we're good, right?' I felt my spine decompress an inch.

Donna waved a hand and a waiter came hurrying over.

'Bag up mine,' she said, 'if you could?' Then she glanced at my untouched panini. 'And hers.' Her nails drummed on the table. 'Unless she's not hungry.' She looked at me suddenly, tilting her head in question. Before I could work out what it was she wanted to me to say, she was up, chatting to Fred across the restaurant. I tried not to watch them. I hoped they were looking at me.

Kay began to hurry me back towards her car, without my panini.

'Hang on,' called Donna.

Kay turned back. 'Is everything okay?'

Donna was looking at Kay's hand, hovering just under my elbow. Her eyebrows were lowered. She moved over to us.

'Where's her mum?'

'Back at the studio. Didn't want to come.'

'Really,' said Donna, without any intonation. She looked at me, and then held out her hand. 'Come on, Belle. You can get in my cab.'

Our fingers linked. Someone handed Donna her salad in a box. There was a hushed silence in the restaurant – which, again, might have been my imagination – as Donna led me out onto the pavement and waved at the black taxi waiting down the street. We left the production crew packing up, Kay speaking quickly and urgently into her phone as the taxi pulled off the kerb.

Donna pulled her seatbelt around herself and dug in her bag for her lipstick. I watched her applying it in her phone camera, mouth slightly open. She closed the lipstick and pressed her lips together once, twice.

'Well,' she said, after a few seconds, 'I think you played that perfectly.'

It was the first time she had ever spoken to me off camera, and her voice was different. Not completely, but noticeably. Slightly deeper.

'Did I?' I said. I wasn't sure how else to respond.

'Confident but not too confident. And definitely young enough. You think well on your feet. And you're very cute. You've got brilliant eyes.' She reached out and, with one perfectly manicured finger, turned my chin towards her. 'Yes,' she said, 'it's because they're so big, I think. And blue.'

58

She smiled, and again, that was different. It was smaller, but she held it more fully in her eyes. It struck me that I was seeing something none of the rest of the girls had seen yet. The real Donna. Donna not on TV.

'I meant all of it,' she said as she let my chin go and opened her box of salad. Her fork dug around for cherry tomatoes. 'I really do think you've got a future.'

'Why?' I asked.

'Why do I think that?'

I nodded. I must have looked nervous, because she laughed and said, 'It's okay. You can speak your mind.'

'I think some of the other girls are better than me.'

Donna considered this. 'They could be. In some areas. Things can swing quickly at this age, though, and often it's the most diligent child in class that ends up pulling ahead. Do you understand what I'm saying?'

'I need to work the hardest.'

'Well, yes, but you also need to work the smartest. That's where I think you'll outstrip the others. I can see that in you.'

She reached over to squeeze my hand – not benevolently, or kindly, but with an urgency that made my heart beat faster.

'There's a quality, Belle, that can't be taught. It goes beyond talent and confidence and it can be hard to spot this early, but I've been looking.' She let go of my hand and offered me the box of salad. 'You must be hungry. There's an extra fork in the bag.'

I wasn't – this was all far too exciting – but I took a cherry tomato and chewed.

'I think you could be great,' said Donna. 'Truly, I do. I think people are going to fall in love with you. But if that's going to happen, you're going to have to trust this whole process. And you're going to have to trust me.' She paused, examining my face. 'Can you do that?'

I nodded. I wanted to make some kind of verbal promise to her, more of a vow, but the words wouldn't come. She smiled again, that new, soft smile.

'Those eyes,' she said. She shook her head. 'Those eyes are going to be on billboards.'

Amongst the exciting, exhausting movement of it all, we had found a moment of stillness. I could have drifted out of the window and down the Thames on a cloud. It was the most special I had ever felt.

She was Donna Mayfair again when we got back, larger than life, her hand resting lightly between my shoulder blades as she guided me back into the studio. 'Run and tell the other girls what filming a lunch scene was like,' she said musically, loud enough for them to hear as they hovered by the crafty table. My pride quickly turned to embarrassment as Kendra's eyes rolled in my direction.

Told you, I saw her mouth to the others.

They were strange with me for the rest of the day. Only Faye was as serene and undisturbed as always. When we went upstairs for a few more hours of school, she hung back with me to ask, 'How was lunch?'

'It was good,' I was unsure how to tell it all, or whether I even should. 'I mean, when we were filming, she was Donna—'

'Sure,' nodded Faye, sagely.

'But then we took a taxi back together and she was different.'

'Nicer?'

'You don't think she's nice?'

'No, she is,' said Faye, running a little to grab the door before it swung shut. 'She's beautiful.' Faye always called it like she saw it. 'What was it all about, then? Why did she want to talk to you?'

The other girls were waiting a few paces ahead outside the door of the schoolroom. Their eyes flickered to us and away. They feigned interest in the production posters on the walls.

'It was just a scene,' I said. 'Just for the show. I think she picked me randomly.'

I knew they didn't quite believe me, but I also knew that they wanted to.

It was the next day when Kendra gave me the dare. Crafty had pizza and we were sat around in a circle in the dressing room, stretching after dance, balancing paper plates and pizza slices as we leant forward over split legs. Crafty always had pizza, but this was the one and only time that I remember us actually eating it. We became more conscious about eating in front of Donna after a while, and the crew became less conscious about making sure we ate anything. By Season Three we were lucky if there were a few pieces of fruit left at craft services by the time we were finished for the day. It was around this time that we began to suspect our limited access to food was deliberate.

We had a class that afternoon followed by a mock audition, our last chance to impress Donna before we went out for *Alice* at the end of the week. Kendra balanced her plate on her knee as she looked at me, head tilted.

'I dare Belle to forget her lines later.'

I held my slice halfway to my lips for a second and then put it back on my paper plate. 'Don't be stupid.'

'It's not a real audition.'

'She obviously can't do that,' said Roni. Roni didn't often speak up, but she had a strong sense of right and wrong that could burn you if you upset it. 'Play fairly.'

'I am playing fairly.' She was sat with her legs splayed, reaching forward to push her toes down. Red hair hid her face. 'Nothing's actually going to *happen* to her, is it? And I bet the crew would love it. It would probably make the show better.' Kendra often talked about what would make the show better or worse as if she considered herself an honorary producer. She sat up to pull her hair back into a ponytail. 'If you don't want to do it you can just say.'

'Okay,' I said. 'I don't want to do it. Would you?'

'You can't copy a dare.' This rule had been established early on, mainly because Kendra had a knack for coming up with the best and meanest dares and didn't enjoy having the tables turned on her. 'You can just do the forfeit, if you want,' she said. 'But you've got to do it now.'

This was also unkind because the team were milling around on their break and the chances of being caught slipping into the production room to steal something were much higher. I looked around the group. They were all suddenly very focused on their stretches.

'Fine,' I said, throwing my plate down. The feeling of Kendra's smile on my back followed me out of the door.

The production room was on the floor below, removed enough from where we worked and studied that the risk of eavesdropping was reduced. When we weren't on camera, we were treated a little like household pets who needed to be strictly confined to their own area. I listened at the top of the stairs for a minute and then, reassured by the silence, I made my way down, barefoot and skittish.

But the room wasn't empty. Sat in the windowless gloom, desk light pointed at a slice of pizza and feet up on one of the swivel chairs, was a man, skinny in his black t-shirt, with rumpled hair and headphones snaking from his ears to an iPod on the desk beside him. He sat side on to me and he was doing what can only be described as air drumming, with closed eyes and a passionate intensity on his face.

I paused in the doorway, unsure whether to laugh or run away.

One eye opened. 'Ah,' he said, pointing at me. 'No, no, don't worry. It's all good. I've got it.'

Baffled, I waited in the doorway. He leapt off the desk and ruffled through the papers under the computer monitors, iPod tucked into the back pocket of his jeans. He was dark-haired, with a messiness to him – rumpled hair, baggy t-shirt – that made him seem friendly and, at the same time, made me nervous.

'Right,' he said. 'Here.' He held out a sheet of paper to me.

It was our first dance class, written out sentence by sentence, with some parts highlighted green. Even what hadn't been said was made clear on the page. *Kendra slaps the door as she leaves. Donna does not like this behaviour.* I smiled.

'Good enough?' he said, as if this hand off was something we'd discussed in advance. I looked up, uncomprehending. 'For your forfeit. I think the little one took someone's sock the other day.' Hannah. We'd nearly pissed ourselves laughing when she'd brought it back.

'How did you know?' I managed.

He gestured to the mic around my neck. 'Those don't turn off.'

My hand flew to it.

'It's fine,' he said, laughing. 'It's pretty standard. I'm not spying on you or anything.'

'Sounds like you kind of are.'

He laughed again. Even in my confusion, I was pleased that I'd made him laugh. 'Alright, trouble. It's just how this shit works. We're only really listening when we're rolling, but sometimes we pick stuff up on your breaks.' There were headsets dotted around the room. I was pretty sure this guy was just a runner – I'd seen him bringing Fred and Rupert their coffee – but apparently even he could listen in when he chose to. And there were members of the crew who never took their headsets off.

My mind raced over our daily schedule. We took our mics off for school, handing them over to a PA and collecting them again at the end of class, but the rest of the time we just left them on. All our chatter in breaks and on lunch when we finally felt unobserved had been listened to, perhaps even recorded. And . . .

A cold sweat broke over me. I didn't take my mic off when I went to the bathroom.

I stared up at him, my stomach dropping down to my knees. He leant down and smiled.

'You let me know if you need anything in the future,' he said. 'I'm Howie.'

I didn't bother telling him my name. He already knew.

Someone had eaten my pizza by the time I returned to deliver the page. I sat down silently beside Faye, one hand clutching the paper, the other tightly squeezing the foam head of my mic.

'Bloody hell,' said Kendra, snatching the paper. The corner tore off and fluttered onto my knee. 'As if you got production notes.'

The others crowded around her to read them as I sat a little way off, pressing my hand tightly into the foam, testing how hard I could push without crushing the hard ball beneath. Across from me, Kendra's eyes scanned the pages, and her face slowly fell.

We were both quiet for the rest of the day. When we did our mock auditions, Kendra fell out of her turns in the dance and Donna said, 'Remember, Kendra, we have to act like professionals and take this seriously. The studio will be open late if you need to stay and practice.'

I didn't take any pleasure in Kendra's meek expression as she sat back down. I wasn't cruel. I was just winning.

Reunion special

They were fast, but not fast enough.

By that evening the picture is circulating on social media. All five of us sit around a Wetherspoons table, Roni resting one finger uncertainly on the dark wood. My back is to the camera but the faces of the others are all visible. In the comments, the same account has been tagged over and over again.

As if they're relaunching without you . . . @pagetdanes

Her page is private. I wonder if she's even seen it yet.

The next morning, it's everywhere. A couple of publications have managed to put out thoughtful pieces overnight about the ethics of it all, but they're mostly just short news articles. The Real Deal *cast spark reunion rumours.* Over on social media, some people maintain that maybe the five of us are just out for a casual drink, but most have guessed the truth, or at least something close to it.

'They'll have a statement out tomorrow,' I tell Cameron.

I'm underestimating them. They have Rupert on a morning talk show that very day. Rupert never did any of the front-facing stuff until people online began to get curious about the show's creators and everyone stopped wanting to put Donna on TV. Fred was never going to talk, so Rupert stepped up. His social media has become a shrine to *The Real Deal*, a rose-tinted scrapbook of old photos and his favourite clips. *What a throwback!* he'll caption them. *Miss those days.*

It does something to deflect the criticism, but not much. He also gives interviews, occasionally, and this is where he shines. Rupert could convince nuclear codes out of the hands of NATO members.

'The way I see it,' he says, open-postured, sat across from the two hosts, 'is that it should all be up to the girls. This is a really important time, culturally, and it's more crucial than ever that young female voices are being heard. If they want to end the story properly and get some closure, then we want to provide them with a platform to do that.'

'But it's not all up to them,' says the trouser-suited woman beside him. She's a prominent feminist journalist, one of the internet variety, and the same woman whose rallying cry indirectly had the show pulled from streaming sites. 'We now know a good deal about what went on the first time around and those children were manipulated, exploited and put directly in harm's way for content. How can you expect people to accept that this isn't just an extension of their trauma?'

Cameron and I sit at the kitchen table, mugs of tea in front of us. He has the remote in his hand as if about to change the channel, only it's been over three minutes and he still hasn't.

'Well,' says Rupert, shifting, tugging a little at the foot he has folded onto his left leg, 'first of all, I take issue with that version of events. Whilst the show should – and does – take some account-ability for being too trusting at times—'

'Trusting of who?' asks the woman beside him.

'The adults we let around those girls.' Rupert nods solemnly, as the journalist looks incredulously back at him. 'They weren't always as well protected as we would have liked them to be. I can't argue with you there. But as far as manipulation goes, the fact remains that *The Real Deal* was, and has always been, a docuseries.'

'Which means what, exactly?'

'Which means,' says Rupert, 'that we are not a reality TV show. We don't manipulate or exploit. We certainly don't deliberately put people in harm's way. I suppose you can say that we don't deliberately put them anywhere. We document.'

'Come on,' says the journalist. 'You make it sound like these girls were just roaming around the West End already when you happened upon them.' Rupert laughs. 'You're hardly the David Attenborough of child stardom,' she presses.

He holds up his hands. 'No, no, you're perfectly right. Someone was calling the shots. But that was never the production company. That was always Donna. The training programme was hers, and she invited us to document it. And that's all we ever did, document the rise of five very talented little girls.'

'Six,' I mutter.

'Six,' says the journalist.

'Yes. Six. Sorry.' He straightens up. 'We're not denying that there were some complicated things going on behind the scenes – some awful things,' he corrects, as the journalist opens her mouth. 'Things we became aware of far too late. This is about the girls getting to tell their story. It's about them taking back their power. For us, consent is the most crucial part, and all the cast members you see in this photo—' It's projected behind them, and I'm suddenly very, very glad that my face isn't in it. '—have willingly chosen to return, catch up and finish the story.'

'So you don't take any responsibility for the trauma that this reunion special might be dragging up?'

Rupert tilts his head to the side. 'You've used that word a few times now.'

'Trauma?'

'Yes.'

'Well,' says the journalist, with a quick look at the hosts, who seem to be transfixed by this exchange. 'Yes.'

'I think trauma is quite a strong word.'

'I don't think it's strong at all. Lots of things can be traumatic for girls that age.'

'Uncomfortable, perhaps, and unsettling, even upsetting. But trauma isn't a word to throw around lightly.'

'You don't think that Belle Simon is traumatised?'

Rupert pauses for just a minute, and his expression is blank.

'We have special measures in place to safeguard Belle,' he says. 'As we do for all the girls.'

'But don't you think that's rather too little too late?'

'I think Belle is stronger than people give her credit for.'

'I don't think "strong" comes into it,' says the journalist. 'I don't think "strong" ever comes into abuse.'

'That's another very heavy word,' says Rupert. A misstep. Despite my churning stomach, it's exciting to see. The journalist leans forward, incredulous.

'So, let me clarify this,' she says. 'A child screams on camera that she doesn't want to be left alone with an adult, that she thinks she's about to get hurt – and you wouldn't say she was being abused?'

Jane drops her hockey stick in the doorway and Cameron changes channel without missing a beat. I take a sip of my tea and try not to look guilty.

'What are you watching?' she says.

'*Antiques Roadshow*,' says Cameron, with a quick sideways glance at the TV to double-check that this is correct. 'Aren't you going to be late?'

'No.' Jane picks up an orange from the fruit bowl and a packet of crisps from the cupboard and throws them both into her ruck-sack, loose. 'Guess what, Belle?' she says.

'What?'

'I've got an audition today.'

'That's exciting,' says Cameron when I don't answer. 'Why haven't we heard about this before?'

Jane doesn't reply but I can feel her eyes sliding over to me. She knows, without knowing how she knows, that this is uncertain ground. 'It's sort of an audition for an audition,' she says.

'For a school play? That seems excessive.'

'No-o,' says Jane, standing on one foot and leaning on her hockey stick. 'For *Billy Elliot*. In the West End.'

Cameron laughs. 'What?'

'Open casting call,' I manage. 'They ask schools to send in students sometimes.'

'Right,' says Jane. 'And so, they're choosing who to send. Mr Croft is going to pick.'

'And you want to do it?' asks Cameron.

She nods, reaching for a second packet of crisps. When she pecks us both on the cheek and rushes out of the door – because she is, in fact, going to be late – Cameron looks at me.

'She really isn't very good, you know,' he says.

I manage a smile.

'You did good there,' he said. 'Very contained.'

'You make me sound crazy.'

'If it helps,' he says, 'you're far less crazy about it all than your mum. She would have handcuffed Jane to a kitchen chair at the mention of the word "audition".'

We smile at each other, and I know we're both wishing that she'd slam open the kitchen door with enough force to knock the cabinet over and shout, "What are you fuckers *thinking?* We're doing all that again *over my dead body.*"

A honk from outside turns his smile to a grimace. 'Good luck,' he says. 'Try not to take any of it personally.'

Impossible advice, but I hug him for it all the same. He still doesn't understand why I'm doing this. He doesn't get why I feel like I never really had a choice.

The set in the Soho studio is exactly the same, and here we all are in the same clothes, sat in the same configuration. There's no camera to greet me this time – they're still setting up and Fred is wandering around exchanging words with crew members. Kendra catches my eye as we sit.

'We're waiting for Rupe,' she says.

It's an excruciating fifteen minutes before he walks in, wearing the same blue-collared shirt and jeans that he was wearing on TV less than an hour ago.

'Hi, all,' he says. 'Sorry. Crisis averted, though, I think.' He tuts at us, hands on his hips, smiling. 'You had us in a bit of a time pressure situation there, ladies. Not the brightest of moves, was it?' No one says anything. I see the slightest of glances pass between Roni and Kendra.

'Not to worry,' says Rupert. 'All good now. And I'm excited to see how this morning's going to go. I'll be hovering nearby, just giving you some prompts, but I want you to pretend I'm not there.' He waves a hand. 'Try and keep continuity at the forefront of your minds. You know the drill. You're all professionals. Ready?'

They start rolling just as I notice that Faye is wearing different earrings from yesterday – big dangling blue stones, impossible to miss. She catches me looking and although her face doesn't give much away, I can tell that she's pleased with herself.

'Let's start with Paget,' says Rupert.

Kendra jumps in smoothly, as if we're already in the middle of a conversation. 'Has anyone heard from Paget?' She leans back in her chair, glass in hand. It's unsettling, like time has wound backwards.

We all shake our heads. 'I guess she didn't want to do it,' says Roni. 'I get it. What happened to her was pretty brutal.'

'Not really. Pretty recoverable, in the grand scheme of things. She was old enough to take it, I think.'

'I miss her,' says Faye. 'She was such a sweetheart, wasn't she?'

'She was a sweetheart. But I don't think she could hack it,' says Kendra. She holds up both hands. 'I'm not being a bitch – it's just true. Belle agreed with me.'

'When?' I ask.

'After she left. You agreed that she probably couldn't hack it.' Her glass is tilted towards me, in challenge.

'At the time I was probably feeling pretty cocky. Now I'm not sure how any of us did it.'

'Oh please,' says Kendra. 'It wasn't too bad, for the most part. You guys are all so glass half empty. Roni and I wouldn't be anything close to what we are if it hadn't been for the show.'

Roni evidently isn't too pleased at being lumped in with Kendra. She takes a sip of her champagne before she speaks. 'I do see what Kendra means,' she says. 'I mean, Paget *was* old enough to cope. Hannah was only nine when it all started and look how well she turned out.'

Hannah blushes. Kendra raises her eyebrows.

'Anything to say about that, Hannah?'

'Shut up,' says Faye. 'Not her.'

Rupert and Fred are optimistically silent, but Kendra never goes after Faye. She raises her eyebrows again and returns to her glass.

'And Paget's mother, Charlene?' Rupert asks. He's stood back behind the camera, out of the lights, but his voice comes to me as if he's crouched down beside me and talking directly into my ear.

'I definitely don't miss Charlene,' says Kendra. 'And I bet I know who else doesn't, and that's Belle.'

There's a collective laugh and I ignore the feeling in my chest and join in. 'God, not at all. It feels so mean to say, because I really did like Paget, but . . .'

'But you were relieved when she left?'

'A little. Is that bad?'

Hannah shakes her head. 'I think we all were.' Hannah used to be terrified of Charlene.

'Who do you miss the most, Belle?' asks Rupert.

He's moved now so that he's directly behind me, not even visible in the corner of my eye.

'My mum,' I say. 'Of course.'

Instant sympathy in the faces around me. He's frustrated – I feel it in the silence that follows. He can't say what he wants to, which is, *yes, obviously, but who else?* Rupert will manipulate you and lie to you and fuck you over for personal gain, but under it all he desperately wants you to think that he's nice. It's his greatest – and possibly only – weakness.

'Not Donna?' Kendra doesn't care about being nice nearly as much as she does about being interesting. She's holding her glass out for a refill, but no one is filling it. No one wants to interrupt this shot.

My eyes slide to Rupert at the back of the room. Predictably, he gives me nothing. I don't reply to Kendra. I just shake my head.

She looks at Rupert, somewhere behind me. 'Is this breaking one of the rules?' Silence, but I know that he's shrugged. I can see it as clearly as if I'm looking straight at him. Kendra rolls her eyes. 'Alright.'

'Come on,' says Faye, a little coldly.

'What?'

Faye shakes her head, lifting her glass.

'I totally get that there are some things Belle doesn't want to talk about,' says Kendra. 'I respect it. But honestly, we can't do this and get all nostalgic and leave massive, gaping gaps in the conversation. That's not exactly fair on the rest of us.'

'How is it not fair?'

'Because what stories can we even tell? She's in every single one. Like, why come back if you can't even handle an insinuation?'

'It was a bit more than an insinuation,' says Faye.

'Barely. I don't want to get berated over something that was barely more than an insinuation.'

'Then move the fuck on.'

I have never once heard Faye swear. It shouldn't surprise me as much as it does – she's an adult now, after all, who has had more than a decade to experiment with swearing – but for a second all I want to do is run to Howie and tell him: 'You'll never guess what. Faye said *fuck*.'

It's always so weird, getting the urge to talk to Howie. It comes over me like a sudden, momentary madness.

'Like, I don't understand what Belle wanted out of this whole thing,' says Kendra, not moving the fuck on. She turns to me. 'We're all ready to open up, to have these unfiltered conversations, and then you turn up and none of us even know you're coming—'

'Because Rupert and Fred didn't want you to know! They said you were all excited to see me!'

There's a pause. Everyone is looking at me, faces frozen and uncertain, and then I realise that they aren't looking at me at all. They're staring at Rupert, looming over my shoulder. They're waiting to be told what to do.

'Belle,' says Rupert. 'Come on. We're not going back to the red card system, are we? I thought we were past those days.'

I say nothing, tugging at the cuffs of my blazer.

'Let's try that again,' he says. He stops just short of calling 'action'.

Heart pounding, I try again. 'I don't know what your problem is with me being here.' She's just told me what her problem is. I'm going to sound like an idiot when they cut this together.

'I only have a problem with you if you're going to try and control the conversation,' says Kendra. There's a general snort of laughter at this. Her lips twitch. 'You know what I mean. Since when am I ever going to censor anyone?'

'I'm not censoring you.'

'*You* and *you*' – she points in turn to me and Faye – 'are trying to tell me what I can and can't talk about. Like I'm going to be insensitive and deliberately upset people. We can't be precious here. That's all I'm saying.'

'No one's said otherwise,' says Roni. 'Calm down.' She looks tired. Perhaps she forgot how different this set is to the ones she's used to.

'I'm calm. I'm just pissed.'

'Just be sensitive,' says Faye. 'That's all we're asking.'

Kendra sits back for a second, drink in hand. Then she says, 'This is so nostalgic. The team up.'

'Let's talk about something else,' says Hannah.

'You all let her off the hook so easily.'

'Kendra, come *on*.'

'When all she's done in the last decade is sulk and lie.'

'I've never lied,' I said.

'What about when you said you'd come to Roni's opening night?'

I stand up. 'I need a break.' I don't wait for permission, unclipping my mic and putting my glass down. None of the girls say anything, but Rupert jumps into recovery mode.

'Do you want some water? Shall we take two minutes? It feels like we're being really productive here. Belle, let's have a conversation about what's wrong. Can someone get Belle another drink?'

'Belle,' comes Fred's voice from the back of the room, 'sit *down*.'

'I need to put a tampon in,' I call, because I know that then they can't say shit to me. Donna taught me that trick.

I don't even know where the toilets are. It doesn't matter – my period isn't for another two weeks. I walk straight out of the building and onto the bus.

Cameron is at the bookshop, perched on top of a wooden step-ladder, stacking shelves. He's stood very precariously on one side of the step, a pile of books beside him. The sun hits the back wall, just grazing his ear and the back of his head, lighting up travel books and the small literary criticism section. Mum used to tell him that he'd romanticised the idea of owning a bookshop to the point where the reality of it would always be disappointing. ('Who *reads* any more, Cam? *You* don't even read.') But Cracked Spine – a name panned by the rest of the family but fought for passionately by Cam – is definitely romantic, and gentle, and softly lit, and ironically kept open by Mum's life insurance.

'Promise me you'll do it,' she told him, before she died. So, two weeks after the funeral, Cam quit a job in finance that was making him want to pull his own fingernails out and rented a small unit in Bethnal Green with faded-green walls and a teashop next door.

I had just turned nineteen. Jane was about to be three and very chatty. She talked the whole way through the funeral, which was hilarious and allowed Cameron and I to focus on something other than the strange finality of the day. Three years of living together by that point, and Cameron and I still felt like strangers to each other, in many ways. I stacked shelves in silence as Cameron painted the doorframe with his headphones in, and Jane ran in circles, small pigtails standing straight up on her head and jiggling, before collapsing in a heap on the carpet.

I wasn't convinced about the bookshop as an investment. I didn't read. The only real reader I had ever known was Faye, and now Cameron. He would sit in an armchair in the living room whilst I was at the table working through my GCSE work and, later, my A levels. I would look over at him sometimes, and his eyes would be darting so fast across the page that it looked as if he was having some kind of seizure. It was just another thing that made him incomprehensible to me, this man in our home who moved in a rhythm with my mum so assured that I hated him for it.

On the last day, when we'd finished setting up the shop and we'd gone home to put Jane to bed, he knocked on my bedroom door. 'For all your help,' he said, and he handed me a book. *Jane Eyre*.

I read it in three days. It was my first proper cry.

I wasn't wrong to be cautious. The bookshop isn't a great investment, on paper. But on slow days, Jane does her homework on her stomach in the middle of the floor. On rare busy ones, Cameron will call us both – 'What are you doing? Can you come help?' We will fly round the store, recommending titles we've never read and petting dogs whilst their owners browse. It all makes me a strange kind of happy: a dusty, buttery, soft carpet kind of happy. It's the kind of happy I used to think other people lied about feeling. If Cam had never opened the bookshop, I would probably still think that. I'm willing to do a lot to help Cam keep the bookshop. I guess I just need to work out how much.

The bell jingles, and Cam turns to look at me. The ladder wobbles.

'You're not supposed to be up there when the shop's empty,' I say.

'Ah, well.'

'Seriously, Cam. What if you fell and no one came in?'

'Someone would come in eventually. This is a thriving business.' He slots a book into place. 'Why are you back so early?'

'I walked out.'

'What happened?'

'Kendra,' I say.

'Ah.'

He carries on putting books away as I walk carefully around him, giving the ladder a wide berth. I jump up to sit on the counter beside the till, legs swinging.

'Are you going back?' he asks.

'Not today.'

'At all?'

'I don't know.'

He nods. 'Can they sue?'

'I don't know. I'm just . . . I'm done for today.'

'That's fair.'

'I'll figure the rest out later.'

'Fine by me.' He nods at the box behind the counter. 'Feel like making yourself useful?'

'In a minute.'

'In your own time,' says Cameron. 'There're biscuits in the drawer.'

I'm in the middle of my third biscuit when the bell tingles again. A man about my age smiles at me, pushing the door closed behind him. Cameron calls a greeting to him from atop the ladder and I jump down from the counter and try to look busy.

He browses slowly, making his way along the walls, ducking under the stepladder. *Bad luck*, I think. Cameron climbs down as the man settles on a volume of J. B. Priestly and tucks it under his arm. He seems about to bring it to me at the till when he makes eye contact and smiles. He isn't bad-looking – a little clean-cut for my taste, but sweet and non-threatening. He walks to the offers table and picks up a cheap paperback on gardening with what looks like very little thought. I stash the other half of my biscuit as he walks to the till.

'Hi,' he says.

'Hi.' He's still smiling at me. I'm not used to guys smiling at me – I haven't dated or anything like it since a brief relationship at twenty-two with a man who I liked largely because he knew every bar in the city. In hindsight, it should have been a red flag. I keep my eyes down as I scan the book through. 'I like your outfit,' he says. I realise suddenly how out of place I must look in my tailored jumpsuit and TV make-up. I give him a quick smile in return.

I go to grab a paper bag as he's paying, but he puts a hand on my arm. On the other side of the shop, Cameron's head goes up. He's very still.

'Can you sign that one?' the man asks, nodding at the paperback in my hand.

I'm so taken aback that I do, quickly and without comment. My signature is still loopy and childish. I've never learnt another one. I try to keep it small on the title page, but the bottom of the 'o' in 'Simon' spills onto the book title.

'That's great,' he says, leaning over. 'Thanks. I love your new hair, by the way.'

'Thanks.' I resist the urge to tell him that it's been this length and colour since I was twenty.

'So, there's going to be a reunion? Are you guys still filming or is it ready to go?'

'Still filming,' I manage.

He gestures to my outfit, hand sweeping the length of me. 'Hence . . .'

Cameron clears his throat. 'Belle? Can you take that box through to the back?' He's heading towards us. I pick up the box and push through the door to the stockroom. Behind me, I hear Cameron, friendly and professional, talking the man towards the door.

He comes into the stockroom and sits down on a box across from me.

'You shouldn't leave the shop empty,' I say. 'You'll get robbed.'

'Sure, everyone's waiting for an opportunity to loot this place.' He nods at the door. 'Quite the gentleman, huh? You interested?'

'I really didn't think people would care that much.'

'That's called denial.' He offers a hand to help me up. 'You're going to have to bring that box back through.'

'I know.'

'We can still get you out of this, if you want.'

'He just didn't look like one of them,' I say, balancing the box in my arms again. 'He bought a J. B. Priestly book. He was wearing a coat with a collar.'

'Well, you never can tell,' says Cameron, as he holds the door open.

He doesn't quite get what I mean. I used to be able to see these people coming. I would catch a sideways glance at a shopping centre or a whisper in a restaurant and I would know that I was being observed. Sometimes I could guess before they'd even seen me if they were the kind of people who would know who I was, and then if they would like me or despise me. I'm out of practice. I never was cut out for this, any of it, but now I feel like I'm trying to play an old game with an entirely new rule book. I don't want to be known. I don't want to be seen, any more.

But I'm what it all rests on, really, this family and this roomful of books, mounted on shaky legs. I used to think Mum loved Cameron because he took care of her whilst everything else was going to shit, but after she died, I realised that she loved him because he let her take care of him. Cameron is not a provider. If he was, he would have been a better lawyer. But I am. Somewhere inside me still exists the ability to steel myself and do what needs to be done. At least I hope it does.

Behind the desk, I sit down on top of the box of books so that I'm eye-level with rolls of receipt paper and dried-out markers. If I tip my head back and stare upwards, towards the ceiling, I can see the top of Cameron's stepladder, and the crown of his head bobbing steadily into view.

Season One

Roni and Hannah were cut in the first round of *Alice* auditions. Roni took it well – she was always good at doing that – but Hannah cried. Some of the other girls stood on the stage of the black box theatre with us looked a little shocked, clutching their headshots in trained, professional stances, but Hannah was nine, and too young for the part, and not ready to pretend to don the cap of a working professional. Donna gave her a hug when she came off the stage and a little speech about how rejection was part of the industry.

'Besides,' she said, 'you're the youngest. You should end up better than any of them.'

Hannah wiped her sleeve across her face and gave her a wide-eyed, watery nod. The boom mic hovered closer, but she didn't say anything and after a while it pulled back, furry grey head bobbing disappointedly.

Kendra, Faye and I made it all the way to the end with four other girls, but by that point I wasn't worried. Every girl who left the stage with a stiff upper lip and a pretty 'Thank you for your time' to the casting table only increased my faith in what Donna had told me in the back of the taxi. I was special. There was no way it was going to be anyone other than me.

Donna got the call in the middle of dance class the next day. She let out a squeak of excitement. 'She's here now. You can tell her yourself.'

'Is this Belle?' came the voice of the very posh producer. 'I have a question for you. How would you like to be our Alice?'

We were in school when the shouting started. The six of us were bent over our desks working on everything from long division to cell structure when we heard Charlene's distinctive, bellowing voice echoing up the stairs, through the closed door. Heads turned to Paget, who was already bright red.

'It's okay,' Faye told her. 'The cameras aren't on down there.'

'How do you know?'

'Well, we're up here. What would they be filming?'

I touched my neck, out of habit, but there was no mic hanging around it. They were in the hands of a runner who would be waiting for us outside class. Sometimes that runner was Howie, the man I had met in the production room who, it turned out, was actually only a boy of seventeen. He would always wink at me when he put my mic around my neck, and the other girls would giggle. I enjoyed these winks – Kendra had called Howie 'cute' before she had ever seen him wink at me – but they were also confusing in a way that made my stomach wrap around itself and squeeze.

Another raised voice. Against the tutor's instructions, Kendra slipped out of her seat and cracked the door open. 'That's Donna,' she said, incredulous. We had never heard Donna shout.

The runner outside the door seemed more than happy for us to leave class, even if our tutor wasn't. As a group, we crept down the stairs, a trembling Paget bringing up the rear.

'It's a joke!' Charlene was yelling. 'We were told we were bringing our children into a professional environment!'

'How *dare* you question my professionalism,' boomed Donna. Her voice was still musical, but it was low and full now, like an oboe.

'You set those kids up! You and all these *crooks*—' We peered around the stairs, through the open doorway. Charlene's finger was wagging at the crew and producers. She was a large woman, white-blonde and pink-skinned, and when she was angry, she turned scarlet. 'You knew exactly who was getting that part before we all walked into the room.'

The cameras were on her. Paget had noticed too – she was breathing very hard in and out of her nose, bottom lip trembling. 'She needs to stop,' she whispered, but not loud enough for anyone except me to hear.

'Charlene,' came my mother's voice. 'Let's just stay calm until we've got to the bottom of this.'

'We've got there! We've followed the money! Donna just admitted it!'

'Calm down,' said Donna. Her voice was softer now, her words slower, like she was talking to a child having a tantrum. 'The people who work on this show have nothing to do with the people producing *Alice*.'

'Okay,' said Mum again, calmly, 'that can't be entirely true. Clearly this isn't all a huge coincidence.'

'Being invited to audition doesn't mean we have a say over the casting—' tried Rupert.

Charlene scoffed. 'Spare me! It's all rigged. You've taken one child and made her your prize pony—'

'The children are listening,' boomed Donna.

Heads turned to see us all in a frightened huddle in the doorway. Charlene beckoned to Paget. 'Pack your stuff. We're going.'

'Charlene,' said Mum, touching her shoulder.

'We're *going*.' Charlene grabbed Paget's arm and pulled her past us, out of the door. Halfway down the corridor, she turned back. 'Belle, honey. Congrats on Alice.'

'Thanks,' I mumbled, as Charlene tugged poor Paget through to the changing room.

They weren't there the next morning. Donna didn't reference their absence, but when we walked in the studio she'd bought heart-shaped lollipops for all the girls and matching purple velour hoodies.

'I am so sorry that you girls had to hear all of that yesterday,' she said, sitting cross-legged on the studio floor with us as we opened our gifts. 'I've had some words with people, and I'm going to make sure that never, ever happens again.'

We decided amongst ourselves that we wouldn't mind too much if it happened again. We loved the hoodies.

Paget and Charlene were out for a day and a half. They turned up that Friday, both red in the face but subdued. Donna made Paget her teaching assistant in dance class and gave her a hug when we were finished. On the mums' bench, Charlene sat primly with her handbag in her lap. She didn't say a word to anyone for the rest of the day. Paget never got a velour hoodie.

I started my period on the second night of *Alice*. My costume was nothing like the film version – it was all flouncy white lace. Babyish, I thought, although of course when Donna asked, I said I loved it.

'You look like the world's cutest marshmallow,' said Mum, tickling me under the chin.

I was midway through my chat with the caterpillar when I felt it – a strange trickling sensation, like the 'slow pee' that Kendra had described when she got hers the month before. ('You'll just *know*,' she'd said, with an air of superiority.)

I flubbed a line and had to be bailed out by the caterpillar. No cameras were there to catch it, but I knew Donna had. I came off-stage flustered with only a minute's reprise before I had to go back on. Hurriedly, out of view of the adult chorus members, I pushed the many stupid lacey layers of underskirt aside and felt something wet. Even in the dim light of the wings, my fingertip was bright red.

In a matter of minutes, I would be turning a cartwheel in front of an audience of hundreds, exposing layers of white lace and potentially an angry blush in the centre of them. No one would ever cast me in anything again.

I was white and clammy for the rest of the first half. The cartwheel moment passed with no audible gasp from the auditorium, but there was no way to be sure that this London audience wasn't just incredibly polite.

I ran offstage at the interval and gabbled a whispered explanation into my mum's ear. 'Okay,' she said. 'It's fine. No one saw.' A pad might shift as I danced, we decided quickly, might become uncomfortable and distracting. I had less than ten minutes to come to terms with my new womanhood and learn to put a tampon in, Mum talking me through it from the other side of the toilet door.

When I came offstage at the end of the show, I knew it hadn't been my best. Donna came into my dressing room to ask if I was okay, looking so genuinely concerned that I wanted to disappear through a hole in the floor.

'Screw it,' said Mum. 'It's one show. You made it through.' The next day, in-between filming and the evening performance, we went out for red velvet cake.

For the most part, I loved doing *Alice*. I had never been anywhere near a production as big as this, let alone been at the centre of it. I wasn't old enough yet for it to feel like work, except for rare moments when I was sweating through a tech run or tap dancing on very little sleep. But as much as I loved it all, I was very aware that between school, shooting and six shows a week, I was exhausted. I often found myself falling asleep into my schoolbooks or yawning on camera. Once, Kendra caught me napping in the dressing room and wrote 'I ♥ Donna' on my arm in permanent marker. I had to scrub it so hard before the evening performance that my whole arm was bright red for the entire first act.

Whilst I was working twice as hard, the other girls were working less. 'We don't film any more when you're in matinees,' explained Faye, when I asked why they'd been able to go for ice cream the previous afternoon instead of training. They'd roller-skate, or go to museums, or hang out in each other's hotel rooms and watch movies. My jealousy made me feel guilty. I knew they each would have traded places with me in a heartbeat.

'Why aren't they filming as much any more?' I asked Donna, who often sat in taxis with me on the way to the theatre when Mum was working.

'To keep it fair,' she said.

'To keep what fair?'

'Screentime. Booking professional work shouldn't mean you get featured less. Besides.' She squeezed my knee. 'I wanted to be around for you.'

She was my biggest advocate and my harshest critic. When I came offstage, I would ask how it had gone, and Mum would say, 'Great stuff, as always. Shall we grab some dinner?'

But we never left for food before Donna and I had sat down and talked my performance through, dissecting the good and bad of it. She would tell me if my delivery had been stilted, if my singing had been nasally (which it almost always was), if I'd come across too knowing, or too young, or too 'stage school', which was one of the worst things she could throw at me despite the fact that I wasn't entirely clear on what it meant.

'Your legs are beginning to jiggle a little,' she said once, when Mum was out of the room. 'They shouldn't really be doing that, at your age. Just keep an eye on it.' I promised that I would. After that, I never touched anything at crafty other than the salads.

Even in class, things were different after *Alice*. I wasn't just one of Donna's students any more – I was, so far, her only success story. When the others weren't picking things up fast enough, she would say, 'Belle, could you?', and up to the front of the class I would go. Kendra's scowl was deeply satisfying, especially when I could see a camera pointed at her, but sometimes the expressions on the other girls' faces made my stomach twist. Donna showered us all with compliments, brought us treats every Friday and told us how much she adored us, but we all knew that I was the one she loved the most.

Roni and Hannah weren't booked that season. Kendra and Paget had a few commercials and Kendra even got to say a couple of lines in a CBBC show, after I had been in *Alice* about two months. She came in buzzing, going on and on about the set and the principle actors and how one of the leading boys, a sixteen-year-old playing a werewolf, had told her she was 'pretty convincing'. Mum bought her a box of chocolates to say congratulations and told me off when I complained about giving them to her.

'She's *awful* to me.'

'Oh, sure, and you rise above it like Mother Teresa.' She placed the box firmly in my hands. 'You have everything she wants. The least you can do is be kind.'

When I handed the chocolates over with a mumbled 'Congrats', Kendra was so surprised that she didn't say anything at all.

By that point we had been training with Donna for about five months, and it had become normal to step over production equipment on our way to class and gossip with microphones hanging around our necks. The cameras circled like friendly fish as we went about our lives. Filming was just something I did before I got to the theatre, and then that was my real life, performing every night with Donna and Mum waiting in the wings to greet me when I was finished. At least once a week Donna took us both out to dinner, sometimes just me when Mum was sat hunched over her laptop, phone pressed to her ear. We would talk about everything from my favourite books to Donna's ex-husbands. There were two of them, and according to her they were both as awful as each other.

'But Gregory was awful in a more obvious way,' she said over chicken salads. 'Franz was a more insidious kind of awful. You know?'

I nodded as convincingly as I could.

None of us even realised that what we were filming was going to be the final episode until it was almost done. We'd had unusual filming days before – we'd shot scenes where Donna took us all out to London Zoo and Buckingham Palace, and one where she'd introduced us on camera to male dancers who Mum had told me on the way home were almost definitely strippers. This seemed relatively innocuous: a viewing party for Faye's film.

'It's all to do with *Alice*,' Donna had told me in the car on the way to the theatre, after Faye had been cast. 'You know that, don't you?'

Faye and I had both made it to the final round of call-backs for the film. I knew I'd had a fantastic final audition. Still, I'd been genuinely happy for Faye when she'd been cast. I wasn't ready to leave *Alice* anyway.

'They wanted you,' said Donna, reapplying her lipstick in the back of the taxi, 'of course, but we couldn't get you out of your *Alice* contract early. You're locked in for six months. So they went with Faye.' She smacked her lips once, twice. 'The thing is, Belle, and I'm only telling you this because I know you'll be a grown-up about it, they knew that from the beginning.'

'Who knew what?'

'Fred and Rupe. They knew you wouldn't be able to do the film. But it was a good storyline, you know, the whole rivalry.' She waved a hand. 'They're master manipulators. If you're ever in doubt about what's real, I hope you know you can ask me.'

'I know,' I said. 'Anyway, I don't mind. I like doing *Alice*.'

'Sure, but we shouldn't do that for longer than these six months. We want people to see you doing new stuff. This was just a small part, but when those big film roles come up, I want you free for them.'

I was quiet, staring out of the window as we edged down Tottenham Court Road.

'Something on your mind?' asked Donna.

'You said I could ask you what's real.'

'You can. Always.'

'Is *Alice* real?'

'*Alice* is a story, unfortunately,' smiled Donna.

'I heard Charlene,' I said. 'That day when she started yelling, after I got the part.'

Coolly, Donna put the lid back on her lipstick with a click. 'What do you think she was saying?'

'I'm not sure, exactly.' I waited, but she didn't jump in. 'Something about following the money?'

'She's a very overdramatic woman.'

'I know. But . . .' I wasn't quite sure how to ask the question. 'How did I get Alice?'

She squeezed my knee. 'Because you were the most talented little girl there. And that is the whole and honest truth.' Relieved, I smiled at her. 'People are always going to make up their own stories,' she said. 'But guess what? When you get up on that stage, none of their stories matter any more.'

Mum let me pick out the box of chocolates we got for Faye. I chose a box double the size of the one we bought for Kendra when she got her CBBC role. If Mum noticed when I brought it to the till, she didn't say anything.

Faye shot her scene, and when Fred asked, the director sent over a rough cut of it, just the five minutes that featured Faye and a bunch of spunky orphan children. The crew turned the studio into a makeshift cinema, wheeling in a huge TV screen, and us six crowded onto the sofa, passing Faye's chocolates back and forth. We were giggly and already a little sugar-high when Rupert crouched in front of us.

'Okay,' he said. 'I'm super excited. You guys excited?'

We nodded emphatically, mouths full of chocolate.

'Good!' he said, clapping his hands. 'Whilst your mothers are still getting ready, let's warm up. I want to see those acting chops. Show me some finale faces!'

Kendra and I caught each other's eyes. The other girls were beaming, fluttering their eyelids. Hannah punched the air with a quiet little whoop. Kendra and I copied them, all of us laughing. We blew kisses into the cameras fixed on us.

'Hey, hey,' said Rupert, laughing with us. 'Ground rules. This is a really big night for Miss Faye—' Cue cheers and clapping from all of us. Kendra wolf whistled. 'Right! And so, if anyone messes with this scene, talks to one of us or looks straight into the camera, you're going to get a red card. That means a fine, which means your mothers are going to have to pay us some money. Got it?'

We nodded.

'Good!' he said. 'Hey, so we've done some big smiles. Can we do them again, facing the TV this time?'

We did, beaming at the blank screen in front of us.

'Amazing!' he said. 'Okay, just to warm up our faces, I want to see your best acting. Give me a frown, like you're really mad. I want to really believe it.'

There was suddenly a camera very close to my face. I scowled as convincingly as I could – not pantomime, like little Hannah was doing, but as if I was really out of sorts. Rupert seemed delighted.

'That's great, girls! Now give me some side eye. Like "What did she just say?" Really sassy.'

We looked sideways at each other until we erupted into giggles.

'Go again,' encouraged Rupert.

'What is going on?' came a booming voice.

It was Donna, striding furiously into the centre of the room in a gold dress and heels. We all stared at her, sparkling under the lights, as she flashed furious eyes at Rupert.

'Get that camera out of Belle's face *at once.*'

The lens was still pointed at me, but the grip took a few steps back. I blinked.

Donna dragged Rupert off to the side of the room.

'She is an eleven-year-old child,' came her voice. 'You have a duty of care.'

'She's fine, Donna.' Rupert was speaking in the same tone that he had used when Faye and Hannah's mum, Alex, had complained about class running late. 'I was just getting some backup footage. It's standard practice.'

'She doesn't know that. She doesn't know all the tricks.'

'It's not a trick,' said Rupert. 'You need to calm down.'

'You are responsible for how she is presented to the world for the rest of her life. Do you understand that?'

'You're overreacting.'

The door swung open and in came our mothers. Mum was wearing a glittery top, which was maybe one of five times I had ever seen her dressed up. Rupert wolf whistled. Mum glared at him. She caught my eye, shot me her 'get a load of this guy' face.

I couldn't respond.

'Okay!' said Rupert. 'Let's all get seated.'

'I'm so nervous,' whispered Faye, beside me. I squeezed her hand, absently.

'It'll be *great*,' said Kendra, putting a protective arm around Faye's shoulders.

Around me, crew members put final touches in place. Someone switched the screen on, pressed buttons on the remote. Faye's face appeared, frozen. Everyone cheered, but I forgot to join in. I could feel Donna's eyes on me. She knew that something was wrong.

The camera was still pointed at me. It had caught that I hadn't cheered, that I hadn't replied to Faye, that I was now looking pale and silent and sullen. It would see all those things, and then it would redistribute them wherever it wanted to, in whatever order it chose, until the story it told wasn't really what had happened at all.

And the thing was, everyone would believe it. Because it would be on TV.

I stared at the lens, and the lens stared back.

'Red card, Belle,' tutted Rupert. 'I did warn you.'

Reunion special

It's never the same driver. 'You alright?' this one asks me, offering me a water. I politely refuse. 'Long day ahead?' I wonder if Production has briefed the drivers, if they actually all know exactly who I am and aren't supposed to say anything. Sometimes I feel as if worrying about being recognised is an egotistical exercise. I'm no Roni.

I watch the navigation open on the driver's phone, our little blue dot making steady progress up the street. News alerts descend from the top of his screen, one after the other, each with a notification that sounds like a gong striking. *Three dead in Manchester crash. The Real Deal: Why are we so fascinated by trauma? Relationship experts weigh in on office romances. Lizzie Hough apologises for leaked photos.* The driver swipes them up and away. I wonder if Jane got the same notifications on her phone. I imagine her staring down at that word, *trauma*, equal parts startled and horribly curious. I crack my window and breathe slowly and deeply, trying to make my stomach settle. You can't will it away, that feeling of being broken open in front of other people. Even when you live your life in fear of it, you're never quite prepared for the fingers clawing their way under your skin.

It's okay, though. I'm going there to end it.

My car arrives just a minute or so after Faye's – I can see her silvery hair through the back window as it sits on the kerb in front of us. I open my door, and she opens hers, and her moment of pleased surprise almost makes me reconsider.

'Morning, you,' she says, closing the door behind me. Then she takes me in and says, 'Oh, no, Belle, really?'

I'm dressed down, no make-up, hair pulled back. I look like I should be helping her out of the car and running to find her mic. She knows what this means. She knows what I've come there to say.

'Sorry,' I say.

She pushes her hair back behind her ears. Then she turns her wrist over in a fluid motion, eyes cast down at her watch. 'Look,' she says, 'I wouldn't call us *late* late for another half an hour or so.'

'So?'

'So, shall we go for a walk?'

We trudge through Soho, which I have never done at 8 am. At that time, the Soho I knew in my late teens and early twenties is still asleep, every bar and sex shop still hibernating, or posing as a breakfast café. Strange to think how relieved I was to avoid the Southbank when now all I want is to go wandering with her along the river, waving to boats.

'How's your sister?' she asks.

'Good. How did you know I had a sister?'

'Rupert,' she says. 'He asked me if you thought she'd want to do an interview at all.'

'Jane? Why?'

'She was born as everything was ending. She's never known you working, really. I can see why he thought it would be an interesting perspective on you.' We walk for another few seconds, past a comic book shop and an independent gallery. The way ahead is hazy. 'Don't worry,' she says. 'I told him you'd never go for it. Can't imagine her dad would either.' There's a chorus of horns on the road ahead of us, the two of us winding down a side street towards it. 'If I could do it all again,' she says, 'I'd probably do it without Hannah. Or maybe I wouldn't even do it at all.'

We emerge onto the main road and find ourselves heading towards the Palace Theatre. It always used to be our favourite. Faye looks at me sideways now and then, small furtive glances that she thinks I can't see.

'Is she much like your mum?'

'Yeah, I guess she is.' Jane is exactly what I imagine Mum would have been like at eleven. Sometimes she speaks with exactly the same intonations Mum did, even though I'm sure she doesn't even remember what Mum sounded like, and it sends a chill right through me. 'She's a really great kid.'

'Well, you had a really great mum. Maybe I'll meet Jane sometime.'

'Yeah, maybe.'

'I'd like to,' says Faye. 'I want to see if she reminds me of you.'

She hasn't changed much, in the eleven years since I last saw her. She isn't much taller than she became at fourteen, when she sprung up like a spruce tree and started to dance on long, willowy limbs. Her voice has settled into a deeper place but it's still sweet and gentle, a little croaky now and then. Her accent is unchanged. She moved back to Manchester after the show and I think she's stayed there ever since. Her hair is still long and fine and almost silver. I wonder if she dyes it. I wonder if I look different to her.

We knew every atom of each other, once. It hurts me to think of all the parts of her I no longer know.

'What have you been up to?'

She laughs at me. 'Oh god. I don't know where to start with that.'

'School?'

'Well, not any more, no.'

'I meant—'

'I know,' she says. 'Yeah, I got my A levels. Didn't do uni. Sort of wish I had. Did you?'

'No. Just A levels for me too.'

'Did you do well?'

'Awfully.'

'Me too,' she laughs. 'I wonder if we actually learnt anything whilst we were on that set. I don't know how Hannah turned out so brainy.'

'What do you do now?' I wonder if it's just her little shop.

'This and that,' she says. 'Bits and pieces. Pottery, at the moment. I'm not very good at sticking to anything.'

'Neither am I.'

'Two peas,' says Faye.

The wind in my eyes is making them water. I blink furiously into it.

'So,' she says.

'So.'

'What are you going to say to them?'

'I'll say, Rupert, Fred, I appreciate the offer, but I've decided I don't want to do this any more.'

'And when that doesn't work?'

'I'll play the dead mum card. Or the mental health card, or the total lack of safeguarding card, or the Donna card . . . I've got a lot to work with.' She laughs, doubtfully. 'They have to let me out of it somehow,' I say.

'Belle,' says Faye, 'why did you come back?'

'Because of the money.'

'Just because of the money?'

'It's a lot of money.'

'Well then,' she says. 'Sure. You should probably quit.'

We walk in silence down Shaftesbury Avenue. A group of girls queue outside one of the theatres for cheap tickets. When we pass them, I see one nudge another, speaking very quickly behind her hand. I speed up, just enough that Faye will match my pace without asking questions. I don't get recognised much any more – it's amazing what a haircut and an adult face will do – but every time I do, it feels like people are looking at me and seeing someone else.

'Do you want me to tell you not to quit?' asks Faye.

There's a place on this road that we used to come to for chips after auditions. Once, after a night out at around nineteen, a boy walked me there and I stood for ten minutes watching him order without realising where I was. Then I cried.

'Don't quit,' says Faye.

She's stopped walking just a few paces from the takeaway. Her hair blows into her eyes and she pushes it back, the bracelets on her wrists jingling. She has a tattoo on the inside of her arm: a line drawing of a sun, in red and black.

'Why not?'

'Or do,' she says. 'But I'd rather you didn't.'

'Why not?'

'Because I don't actually want to do this without you, very much.'

When we turn and head back, the girls outside the theatres who noticed us the first time start screaming our names and jumping up and down. We're on the other side of the road, but we can see them in-between cars and buses, waving their arms in the air. I stare straight ahead but Faye waggles shy fingers at them, then takes my hand and waves it back at the girls, high above our heads.

At the studio, the others are all waiting for us. Between last night and this morning, I now have fourteen missed calls from Rupert on my phone. Faye has six. I'm expecting a telling off, but when we walk in together, I see him push down his frustration and breathe out.

'Belle,' he says. 'So glad you're here.' He looks me up and down once but doesn't say anything else.

'On your own time,' says Kendra. She doesn't comment on my appearance either. Actually, she looks quietly pleased.

The studio isn't set up for us to sit down and chat. I apply lip balm in my phone mirror and comb my hair out with my fingers as Faye asks, 'What's going on, Rupe?'

Rupert is busy chatting away to one of the production assistants, but Fred, stood to one side in a white shirt and navy jacket, gestures to the door.

'It's going to be a field trip day today, ladies,' he says.

They've pulled a limo around for us. We're ushered out onto the pavement with the cameras trained on us. I think they're expecting an excited squeal, but no one reacts beyond a monotone 'Neat,' from Kendra. We're not thirteen any more. We've all been in a limo by now. We've probably all been in one wishing we were somewhere else.

Inside they have bottles of champagne waiting for us in buckets of ice and, naturally, more cameras. They've managed to squeeze a handheld one in there too. The five of us squish uncomfortably onto the back bench and the operator sits facing us on the other side, expression neutral.

'Where do you think we're going?' asks Roni as the car pulls away.

Faye says nothing, but she stares out of the window with her face blank, as if she knows.

We pop the champagne and pour ourselves a glass or two for the road, because a limo is a limo, after all. After a few minutes it becomes pretty obvious where we're headed, but we still have to gasp and clutch at each other's shoulders when we pull up.

'Oh my god,' says Kendra. 'It hasn't changed at all.'

The Italian restaurant that used to be next door is now an Indian, but other than that she's right. The Southbank studio stands where it always has, tall and brick-built, painted white. Through the windows I catch glimpses of rooms so familiar it feels as if Howie's face might appear at any one of them.

'Who's Lee Frazer?' asks Hannah.

Then I notice the one thing that is different: a sign over the door that reads: *The Lee Frazer School of Performing Arts*.

'I think she bought the place from the production company a few years after the show ended,' says Kendra. 'Supposedly she's kept it pretty true to how it was when we were here, though. She's meant to be a big fan.' Someone's prepped her with that information. Still, Kendra makes the exposition dump sound impressively natural.

Rupert and Fred, who followed in a production van, tail us behind the cameras as we open the door. The hallway is long and dark and seems to tip as I look into it, so that I'm not sure if I'm staring ahead of me or straight down, into a long, vertical nothingness.

'Huh,' says Kendra. She's looking up and to the right. I follow her eyes. The Lee Frazer School of Performing Arts has been thoughtful enough to hang framed black and white photos of our younger selves on the walls of their entranceway. We obligatorily 'aw' over them as we make our way through. Secretly, I think we're all hoping this is just a production gimmick and that Lee Frazer isn't actually *that* big of a fan. There's only five, I notice. No Paget.

We climb the stairs to the dressing room and stop to take stock. 'We met Kendra and Belle in here,' says Hannah to Faye. Faye is gently dazed, as am I. She keeps to the edges of the room as she walks around.

'I forget you guys were all in the same audition group,' says Roni. 'That must have been an exciting day for Production.'

'Except they didn't actually want to cast Belle, at first,' says Kendra. She laughs. 'Right, Belle? Donna stepped in.'

'Yeah, she did.' I move smoothly past her and fall into step with Faye, who is now leading the way into the dance studio. Maybe she's thinking that the quicker we get through this, the quicker we can get out.

The walls of the dance studio are lined with faintly faded squares, photos of Lee Frazer students, I imagine, carefully excavated by Production. There's a CD player in the corner which I'm certain they've also placed there, and the same wooden barre we used to grip with our small hands. It really looks as if we just arrived for our morning class. In the mirror, our older selves seem edited onto the background. We don't belong here any more.

'Anyone remember any of your old routines?' asks Rupert from somewhere off to the side. Roni unexpectedly launches into her *Charlie and The Chocolate Factory* audition piece, or at least the parts that are still ingrained in her. We're all laughing, and part of it feels real and light and lovely, like we really are twelve again and not even convinced that this TV show is real. At the same time, it's taking everything in me not to give Rupert the satisfaction of an on-camera cry.

It's such a relief when we move out of the dance studio and into the music room that it takes my mind a second to catch up. Faye is lightly touching notes on the piano and Hannah is gazing out of the window when there's a click in my brain, like the pieces slotting together, and I look down and see the exact spot on the floor where I spilled vodka, the section of the window frame that Howie would tap ash onto, the corner where Faye sat and threw up into the bin.

Faye touches a high G, her foot on the pedal, and looks back at me. Wordlessly, she comes to stand beside me. Her hand slips into mine.

It's the warmest, strongest thing I have felt since I first held Jane. But over my shoulder, and beside me, and everywhere, the lenses are looking on. I drop her hand and walk over to join Hannah at the window.

'Isn't there another room you guys were always pretty curious about?' asks Rupert.

It takes us all a second to understand him. Our minds all go to the same place, I think, but we still don't quite believe him, because being back here with the cameras and the crew and Rupert and Fred following a few paces behind makes us feel young, and when you're young there are certain things you just aren't allowed to do.

Even over a decade later, walking down those stairs still feels illicit. At the foot of them, Roni gives me a jokey push forward. I lead the way, resisting the urge to tiptoe.

The production room is different from how it looked when I was twelve and nervously completing my forfeit. The monitors and keyboards and headsets are gone. It's a storeroom now, filing cabinets along one wall and shelves of dance shoes and props and accessories along the other. It isn't so scary any more, or so exciting. All our secrets have been excavated and moved to other, shadier locations.

But Howie is still there.

'Hey, Belle,' he says, sat on the desk in his black t-shirt. He waves at me.

'Belle,' prompts Rupert when I don't speak. I suppose I must have been quiet for quite a while, for him to step in. There's no way to tell how long. Howie goes on looking at me.

I can feel the other girls crowding in the doorway behind me, delayed inhales of breath as they figure out who he is. He looks different now, bearded, a little wider – but I will always recognise Howie. I think I see him in the street every day. He's one of those people that I'm always watching out for when I step onto a bus or pass a restaurant window. I always wonder if the man in front of me with dark hair will turn his head and have Howie's face. But to actually see it doesn't seem real. Howie is a body I buried in LA. He's a spirit I was supposed to have laid to rest.

'You look great,' he says. 'God, how old are you now? This is weirding me out.'

I will not give them this. Not any of them.

I take a breath.

'Twenty-six,' I say. 'You?'

He laughs. 'You do the maths. This is so weird. It's so good to see you.' He stands up and comes straight at me, and I want to back up but I know I'll bump into the girls behind me. His arms come around me crushingly. 'How are you?'

I wait out the hug. 'I'm good,' I say, when he finally lets me go.

'And all the rest of you?' He takes in the others. 'Faye. Hi. You're prettier than ever.' She's stood against the far wall with her hands behind her back. I think Howie can tell he's not getting close enough to Faye for a hug.

There's an uncomfortable silence as Howie waits for someone to answer his question. Kendra breaks it.

'I'd like to go see our old classroom,' she says.

'Belle,' says Howie. 'Stay and catch up.'

'Belle wants to see it too,' says Kendra. 'Don't you?'

She turns her back on Howie, decisively, her arm through mine. Of all the people to save me, I wouldn't have expected it to be Kendra. As we head back up the stairs, I feel Faye breathing next to me, faster than she was before.

They've dug our desks out of storage. *BFF*, reads the corner of mine, with a small heart underneath. I trace the outline of it with one finger. I see Faye feel for the grooves in the underside of hers. We catch each other's eyes, but she's wary of approaching me now. I move away instead, floating over to the window.

Behind me, Kendra, Roni and Hannah are flicking through old schoolbooks. Production really seem to have kept everything. They're laughing at Kendra's spelling, which was always atrocious. Outside, Howie is leaning on the wall under Lee Frazer's sign, his smoke rising gently upwards, towards me. He doesn't look up, but I still think that he can see me, somehow, that he knows he's being watched.

When Fred calls a break, I slip out of the room and down the stairs towards the entrance hall. I avoid eye contact with my own beaming thirteen-year-old face.

Howie has nearly finished his cigarette. He puts it out when he hears the door open, turning. He smiles. 'Princess Belle. How's it going?'

'Don't stop on my account.'

'Wouldn't want you breathing all that,' he says.

I let the door close behind me and stay stood with my back against it.

'Come over here,' he says. 'Let me look at you.' I stay where I am. He walks a few paces closer to me instead. 'You really do look great,' he says. 'You look way more natural than the others. What's up with Kendra's cheeks?'

'Filler,' I say.

'Ah.' He grimaces. 'Never good, is it?'

'I thought you stayed in LA?'

'Rupe called and offered me some work. I'll be here for a few weeks, then back home to the wife and kids.' He sees my face. 'I'm joking. There's been girls, but none of them stuck around.'

Shocker, I think. He's thirty-two now. He still looks good, but he still has the energy of a seventeen-year-old nepotism hire wandering aimlessly around a television set.

'It really is good to see you,' he says. 'I get why you never reached out.' This is a lie. 'But we should catch up sometime, for real. Since it's been so long.'

I shake my head.

'No?' he says. He's still smiling.

'I don't want to catch up with you.'

'Why not?'

'I don't want anything to do with you.'

His face falls. 'Don't do that.'

'Don't do what?'

'Don't lump me in with the rest of them.'

I don't say anything.

'I helped you.'

I press my back firmly against the door. Behind me, my hand finds the doorknob.

'I'm probably the only person in the world who knows what you actually went through.'

It could be a threat. It's hard to tell, with Howie.

'You don't know how much I've thought about you.' He drops the cigarette. 'Shit, Belle. It wasn't meant to go like this. I'm sorry for ambushing you. That was Rupert and Fred.' He holds up a hand, anticipating an interruption that never comes. 'I shouldn't have agreed to it. I know that. I just wanted to catch up.'

'I don't want to talk to you.'

'We don't have to talk on camera.'

'I don't want to talk, Howie. On camera or off.'

'How about on mic?'

It takes the words a second to sink in. Howie watches my face and grins at me from under rumpled hair. I reach up and pull the mic off the neck of my t-shirt like it's burning me. It lies, round and black, in the centre of my palm. We both stare at it.

I fold my fingers over it tightly.

'You should have stayed in LA,' I whisper, as quietly as I can.

He looks at me with big, hurt eyes. 'Maybe you shouldn't have taken the money.'

The mic presses into my palm as we watch each other. He takes a few paces towards me. I back up into the doorway. He puts a hand on my shoulder.

'Why are you scared of me?' he asks. I don't say anything. 'Look,' he says, 'Belle, I'm going to be in town for a while, at least a few weeks, and then I'm gone and I don't know when I'll be back. I don't imagine you'll be heading out to LA anytime soon.'

I shake my head.

'No, didn't think so. Let's get dinner. Or coffee, or drinks, or *something*. You understand that I didn't need to take Rupe's money, right? I came back because I wanted to see how you were doing.' He puts his head on the side. 'I've missed you.'

Behind me, I find the doorknob again and push. Howie stumbles forward a little as I step back into the corridor.

'Please,' I say.

His disappointed eyes stare me down even after I've closed the door.

Rupert makes us sit cross-legged in a circle on the floor of the dance studio for almost three hours that afternoon, reminiscing until the conversation starts to flag. Hannah hasn't said a word in twenty minutes when he finally sighs and raises a hand, and says, 'Okay, girls, that's great. Thanks.'

We get up slowly off the wooden floor and rub our lower backs.

Outside on the pavement, with mics removed and cameras being packed away, we wait for someone to order our cars. Howie's cigarette is still lying next to the wall, crushed. There's a relieved silence for a few minutes. We rest our voices.

'Those pictures,' says Kendra suddenly.

'Fucking hell, I *know*.' Roni lets out a bark of a laugh. 'Eerie.'

I ask Kendra if she knew where we were going. She nods. 'They called me last night and sent over some stuff to memorise.'

'Could have given us a heads up.'

'And ruin your authentic reactions?'

I'm staring down at my shoes when she says, 'I didn't know they'd invited that creep along.'

I hadn't even realised that my head was hanging low. I stare out over the river instead. 'Oh, right.'

'Honest. I would have prepped you for that one.'

'We probably should have guessed,' says Roni. 'We all know what they're like.'

Faye is watching the river too. She doesn't seem like she can hear us.

'It was a dick move,' says Kendra. 'Just pushing him on us like that. There's something scary about that guy. Always hanging around when we were kids. There's a reason guys like that don't have friends their own age.'

'Yeah,' I say. 'What a freak.'

I do my best to ignore the guilt that gnaws at my stomach the entire drive home. As much as I can't bear to be around Howie any more, the facts are the facts. I owe him.

Season Two

It was made very clear to us that Season Two was not a guarantee, and so our goodbyes were tearful and overly dramatic, with assurances that we would swap letters and call and visit, promises that we knew at the time we probably wouldn't keep. Even Kendra was effusive, squeezing me tightly and saying, 'Belle, I don't know what on *earth* I'm going to do without you.' Maybe she meant it. I liked to think that Kendra didn't have any other rivals as interesting as me.

Faye hugged me once, briefly. 'I think we'll all be back,' she said.

'How do you know?'

'I don't. I just have a feeling.'

I still had six weeks left in *Alice*. Production weren't paying for the hotel when filming stopped, so we rented a bedroom from a woman in Camden who gave us a list of restaurant recommendations that were all out of our price range and asked us to pay in cash. Mum and I shared a double bed, and, as the weather got colder, a plug-in radiator that didn't do much except make strange popping sounds in the middle of the night.

On the last night of *Alice*, the cast presented me with a big bouquet of red roses onstage and I sobbed into them like my heart was breaking. But the whole bus ride home, as I clutched them between my knees, I was thinking of Cotswold hills, and my favourite café, and the bookshop that Mum and I would put our coats on to visit when it rained.

Rupert called, after we'd been back a few weeks. 'Tell your daughter she's going to be on TV tonight!' he said. Mum had the phone pressed to her ear but I could hear his voice booming through our little wooden kitchen.

Mum and I stared at each other. We were both wondering how to play this.

In the end we invited my friends from school round, and Mum's friends, and the neighbours. Stella Malone told me how glad she was she hadn't been cast on the show and had to move to London. 'I wouldn't have met my boyfriend otherwise,' she said, popping a mini cocktail sausage into her mouth. Suddenly, prancing around on a stage in a white lacey costume seemed far less cool than actually having a boyfriend.

I was jittery, bumping into people in our small kitchen, knocking over two drinks. Mum took me by the shoulders and manoeuvred me into the corridor.

'Belle,' she said, bending down to stare into my face, 'it is just TV. And if the person on the screen looks totally different to the person I'm standing in front of right now and they haven't got any of it right, then it will be *funny*. We will *laugh*. Okay?'

'Okay,' I said, unconvinced.

But they actually got a surprising amount of it right. They'd caught one moment on my face in the audition that may or may not have been a dirty look at Kendra – I honestly couldn't remember it well enough to know if the editing was honest – but other than that, I came across well, if a little keen at times. The fairy godmother line was as awful as I had anticipated, though. Stella Malone raised her eyebrows at me from across the room.

'Well!' said Ms Winnow, my effusive drama teacher, perched in our nicest armchair with a cup of tea and a custard cream. 'What did I tell you, Sofie?'

As we were cleaning up, I asked Mum if we could have a party for every episode.

'Absolutely not,' she said, shoving crisp packets into the bin.

'But it was so much fun.' I desperately wanted to see Stella Malone's face when I was cast as Alice, when I came offstage after my opening night, when I helped Donna coach the class and corrected Kendra's turnout.

'It was a lot of fun. But people have better things to do with their weekends.'

I hopped up onto the counter to finish the rest of the Indian selection plate. 'Do you think the person on TV was totally different from me?'

Mum slowed in her cleaning efforts. 'No. Not totally different.' She turned to me, one hand at her hip with a dishcloth clutched in it. 'Do you think you're like that in normal life?'

'Yes,' I said, taking a bite of an onion bhaji.

'It was a great episode,' said Mum. She went back to scrubbing the sides. 'Me and you will watch all the rest. We'll just be quieter about it from now on. I'm sure everyone else will still be watching too.'

They were, and as time went on, I began to wish that they'd stop.

It began subtly. Eye rolls from the other girls stitched in after Donna complimented me, my frowning face when someone talked back or showed Donna what could be interpreted as a modicum of disrespect. They'd had cameras in our car rides sometimes – not when we took taxis, but when we drove in cars Production had sent for us. I'd been too inexperienced to tell the difference. I saw myself, eyes bright and wondrous, drinking in every word she said. I looked at Donna like I was in love with her.

I had been given my own laptop for Christmas. 'For school,' Mum had said. Three episodes in, I searched my name online and found a fan site – which was apparently my 'official' fan site, although no one had told me – and a few articles about the first episodes that were mainly descriptive. I wasn't on Twitter. Instagram wouldn't exist for another year. I was far safer online than I was in the real world.

Boys at school teased that Donna was my girlfriend. Girls stopped telling me they'd watched last night's episode and started exchanging subtle looks when I approached. Mum and I watched three episodes and then we stopped, distracting ourselves with rented romcoms or board games when the show aired. I'd been so excited to get home and make plans with friends, even go to school, but now I didn't want to leave the house. It was that feeling of being seen, all the time, perceived everywhere I went. I was only just beginning to understand what it was and I already knew that it was my least favourite thing I'd ever felt.

I told Mum that I didn't want to go back to school after Year Eight.

'I don't have time to home-school you,' she said.

'I can teach myself.'

She shook her head and said, 'Belle, I'm sorry, but you're going to have to find a way to get on with it all.'

But I didn't have to, as it turned out, because the next day Donna called and said, 'Is there a very, very small chance that you and your mum can be in London as soon as tomorrow?'

She'd got me a part in a music video. 'It won't be part of the show,' she said. 'It's a favour for a friend.'

'Is she getting paid?' asked Mum.

'Of course she's getting paid. She's a professional. It's a short shoot, just one day.'

'I can't get off work tomorrow,' said Mum.

'Send her on her own.'

'I can't do that either.'

'I'm her manager. I'll be there the whole time. And she's old enough to get a train by herself, isn't she?'

I loved the way Donna spoke, like anything was possible as long as you wanted it enough. I begged and pleaded, and Mum wrote me a sick note, and the next day I was on a train to London with my pyjamas and toothbrush in a rucksack.

The shoot didn't even take the full day. It was mostly crowd work with a group of other girls – all of whom knew each other and paid me very little attention – but I had eight bars of a solo in front of a fountain in Hyde Park. I was in a fur-trimmed winter jacket, and when I bent my leg behind my head, I heard a sigh from the director and a murmur from Donna – '*I told you.*'

At her house that evening she let me order pizza for dinner – 'Enjoy this metabolism whilst it lasts, Belle' – and ice cream for dessert. I sat on her sofa eating it, in her high-ceilinged, white-walled Barbican apartment. From the window I could look down and see what felt like all of London spread out below me, like a map on a novelty tea-towel.

She put on *Bright Eyes* starring Shirley Temple and said, 'I wanted to be Shirley Temple so badly when I was a little girl.' Shirley Temple seemed like a far more embarrassing version of who I was being on TV, only young enough to more or less get away with it. I nodded anyway and tried to act as if I was enjoying the film.

Later, I put on my pyjamas in the guestroom and she knocked on the door as I was climbing into bed. 'This is the room I always thought I'd put my daughter in, if I had one,' she said. She leant in the doorway, mug of herbal tea in her hands, and took it in – the pink room with the lace curtains and me, tucked up in the bed.

'Did you want to have a daughter?'

'Oh,' she said, 'very much. I think the daughters of bad mothers often want to have daughters of their own.'

'Why didn't you?'

'I was too scared. I think the daughters of bad mothers often are.'

'What was bad about her?' It felt as if I could ask her anything right then, in that dim, pink light, and she would answer. Donna had such a ready honesty about her, if you were willing to listen. When it was just you and her, in a space without cameras and eavesdroppers and people who all wanted something from her, she would open up gently and easily, like a kind of blossoming. She would become more real to me.

'I wasn't as lucky as you,' she said. 'I didn't have a mother who would have done anything for me.'

She walked over to tuck me in, even though I was already under the covers. The duvet was heavy and enormously puffy. Her hands patted it tightly down on either side of me. Through the material I felt the tips of her fingers sliding beneath my ribs. I settled in. 'Thanks for letting me stay,' I said. 'And for the pizza, and everything.'

'You're welcome, Princess Belle,' she said. The nickname didn't register until she was halfway down the corridor, and by then it was too late to call out and ask her not to use it.

If she already knew then that we were getting a second season she didn't say anything to me. We got the call from Rupert two days later, and within the week we were packed and heading back up to London. Mum asked me if I was sure.

'You've been so stressed out lately,' she said.

'I'm sure.' I just needed to get out of that school and back into my little bubble with Donna and the girls, where everything was still present, unedited and unaired. Somehow, in my mind, I

111

would be okay as long as I could stay in that space. And never look at myself on a TV screen again.

It had been three and a half months and we all looked older. Faye and I had had birthdays, joining Kendra in her teens, and Hannah was now in double digits and very happy about it.

'I got my own phone,' was the first thing she said to me after 'hello', showing me a small white phone identical to Faye's. Faye abandoned her conversation with Kendra in order to run over to me and fling her arms around my neck. I gave Kendra a smug smile over her shoulder.

Faye was taller, still slender, still silvery. When you caught her in an evening light, under a window or in a doorway, she looked as if she had the moon in her eyes. She sang as she unpacked her dance bag and I sat and listened, and closed my eyes when I knew no one was looking.

Paget's birthday had passed as well. She had turned fourteen just a few months before, but she looked far older, despite the braids in her hair and her nervous manner. Her body seemed to have grown to fit her gangly limbs and when she stood beside us in her black leotard she looked like a young woman standing amongst children.

Fred and Rupert talked between themselves at the side of the room, casting frequent glances at Paget. Fred put a hand to his forehead. Without anyone actually verbalising the plan we took it in turns to wander dangerously close to them and eavesdrop.

'Okay,' Faye heard, on her turn. 'Let's reach out and see if he can get it faxed.' The rest of us returned with nothing intelligible.

Lining us up and keeping us in our places was like herding cats, but when they managed it, Donna emerged. She was dressed for winter, in a long white knitted dress and a fur-trimmed cape, which she removed and placed over a chair. Then she turned to face us with a smile, red lips bright and stretched wide between a mass of brown curls.

'Goodness!' she said. 'Haven't some of you grown!'

The first audition of the season was *The Sound of Music* – a real West End production, this time. We watched the film in the studio, sat on cushions with it projected onto the blank wall in front of us. It wasn't a particularly comfy way to watch an almost three-hour film but Rupert said it looked lovely on camera.

'Doesn't Paget look like Liesl?' said Kendra, during *Sixteen Going On Seventeen*.

'Yes,' said Donna, 'she does, rather.'

Paget, sat silently behind Donna, turned red.

On our break, before we went up to school, we sat around cross-legged in the dressing room and took a poll of everyone's current bra size and who had or hadn't started their period.

'A girl at my school got hers in PE,' said Kendra. 'It ran down her leg and everyone saw.' We shuddered at the horror story. 'She made some bitchy comment about me being jealous of Belle – you know how they made it look – and I told her, "Shut up, Mary, you don't even know how to use a tampon."'

'Did everyone at your school watch?' asked Faye. 'Everyone at mine did.'

'Mine too,' I said.

'I hate it,' said Roni.

'Really?' Kendra let out a surprised laugh. 'Why?'

'It's awful. The show's awful, and people online are awful.'

'Then why come back?'

Roni picked at a piece of fluff between her toes. 'They'd say I left because I wasn't good enough.'

Kendra took in our downcast faces. 'You're all mad,' she said. 'I love it. Do you know how many people would kill to be us?'

She had returned from the break as sharp as ever and now uber-focused, on top of every note and step and syllable. In class she was nearly impossible to critique, but Donna always found a way. Sometimes her face wasn't engaged enough and then it was too engaged – the word 'precocious' was thrown around and, despite Donna's self-professed love of Shirley Temple, it definitely wasn't a compliment. Kendra never faltered in front of the cameras, but as we pushed through the double doors and made our way up to the classroom, sometimes I caught the moment that her face dropped and twisted.

Paget, despite how mature she now looked, seemed to have regressed. Donna watched her with a cold eye, sometimes failing to give corrections and instead turning away without a word. Then Paget's limbs failed her and her gangly, awkward self returned as she flailed, desperate to get it right.

We were only a few days into our prep for *The Sound of Music* when Mum and I turned up to set to find no Donna, and Rupert organising the other girls into a line. 'Belle!' he said. 'Brilliant. Stand here.'

'What's going on?' asked Mum, taking my bag from me. We didn't wait for Donna in a line unless it was an important occasion. I scurried over to stand next to Faye, who gave me a shrug.

We waited in our line for fifteen minutes, craning our necks to watch assistants and runners exchange pieces of information – 'How long does she need? Five minutes? Can you hurry her up?'

'Hey, Rupe,' called Kendra.

He turned around, amusement on his face. Us kids never called him by his nickname. 'Can I help you, Miss Kendra?'

'How long are we going to be standing here?'

'Not too long,' he said. 'We're just waiting for Donna. Perfection takes time.'

When she did walk in, she was in a black blazer and cream trousers, shiny brown hair slicked back into a bun. She carried none of her usual sunshine with her. All of her edges were severe, and her expression was one of concern.

'I'm sorry, girls,' she said. 'This isn't fun news.'

Anxiously, glued to our places, we readied ourselves.

'When we started this journey,' she said, 'we were searching for girls of very particular ages. Do you remember what they were?'

She was looking at me, but Kendra answered. 'Anything from ten to thirteen.'

'That's right,' said Donna. 'I wanted girls that age because they would be easy to train. Not babies, girls with a foundation, but not girls who were so old that their bad habits were already set. Not girls who would grow into adulthood too quickly before I had time to really make an impact with them.'

A chorus of nods.

'We made an exception for one girl,' she said. 'That was you, Hannah. You were only nine, but you were very good for your age, and it was so nice to see you working with your sister.' She stopped walking. She held up a finger. 'And this is very important – you were *honest*.'

And then Paget burst into tears.

We were ordered out into the corridor by our mothers when the screaming started. Unsupervised, we were free to crowd against the door and press our ears to it. There wasn't any need. We could have heard them from halfway down the corridor.

'You contacted my ex-husband?' Charlene was screeching. 'Are you *serious*?'

'Mum,' came Paget's voice, pleading. 'Stop.' She was crying. When we'd left the room, I'd thought she was with us until I looked back, the door closing, and saw her standing there in a panic with Rupert's authoritative hand on her shoulder.

'You signed a contract with us under false pretences.' Donna's voice wasn't loud exactly, but there was a size to it that made us look to each other, to check we were all hearing the same thing. 'I vouched for your daughter – I sent her on auditions and talked her up to *my* industry contacts. *My* friends.'

'So we told a white lie to get her in front of you. You still liked what you saw! She's still just as much of a star!'

'I thought your daughter was good for fourteen,' came Donna's voice. 'It turns out she's just above average for sixteen.'

'How dare you?' shrieked Charlene. 'She's a *child*.'

'She's not a child. I moved out at sixteen. I built a career for myself. The *children*, the ones I am trying to help, the ones she lied to, are out there!'

Even through the wooden door I felt her finger pointing right at the centre of me.

'There's only one little girl out there you're trying to help,' hissed Charlene. The centre of me ran cold.

That evening, Donna took Mum and me out for dinner to show us the rough cut of the music video. Mum watched me raising my leg above my head in the fur-trimmed jacket and said, 'That's very pretty. Is the artist a big deal?'

'She's up and coming, I'm told,' says Donna, 'although I think Belle will be far bigger than her in a couple of years. She's not as lucky as Belle – she won't still be pretty by the time she's twenty-five.' She winked at me. I winked back. Donna slipped her phone into her pocket and took one of my hands across the table, and then one of Mum's, and pressed them both once, briefly. 'How are you both feeling?' she asked.

I looked sideways at Mum. 'Strange,' she said.

'That's understandable,' said Donna. 'What happened today was out of the ordinary.'

'It was cruel,' said Mum.

The wind went out of me. I pinched my straw tightly between my two fingers. Across the table, I saw the word had knocked Donna backwards too. I saw her mouth pinch.

Then she nodded slowly. She caught my eye and smiled, reassuringly, to let me know that she wasn't upset, and took a sip of her mojito. She wore a gold ring on her finger with a small pink stone – it caught the light as she lifted her glass. She'd bought us matching ones recently, but Mum wouldn't let me wear mine out, in case I lost it. I kept it beside my bed in a jewellery box and opened it now and then just to stare at it.

'I guess it looked that way,' said Donna.

Mum spread her hands, questioningly.

'The thing is, Sofie, that age and lying about it is a serious thing in this industry.' She sighed. 'Say a casting director tells me that he only wants little girls aged thirteen and under, because he's planning a multiple-season TV show and he doesn't want his actresses to hit puberty too soon. Imagine if Paget had walked back onto *that* set yesterday.'

'Girls grow at different rates,' said Mum. 'It'll never be an entirely predictable thing.'

'Or say, in two or three years,' pushed Donna, 'I get a call for her to play a romantic lead in a teen film. She's supposed to be sixteen or seventeen, and they may cast a fourteen or fifteen-year-old boy alongside her – not an unsuitable age gap, but if Paget is actually eighteen or nineteen and lying about it then things become a little more complicated.'

Mum's eyes went down to her plate. She stirred her pasta without taking a bite.

'I hated doing that to poor Paget,' said Donna. 'Trust me, I did.'

'So why did you?'

'Because it's TV,' said Donna. 'I know how that sounds. I know it's hollow. But it's the truth. And I had a false assurance from Fred that Paget would be allowed to leave the room during the commotion, which of course turned out to be a lie—'

'You knew Charlene would flip out like that?'

'I don't think it was a surprise to any of us. That woman has a temper.'

'So,' said Mum, 'you, Fred and Rupert, the three of you, you set this up. You got the photo of the birth certificate from Paget's father and you staged the scene.'

'It's TV,' repeated Donna. 'That's just what it is. You lie, you deal with the consequences on camera. That's what all of us have signed up for.'

'Is that what Belle has signed up for?'

'Belle doesn't lie.'

'She makes mistakes. All kids do. Is that how she'd pay for them?'

Donna's eyes landed on me. Her face softened. 'I would never do that to Belle.'

'How can I be sure of that?'

'You can't, Sofie,' said Donna simply, picking up her fork. 'You're just going to have to trust me.'

'Do you trust her?' asked Mum in the cab on the way home.

'Yes,' I said, instantly.

She nodded, twisting her watch around her wrist.

'Do you?'

'Hmm,' she said, which wasn't really an answer.

Reunion special

I come home from the bookshop to find that Jane is making dinner. Chicken strips and Potato Smiles – when I walk into the kitchen, she is standing with the oven door open, prodding them with a fork.

'They won't cook if you keep letting the heat out.' I take the oven gloves from her and stand in front of the oven door so that she can't get to it. 'Does your dad know you're using the oven?'

'He said I should practise.' She holds up her left thumb, which has a small pink mark on the side. 'I burnt myself a little.'

'She burnt herself,' I call to Cameron, who has followed me in and is hanging his coat up by the door.

'Burning is learning,' Cameron calls back.

'You're a terrible parent.'

Jane and I run her thumb under the cold tap. She dries it in a tea-towel and then stands very still, holding it out in front of her.

'I can feel my heartbeat in it,' she says.

'Can you? That's nice.'

'Not really. It hurts.' She eyes the oven. 'Are the Smiles ready? I threw the packet away so I don't know how long they're supposed to be in there for.'

'That wasn't smart. Why are you making them?'

'To cheer you up,' she says. Sometimes she just seems to know things, without anyone telling her. I wonder if maybe she crouches on the stairs and listens to us after she's supposed to have gone to bed.

Over dinner, she holds out one of the Smiles and says, 'These are your fears. Eat them.'

It's something Cameron used to do for her when she was little. I bite the face between its two gaping eyes and chew. Jane applauds. It's a strange ritual, but I love that I'm part of it.

'Did you tell her?' Cameron asks me, after she's gone to bed.

'No. Did you?'

'I don't remember telling her.' He sips his tea. 'She's like one of those horrible omniscient children in romantic comedies.'

'How'd you mean?'

'The ones who look up at the protagonist and say, "But you love her, right?"'

'To be fair, I can imagine her saying that.'

'Can't you? I'll have to beat that out of her.'

'She's alright,' I say.

'So. Interview to camera.'

'Yup.'

'The thing is, Belle,' says Cameron, 'unfortunately, you're bringing all of this upon yourself.'

'It's healthy to face your fears. Isn't it?'

He considers. 'Depends. I wouldn't recommend someone with a fear of wasps went poking around their nest with a stick.'

'I see your point.'

'But I understand why you're doing it. I think.' He crosses to put his mug in the sink, squeezes my shoulder as he goes. 'Don't let them get to you. That's all I ask.'

'I won't,' I say. 'I'll try.'

I'm early to set the next day. Rupert does a double take when he sees me.

'This can't be our Belle. So on time?'

'Traffic was in my favour,' I say.

'You look *fantastic,*' he says, which sounds like a compliment but is actually a dig at my dishevelled appearance the other day. You have to work with Rupert for a while to pick up on these things. 'We're ready to start whenever you are.'

'Yeah? Okay.'

'I'm going to get Make-up and Hair to touch you up,' he said, 'just gilding the lily stuff, and then we'll sit you down and have a chat.' He waves his hands. 'Super calm, super easy, nothing to stress about.'

'Sure,' I say, my heart in my throat.

Someone hands me a drink whilst I'm in the make-up chair. I shake my head at first, but one of the producers says, 'Go on, Belle, you've earned it.'

How? I think. I'm too nervous to refuse a second time. It's a vodka tonic. It goes down a little too easily.

'Okay!' says Rupert when I'm finally settled in front of him. 'Fantastic stuff. Doesn't she look great?'

I realise he's talking to Fred, who is standing, like he always is, in the very corner of my eye. 'You look great, Belle,' he says. 'I hope you're not nervous.' This is practically warm from Fred.

'I know this isn't the kind of thing you're used to,' says Rupert. 'But you're in great hands.' He gestures to one of the women stood next to him, dressed in a grey jumper and severe black glasses. She walks forward to shake my hand.

'Hi, Belle,' she says, 'I'm Sara. I'll be chatting to you today.'

I look back at Rupert, confused.

'Sara's a pro,' he says. I've never worked with Sara before but she gives me a knowing nod to confirm that yes, she is, and I suppose I have no choice but to believe both of them.

She sits across from me, no notes, just a keen gaze and an air of anticipation. There's a camera just to the left of her, and another on my right, some distance away but no doubt trained in on my face. I can almost feel the heat of it.

'Don't look into it,' says Sara.

I start. 'Sorry.'

'It's fine. Just look at me.' She gives me a minimal effort smile. 'Shall we?' I nod. 'Great,' she says. 'What's it been like being back with the girls?'

'It's been great,' I say. 'I haven't seen them in so long and they were like my family at one point – they still are, in a way. It's always good to catch up with family, I guess.'

'So you've missed them.'

'Yeah. Yes.' I shift in my seat.

'Are you comfortable?'

'Yes. Sorry.'

'It's fine. And do you find that things are very different between you guys?'

'Oh, no,' I say, as a reflex. 'Well. Obviously. A bit. I mean, all this time has passed, you know?'

'How are they different?'

'We're just older.'

'Tell me more about that,' says Sara.

About ageing? 'Um, I suppose when we were kids who still had everything ahead of us we became very close very quickly and now we've all gone in very different directions.'

'So you don't feel that close bond any more?'

'No, no, I still do. I suppose it's like . . .' *What is it like?* 'It's like seeing old schoolfriends,' I say, relieved. 'You still have those memories but you're not all kids together any more.'

'But you guys went through something more intense than the aver-age school experience,' says Sara. 'I mean, you became famous together.'

I'm waiting for the question but it seems like Sara is waiting for an answer. 'Yeah. We did.'

'Do you think that caused some tension? Maybe there's a little jealousy there?'

'I don't think there's any jealousy, no.'

'Who did Donna think was going to be the biggest star, when you were all training together?'

I swallow. 'Me. I guess.'

'And who is the biggest star?'

'Definitely Roni.'

Rupert waves a hand. 'Belle?' I blink. 'You're doing great,' he says, 'but remember, we want as little of Sara's voice in there as possible, so try to acknowledge the question in your answers.'

'Right.' I knew that. 'Sorry. Sorry,' I say again to Sara.

'It's fine,' she says. 'Give us that comparison between you and Roni again.'

'Donna thought I was going to be the biggest star, I guess,' I say. 'But I think it's pretty clear that the biggest success to come out of the show is Roni.' Rupert gives me a thumbs up, just in the corner of my vision. 'Kendra's done very well too,' I add.

'You don't resent them for that?' asked Sara. 'You aren't jealous, not even a little?'

'I'm not jealous of them at all,' I say honestly.

'Didn't you like what you did?'

'I liked acting and all that for a while. But I'm glad I don't do it any more.'

'Tell me about that,' she says.

This means that she wants a paragraph. 'It was just very intense,' I say. 'And I was very young. And – and I don't think it was very good for me. I don't think I was ever supposed to be in that world.'

'Why do you think that?'

'I don't know why I think that. I just know it. It's just the truth.'

'This is only going to work if you're willing to be open with me,' she says, like she's my therapist. I think about making the joke out loud but I'm not sure I want to say on camera that I've been in therapy. It was just for a bit, when I was still a teenager. I don't do it any more. Not because I don't need it, but because it used to worry me that my therapist might find me annoying.

I take a breath. 'I suppose people told me I was, when I was twelve. That I was perfect for it. And so every time I felt not perfect for it, when I was growing up, it would make me feel awful. It just started to not be fun. It started to make me feel awful. But for Kendra and Roni, it's still fun. I think that's the difference.'

'When did it start to not be fun?'

'It was gradual,' I say firmly.

She moves on, thankfully. 'Was there anyone you were particularly excited to see?'

'I was excited to see everyone,' I say.

'So, there wasn't one bond closer than the rest?'

'No.' I'm trying so hard not to hesitate that it comes out a little too forcefully. Sara blinks.

'Okay,' she says, 'anyone you didn't want to see?'

I'm reminding myself to breathe, which is never a great place to be in. 'No, I was excited to see everyone.'

'The last time you saw most of these girls they weren't too happy with you,' says Sara. 'Were you worried that there would still be some old resentments there?'

'I guess I was a little worried some of the old stuff would get in the way,' I say. 'But we're all adults, and we get on really well these days. We always did really. It was just complicated now and then.'

'In what way?'

I wave a hand, and then wish I hadn't. The camera will see it shaking. 'You know what teenage girls can be like.'

'Tell me about Faye,' she says.

'Um.' I hate how open-ended this is. 'Faye's great. We were very close when we were younger.'

'Has it been nice to get close to her again?'

'It's been lovely to see Faye.'

'She taught you to sing, didn't she?' asks Sara.

I smile. 'Faye helped me a lot with my singing, yeah. She was a great teacher. She was always the one that made it all easier for me. She still does that.'

'Do you think you'll stay in touch after this?'

'I hope we'll stay in touch. All of us.'

'How about Donna? Any contact there?'

My eyes flick to Fred and Rupert, standing just past Sara, a little way off.

'Keep looking at me if you can, Belle,' she says.

'Sorry.'

'It's fine. Any contact with Donna in the last decade?'

I shake my head.

'Could you give that to me verbally?'

'I haven't had any contact with Donna, no.'

'How about any crew members that you were friends with? Producers? Your tutor, perhaps? Other people on set?'

'No,' I say, over dry lips.

'Acknowledging the question?'

'No, I haven't stayed in touch with anyone from the crew. Or any of the producers.'

'So, you haven't stayed in touch with anyone from the show since you left? Why was that?'

'I don't know why,' I say. 'I guess it just didn't work out like that.'

'You wouldn't say you chose to cut everyone from *The Real Deal* out of your life?'

'Kind of,' I said, 'maybe. I guess.' She really was starting to sound a little bit too much like my therapist.

'Why did you do that?'

'I guess the chapter was closed.'

'Which means?'

'I don't know. I was just done with it.'

'What made you so done with it that you couldn't stand to contact anyone from the show?'

'It wasn't – I don't know.' I'm mumbling.

'If you could speak clearly for the audio, Belle,' says Sara.

'Sorry.'

'It's fine. I get the feeling you don't like this line of questioning.'

'I just don't really know what to say.'

'Give it a go,' she says.

'It was – hard. It was hard to be on the show, and it was hard to leave. I don't like remembering it, really.'

'Why was it hard?'

'To be on the show?'

'Sure.'

'I was very young,' I say, 'and I didn't think I was, and I think that's a dangerous combination. Because I felt like I could take on things that I wasn't equipped to take on, and I didn't think about what they would mean for me later in life. How they would stay with me.'

'What's stayed with you?' she asks.

'Things casting directors said about me. That sort of stuff.' Not technically a lie, but only half of the truth.

'Anything else?'

I look back at her, blankly.

'We learnt in Season Five that Donna was abusive to you.'

I swallow my breath.

'That argument, and the moment you blew the whistle and told the crew what was going on. Can you tell me more about that moment?'

Her face is all I can see, blown up to monstrous proportions, her eyes black. Then everything zooms out and she's very far in the distance, a miniature woman in a grey jumper with neatly crossed legs. My ears are buzzing. The camera comes right up into my face, draws back, comes up, draws back.

'Hang on, Sara,' comes Rupert's voice. 'Belle's not going to be talking about that.'

'Oh,' says Sara. 'Apologies.'

'No harm, no foul. We'll just move on.' Distorted, his voice wobbles around me. 'Belle? Are you ready to move on?'

I sit rigid in the chair, with no idea what my face is doing. Whatever it is, they've got it on tape.

'Belle?' asks Rupert. 'Do you need some water?'

I shake my head.

'Some air?'

'We're in the flow of things,' says Fred. 'And we've got to get the next one in after her.'

'It's fine,' says Rupert. 'Go on, Belle. Get some air. We'll be back in five.'

The river outside of the Southbank studio is never peaceful. People are always drinking cans or bottles at its edge, walking along its banks, running for the bus or the tube towards its bridges. Today there is a party of hot tub boats floating past me. The men whoop and holler, waving damp arms in the air. A leaf lands in one of the hot tubs. They drift uncomfortably slowly, energy dipping the longer they know I can see them, until they reach a group of teenagers crowded around someone's phone and are reinvigorated.

There are two kinds of peace. One is the sun-dappled walls of a bookshop, the gentle emptiness of your own bedroom – a kind of undisturbed, predictable peace in which you are only ever exactly what you are. The other is the peace that comes when no one sees you as anything more than another piece of a crowded picture. As soon as they turn away from you, you don't exist. This is the peace I find in central London, on the days when no one recognises me. That feeling of disappearing into the noise.

I'm standing just down the bank from the Globe. It's colder today than it has been in a while. I've got a jumper in my bag, but right now I'm happy to just let myself feel it. Had I really thought that Rupert would keep his word? In my head I'd been prepared from the beginning, wise to his usual his tricks. I don't know any more.

As I stand there, shoulders stiff with two hands on my bag like a pensive living painting, a car pulls up. Kendra gets out, swinging her heels out of the door first, *Devil Wears Prada* style. She blinks at me.

'Are you done already?'

'No. I don't know.'

She's staring very hard at me, like I've got something on my face. 'What?'

'Are you good?'

I shrug.

'Did they pull something?' she asks. 'You look pissed.' I don't say anything, but she nods like my silence is all the confirmation she needs. 'I don't know why you thought you could trust any promises made by Rupe.'

'Please. You cooperate with him more than any of us.'

'Obviously,' says Kendra.

'Doesn't he make you promises?'

'The only thing Rupe promises me is a pay cheque. I don't ask him for any kind of protection. What's the point?'

I might have been Donna's favourite but Kendra has always been Rupert and Fred's. She understands the trade-off. 'Fact is,' she says, 'I'm in work because of them. Most people don't like their bosses, but they still cooperate with them. You know?'

'So I guess you're going to be employee of the year.'

She laughs. 'Yeah, why not,' she says. 'As long as I'm doing this, I'll be employee of the year.'

I wait for her to walk towards the studio. She goes on standing there, looking at me with her arms folded.

'Are you going back inside?' she asks.

'I don't know.'

'What happened?' she asks. 'Exactly?'

I tell her. I give her the exact wording of it all. Her face doesn't change, but after a minute she looks down and pushes the toe of her boot gently into the ground.

'Fuck,' she says. It's oddly validating, that soft swear word.

The hot tub boats are far away now, small red dots travelling upstream.

'That's fucked,' says Kendra.

She comes to stand beside me, following my eyes to the farthest curve of the river. I feel her jacket brush my bare arm and I realise that I'm shivering. Kendra takes a carton of cigarettes out of her pocket and lights one. The smoke drifts away from me on the wind but I can still smell it. She catches me looking and rolls her eyes.

'Curb your judgment.'

'I'm not judging.'

'Never.' She takes another drag. 'Hey,' she says, 'you know the other day, when you and Faye went for that little walk around Soho?'

She keeps her eyes on the river, even as I turn to look at her, but I can see from the slightly upturned corners of her mouth that she's glad to have my attention.

'Rupert asked her to do that.'

'What?'

'Yeah. So you wouldn't quit. He figured you were a flight risk.'

'Oh.'

'Thought you should know,' she says.

'Why Faye?'

'Please,' snorts Kendra.

Don't quit, she'd said quietly, under the chip shop sign, silvery hair pushed back behind her ears. Eyes wide, like it really mattered. Fourteen years since my first audition and I still couldn't tell when I was being played.

'I don't know why you care about any of this,' I say.

'That's kind of dramatic.'

'You've made it pretty clear how you feel about me.'

She turns to me, exasperated. 'Is this about the other day? Me saying you'd lied? That was Fred's line.'

'You said it.'

'That's how this works. How do you not get that yet?'

She's speaking so calmly. I wonder if it really is that black and white for her.

'I'm sorry about what they did in there,' says Kendra, nodding towards the studio. 'Honestly, that's a fucked-up thing for them to ask you.' She inhales, and then continues, louder: 'But, also, I don't get you at all, Belle. You should know more than any of us what you're letting yourself in for and you let them do this to you, over and over.' She takes another puff. 'Like they're gonna do a *Real Deal* reunion and only talk about the shiny stuff. Like they're gonna spew this stuff about letting us "finish our story" or whatever and not address that you originally finished it by screaming at a camera and running off into the night. You can't drift through this process and hope that everyone else is looking out for you, because we aren't. We're looking out for ourselves. Be an adult.'

My phone rings.

'Or,' she says, as I fish it out of my pocket, 'quit.'

It's Rupert. He'll call a couple of times, and then he'll walk out of the studio and ask if I want any water, or if I'm feeling okay, and slowly but confidently he'll lure me back in like an escaped puppy.

I shove my phone into my pocket and start walking towards the bridge.

'Good chat,' calls Kendra.

The tube back to Bethnal Green is quiet, just me and a mother and her daughter. The girl is about six or seven and her mother is reading softly to her out of a Ladybird book. The girl leans up against her mother, the edge of the woman's camel coat draped across her knees like a blanket. I change lines earlier than I'd planned to. Mothers and daughters are hard for me to watch, these days. On the next train, I sit next to a paper with a picture of my fifteen-year-old self on it. *Belle Simon 'incredibly anxious' over the return of reality show.* I wonder who gave them the quote. Probably Howie. Anxious is fine, though. Everyone feels sorry for anxious. Just because they're talking about me doesn't mean they're mad at me. I breathe out and through.

I'm angry at Fred and Rupert and Kendra and Faye and all of them, every last person who ever touched this godforsaken show. But the anger is a raft. I know that if I let go of it then I'll have to contend with the uncomfortable truth that maybe I'm just made of different stuff from the rest of them. Softer, smaller, more vulnerable stuff. The kind of stuff that bruises like peaches and sinks in storms.

I don't go to the bookshop. I go to bed, which I know will not make me feel better, and I draw the curtains closed and I put the tennis on because it's there and I'm not in the mood to make any choices and also I don't care about the tennis. Cameron comes in later in the afternoon and pauses in the hallway, cutting off a creak halfway, but then I hear him turn and walk back out. Maybe he thinks I'd rather be left alone, or maybe he's just not in the mood.

He returns later, in time to make dinner so that it'll be ready for Jane when she returns from hockey practice. I switch off the tennis and just listen to the noises he's making for a while, the clanging and chopping and pacing. When I hear him coming down the corridor towards me, I turn it back on and make myself sit up straighter in bed.

He knocks. 'Belle?'

'Hey,' I call.

He puts his head around the door. 'How are you doing?'

I raise a finger. 'Hang on. Match point.'

He glances at the TV. 'No it isn't.'

'I'm still learning the lingo.'

'What happened?' he asks.

'I quit.'

He looks as if he isn't sure whether to believe me. 'For real?'

'For real.'

'You told them that?'

'Not yet. I just walked off.'

He hovers in the doorway.

'What?'

'You'll probably need to put it in writing.'

'Yeah, I will.'

'We need to take a look at your contract as well. Check that there's nothing they can bring against you. You know they will, if they can.'

I don't reply. Cam nods to himself and then closes the door softly. I watch the ball go back and forth, back and forth.

The front door slams. Jane's quick footsteps come running down the hall. 'Belle!' she calls.

'Belle's not feeling great,' comes Cameron's voice.

I push myself upright again and force a smile onto my face as she comes crashing through the door, dropping her mouthguard and lunchbox onto the carpet. She launches herself onto my bed, shinpads and all.

'Woah!' I wrestle her into a sitting position. 'What's up?'

'I've got exciting news,' she sings.

Her PE clothes are still slightly too big for her – she's been promised she'll grow into them but she's still the smallest in her class and the only one whose skort reaches down past the middle of her thighs. She sits cross-legged in the centre of my bed, swamped by her clothes and my white bedsheets.

'Did they pick you for the audition?'

Her face falls. 'That's not fair. I wanted to tell you.'

'Sorry. I'm a good guesser.'

'I'm going in on Monday,' she says. 'To the *actual theatre*. I think the acting and dancing will be fine, but I'm a bit nervous for the singing. What did you do when you had to sing?'

She's a very small, very excitable speck in the white expanse of the bedsheet, chirping away like a little bird. She could be crushed by a boot heel or a person's thumb. One wrong word delivered in the wrong tone could occupy her small mind for ever.

And they're still doing this. *How* are they still doing this?

'You're not going,' I say. I turn the tennis back on.

She starts, crestfallen. Her face slips so easily between emotions. 'It's a real West End show,' she says.

'Exactly. What's wrong with school drama?' One of the women onscreen hits a ball into the net.

'This is like, *real* acting.'

'But you don't want to be an actor.'

'*Please*, Belle.'

'I'll talk to your teacher. Or your dad will. They should never have dangled this in front of you in the first place.'

'I want to do it!' Her fists are balled.

'Of course you do,' I say. 'You're eleven. Of course you want to do it.'

'So why can't I?'

'Because you don't really know.'

'I do!'

'You don't, Jane. Drop it.'

'I know it'll be hard work. I know I'll have to miss out on other stuff. I know they might be mean at the audition—'

'You don't know SHIT!'

I have never shouted at Jane before.

Her lip quivers. I realise that somewhere in all of that I went from sitting to standing and now I'm bent over her as she cowers in the centre of my bed. She sniffs.

'Jane,' I hear behind me. 'Come here.'

Cameron doesn't ask me to apologise. He doesn't even look at me. He just takes Jane's hand and walks her gently out of the room. I hear her sniffs growing distant down the corridor. On screen, one of the tennis players throws her racket at the ground. It bounces once, comically, before settling beside her foot. The other one is crying happy tears. I missed the real match point, apparently.

There's a knock on my door. Cameron is back.

'Jane's having dinner,' he says.

I don't say anything.

'You chose to put yourself through this again,' he said. 'Lord knows why, but you did. I won't have you taking it out on her like you took it out on your mum. Do you understand?'

I still don't say anything.

'Fine,' he says. 'Sit there and feel sorry for yourself.' He slams the door behind him.

My phone lights up, but it isn't Rupert, like it has been all afternoon. It's a message from Howie.

Hey, Princess Belle. Thoughts on that drink?

His timing is impeccable. People like me and Howie deserve each other.

Season Two

None of us booked *The Sound of Music*. The call-backs stretched out for weeks, but when we stopped hearing from them Donna chased and delivered a solemn 'no' to the class. I was crushed. Kendra was furious.

'I know I was good,' she said.

We all avoided saying what we knew to be true: that Kendra was too precocious even to play a von Trapp. Where before she had appeared confident, self-possessed, quick-witted, now her manner onstage was almost manic. She was undeniably talented, but I could see the look in casting directors' eyes sometimes when they spoke to her. They were thinking: *This child would be a nightmare to work with.*

Paget was a shambles in the dance call, nervous and inarticulate when they spoke to her. She was called to sing for the casting agents and left the room almost in tears. We felt sorry for her, but she also embarrassed us. Sixteen was nearly grown up. Donna had her own flat in London by that age. We couldn't understand why she didn't pull herself together.

'After all,' Kendra whispered, 'we all just get on with it. And we're *much* younger.' We nodded, sadly and condescendingly.

After the debacle that was *The Sound of Music,* Donna began to limit the auditions that Paget could go on. No more big stage roles or TV guest stars, but bit parts and commercials. Whilst we were all being handed scripts for long-running BBC dramas, Paget was attempting to sell school shoes with lipstick in the heel.

'Let's hear it again,' Donna would say, and Paget, bright red, would recite the mortifying dialogue with a false brightness in her trembling voice. It was always awful. No wonder Donna didn't send her out for anything real, we thought. She couldn't even get through the easy stuff.

Paget didn't hang out with us on breaks any more but read on her own in the corner. Charlene raged at Donna on an almost daily basis, and when the fights happened and we were ushered into the corridor, Paget would sit with her back against the wall and cry quietly. Sometimes we went and put our arms around her, but mostly we just let her be. It didn't seem to make a difference either way.

The truth was that Donna's words had made an impression. Paget had lied. I recited the speech Donna had given to Mum, about why Paget's age mattered so much, and the other girls agreed.

'It's sad,' said Roni. 'She's nice.'

'We can't trust her, though,' said Kendra.

This idea settled in our heads, and the more we sat with it, the more it became clear to us that we couldn't trust Paget in any capacity. When she walked into the room, we would clam up. We would communicate only via glances. She was fake, and so we owed her no part of ourselves. We cut off her access to us.

'They won't be around too much longer, Paget and her mum,' said Howie. 'Donna wants them gone.'

He'd started to come up to me when we caught each other off camera, on our breaks. When I stayed late in the studio to practise, we would often run into each other on my way out. 'Alright?' he'd grin.

'Alright,' I'd say, pushing open the door.

On the way home I'd daydream about showing up in the Cotswolds with Howie and running into Stella Malone. *How old was your boyfriend again, Stella?* I'd ask, hanging onto Howie's arm.

I wasn't nervous around Howie any more. He treated me like a friend, which was exhilarating since he was so much older. I returned the favour. I felt that maybe, in a year or so, when my boobs came in, the dynamic of our relationship might shift. For now, our relationship was comprised of quick exchanges, titbits of gossip that I'd relay to the other girls. When we caught each other in the upstairs corridor by the schoolroom, he had his phone in one hand and a Cornish pasty in the other (another crafty treat that we never quite seemed to get our hands on). He told me that my hair looked nice, and then he said, 'Hey, are you close with Paget?'

'Donna wants Paget gone,' I told the others.

'Did she tell you that?' asked Kendra.

'No. I just heard it.'

'From your boyfriend?'

'Shut up,' I said loftily.

'I don't believe it,' said Faye. 'What Paget did was wrong, but Donna wouldn't actually kick her off the show.'

'Of course she would,' said Kendra.

'She's not that mean.'

'It's not mean. It's business. We're all here to do a job. It's like Paget lied about her qualifications. That would get her fired in real life, wouldn't it? It's the same.'

We considered this. It made sense. Kendra sat back.

'I hope Donna does let her go,' she said. 'I'm sick of all the arguing.'

We waited for the day we'd all be told to stand in a line and Donna would enter in business casual to tell Paget she was going home. It didn't come. Paget continued to be sent on auditions for children's toys and back to school offers, and Donna continued to virtually ignore her in class, only offering occasional corrections. When she did, she no longer used Paget's name. Instead it was 'you', or 'girl at the back', or once, to one of her assistant teachers: 'Do you see how the big one is just struggling along behind the others?'

None of us had thought of Paget as big. But now we looked at her, she wasn't as wiry as she used to be. She was gaining a thickness on her thighs and bum and upper arms that hadn't been there before. We would have to be vigilant, to make sure the same thing didn't happen to us.

'I feel bad for her,' I said to Howie, the next time I ran into him. We were chatting outside the dressing room on my lunch break. 'I get why Donna's upset, but I'd hate it if I felt like she didn't even want to look at me any more.'

'Well,' said Howie. 'You have the opposite problem.'

'What's that?'

'Donna likes you too much.'

I grinned. 'I don't see how that's a problem.' Despite the comments online, I liked being the favourite.

'It fucked *The Sound of Music* up for you, right?'

I stared at him, the salad in my hand forgotten.

'You didn't know?'

'What are you talking about?'

He looked around conspiratorially, then leant in.

'You know how you got a bunch of call-backs?'

'Yeah?'

'Well, they loved you, but if you took the job then you would have been on camera way less. This is a big show and what with child labour laws and everything there's no way they could have had you doing both. They were already pushing it with *Alice*.'

'They were?'

'Oh, yeah,' he said. 'I'm pretty sure that schedule you were on was totally illegal.' He shrugs. 'But *technically* this is a docuseries, not a reality show, so it's a bit murky.'

'Wait.' My head was spinning. 'So Donna had me cut from *The Sound of Music*?'

Howie shrugged. 'That's what I've heard. I thought she would have talked to you about it, with you guys being so close.' I pushed my fork slowly through my salad. 'Obviously not,' he said.

'Belle?' called a voice. Howie gave me a parting grin and scarpered, tossing the remains of his pasty in the bin as he went and wiping a hand on his t-shirt. Donna appeared, pushing open the double doors. 'There you are,' she said.

'Am I late?'

'No, no, I've asked them to give us longer. We're going to do lunch.' *Doing* lunch meant filming. Outside the window, crew members were already packing up the production van.

'I promised Faye I'd braid her hair for her.'

'That's adorable,' said Donna. 'Maybe tomorrow?'

She had me in my coat and out of the door before I had a chance to explain. I pictured Faye waiting for me in the dressing room with her hairbrush and felt a guilty stab in my stomach.

I went in Donna's cab, like I always did these days. I wasn't sure if anyone had even told my mum I was leaving set. 'Right,' she said. 'Quick summary.' She saw me looking up at the car ceiling. 'No cameras, don't worry.'

'Okay,' I said.

'I've told you before that I want to do the whole triple threat thing with you. How do you feel about singing?'

'I like singing.' I hesitated. 'But—'

'It's your weakest area,' she said. 'You still have a lovely little voice.'

'Faye's much better than me.'

'That's true, but don't say it on camera. And Faye doesn't have your presence. It takes more than a pretty voice to be a pop star.'

She saw my horrified expression and laughed. 'Belle, doesn't every little girl want to be a pop star?'

'Sorry.' I rearranged my features. 'I want to be an actress more.'

'I know,' said Donna. 'I love that. But if we want to do this singing thing on the side then we need to start feeding it in now. That's what this lunch is about, okay? I'll ask you about music, and you'll say—'

'I love singing.'

'There we go!' she says. 'And we'll talk about doing a song and maybe then an album, and you'll get all excited. Show me those acting skills.' She put her hand on my knee. 'This is just us laying the foundations. Understand?'

I nodded.

'I never want you to do anything you don't want to do. So if you don't want to do singing, best to tell me now.'

'No, I want to.'

'You're a pro,' she said, squeezing my knee. 'It'll be great. Trust me.'

Over lunch, in front of the cameras, I feigned enthusiasm. She asked me who I'd like to be as big as, one day, and I listed ex-Disney acts and family-friendly favourites.

'I've got you a great opportunity,' she said, as we were wrapping up. 'It's a very different kind of job. One of my industry contacts is throwing a big party and they'd love to have you come and perform. Dance, and maybe sing as well if you feel like that's something you could do.'

'That sounds amazing.' I couldn't quite picture what that would be like, performing at a party. 'Is everyone coming?'

'Just you and me,' said Donna. 'It's going to be a very important night for you.'

I wished she had brought this up on our way there, so I could have quizzed her about how I was meant to react. In the car on the way home she directed the taxi into a drive-thru and bought me an ice cream.

'Wonderfully done,' she said.

How could I ask her, as she handed me my treat with a gracefully outstretched arm and beaming smile, gazing down at me in all her loveliness like I was her very own little girl, if she had anything but the best intentions?

'Are you staying late?' asked Faye, putting her head around the door of the music room. Her hair was still loose around her shoulders.

I was stood by the window, fiddling with the CD player. 'I wanted to practise my singing.'

'We don't have a singing thing coming up,' she said. 'Just that crime show.' We were both auditioning to play a teenage drug addict.

'I know. It was just something Donna said I should work on.'

'Okay,' she said. 'Is your mum still here?'

'She's coming to pick me up later.' The frequent bust-ups between Donna and Charlene were getting to be too much for Mum. It wasn't what she'd signed up for. As soon as our morning of filming was over, she was happy to leave me in school and head back to the hotel to work. 'I'm sorry that I didn't do your hair,' I said.

'That's okay. What did you guys talk about?'

I hesitated. Then I pulled her into the room, closing the door behind her. 'She wants me to work on my voice.'

'Why?'

'I think she wants me to be a singer. When I'm a bit older.'

Faye was very aware that she was more talented than me. She paused for just a second, and then she took the CD player from my hands. 'Go on, then.'

'Sing?'

'I can help you,' she said, 'if you want.' Alex, her mum, was a singing teacher and Faye had been raised not just on music but on theory and technique. There was definitely an argument to be made that she knew more about it all than Donna.

141

'Yes please,' I said.

I sang the Vanessa Carlton song through three times. After the first time, Faye stood up, pacing around me as she delivered her notes. Sometimes I would deliberately get things wrong, just because her impatient 'no, no' was so funny to me. After the third time, she said, very seriously, 'That was beautiful, Belle.'

It was that kind of light again, coming in through the window, that made her look not quite real.

There was applause from the doorway. Howie was leaning in it, grinning at us.

'Beautiful,' he echoed. 'You must be a good teacher, Faye.' I'm not sure he'd ever spoken to her directly like this before, using her name. She smiled uncertainly.

'Are you locking up?' I asked.

'I can wait around a bit. Got nothing better to do.' He sat down beside Faye and brought out a flask from his pocket. 'Cold in here, huh?'

'Is that coffee?' she asked as he took a swig. He laughed at her and I joined in, without quite knowing why.

'Howie,' I said, jumping up to sit on the window ledge, 'tell Faye what you told me earlier. About *The Sound of Music*.'

Amused, he related it to her. Faye's eyes widened.

'Why would Donna do that?' she asked.

'To keep Belle around. Haven't you noticed that Donna worships the ground she walks on?'

'She does not,' I scoffed.

Howie and Faye exchanged a look that made them both burst into laughter. A little annoyed, I hopped down from the window ledge and made my way over to him, holding out my hand.

'I want some of your coffee.'

'It's not—' He caught my smirk and laughed again. 'You're too young.'

'I'm not. And I'm cold.' Faye was staring at me, not scandalised, like I'd hoped she might be, but interested. 'I'll tell Fred and Rupert you were drinking around us,' I said.

'You're a bitch,' said Howie, with a wink. 'Don't blame me when you don't like it.' He held out the flask.

It was awful. I hid my grimace as best I could. 'What is that, whiskey?'

'Vodka,' said Howie, with another laugh. He offered the flask to Faye, who hesitated.

'Dare you,' I said.

She surfaced, spluttering. 'That's *awful.* Why do you drink it?'

'It makes you feel nice.'

'He means it makes you dru-unk,' I sung, back up on the window ledge with my legs swinging.

'Please,' laughs Howie. 'You wouldn't know what drunk was if it bit you on your little butt.' Faye and I giggled. 'You ready to call your mum?'

'No,' I said. 'I want another sip.'

'Next time. That's enough for now.' He slid the flask back into his jacket pocket. 'Call your mum. You too, Faye.'

He saw us out the door when Mum and Alex arrived, waving us off as we went to join them on the bridge.

'Who's that?' asked Mum, as Howie lingered to lock up.

'He's on the crew,' I said. 'You've seen him.'

She squinted. 'Really? He looks very young. How old is he?'

'I don't know. Eighteen, I think.'

'Were you in there on your own with him?'

'No,' I said. 'Faye was there. Anyway, it's just Howie.'

By the time the first season had almost finished airing, it was clear that we would be back for Season Three. Fred and Rupert were thrilled with the reception. Donna talked to our mothers about social media – we got set up with accounts on various platforms. 'Managed by mum' read our bios, but really we were the ones on there every day. We would sit in a circle in the dressing room and show each other the clips of us that fans had set to music, all the nicest comments we could find. We usually scrolled past the negative stuff as if we didn't see it, none of us wanting to acknowledge the fact that we might not be universally liked. But we all cried sometimes, Paget most of all.

Charlene and Donna had graduated from brief, loud exchanges to full-on battles, both of them venomous towards the other, finding something to tear each other apart over almost every day. The first raised voice was like an air-raid siren – we were neatly filed out of the room and left to make a safe zone for ourselves in the corridor whilst inside the dance studio, accusations flew. Donna accused Charlene of living vicariously through her daughter, Charlene accused Donna of deliberately sabotaging Paget, and Kendra accused everyone of taking it too seriously.

'Charlene knows what she's doing,' she said. 'This is all going to be great for Paget, trust me. Everyone will remember her way more than any of us when this airs.'

Paget, sat at the other end of the corridor with her head on her knees, let out a small sob.

'It's awful,' Faye told Howie when he next came to join us in the music room. 'She just cries all the time, constantly.'

'She's just not cut out for it,' I said.

'You sound like Kendra,' said Faye, chewing her lip.

'Well, she's right, for once. Paget's only a couple of years younger than Howie.'

'Do you ever cry, Howie?' asked Faye.

'I've cried over girls before,' he said. 'Not much else. Want another sip?'

What girls? I wanted to ask. I took the flask and braced myself for the taste.

Over time he started letting us have three sips each, never any more than that. 'You're too young,' he'd tell us when we tried to wheedle a fourth out of him. It wasn't that we wanted to drink it, but we wanted the moment of admiration after we'd swallowed our sip, the cheers from the other two. And three sips in, Faye and I would feel it a little, that warmth that Howie described. The whole thing was addictive.

One day, Donna came into the studio with a film audition. These were always the ones we got most excited over. Faye and I were both in the middle of jobs, me shooting a three-episode arc on a medical drama and Faye doing educational videos for a campaign against teenage pregnancy. She brought her bump onto set one day and we shrieked with laughter when she wore it to dance class. Donna let her keep it on for a full ten minutes, joining in the giggles as Faye's stomach jostled us at the barre.

'This is going to be a tight turnaround,' she said, 'so Faye and Belle are out, I'm afraid. They're looking for someone to play an anxious sixteen-year-old runaway in some reshoots. It's just one scene, only a handful of lines, but the film itself is awards bait so there could be some good exposure in it.'

Charlene sat up straighter in her chair. Even Paget raised her head a little, almost looking Donna in the eye.

'I'm sending Kendra in,' said Donna, handing her the pages she had to learn, or the 'sides', as we now had to call them.

'Oh,' said Charlene, 'you are fucking *kidding*—'

'Out you go, girls,' said Alex, with a weary gesture towards the door.

We sat in the corridor with our legs stretched out in front of us and half-listened to the yelling. Paget went to lock herself in the bathroom.

'It is a bit harsh,' said Roni.

'Well, sure,' said Kendra. 'It's like if a role came in for a mute ten-year-old with a bowl-cut and no one suggested sending Hannah.'

'Hey,' said Faye, sharply.

Kendra rolled her eyes. 'Did I hurt your feelings, Hannah?'

'No,' whispered Hannah.

'See? She's fine.'

'Maybe you should turn down the audition,' I said. 'You know, in solidarity?' Kendra stuck her middle figure up at me.

'Hang on,' said Roni, who was closest to the door. She shuffled closer. 'Hear that?'

'We've heard it all before,' said Kendra, picking at her nails.

'No, but that's Belle's mum. She never yells.'

'What?' I flew to the door. She wasn't yelling exactly, not like Charlene and Donna did, but her voice was raised above the others.

'You know this is fucked up,' she was saying. 'You're singling one girl out and making an example out of her.'

'Sofie,' said Donna, 'let me handle this. You just worry about Belle.'

'I am worried about Belle. I want her career in hands I can trust!'

'Have I *ever* given you cause to doubt—'

'Yes!' came Mum's voice, with an incredulous laugh. '*This* is cause to doubt!'

'Shit,' murmured Kendra, as Charlene took over again. 'Your mum really laid into her, Belle.' She looked delighted.

I sat against the wall and seethed. When the door finally opened, the other mothers had dispersed, but Mum and Donna were stood to the side of the room, talking softly and intensely. A camera was watching them from a distance. I couldn't intervene without putting myself in its line of sight. When Mum finally walked away, I saw the rage in her face, white-hot and unstable. Donna's expression was unreadable.

I rushed over to Mum. 'Why did you do that? What did you say to her?'

Her voice was flat. 'I told her that if she didn't let Paget audition, you wouldn't be going to her fancy party.'

'*What?*'

'Shush,' she said.

'Why would you say that?'

'I'm not open to discussion about this, Belle,' she said.

Paget got her sides. I went to the party.

'Don't worry,' said Donna in the car on the way there. 'I don't hold *you* responsible for any of it.'

I breathed out. 'I'm still sorry.'

She patted my knee. 'You have a great mum, Belle. She loves you a lot.'

'I know.'

'So don't think I mean anything bad by this, but it's worth saying that one day you won't be beholden to what she says you can and can't do. And then it's a whole other ball game. Just see what we'll make of you.'

The words sent a thrill through me. Donna dug around in her purse.

'Here,' she said, producing a little parcel wrapped in silver paper. I took it reverently. It was a charm bracelet, with a little silver heart dangling off of it. 'For the Queen of Hearts,' she said. 'For *Alice*. I thought maybe we could add to it as you go. Whenever you get your next role, and your next, we'll add a little charm. How does that sound?'

I leant into the arm she put around me and held my wrist up so that she could do the clasp. She fiddled with it, my arm outstretched in front of me, both of hers encircling me, her hair tickling my cheek.

'I'm sorry about *The Sound of Music,*' she said.

Maybe she knew, somehow, that Howie had told me. Maybe she didn't. 'It's okay,' I said. Either way, I forgave her.

She released me, and then she put her finger under my chin, turning it towards her like she did when she was looking for something in me. I never knew what it was. 'You look beautiful tonight,' she said, letting it go. 'Silver is your colour.'

'Gold's yours.'

She laughed. 'I know. Isn't that perfect?'

I nodded, because it was. We were like two stars.

Mum was asleep by the time I got back to the hotel. Production had upgraded us to a suite this time, with two bedrooms and a small, shared kitchen. I lay on my bed and ate crisps in my silver dress and I thought how nice it was to be just back from a party in a huge London house made of white stone, where people in fancy clothes had watched me dance and listened to me sing (not too badly, thanks to Faye) and told me that I was 'something special'.

'I've been just *loving* you on that show,' said more than one person. A woman who I vaguely recognised, although whether she was an actress or a singer or a reality star I couldn't say, walked up to me and grabbed my face in her hand, white acrylics digging into my cheeks. Her breath smelled like wine. 'Darling!' she said. 'The cutest face!' She gave me a peck on the lips and laughed when I recoiled. Parties were a strange place, I decided – dazzling and exciting, but it was an unsteady kind of excitement in which I couldn't anticipate how the adults around me were going to behave next. I wasn't used to adults being so unpredictable.

After my performance, I sat by myself at a table eating a strawberry tart and watched Donna making the rounds. Across from me were two men who had both been on *I'm a Celebrity, Get Me*

Out of Here. They were engaged in a loud conversation, completely oblivious to me.

'Jenna's are bigger,' said one, eyes following a dark-haired actress hanging onto the arm of her blonde friend, 'I'll grant you, but Lizzie's are so bloody perky. Bigger isn't always better, you know.'

'True,' agreed his friend, gracefully.

I hoped my boobs would be like Lizzie's when they came in.

A man with a round face and a blue bowtie appeared at my elbow and knelt down close to me. He smelt like soap and sweat. 'Donna tells me you'd like to be in music,' he said.

Donna was talking to a beautiful dark-haired woman who had been on *Strictly* with her. She clocked the man and I immediately and glided over to us, gold skirts sweeping the floor.

'You've got a really sweet little voice,' said the man. 'And you'll definitely look the part in a couple of years. Maybe even less.'

'I think she could be excellent,' said Donna, reaching us. 'Belle, darling, this is Tony.' The man stood up to embrace her, kissing her on both cheeks. 'We'll keep this on ice?' she asked him.

'Absolutely,' he said. 'You give me a ring when she's ready.'

'I do want to get her started young,' said Donna.

'I'm with you there,' said Tony. 'But I agree, she's still cooking.' He grinned at me. 'You want to be a popstar then, Belle?'

I swallowed my mouthful of strawberry tart. 'Absolutely.'

'Let's see if we can't make that happen for you.'

Back in the hotel room, through the open door to the other bedroom, I watched Mum's chest rise predictably up and down. I matched my breathing to it, and suddenly the room full of glossy people with too-loud laughs and perfect teeth felt very far away. I hadn't been sure what any of them would do, at any moment. But Mum would always breathe like this. She would always get mad at me when I left my clothes in a pile and she would always swear at the TV during *The X Factor*. I watched her, the steady rise and fall of her chest under white sheets, and I felt comforted in a way that I hadn't known I needed.

I rolled off the bed and crept into Mum's room in my bare feet. She'd left the window open and the room was freezing, heavy hotel curtains rippling slightly. Our new suite had floor-to-ceiling windows and when I snuck behind the curtain, pressed right up to the glass, it felt like I was hovering over the street below. I pulled the top window closed and slipped out again.

'Mum?'

'Hm,' she said.

I slipped into the bed beside her, under the cold sheets.

'I think I'm going to be a popstar,' I whispered.

'Hm.'

'I wish you'd come tonight.' I wanted us to sit on my bed together and unpack the evening. I felt as if I had moved through it all like a dream.

I fell asleep without meaning to. When she woke up in the morning and found me beside her, in my silver dress with my pretty clips slipping out of my hair, she laughed.

'My glamorous girl,' she said, gently shaking me awake. 'This lifestyle suits you.'

I struggled up on my elbows and stared mournfully down at my skirt. 'I've creased it.'

'It's just a dress. Come on, get up.'

'We'll be early.'

'We're not going to the studio,' she said.

'We aren't?'

'We're going to Paget and Kendra's audition.'

We never went to each other's auditions. I had been doing this for long enough now to know it wasn't a particularly professional move, to pile five girls, their mothers and a camera crew into a waiting room all for one auditionee. Mum saw my face.

'Rupert said they felt Paget could do with the support. It's been a tough season for her.'

'Don't you want to hear about my night?'

'Tell me about it on the way,' she said, throwing a jumper at me.

I gabbled out everything I could remember as we sat on the tube, including the ex-member of a 2000s girl group who got drunk and took her top off very early in the evening, and the famous reality TV couple who had got into a big argument over the main course. I left out the woman who had kissed me on the lips, because remembering how her breath had smelled still made me feel a little ill. She asked if there had been any other children there.

'Just me.'

'Did Donna take care of you?'

This was a loaded question. I tried to speak lightly. 'Yes, she introduced me to everyone. And we didn't stay that late.'

'So it was good.'

'It was good.'

'I should have come with you.'

'I said it was good.'

'I know.' She was frowning, though. She'd tried very hard to talk Donna into bringing the both of us, but Donna had explained that it wasn't a good look.

'This industry wants children to behave like small adults, in a way,' she said. 'It's disturbing, I know. But if Belle's there holding onto her mother's hand, it won't leave a good impression.'

It made sense, and Mum backed off with a lot less resistance than usual. But I could see that she was worried, searching me for signs that she'd made the wrong decision. I pulled the sleeves of my jumper down over my hands and decided not to get into a conversation about music. I knew what she would say. Donna had first mentioned the idea to her over lunch in Season One. Mum had laughed and shaken her head, as if me and a recording career were totally incompatible entities.

When we met the other girls outside the building, the cameras were already there. They seemed more eager than usual, trained on us immediately if we so much as yawned. None of us dared to ask questions. Kendra was muttering her lines to herself, walking back and forward in front of the entrance. Paget was stood on her own, gripping her sides so tightly that I thought she might rip them.

'Okay, girls,' said Rupert, clapping his hands together. 'Shall we go inside?'

The waiting room was empty. Instead of a crowd of other little girls and their mothers, there was only our small group and the film crew following us. Faye's eyes found mine. Even Kendra hesitated.

'Where's everyone else?'

We were rolling, so no one answered her question. She repeated herself.

'Rupert, where's everyone else auditioning?'

'Red card, Kendra.'

'Answer her,' said Charlene.

Rupert gave a tight smile. 'This is a pretty big entourage you girls are dragging along with you. Not really fair on the other audi-tionees, so the casting directors saw everyone else yesterday.'

Kendra looked as if she wanted to ask a follow-up, but the red card had knocked her confidence. She'd never received one before. She took a seat. The rest of us followed suit.

'Where's Donna?' Faye whispered.

A woman with grey hair and a pair of red glasses opened the door to the audition room. 'Kendra Hale?' she read from her clipboard.

We wished her luck. She moved towards the door as if she hadn't heard us. We sat in silence waiting for her to emerge, pretending we couldn't hear Paget nervously muttering her lines under her breath.

When she came back out, she put her folder down on the chair next to her and took a breath. Then she said, 'Donna's in there.'

'What?' came the question, from three different directions.

'She's in there with the casting directors. She's chatting to them.'

'Jesus,' said Charlene, putting her head in her hands. 'It's another fucking set-up.' Paget had gone white. Charlene reached out and took her daughter's hand. Uncharacteristically quiet, she pulled Paget onto her feet and started for the door.

Sound operators and camera men blocked her way. Charlene stood and looked at them, Paget hanging onto her hand. She seemed to be deciding whether to push her way through or back off. To everyone's surprise, she chose the latter. She and Paget disappeared to the far corner of the room. I watched Charlene put her hands on Paget's shoulders and look her tall daughter in the face. Her back was to me, but I could see Paget's lip trembling.

'Can anyone hear what they're saying?' hissed Roni.

Kendra shrugged. 'Doesn't really matter. We'll watch it on TV.'

The lady with the clipboard reappeared. 'Paget?'

'Are there cameras in the room?' I asked Kendra as Paget made her way unsteadily over. Charlene remained at the far side of the room, one hand on the wall, the other on her stomach.

Kendra nodded. 'I wonder if the job's even real,' she said. 'I hope it is. I did great.'

Paget turned back once as she entered the audition room. Her eyes were empty. I knew, then, that this would be it for her.

'I'm coming in with her,' said Charlene suddenly. She strode across the room, slipping through the door before the casting lady had time to close it. I saw a quick look exchanged between Fred and Rupert. Rupert's lips curled upwards.

We sat in awful silence. Voices murmured indistinctly – I caught Paget's, then Donna's, then Paget's again. For a while there was only the gentle background hum of her performing her sides.

Then Donna resonated through the floorboards, gently vibrating the soles of our feet.

It escalated quickly after that.

'You're a witch!' came Charlene's screams through the wall. 'You're a self-obsessed monster! Why would you put a child through this?' Paget appeared in the doorway, finding her way out of the room with her flat palm on the wall. She was crying in violent, desperate gasps. We crowded around her but she batted us away ineffectually. Inside the room, Charlene was still raging. Her words were clearer now thanks to the open door. 'How can you say things like that about a young girl?'

'I need to be able to defend my reputation,' came Donna's voice. 'I don't want people thinking I *chose* to put this in front of a casting agency.' She spoke lower. 'Frannie, Craig, I'm so sorry about this. I will make sure this woman and her child never bother you again.'

Charlene's tirade was almost unintelligible now. Paget's sobs were animalistic. I looked around me, for Fred or Rupert or somebody to do something, and made eye contact with the camera.

'Red card, Belle,' said Rupert, coolly.

I stared at him. Right at him. He looked straight through me.

Mum had come to stand behind me, her hands trembling on my shoulders. 'It's okay,' she said, 'it's okay, we'll go home soon.' Then she gripped my shoulders and muttered to herself, "What the fuck is happening? What the *fuck* is happening?" like she didn't know I could hear her. I was numb. She made a move toward the room, but Fred stepped into her path.

"Sofie, this is a professional situation," he said.

Mum didn't say anything to him, but she looked at him like he was something she'd just scraped off the bottom of her shoe. She reached for Paget instead, who had sequestered herself in the corner of the room. Her hands left my shoulders and she took hold of Paget's arms instead, and stroked her forehead, and then pulled the tall girl into her chest and rocked her slowly, saying something that I couldn't make out.

Donna emerged from the room in a cloud of nut-brown hair and Chanel perfume. She didn't seem to see any of us, as she bit back at Charlene and swept over the waiting room floor. She was immersed – which, I realised, meant that she was acting.

Our mothers were trying to clear us an exit path but it was clear that, this time, Production wanted us in the room. This was going to be their finale, I thought. It had to be. Funny how they would just decide how they wanted to end the chapter, and we wouldn't know it was happening until we were in the middle of it. These people were pulling strings for me, and against me, and around me, and I wouldn't be able to tell which was which until I was right in the middle of it. For the possibility of something great, I had to put my trust in the hands of people who I was fully convinced would dismember me for good TV. And I had to be grateful.

Donna still didn't look at any of us, but as she walked across the room, crew members cleared. It was only after a second that I saw how she had parted them like the Red Sea and left the way to the door open for us. Eyes still on Charlene, her hand beckoned me forward.

Something clicked.

I scarpered quickly down the path, the other girls following. Donna blustered and raged as we ran for cover, bursting through the doors. Paget was left behind, of course, still sobbing with her entire chest, fists clutching at the front of my mum's shirt.

Hannah was crying too. 'Why would Donna do that?'

'It's the finale,' I said. It was all slotting together in my head.

'So?' said Faye.

'So, they were never going to bring Paget back for another season. She'd be seventeen. The ages just don't work.' This made sense. It all made sense.

'She didn't have to do that to her,' said Faye.

'She did,' I said. 'She's sacrificing Paget to protect us.'

Rupert went to Donna and said they wanted a big, explosive end to the season. So Donna, wanting to protect the children in her care, the ones who had always been honest with her, made the difficult decision to go after the young adult who lied. She had built a finale that involved just her, Paget and Charlene, and left all the rest of us out of it.

I explained this to the girls as best as I could. Donna was looking out for us. She loved us. Through the window, we could see her tossing her hair over her shoulder, her finger in Charlene's face. None of us liked Charlene anyway. Donna was a knight slaying a dragon.

And Paget would be fine. So she'd witnessed her mother in a few arguments, done a couple of embarrassing auditions, received a few harsh words for a lie she'd told. She'd forget it all, in a few years. Those were hardly things that would traumatise a person for ever.

When I looked in through the window, she was curled up very small and frightened in the corner of the room, with her hair falling over her face. My mother on one side of her, gently rubbing her back. A camera on the other.

Reunion special

In the morning, when I still haven't answered him, Howie sends me a video link and a smiley face. The title reads: *The Real Deal s2e7 cute moment.* Thirteen-year-old me works on a routine in the corner of the studio with her eyes squeezed tightly shut. Faye, with a finger on her lips and a gesture at someone off camera, sneaks up and grabs me around the waist. I shriek. A voice – unmistakably Kendra's – says 'Ouch'. There she is, plugging her fingers into her ears as she sits on the floor with her sides. Faye and I grab an arm each and drag her across the studio floor as she shouts at us.

They used to be so little! reads the top comment. Hundreds of likes. I scroll down.

Guess Belle and Faye have always liked playing with each other ;)

The username is nondescript, just a collection of numbers and letters. *What do you mean???* someone has asked underneath.

I used to work on that set and let's just say . . . I saw some things

Replies are mixed. Most call bullshit. *Gross, they were kids,* says one. *HOT,* reads another, with a flame emoji. Another: *damn . . . your a lucky guy!* I slide my phone under my pillow and stare at my ceiling for a few minutes.

There's a knock on my door.

'Are you going in?' calls Cameron. 'There's a car here for you.'

'I told you, I quit.'

'I'm not sure they know that.'

I roll over and pull the duvet over my head.

'Belle?'

'Tell it to go away.'

He wants to shout, *tell it yourself.* Instead he slaps a palm gently on the door and walks off down the corridor. Outside, on the street, I hear a car pull away. Cameron leaves for work at the bookshop a few minutes later, without another word to me.

I pull my phone out again and text Howie back. *Did you comment?* He replies instantly: a winky face. I put the phone down.

It was funny! he chimes when I don't reply. *Didn't mean to attract the pedos. My bad.*

I only wanted the confirmation. Still, I find my fingers moving over the keys on their own accord.

That drink isn't happening by the way.

I like that Howie replies instantly. That was always the comforting thing about him – he's never been the type to leave you wondering what he's thinking. *Sure sure,* he says. Then, *I can wait.*

I put the phone down before I'm tempted to reply again. There's a taste in my mouth like I haven't brushed my teeth in a week and my chest is tight. When I make it to the kitchen, phone left behind on the bed, I sit down next to the fridge for a few seconds before I actually manage to open it and take out the butter. Marmite toast was Mum's cure for any illness, mental or physical. It stays down, but it doesn't get rid of the gnawing, nibbling sickness.

From my bedroom, my phone rings. I listen to the rhythmic buzzing. I wait until it's finished before I swallow. When I finish my last crust, it starts to ring again. I imagine Rupert staring at the call screen in the middle of the studio, holding back his frustration, flashing his infuriating smile at the rest of the team. Once, as a kid, I watched him out of our classroom window, chatting to Donna and other producers by the studio entrance. He nodded and smiled, and then as soon as everyone had gone inside, he kicked the ground hard. For the rest of the day, I couldn't stop staring at the muddied tip of his left shoe. I had seen Fred mutter swear words, slap walls, bark at crew members – but none of it had startled me as much as the muddy tip of Rupert's shoe.

I leave my plate in the sink and walk back into my bedroom, where the call is just ending. It isn't from Rupert. It's Faye. Two missed calls appear beside her name on my lock screen. I'm still staring down at it when she calls again.

'Hello?' she says, when I pick it up.

'You called me.'

'You weren't saying anything.' A pause. 'Still aren't.'

'You called me.'

'Sorry. Jesus.'

'What's up?' I say.

'You sound mad.' I can hear the bustle of the studio in the background.

'Are you working right now?'

'I'm filming an interview to camera today,' she says. 'Rupert's been wondering when you'll come in. Apparently there's a little more they want to do with you.'

'Right.'

'He didn't ask me to call you,' she says quickly.

'Like he didn't ask you to talk to me the other day?'

She sighs. 'Kendra told you. I thought she was looking pretty smug today.'

'I'm not coming in,' I said. 'You can tell him that.'

'I don't— I'm not telling him anything.' A pause. She sighs. It's strange to hear Faye flustered. She so seldom is. 'Belle, I feel awful. About not being honest with you, about what happened here yesterday—'

'How do you know about that?' A stupid question. 'Oh.'

'She's actually worried about you,' says Faye. 'Which may never happen to you again, by the way, so I'd enjoy it while it lasts.' She pauses. 'I didn't really plan what I was going to say.'

'I can tell.'

'Belle, come on. Please don't make this into some sort of . . .' Another deep breath. 'He asked me to talk to you and I did, because I wanted to. That's – that's not awful.' I'm still quiet. 'What do you want?' she asks. 'Do you want me to come over there?'

'Okay.'

'I'm meant to be filming in, like, five minutes.'

'Don't offer then.'

'Shit,' she curses. 'Fine. Okay. I'll leave. What's your address? Can you text it to me?'

Disbelieving, I do. Then I climb into bed and watch the show Jane likes about a group of Year Eight students who start a girl band. They aren't half bad. I'm sure Tony would have signed them.

Half an hour later, there's a knock at the door. I still don't expect it to be her. But here she is, standing there, out of breath like she ran all the way from Soho. The rapid rise and fall of her chest almost makes me smile.

'Fuck you,' she says. 'Fred and Rupert are going to kill me.'

I stand aside to let her in. She walks through the hallway into the kitchen, stopping briefly in front of the fridge to look at Jane's school report and her Year Six art project. It's a painting of me. It's not a particularly flattering one.

'This is lovely,' she says.

'The picture?'

'And the place. How long have you guys lived here?'

'Over a decade now. We moved in just after Jane. Mum wanted to get out of the city, but Cameron and I wanted to stay.'

'You didn't want to go back to the Cotswolds?'

'Honestly? I couldn't stand the thought of it. Ending up back where I started.' She sits down at the table like she's waiting for me to offer her tea. I sit across from her. 'Go on.'

Faye brushes silvery hair out of her eyes. She's still in her coat. For a northerner she's always been surprisingly cold-blooded. 'I'm sorry,' she says. 'It was stupid of me. He made it sound like it was for you, to stop you backing out on all the money just because you were scared – I know,' she adds, in response to my look, 'but come on, you know what he's like. And I really, honestly, am glad you're doing this too. I was really happy to see you when you turned up.'

I raise my eyebrows at her.

'Okay,' she says, with a laugh, 'after I'd processed. I was, I swear. It's been way too long. And – and we had something good, for a while.'

'As kids.'

'Sure. As kids. But it was still good.'

I stand up to make the coffee. Faye sits quietly and watches me as I puzzle my way through the process of using Cameron's industrial coffee maker. I don't drink coffee much. I'm jittery enough. I hit a button and jump as the milk frother roars at me. I can feel her smiling.

'This thing is awful,' I say.

'I'm happy with water.'

I persevere. I don't know if what makes it into the mug is good coffee or not, but either way I'll be able to tell by her face. She's looking at me thoughtfully as I carry it over.

'You're quieter,' she says.

'Am I?'

'I think so. You weren't ever loud, when you were a kid, but you had things to say.'

'Oh, well thanks very much.'

'It's not a bad thing,' she says. 'We're all different. I think you're the most different though. I mean, I think you've changed the most.' I hope that's true. At fifteen, I truly sucked. 'I suppose it makes sense,' she says. 'I suppose it's fairly common. God, I can't believe they asked you that about Donna and Season Five, the other day. I don't blame you for walking.'

It's not that I don't want to reply to this, but there isn't anything to say. I don't know what I'm supposed to share with her. I don't know what to ask her. When we were younger I would run my mouth to her like a faucet that couldn't turn off. I've forgotten how to do that.

When I look up, she's smiling. There's nothing uncomfortable or pitying in it. It's just kind.

'Can I see your room?' she says.

She walks around it slowly with the mug of coffee clutched to her chest. There are pieces of Jane everywhere, from handwritten notes stuck to my walls to photos framed on my desk. Her shoes are kicked off in the corner, with a single sock beside them. Her hairbands are on my nightstand.

'Sometimes I wish I'd been a few more years older than Hannah,' says Faye, as she looks around.

'Really? Why?'

'I think it would be so lovely if I'd been old enough to think about her almost like a mother would. We were too close in age. I wasn't nice enough to her growing up.'

'You always looked out for her.'

'Yes,' she said, 'but I could have been better.'

She sits on my bed. I sit beside her. 'I'm not always nice to Jane,' I say.

'Aren't you?'

'Not always,' I say. 'Not when I'm scared.'

It all sort of pours out then. It's probably the most words I've said to her since I first walked into the reunion and for a second I forget myself and talk and talk like I don't do to anyone these days, not even Jane or Cam. She sits and listens with her legs crossed in front of her, propped up against my pillows, taking occasional sips of tea.

'That's stupid,' she says, when I'm finished.

'Oh, cheers.'

'I get it, really, but it's an audition. What's the worst that can happen in an audition room?'

'Someone could say something horrible to her. They could make her cry, they could make her feel bad about herself—'

'Right,' says Faye, 'because that never happens to kids otherwise.'

'It doesn't have to.'

'Belle,' she says. 'Yes it does.'

'Okay, but I can try to minimise it.' That's my job – to minimise the amount Jane gets hurt. Not to put her directly in the firing line.

Faye's shifts on the bed, two hands on her mug to balance it, settling herself against the pillows.

'Go on,' I say.

'I don't need to. You know how that sounds.'

I pick at my nails. Faye says, 'Belle, just let her do it. It's like, exposure therapy. For you,' she adds, as I open my mouth, 'more than her.' She watches me peel a piece of skin from around my thumbnail. 'It won't be like it was for us. It's different.'

'Is it?'

'God, yes. I'm not asking you to hand her over to Fred and Rupert or throw her onto the Disney treadmill. Tons of kids do theatre in London. The majority of them love it. Remember how much you loved *Alice*?'

I nod. I want to tell her that I'm scared to have the kind of regrets that Mum had. That Mum named Jane the way she did – sensible, plain, un-princessy – for a reason, and I'm scared to be the one that breaks the spell. She knows, though. She's still right.

My phone rings again. There's a moment where both of our eyes dart over to the screen, but it isn't Rupert.

'Jane's school called,' says Cameron when I pick up. 'Apparently she isn't feeling well.'

'What kind of not well?'

'Sore stomach. I'm prepared to bet it's a little more in her head than she'd like to admit.'

'I'll go grab her,' I say. More often than not, Jane's sick days are the days she repackages emotional symptoms into physical ones. Eleven-year-old girls without mums get to take lots of sick days, if they want to.

Faye, to my surprise, doesn't utter a word about heading home. She climbs quietly into the Uber with me and squeezes my hand. As we drive, I watch her face, changing as the light falls on different features.

At Jane's school, a receptionist calls her out of the sick room and helps her put her jacket on. I can see why they've sent her home. She does look pale. She avoids eye contact with me as we walk out, but when she sees Faye in the Uber she can't help but shoot me an incredulous look.

'Jane, this is Faye,' I say, opening the door. Faye gives her a wave.

'From the show?' asks Jane. Faye nods. 'Hi-i,' she says uncertainly.

'Sorry you're not feeling well,' says Faye.

Jane shrugs. I put my arm around her. She pulls the cuffs of her school jumper down over her hands and rests against me. After we've driven for a few minutes, she says, 'It's a bit better now.'

Faye and I exchange a smile over her head.

'Are we going home?' asks Jane.

'Sure. Do you want to go to bed?'

'I'm not really tired.'

I give her a look. 'Okay, miss. What do you want to do?'

If you give Jane a choice, that choice will always be the Natural History Museum. 'She's weird,' says Faye as Jane practically dances through the wooden doors. 'Were we weird like this?'

'You were worse. You liked the Science Museum.'

'Come *on*,' calls Jane.

'What does she like about it?'

'When she was younger it was the bugs. Now it's the dinosaurs.'

'Kendra liked the V&A,' says Faye as we hurry after Jane. 'Pretentious twat.' I laugh. 'Well, nice that her dream afternoon out is a free one.'

'That's our Jane.' Our Jane is currently reading a display board about meteorites. 'You can leave at any time, by the way.'

'Oh, well thanks very much.'

'This is a kindness,' I say. 'She's going to want to look at everything.'

'Everything?'

'Every moth, every fish, every rock.'

'Jesus,' says Faye. 'I didn't think she was this much of nerd. I thought your Mum had finally managed to raise a cool kid.'

'She gets it from her dad.'

'He's a nerd?'

'Biggest nerd you'll ever meet.'

165

'Ah, well,' says Faye, as Jane leans in to look at a case of fossils, her face glowing. 'When all's said and done, I reckon those are often the best ones.'

Faye asks a stranger, who thankfully doesn't know her, to take a photo of the three of us by a model of a T-Rex. We tell Jane to give us her best terrified face and she rolls her eyes at us, but then clasps her hands to her cheeks and opens her mouth wide in a mock scream.

Faye takes her phone back and examines the picture. 'Brilliantly done,' she says. 'You're going to crush that audition tomorrow.'

Jane looks sideways up at me. When I don't say anything, she slips her hand into mine with a smile so wide it hurts me.

Rupert does call me later, after Faye has driven off and Jane has gone to her room to do her homework. I put my phone on silent, and back in bed I pray that Rupert will get into a car accident or hit his head really hard on an open cabinet door and entirely forget who I am.

But he calls again as we eat dinner, and again the next morning as I make Jane waffles. My phone is still on silent but I can see the glow out of the corner of my eye as I serve Jane her breakfast. She stares down at her plate doubtfully.

'What?' I say.

'I might be sick.'

'You won't be sick. This is the breakfast of champions.'

'It's got a lot of whipped cream on it.'

'That's full of sugar. It's good for energy.' She's still staring down at her plate. 'Hey.' I click my fingers at her. 'Which of the two of us has done this before?'

'Okay, okay.' She digs in without further encouragement.

My phone lights up, but it's just a text. Howie's sent me a photo of a sexy Princess Belle costume from a party storefront. The skirt is lurid yellow and very puffy. It comes with matching stockings and underwear. *Would you believe I passed this on my way to get coffee?* he's texted.

I bury my phone in my pocket. Jane watches me over her waffles.

'What?'

'Nothing.' She goes back to eating.

She's quiet in the car, headphones in, listening to her audition song. I leave her to herself and make stilted conversation with the driver, who, to my horror, *knows he knows me from somewhere.*

'That's funny,' I say. 'No idea, sorry.' I stare out of the window and brainstorm a facial expression that will make me look less like myself.

In my lap, there's a buzz. Rupert never texts.

Hi Belle, give me a call when you can. We need to discuss your contract.

'I've got it!' says the driver. He's been looking at me in the rear-view mirror. 'The theatre show, right? My daughter loves it.'

How old is his daughter, I wonder? Jane's age? Younger?

It also crosses my mind, briefly, that the moment he recognised me is the same moment my face fell. I suppose the facial expression that will make me look least like myself is undisturbed peace. It's going to take some practising.

The women around me are largely calm. They chat away to each other about new uniforms and birthday parties and how old is old enough to invite *boys* to a birthday party. One calls down the corridor: 'Sally, hi! God, this is stressful, isn't it?' Giggles.

'Yours will do wonderfully,' Sally calls back. 'Mine has the flu I think, bless.' Beside her, her daughter sniffs loudly, wipes her nose on her sleeve.

These are not theatre mums. These are school mums indulging an extracurricular. Real theatre mums are laser focused. When you sit down across from them and their daughters on benches or plastic chairs they will whisper to each other behind their hands, over the neat heads of hair on their daughters, and then they will shoot you pained smiles. When they whisper-call to your mother, 'Is this her first time?', and your mother shakes her head, they will drop any pretence of whisper and say, 'Really? Good for her! Why don't I know her then?'

One of the very best parts about the show taking off was the fact that when I walked into those audition rooms, none of them could say shit to me. They all knew who I was.

The children go in for the dance call, and the mothers reshuffle themselves. They group like girls at the back of the classroom, in parties of three or four, and they whisper their anxieties to each other. They talk about their other children, particularly their sons. There are only three fathers in the vicinity. They don't group, but they do nod at each other across the corridor, over the tops of their phones.

Jane emerges from the dance call amongst a flood of other little girls, calm and collected in her leotard. 'Did it go well?' I ask. She gives me a curt nod.

Around me, mothers press their children for information – 'Well, go on then. What did they *say*?'

'They told me to tuck my hip under,' says the girl beside me. She scratches the side of her nose, cardigan sleeve stretched over her fingers.

'Oh,' says her mother, 'well, I've told you that.' She may not be a theatre mum yet, but she's a fast learner. I read Jane's sides over her shoulder.

We wait for twenty-five minutes before she's finally called in. She stands up, gives herself a little shake.

I do my best to hide my laughter at the shake. 'You good?'

'I'm good.' Her drama teacher has said something to her about professionalism – I can see it in the little choices she's making, the restrained hellos she gives to classmates when they run up to her and her refusal of a drink from the vending machine. It feels as if she's already acting. I buy her a drink anyway, and when she eventually unscrews the bottle of Coke with a cautious glance at me, I pretend like I haven't noticed.

A woman with a clipboard appears – there is always a woman with a clipboard; she is a figure that haunts my dreams – and calls a name. Off goes the girl it belongs to, ballet bun as solid as marble as she marches off down the corridor. 'Good luck!' whisper-calls her mother. The girl glances back, mortified.

Jane and I sit and watch them go and reappear, one by one. After a while, she joins a friend sat close to the doors. They pool their intel. She looks excited, suddenly, like she's actually enjoying herself. I have never felt like this at an audition. Maybe, as I have long suspected, Jane really is made of much tougher stuff than me.

The woman with the clipboard reappears. 'Jane Keeley?'

I don't call down the corridor to her just before she disappears out of sight and tell her to knock 'em dead. I don't even watch her go. I stare at the wall ahead of me and remember that she's probably talented, and she's very funny, and this is all supposed to be fun.

She comes out with her little chin tilted upwards in the air. She gives a polite thank you to the woman on the door. When she gets to me she is composed, face neutral, arms very straight. I ask her if it went well. She nods, and then, keeping her arm very still, she makes a small but frantic hand gesture down by her side.

I walk. Jane leads the way, small feet pattering faster and faster, out of the doors of the theatre and around the corner. She waits until she feels as if no one except me can see her – and then she cries, tears spilling out half in relief.

'Oh shit,' I say, before I can stop myself. I'm crouched in front of her, hugging her small body to me. My bag lies abandoned next to me. Jane wraps her arms around my shoulders and pulls me towards her tightly, crying hard into my hair. I hold her. *How could you let this happen? How could you let this happen again?*

I pull away, grabbing her face between my hands. Tears roll over my fingers and down my arms. Her cheeks are puffy.

'What happened?' I ask, frantically. 'What happened? What did they say? Did someone say something to you?' She's just crying, looking at me with her big watery eyes. It hurts me sharply and repeatedly. 'Jane, what happened? Please just tell me what happened.'

She's trying. The sobs are moving her little shoulders up and down so violently that it's hard for her to get the words out. 'I-It—'

'What?' I'm still clutching her face between my hands. 'Jane?'

It comes out in a tumble. 'It went really *bad*.'

'Why?'

'I forgot the lyrics,' she sobs, 'and I asked to start again, but then I was nervous and right at the end I—'

'What?' I ask when the sobbing resumes.

'I—I—' Her eyes are very wide. 'I *hiccupped*.'

We stare at each other.

'What?' I say, eventually.

'I hiccupped. Right before the final note. I-I did a big, giant hiccup.'

And, with timing Richard Pryor would envy, the near-empty Coke bottle rolls out of my abandoned bag and onto the street.

I look at it, then back at Jane. My lips twitch. '*Don't*,' she reproves, horrified, but it's too late. 'It's not funny,' says Jane, but her nostrils are twitching. The next sob is more of a gulp, and then there's a definite giggle in it. I sit back against the wall beside her feet and laugh like I'm exorcising something. Jane sits down next to me. Her cheeks are still wet, but she's laughing too.

'I'm sorry,' I say at last. 'You said you didn't want a drink. It's my fault.'

'It was so embarrassing,' she groans, head in her hands.

'I know.' I rub her back. 'But I'm sure they didn't think anything of it. You're a kid who hiccupped. You think that's the worst thing a West End casting director has ever seen? We heard horror stories, in my day. Kids wetting themselves. Throwing up in bins. A hiccup is nothing.'

She picks at her nails. 'Lydia Frey forgot her own name.'

'What? How do you know that?'

'She texted me. They asked her what her name was and she said "Laura". That's her sister's name. And they looked at her notes and said, "No it's not." She was mortified.'

We're laughing again. 'See,' I say, tapping her knee, '*that's* embarrassing.'

'I guess.'

'Did I ever tell you about the time I got my first period?'

She wriggles away from me. *'Ew.'*

'It was onstage.'

'No,' she says, eyes wide.

'I was in white lace. Head to toe. I had to turn a cartwheel.'

'*No.*'

'This is an embarrassing business, kid.'

'Well,' she says, 'maybe my next one will be better.'

She doesn't look at me, still picking at her nails. I separate her hands, squeezing one.

'Maybe it will,' I say.

'This street smells like piss.'

'Never sit on the ground in the West End. That's a basic rule that we both failed to follow today.'

'Your fault.' She holds out a hand to help me up. Then she lets go and uses it to wipe her cheeks, a tear running off the end of her finger. 'Do I look like I've been crying?'

'Yes. So do half the girls walking out of that theatre.'

'I'm still a bit sad,' she says, clinging to my hand as I call an Uber.

'I know,' I say. 'That's okay.'

She cries again later that evening, when she tells the story to Cameron. She laughs too. She's impressively resilient and, equally, totally distraught. The story is funny, but it would be a whole lot funnier if it had happened to someone else.

When she goes to bed, Cameron makes me a gin and tonic. 'She was definitely glad you were there rather than me,' he says. 'Even though you were probably more stressed than she was.'

'Yeah, I really panicked for a minute there.'

'So she told me.'

I take a sip of my drink. It's a pink gin, and he's put fresh raspberries in it. He must have gone out and bought them.

'It's just kid stuff,' he says. 'Getting knocked down, getting your ego bruised. Being embarrassed or unsure of yourself. I think you forget that sometimes. Some pain is normal.'

I know he's right. Some pain is normal. It's just hard for me to tell which kinds.

I tell Faye this later when she calls to ask how it went.

'Me too,' she says.

'Really?'

'I've got a little cousin a couple of years older than Jane. I find it so hard to give her advice. Sometimes it feels like I'm telling her to live her life on survival mode – don't drink, don't go too far with boys, don't go to parties . . . I don't know. Even little things. She's thirteen. I don't know what's normal for thirteen. I just say she's too young for all of it. I don't even know if it's true.'

I roll onto my back. My phone lies next to me on my pillow.

'I don't know what I'm meant to be protecting her from,' I say. 'I just sort of feel like it's everything.'

'You can't protect her from everything.'

'I know that. Obviously. But then—'

'I know,' says Faye.

There's silence for a minute.

'What if she wants to be an actress?' I say. 'That'll be even worse. I mean, she'll look to me even more then. And what can I tell her?'

'I don't know,' says Faye.

'Like, do I tell her not to do it? Because that's what I wish someone had told me.'

'Do you really?' she asks. 'Do you wish you hadn't done it? Any of it?'

'No,' I say, eventually. 'But then I don't know which parts I'd keep. I couldn't keep the fun bits, or the money, without keeping the bad parts.' I swallow. 'I couldn't keep you.'

I swear, I can hear her smiling.

'It's all redundant,' I say. 'Nothing is ever all bad. Even really shit stuff sort of . . . gets you somewhere. Sometimes. Makes you something you wouldn't otherwise be. It's hard to go back and wish parts of your life away. It's like wishing yourself out of existence.'

'But if you could rewrite it?'

There's a lump in my throat. 'Then it would be six little girls growing up together and taking dancing class before school.'

'And that would be it.'

'That would be it.'

'I would have liked that,' whispers Faye.

Later, when we're off the phone, I open Rupert's message just so he can see that I've read it. Then I go onto social media and I do something I never do – I post. I choose the picture of Faye, Jane and I in front of the dinosaur, doing our best terrified faces. *Fuck you,* I think. I post it with my middle finger, which is childish and absolutely ineffectual, but also oddly satisfying.

Howie messages me instantly. *So that's all happening again?*

None of your business, I reply.

I'm on set tomorrow, he says.

My heart drops. *Why?*

Filming an interview. We should get a drink after.

Fuck. Why are they interviewing Howie?

I'll even pay, he sends when I don't reply.

I'm not going back.

Enjoy getting sued then.

They wouldn't sue me, I thought. With their reputation, they'd be stupid to. Imagine how it would look. *Former child star of* The Real Deal *finds reunion filming too traumatic to continue so production sues for breach of contract.* Or to put it in tabloid terms: *Belle Simon SUES. Friends say: 'She can't take it any more!'* They'd be cancelled instantly. Fred and Rupert can't keep dodging bullets forever.

Howie messages again, just as I'm putting my phone away to go to sleep.

You'll miss the fun if you don't come, he says. *I wonder what they'll ask me?*

Season Three

We knew before we even made it home again, me and Mum, that we wouldn't be there long. The farm sold quickly – more Malone types, looking for their Cotswold retreat. We packed up our life and waved goodbye to our cold farmhouse and our slanted fields, and we followed the trucks to our new central London flat. When I looked behind me out of the back window of the car, I saw Stella Malone sat on the front step of her house, her new BlackBerry in her hand, her boyfriend's arm around her waist, watching us go.

We'd packed up in record time and were back in London within a couple of months. Still, Donna was impatient. She called constantly. 'People are so disappointed you can't come in for things this week,' she says. 'They want you for *everything*.'

I'd felt like everyone in the world had been watching the show in Season One. They hadn't been, but they were now. Paget and her age and her tears and her mum had put our show on the map. Donna was fielding offers constantly, brands were begging to work with us, casting directors wanted us in for meetings. Teen magazines were all over us. 'We *love* your girls,' they said, and, wherever she could, Donna sent them me.

'Not that they don't ask for you more than any of the others anyway,' she said. 'They're thinking long term with you, Belle. You're an investment. Everyone wants to get in on the ground floor.'

I did a few phone interviews from our kitchen, sat at a wooden chair with Mum across from me, giving me an encouraging thumbs up. 'What's it like working with Donna?' they'd ask.

'It's amazing,' I'd say. 'She's like my best friend. She says we're twin souls.' They would always ask me if I had a boyfriend. I'd always try to sound bored when I said 'no', like lack of interest was the only thing preventing me from having a boyfriend, but these were print interviews, so my tone didn't really matter.

Everyone was asking for Donna too. She'd had a BAFTA-nominated turn in a TV thriller and she was going to be making new music for the first time in years. She invited me to be in a music video with her, playing her reflection in a mirror like she was staring into her own past.

'God,' said Mum when she watched it. 'You really do look alike.' I had never felt more beautiful.

For the first time in our lives, the money was coming in steadily. We had our wages from the show, plus the money I'd made from the few small screen roles I'd landed so far (*Alice* hadn't paid very much), and now the sale of the farm. We bought a flat in an Elephant and Castle high-rise with security on the door. Mum signed up to a dating site that advertised on TV before *Take Me Out* and started going on dates, something she'd barely ever done at home. It took me a while to realise that she was doing this because she was lonely.

When Mum went out, I got the tube to Donna's house in Chelsea and stayed in the pink bedroom. We would watch classic films and Donna would paint my nails for me, so that when people on various sets and in various casting offices told me they looked nice I could say, 'Donna did them.'

'So *cute*,' they would say, and Donna and I would smile at each other.

Things had been strange, after Paget. She'd asked Mum and I for dinner that night, after the audition debacle, and Mum had said, 'No, thank you,' in a clipped tone that left no room for argument. Donna tried anyway. We had to understand how this all worked – this was a finale, and finales were tricky, but it had been made clear to Paget and Charlene that they would be leaving the show ahead of time.

'You'd already fired them?' asked Mum.

'Fred and Rupert,' said Donna, 'not me. And no. It was just made clear to them.' Mum didn't ask what exactly that entailed, or how sure they all were that Paget and Charlene had gotten the message.

I lay awake that night and worried that she was going to pull me off the show. But I already had jobs lined up in London, commitments that neither of us wanted to back out on. When Season Three happened, we would be here anyway. There was no point in jumping off the conveyor belt now, and Mum knew it.

'Call me if you need me,' she said, and sent me off for my first sleepover at Donna's in months.

She had face masks and nail polish and feta salads, and she'd bought me three new pairs of pyjamas. They were waiting in the drawer in my bedroom. When she opened the drawer to show me, I felt her anxious gaze on me and I realised how much it mattered to her that I liked them.

'I know you must feel weird about what happened at the end of the season,' she said. 'We can talk about it, if you want.'

But I told her it was okay. And it was, really. I had made my peace with it. It had all been done out of love.

About a month after Season Two started airing, I was booked for my first film. It was a family drama and I was playing the youngest grand-daughter of a well-known Shakespearean actor, who was good-naturedly gruff between takes and had a laugh that sounded like a gun going off. When Donna came to set with me, he would wander over to flirt with her, and I would hear her musical voice drifting over to us from craft services. Sometimes she would catch my eye and shake her head amusedly, and I would grin and shake mine back.

A few weeks into the shoot, she came over to me, eyes dancing. 'Do you know what that ridiculous man said?'

'No.' I was nervous to hear it. 'What?'

'That daughter of yours is a talent.'

'Me?' I asked, surprised. 'He's met my mum.'

'He thought she was a chaperone, apparently. He was astonished when I set him straight. Isn't that cute?' After the shoot she took me to her favourite ice cream parlour in Covent Garden – a rare treat, as these days we were more careful about my diet. I'd been asked to wear a chest binder on this shoot.

'It's exciting!' said Donna when I'd cried embarrassed tears on our lunch date. 'You're becoming a woman.'

'But it's better if I look younger.' She'd told me that. It made me more bookable. We couldn't control some of the changes in my body, but we could control my skinny legs and arms.

I only ate half of my ice cream before I threw it away. 'Oh, it's horrible, isn't it?' sighed Donna as I walked back towards her, half-full cup of rocky road left lying in the bin. 'It really shouldn't be like this.'

'But it is.'

'But it is.' She squeezed my shoulders, leaning down to kiss the top of my head. 'You're so good.' Later that day, she gave me a new charm for my bracelet. It was a little camera. 'For your first film,' she said.

When filming resumed for Season Three and we all came back to set, only Hannah looked the same. Kendra had more of a figure than ever, and Roni's sweet, round face was maturing and gaining character. Faye had sprung up into something willowy and ethereal, her features soft and romantic. She was fast becoming the most beautiful of us all. Sometimes I thought she was even more beautiful than Donna. I found it hard to hold her eye at first, when she looked at me, until she came over and touched my arm and said, 'Did you miss me?'

'Yeah,' I said, 'a lot,' because I had.

When we bumped into Howie, Faye and I walking down the corridor to the classroom arm in arm, I saw him noticing her. But all he said was, 'Jesus, Belle, you grew up a bit there.'

I hit him on the arm and he pretended that it hurt him. He was nineteen now and had not progressed much further in his career, as far as I could tell, still running back and forward between the coffee shop and the studio. I was glad of this. I wanted to know that he would always stay where he was, just in case I needed him.

In the dressing room, we did a quick run through of everyone's last few months – Faye and Hannah's Portugal trip, Roni's cat dying – and then we compared social media followers. I was leading, but Kendra was catching up disturbingly quickly. A few choice guest-star spots on popular teen dramas had started to legitimise her in the TV world and I knew that Rupert had suggested she go with Donna to the BAFTAs. I told her this. She rolled her eyes.

'What? Aren't you excited?'

'Oh,' she said, 'piss off.'

She'd discovered drinking over the break. It was funny to hear her brag about it, Faye and I shooting each other smug looks. She had half a bottle of Sainsbury's vodka in her bag, which she waved at us.

'Go on, Hannah. Try it.'

'She's too young,' said Faye. Hannah looked relieved.

'My friend can drink this stuff like it's water,' said Kendra.

'Well,' I said, 'it's not like it's hard.'

She passed the bottle over with raised eyebrows and a smirk. Maintaining a straight face whilst I took a swig was a battle, but there was no better reward than Kendra's obvious shock. Thank God for Howie's cheap taste.

It was strange to be without Paget. Her quiet, damp presence had been unsettling, but her absence was even more so. We avoided mention of her. We pretended like we had only ever been five.

When Donna welcomed us back, she ran quickly through Kendra's achievements, made a brief stop at Faye and Hannah's, and she didn't mention Roni at all, who hadn't booked much beyond bit parts and adverts since we'd all begun. She talked so long about me that I found it hard to sustain my smile.

'Belle is flying,' she said. 'But I think we've got some more stars in this group, and I'd like to show off our little TV star at the BAFTAs with me next week.' I was so astonished that I forgot to look happy. Teasing Kendra was fun but not for a second had I thought she would actually be chosen over me. 'Fancy it?' Donna asked Kendra.

'Definitely,' said Kendra.

'It's a joke,' I seethed to Faye and Howie later as we sat around in the music room, passing Howie's flask between us. 'I've done everything she's asked me to do over the last few months. And she's taking Kendra?'

'Sorry, Belle,' said Faye. 'You deserve it.'

'Obviously.' I took another swig, wincing. Howie watched me from against the wall. 'Aren't you going to take this off me?' I asked, waving at him.

'Nah,' he said. 'You can set your own limits.'

'Woah.' I grinned, chucking the flask to Faye. 'You've changed your tune.'

'What are you now? Fifteen?'

'Fourteen.'

'Old enough,' said Howie.

He was lying languidly against the wall, hair and t-shirt rumpled. He smiled sleepily as he said it. He was beginning to lose the boyishness in his face, his nineteenth year revealing a jawline, cheekbones. I watched him run a hand over the stubble on his chin and knew, suddenly, all in an ageing rush, what it was to want someone.

Faye and I had missed him. Or rather, we had missed this – the three of us, sat in a room together, being grown up. Howie didn't treat us like little sisters any more. He teased us if we couldn't keep up with him, dared us to take one more sip when we said we were done. We became experts at getting tipsy and pretending not to be. The one time Mum told me I smelt of vodka, I said that Howie's cleaning products had spilt in the bathroom. We kept emergency toothbrushes in Faye's dance bag after that. When Faye threw up into the bin, whimpering, 'Sorry, sorry,' as I stroked her hair and Howie's hand moved in circles on her back, we told Alex that she'd eaten something dodgy.

'Hm,' said Alex.

Faye called me the next day. 'Pretty sure Mum knows.'

'Shit.' I wasn't ready to give it all up. My friends from home were starting to go to parties and date boys. I needed something that made me feel like a teenager.

'Sofie hasn't guessed at all? You've been steaming some nights.'

Mum hadn't guessed. She hadn't had the chance.

The first time I'd gotten drunk, too drunk to disguise as tiredness, I hadn't realised it had happened until Howie stood over me and said, 'Belle, is your mum picking you up?'

I was lying on the carpet, I realised. I'd been dancing a minute ago.

'Yes,' I said, struggling up onto my elbows.

'Think of a lie, then,' he said, chucking my jacket at me. 'Don't fucking get me fired.' He'd never looked angry with me before. I couldn't bear it. I reached for him, and found Faye's hands instead, helping me up. Her phone was ringing.

'Coming,' she said into it. She looked at me, chewing her lip.

'I'm fine,' I said. Howie snorted.

'She asked if you wanted a lift.'

'Tell her Belle's getting the tube,' said Howie. 'Gives her a little time to sober up.'

He walked me to the tube stop. Everything was hazy in an alarming sort of way. Up until now, drinking had always made me feel good. I felt something land on my shoulders.

'You were shivering,' said Howie, as I reached for it. It was his jacket. 'You know where you're going, right?'

'Yes.'

'You're sure?'

'Fuck's sake, Howie. I'm not a kid.'

'Alright, Miss Belle,' he grinned. 'Be safe.' He nodded at the jacket. 'And I want that back.'

On the tube, I wrapped the jacket tightly around me, and tried to work out in what way the nickname 'Miss Belle' was supposed to be taken.

I didn't go home.

'Belle?' said Donna, opening the door to find me cold and bleary-eyed, wrapped in a man's jacket. 'Are you alright?'

'I'm fine. Can I stay here?'

'Have you been drinking?' She asked it in a way that meant she already knew the answer, so I just shrugged. 'Oh dear,' she said, with the slightest hint of a smile.

'Can I stay here?' I bleated.

She tucked me up with a glass of water and two paracetamol on the bedside table. When I rolled over, away from her, she pushed the hair back from my forehead and planted a kiss on my ear before she left me to sleep.

I woke to her shaking me gently, gesturing with her eyes to the phone in her hand.

'Yes, yes, she's here,' she said. 'She wanted to get an early jump on rehearsals.'

She handed the phone to me. Mum was seething. '*Don't* do that. You should always come home unless I explicitly tell you otherwise.'

'This is home too. I'm in my bedroom.'

'You can't impose yourself on Donna's hospitality whenever you feel like it.'

'Of course she can,' said Donna. 'Sofie, you need your own space sometimes.'

'I need to know where my daughter is.'

'Like she said,' said Donna. 'This is her home too.'

She took the phone back from me and wandered out of the room as I lay under the covers, going over the events of last night in my head. Howie's jacket was draped over the back of an armchair. I should have taken it off. I didn't want to get him into trouble.

'Well,' said Donna, returning, sans phone.

I gave her a tentative grin from under heavy eyelids. She returned it.

'In the rebellious years, are we?' she asked me.

'It was stupid. I was just with a couple of friends and someone had some vodka . . .'

'Seems like one of your friends might be missing a jacket,' she said, nodding at the armchair.

I flushed. 'Don't tell Mum. Please.'

'Did you do anything?'

I shook my head automatically, and then realised what she meant. 'No! Nothing like that.'

'Then I don't see why Sofie needs to know anything.'

I sat up and threw my arms around her. The force of the hug made her laugh.

'You're a teenager,' she said. 'It's hard for Sofie to see that, I think. But this life isn't normal, and I think it's good for you to get to do some normal stuff here and there. As long as you're always careful, and as long as you always come here afterwards so I can make sure you're okay.'

I couldn't believe my luck. As we sat in the back of the car together on the way to set, I watched her out of the corner of my eye, the way the light hit her face, the glint of her rings as she pushed her hair behind her ear, and I felt more than ever how strange and wonderful it was that I'd been chosen out of every girl in the country to grow in her wake. To tread in her delicate, impossibly luminous footsteps.

Mum was waiting with folded arms on the pavement when I stepped out of the car. She pulled me close. I felt the rapid intake and output of her breath. 'Sorry,' I said, muffled, into her chest. Donna stepped away to give us space. I watched her over Mum's shoulder, clicking off into the studio in her heels. She never wobbled.

'Charge your fucking phone. Send me a fucking text. It's not hard.'

'I know.'

'Donna's is not home. If you want to sleep over some nights, that's okay. But it's not the same as going home. You always need to tell me. Okay?'

'Okay.'

'Trust is fragile,' she said. 'Remember that.'

'I know.'

'I want to be a cool mum, Belle, but I'll be a tiresome nag if I have to be.'

'Don't say you want to be cool. That's the least cool thing you can say.'

She grimaced. 'Shit. It is, isn't it? Tiresome nag it is, I suppose.'

'Don't be that either.'

'There are worse things to be,' she said.

After Mum and Alex caught on, those nights with Faye and Howie became less frequent. But I would still walk over to Donna's sometimes, after shooting, past terraced Chelsea townhouses, and I would knock on her door. She would say, 'Belle, come in, your room's all ready.'

'I'm sorry about the BAFTAs,' she said, one night, sitting on the end of my puffy duvet. 'I wish I'd been able to take you.'

'It's okay.' I'd felt sick when I'd known the cameras were going with them. I didn't want Kendra and Donna to have any kind of storyline that didn't involve me.

'You know I wanted to,' she said. She stroked my hair. 'The thing is, we have to jump through of Rupert and Fred's hoops sometimes.' She pulled a face. 'I hate it as much as you do.'

'Yeah, it sucks.'

'Don't worry,' she says. 'It's all headed somewhere. I've got a plan. You're just going to have to trust me.'

By that point, Kendra always had a bottle of Sainsbury's vodka in her bag, decanted into a pink metal water bottle. She was friends with a sixth former from her old school who worked in the one near Tottenham Court Road, who would scan it through for her without asking for ID. She got through them very slowly, bringing them out in-between classes for the smallest of sips, making eye contact with us over the top of the bottle. I always took a bigger sip than her, if she offered. So did Faye. Those sips of vodka in the dressing room became pre-drinks for us. Suddenly it wasn't just the evenings that we spent tipsy, but the afternoons as well. One day, when Kendra was in a particularly good mood, Donna walked into the dressing room to find us giggling around her dance bag.

'What's going on?' she asked. We were ten minutes late for class. We stashed the bottle in-between every sip, constantly vigilant, but our cheeks burned as if we'd been spinning it on the carpet. Donna looked at the bag, and then back at us.

'Is this getting to be a problem?' she asked me when I turned back up at her door that evening.

'No.'

'I've been nothing but supportive of you having your fun, Belle, but I don't want it to interfere with your training. Or your work, more to the point.' She tucked a strand of hair behind my ear. 'Refocus. Yes?'

I nodded. I could go without those sips from Kendra's vodka in the dressing room, but I knew I wasn't going to stop drinking with Howie.

We were famous now. We weren't household names, but we were known. We felt it when we went outside and people shouted our names, or when we went online and found edits of ourselves set to pop music. Kendra got in trouble with her mum for posting photos of herself in a very small bikini after they went viral on fan accounts. Going out together as a group became a hazard. On one occasion, word spread so quickly about our trip to Westfield that security had to rescue us from a frighteningly packed Claire's Accessories.

Commentary on all of us became repetitive. Kendra was bad and kind of mean, but she was also cool and witty. Hannah was sweet but too quiet, and Faye was grounded and sensible and everyone's favourite. I was talented and going to be a star, which split the show's fanbase down the middle – they either loved me or hated me, but either way they'd make sure to let me know. And Roni, they said, shouldn't be there. She wasn't as good as the rest of us. Even Hannah had more star potential than her. After all, we were on Season Three, and she'd barely been cast in anything.

Then, shortly after I wrapped my film, Roni booked a job. It was her first-ever stage work, as Young Fiona in *Shrek: The Musical*. The fight to hide my jealousy on camera was so exhausting that afterwards I locked myself in the toilet and spent three minutes completely relaxing my face muscles.

'Of course,' Donna said later, in our dance lesson, 'you won't need to dance really, Roni.'

'I know.'

'Or act much, really. It's just one song. And some chorus work, isn't it?'

'Yes,' said Roni.

'*Alice* took a lot out of Belle. Carrying a whole production at only twelve.'

Roni said nothing.

'Lucky, isn't it, that they're trying a black Fiona?' Donna clapped her hands. 'Faye, come up to the front. I want to see your scorpion.'

Faye walked up to the front and started to pull her leg over her head. I watched her fingers grab at the back of her calf. Kendra tugged me backwards. With quick glances to the front of the room, to check that Donna's attention was still on Faye, she placed a hand on my shoulder. 'You need to stick up for her.'

'Why me?'

'Well, you're the one she's being compared to.'

'She's not comparing.'

'Are you deaf?' asked Kendra. 'Either way, you're the only one she ever listens to.'

A camera was watching us, just to the left of Donna. I lowered my voice, as if I wasn't wearing a microphone, and tried to adjust so that it couldn't see my lips moving. 'Roni can speak up for herself. She's not . . . She's tough.'

Roni heard her name. She moved cautiously over to us. 'Kendra, drop it.'

'Belle should say something.'

'Yes, but I don't want a fight.'

'What do you mean, yes?'

Roni sighed at me. 'Belle, you should say something every time she pulls this crap. When she tells Hannah that she worries she won't be where you were at twelve by next year or she asks Kendra what she's had for lunch and dinner this week or when she makes you an assistant teacher in vocal class when Faye sings circles around you.'

'This is bullshit.' My face was hot. 'I'm not going to tell her to like me less.'

'What's going on?' called Donna.

'Nothing,' mumbled Kendra.

'Belle?'

Donna was looking at me, not accusingly, but with an asking, reassuring look. I swallowed.

'They're saying I should stand up to you—'

'Snitch!' cried Kendra, throwing up her hands. Roni walked quickly away from us. She stood to the edge of the room, like she was hoping Donna would forget she was there.

Donna stood there, observing. Kendra subsided, folding her arms and staring off at the far wall. 'I won't have infighting,' said Donna eventually. 'You're not those kinds of girls.' She walked back over to Faye. Then, almost as an afterthought, she added, 'And Belle will not take the fall for other people's sloppy work. Is that understood?'

She waited.

'Yes,' said Roni.

'Yes,' mumbled Kendra.

Howie had slipped in through the door to hand a coffee to Fred. I watched him in the reflection of the mirror as he laughed, silently. When he saw me looking, he curled his fingers and made a jerking motion with his wrist.

Even though it became harder for our little club to meet, we still found ways. Faye and I entered a duet into a local competition, with Donna's blessing. It was two months away, which gave us a solid alibi for a whole eight weeks.

'I'm going to be late tonight,' I said to Mum on our break. 'Duet rehearsal.'

'Give me a call when you're done and I'll come meet you.'

'Sure.' That meant I could drink, but not much. I walked past Howie in the corridor and gave him a subtle thumbs up.

Faye grabbed me around the waist on our way out of the classroom. I shrieked.

'Shush,' she said. Kendra turned around to shoot us a suspicious look. We both waited for her to turn back around. 'We're on?' she asked.

'We're on.'

She did a little dance on the spot which made me throw my arms around her and say, 'Fairy Faye, you are my favourite person in the world.'

'Even more than Donna?' she asked, grinning.

I gave her a shove. 'Oh, shut up.'

'Howie,' she told him later as we sat around in the music room, 'Belle says she loves me more than Donna.'

He laughed. 'Belle's lying to you.'

'I do.' I was two shots down at this point. 'I love her.' I threw her to the floor, planting kisses on her cheeks and forehead. She shrieked with laughter, wiggling away from me.

'You're a fucking predator, Belle,' said Howie with a grin. I sat up, pushing my hair back behind my ears. Faye and I shuffled away from each other. 'Has Donna ever done that to you?' he asked.

'You're gross,' said Faye.

'Hey,' he said, 'it's what you do to people you love. And God knows Donna loves Belle. You should see the kind of shit people put online.'

I'd seen it. We both had. There were whole blogs and pages dedicated to discussing whether we'd done things we didn't even really understand. We never talked about them, because to talk about them would be to acknowledge that they had something to do with us and our real lives, and that produced a suffocating kind of anxiety. It was easier to pretend that they were written about other people. Howie saw our faces.

'Forget I brought it up,' he said. 'People are weird.'

Faye and I had both admitted to each other, sat whispering on the floor of the dressing room with our hands tightly covering our mics, that we were in love with Howie. It was such an absent, easy, nonconfrontational sort of love that we didn't even mind the competition. Actually, there was a pleasant companionship in it.

'Maybe we'll be sister wives,' Faye had giggled. It was funny, but also it wasn't a terrible idea.

'Have either of you ever kissed anyone?' asked Howie later, in the music room.

I waited for Faye to admit that she hadn't first. 'No,' she said, taking a sip. You could always count on Faye's honesty.

'Belle?'

'Me neither.'

'Aw.' He pouted. 'So cute.'

'Shut up,' said Faye, sticking her leg out to kick him.

'Seriously. You're both fucking adorable. Fourteen and never done a thing. It's a shame you don't have a dad, Belle – you're every man's dream daughter.'

'And you're every dad's nightmare,' I said. I was pretty proud of that line. Even Howie looked impressed.

'Fuck yeah, I am,' he said. 'Chuck me the flask.' He caught it deftly. 'You should just teach each other,' he said.

We looked at each other sideways. 'Teach each other what?' I asked.

'To kiss. Don't girls do that?'

'No,' laughed Faye.

'They do in porn.'

'Howie!' she said, kicking him again.

'Sorry, sorry. Jesus, you're so easy to shock.'

He smiled at us, smug with all the things he knew that we didn't. I shuffled around to face Faye. 'Okay,' I said. 'Let's teach each other.' She knew I was joking. We mimed kissing, several centimetres away from each other and fell about laughing.

'Cowards,' said Howie, taking a sip.

I reached for the flask. He held it out of my reach. 'Give it!'

'Sorry. Drink is for those who complete their dares.'

'You didn't dare us.'

He pointed at me. 'I dare you . . .' His finger moved to Faye. 'And you, to kiss.'

Faye shook her head, laughing. 'What's the forfeit?'

'Hey, come on. Belle?'

'You heard her. What's the forfeit?'

He pretended to think. 'Forfeit is . . . you've both got to kiss Kendra.'

'Fuck, no,' I said, at the same time as Faye broke out with, 'Howie, that's not *fair*.'

He shrugged. 'Fine. That's all you get.'

Faye and I looked at each other for a second. Then she leant forward, and so did I, and our lips touched for the briefest of seconds. It was the slightest, smallest peck, but the moment of contact made my stomach do an unexpected dive down to my toes. Howie whooped.

I couldn't look at either of them. My gaze shot down to my lap.

'Alright, alright,' I heard him say. 'Barely a kiss.'

'You're a perv,' said Faye. 'Give us the flask.' She took a drink from it, but when she offered it to me, I shook my head. I still couldn't look at her, my hands trembling in my lap. 'Belle?' I felt her hand slide into mine. 'Do you want to go?' she asked, her voice suddenly quiet. I wasn't sure how to answer her. I was feeling very strange.

'She's fine,' said Howie. 'Belle? You're not gonna throw up, are you?'

I shook my head again.

'Neither of you have ever watched porn then?' he asked us, lounging against the wall, chucking his lighter from hand to hand.

'Why would we do that?' asked Faye, with an exaggerated shudder.

'It's educational. Can't imagine Donna's curriculum covers sex ed. You should learn this stuff somehow.'

'We're not children,' I said.

'Exactly my point. You should know this shit. At your age, you should be out there practising this shit. God knows I was.'

Faye was looking from one to the other of us. 'Belle,' she said, 'we are sort of children. Strictly speaking.' I flushed. This was such a Faye thing to say, and for the first time, I didn't find her frankness endearing. 'Come on, Howie, you had sex at fourteen?' she asked him.

'Thirteen.'

'That's bullshit.'

'It's true,' he said. 'I was shagging anything that moved.'

Faye looked down. 'Well, maybe it's different for boys.'

'And I wasn't half as mature as you two are. I mean shit, you have *jobs*. For all intents and purposes, you're adults. And you know the kind of shit that's out there online about you both.'

'Yeah,' I said. 'Weird people.'

'Okay, but how much have you looked at? I mean, do you know there're photos out there with your heads on the bodies of porn stars?'

I tried to look as if I had known that. A sick feeling washed over me. 'That's not true,' said Faye.

'Look it up then.'

'No. People couldn't do that. It would be illegal. We're kids.' I wished she would stop saying it.

'I mean, you're not tiny,' said Howie, 'are you? It would be one thing if you were, like, nine.'

I was tried to imagine what these photos of me but not me would look like. In my head, they were obvious fakes, two magazine photos with raw edges taped together, like a collage. My head on some obviously adult women's body. Nothing that actually looked real. This was comforting.

Faye reached for the flask. Howie held it out of her reach. 'Go on, kiss her again.'

'No.'

'You won't even have another peck? Jesus, Faye, it's just a laugh,' he added. Her lip was trembling. 'Fine,' he said, throwing the flask to her, 'have another shot first. Liquid courage.'

'I don't want any more,' she said.

'Belle?' I shook my head again. 'Are you sulking?' I didn't answer. He threw the flask at the ground. 'Jesus, this is what I get for hanging out with fucking babies.'

I almost grabbed her face then and went for it, just to shut him up, but she stood up suddenly. 'I need the toilet,' she said. She sounded very young as she said it, like a child tugging her mum's hand.

'No you don't,' said Howie. 'Sit down.'

'Come with me,' she said, holding her hand out to me. Her eyes darted back and forth over my face. I grabbed her hand. Her fingers clung very tightly to mine as she pulled me up. Even when I was standing, they didn't let go.

'This is so fucking childish,' groaned Howie. 'I thought you guys were cool.'

Silent, Faye tugged me out of the room. Her face was set. Once we were in the corridor she started running. I ran with her, scared without even really knowing why. I could hear Howie's footsteps behind us, slow at first, then faster, getting closer. That corridor had never felt so long. With every inch that Faye tugged me forward, the doors to the staff toilets only got further away.

The lurch of relief in my chest when our hands touched the wood was sickening. Faye pulled me inside, locking the two of us into a cubicle.

We stared at each other. She took my other hand and we stood, facing each other, gripping each other's fingers down by our sides, our foreheads very close together. I could feel her rapid breath on my face.

'Are you actually locking me out?' I heard him call. His voice took on an echoey quality when he entered the toilets. 'I gave you the fucking idea!'

We stood frozen, socked feet on the toilet floor. We'd left our shoes in the music room, along with our dance bags. Faye followed my eyes downwards and tightened her mouth when she realised, her eyes glassy.

A loud thump on the door made us both jolt. I squeaked slightly, prompting laughter from Howie.

'Come on! What are you doing?'

He banged on the door again.

'Come out!'

Faye shook her head at me. I couldn't have moved even if I'd wanted to.

'Do you want me to lock up and leave you in there?'

Faye gripped my fingers tighter and shook her head at me. *He won't*, she mouthed. She was right – there was no way he'd have been able to explain that to Fred and Rupert the next morning. Faye let go of my hands, reaching for her pocket. I watched her type a message to her mum.

Belle's phone is dead can u come and get us both?

I'll call you a taxi, came Alex's response. Hannah had the flu and the two of them hadn't left their hotel room for the last few days.

I dont feel well, sent Faye.

If you've been drinking again then you need to tell me.

I shook my head at her frantically but she wasn't paying me any attention. Howie thumped on the door again. The phone nearly came out of Faye's hands and into the toilet, but she managed to hold onto it.

We found some vodka, she said. I put my hands in my hair, horrified. *Don't tell Belle's mum she didn't have any it was just me*

I'm on my way, she sent.

I thought that maybe, in the fifteen minutes it took Alex to arrive in her cab, Howie might lose interest and wander back to the music room to get high. He stayed, occasionally thumping on the door or shouting something to us, but mostly just quietly waiting. We could hear him breathing as we stood there, shivering, clutching each other's hands.

It wasn't until Alex opened the front door of the building and called, 'Girls! Let's go!' that he scarpered. We heard him retreat down the corridor to the music room and slam the door.

Slowly, Faye unlocked the door. She didn't move. I took cautious steps out into the corridor. It was empty. We scrambled down the stairs and arrived in front of Alex breathless and sweaty, closing the door firmly behind us.

'Where's your stuff?' she asked. 'Where are your shoes?'

'We'll get it all tomorrow,' said Faye, pushing past her and out into the street.

'What's happened?' asked Alex, following her.

'Nothing,' said Faye. 'I'm just tired.' She tilted her head up, taking evening air in through her nose, and she wrapped her arms tightly around herself, as if to check that she was still all in one piece.

We watched over each other, after that. If he attempted to crack a joke with one of us or pull us aside for a chat, the other one was always there to intervene. We were never rude to him, but we were distant, nervy, and after a while he stopped trying.

Roni, gearing up for her opening night, was too busy to notice the change. Hannah lived in her own little world. But Kendra was always quick to pick up on these things. She was gripped by it.

'What happened between the three of you?' she asked.

'What do you mean?'

'You all used to be so buddy-buddy.'

'He's old,' Faye said. 'He's on the crew. We were never friends with him.'

Gaslighting Kendra wasn't effective. She was always too sure of her own reality. It was why, no matter how many comments Donna made about her eating habits, she would still ignore the fruit at the crafty table every lunchtime and walk down the street to get a slice of pizza and a Twix.

Faye and I were still close, but with the break-up of the little club we began to drift. The distance between us hurt me, and so I ran to Donna. There wasn't a lunch I didn't spend out with her, sometimes without cameras, often with. The lines between off and on had begun to blur and I was starting to realise that it didn't matter what I knew was real and what I knew was contrived – when it was out there, on a screen, it was the truth, and anything I knew became irrelevant. The apathy took me like a tide. There was no point in fighting it.

So I was the bootlicker. Donna's favourite, her biggest admirer, the cocky, privileged one that no one was ever rooting for. Kendra, perversely, became the scrappy underdog – more talented than me, many people thought, and more beautiful, and with more personality, but not afforded the same opportunity. It didn't matter that she hurt more feelings and caused more rifts than the rest of us combined. On camera, she was honest. She told it like it was. She wasn't afraid to stand up for herself. These were qualities people liked much more than being nice.

When I stopped caring, it stopped mattering. I was working. Casting directors loved me. Music execs were beginning to swarm around me. I had money and praise, and girls much prettier than me would stop me and ask for pictures in the street. If the camera and I had to learn to coexist in order for me to keep all of that, so be it.

I suppose I felt that way because by this point, I could always see the machinations. I could watch the wheels turning. I knew the stories they were trying to tell and the pictures they intended to paint. I could always see it coming. Until I couldn't.

Preparations for Roni's opening night began early. Fred and Rupert were insistent that this time, they had to find a way to get the cameras into the theatre. They wanted all of us in the front row of the stalls and they wanted footage of us reacting to Roni's big moment and cheering for her at the end.

'Oh,' said Donna, 'that'll be a *lovely* little scene.'

They wanted jealousy and satisfaction and a comeback story for Roni. No one acknowledged it, but everyone knew it.

To everyone's surprise, they managed to swing it with the theatre, because Roni's contract was for a year and there was every hope that the show would run far beyond then. 'Publicity is the golden word,' Rupert told us all.

Roni barely spoke to us in the weeks leading up to that night. She spent her time on set rehearsing and stayed late in the music room to practise her song. I would sometimes wonder if she ever spoke to Howie, when she did this, and feel a guilty brand of jealousy.

The day before the show, before she left for a tech run, she sat with us all in the dressing room and said, 'I'm the most terrified I've ever been in my life.'

We knew why. We'd all guessed that the season was wrapping up, and that maybe the cameras were coming to this performance because Fred and Rupert wanted footage for their final episode. If Season Two had taught us anything, it was that finales were a dangerous business.

Mum woke me up the next morning by walking into my room and coughing her lungs up.

'Gross,' I said, the duvet over my head.

'Sorry.' She'd caught her boyfriend's cold. 'That bastard,' she said, but I could hear that she was smiling.

I flung the duvet off. 'So you can't come tonight?'

'Donna was insisting on driving you anyway.'

'Really?'

'They probably want to film something in the car.' She coughed again, violently. 'Hey,' she said, when she was finished. 'He really wants to hang out with you some time.'

'That's weird.'

'Don't you want to meet the man who gave me these germs?' They'd been dating for some time now but I didn't know anything about him, mostly because I hadn't asked. When it came to her dating life, Mum only ever told me what I wanted to know. 'He's lovely,' she said. 'He's called Cameron. Have I told you that yet?'

'No.'

'Well, that's his name. Fancy dinner with the two of us sometime?'

'Maybe,' I said, in a way that meant no.

She helped me get ready that evening, painting over my French tips – courtesy of Donna – with a sparkly silver.

'You look like a movie star,' she said, as she pinned up my hair. 'Is there a red carpet?'

'There's a carpet, but it'll probably be green.'

'Green?'

'*Shrek.*'

'Ah.' She laughed. 'Show openings are fun. I'm jealous.'

'I don't really want to go,' I said.

She knelt down next to me to pin my hair. 'Whatever they've got up their sleeves,' she said, 'if indeed they do have something up their sleeves, then you don't have to worry. You're luckier than the rest of them.'

'Why?'

'Because Donna will protect you,' she said. 'And I can't say that for sure about any of the rest of those girls, but I can say that for sure about you. She adores you.' She kissed my forehead. 'It's the one thing the two of us will always see eye to eye on.'

'The one thing?'

'It's an expression.'

I watched her tidy up my make-up table in her dressing gown, occasionally stopping to cough into her sleeve. I wondered if she minded all the time I'd been spending with Donna this year. I wondered if, despite her boyfriend and his germs, she ever got lonely.

Donna arrived to pick me up in her cab. She pretended to go into raptures when she saw me. Donna only did bits like this when she was in an especially good mood.

'I've got a surprise for you tonight,' she said.

'Yeah?'

She tapped her nose. 'Your fairy godmother has been working overtime. Just you wait and see.'

I waved to Mum as she stood in the window upstairs. Donna looked back as we drove off, watching Mum for a while.

'Your mum is so pretty,' she said. 'I don't know why she doesn't do more with herself.'

'She's got a cold.'

'Ah, well. There's always an excuse, I suppose. Promise me you'll never let yourself go, Belle. The most depressing thing a beautiful woman can do is to stop ever trying to be beautiful.'

We were driving through St Paul's when the car pulled up on the pavement. I blinked at Donna, who gestured to the car door.

'It's still a long walk from here.'

'There's been a change of plan,' she said.

She pointed upwards, towards a rooftop bar opposite the cathedral.

'Up there,' she said, 'there is a table of very important people who work in the music industry. They have heard tapes of you singing and they have seen pictures of you, and they truly believe, as do I, that you could be the next big thing in pop. I mean, you should have seen how excited they got. It's like they've unearthed a young Britney Spears.'

I stared at her, uncomprehending.

'Belle,' she said, her voice taking on a note of irritation, 'don't look gormless.'

'What about the show?'

'She's signed for a year,' said Donna. 'There'll be plenty of opportunities to go and watch her. Listen, I've squared it with Production. Everyone's aware. There's a crew up there and they're going to be filming.'

'Aren't they filming Roni?'

'Yes, they are.' She squeezed my hand. 'A triumphant finale, Belle. That's my gift to you. To all of you. A big, happy moment for Roni, after all her struggles. After my bullying—' She grinned as I protested. 'Belle, you're a smart girl. We both know how this works. Roni gets to prove me wrong, and you get to walk in and meet important people in the music industry and talk about how far your star is going to rise.'

I looked up at the bar, neon lights against the darkening sky. 'High, apparently.'

She laughed. 'See, this is the form I need you on tonight.'

'Rupert and Fred agreed to this?'

'Why wouldn't they? It's the perfect contrast to what happened with Paget.'

'Okay,' I said, 'so what about Season Four? What's the contrast to this?'

'You let me worry about that,' she said. 'All you have to do is go up there and be amazing.'

I stared at her then, sitting across from me on the leather seat, beaming. She was the brightest, warmest thing I had ever seen. And she was clever, always making this machine work to our advantage. Always making sure, when the dust settled, the two of us were still climbing upwards.

'I love you,' she said. 'Your future is always safe with me.'

And it was, I thought. It would be. As long as I always left it sitting there in Donna's slim, perfectly manicured hands.

Reunion special

'Turn your phone off,' Cameron says at breakfast.

'I'll silence it.'

'That's no good – I'll still hear it buzzing.'

It goes again, interrupting him mid-bite. He chucks his toast down on the plate.

'Belle, turn it off or answer it. You're going to have it out with them eventually.'

'I know.'

He nods at the phone.

'It'll be awful,' I say, dragging my spoon through my cereal.

'Will it be more awful this morning than tomorrow morning?'

'Probably not.'

'Then,' he says, 'answer the phone, tell them you quit, and let's let it lie. Let's have it done.'

Rupert sounds astonished when I actually answer the call. 'Belle. Hi.' I suppose at this point he's been ringing on autopilot. 'I'm so glad I finally caught you.'

'I'm not coming back,' I say, my mouth full of cereal. Cameron nods reassuringly at me from the other side of the table.

'I thought you might say that.'

'We had a deal. You broke it.'

'I can only apologise for Sara,' he says. 'She's new. Very keen. Young.'

'She wasn't that young.'

'Besides,' he says, 'our deal wasn't broken. I said you wouldn't have to talk about it.'

'Yes, you did. And then I did.'

'The way I remember it, I jumped in to bail you out and you didn't say a single word. That all sounds fine and above board to me.' I'm quiet. I can hear the smile in his voice when he speaks again. 'Well, perhaps not exactly above board. But technically fine.'

He thinks he has me. My mind races through the ways I might have fucked up. What haven't I thought of? 'You aren't going to sue me.'

'No?'

'No. How would that look? You won't do that.'

'You're right,' he says. 'See, you're smart. I've always said that about you.'

'So? What's the play?'

'All I'm asking is that you behave like a professional,' he says. 'You signed a contract with us. You were booked for a job. And here you are storming off set whenever you feel like it, dodging our calls, ignoring your call time. What would Donna say if she knew you were behaving like this?'

He waits for me to answer. I don't. Cameron, brow wrinkled in concern, gestures for me to put the phone on speaker.

'The thing is, Belle,' says Rupert, as I lay the phone on the table, 'and I hope you can understand this, we're going to be telling this story one way or the other. We wanted to bring in all these different perspectives, to make sure everyone's able to tell their side in their own words. But if you're not here to speak for yourself then other people are going to have to speak for you.'

I meet Cameron's gaze. He hasn't understood the threat in this.

'Can you hold on?' I asked Rupert.

'Sure. I'll be here.'

I mute the call and put my head in my hands.

'What is it?' asks Cameron.

'They're going to do a smear job.'

'What do you mean?'

'You heard what he said. If I don't tell my side of the story, other people will tell it for me. As in, they'll take all those things they've already been feeding to Kendra – that I'm manipulative, I was Donna's puppet, I'm ungrateful – and that'll be the version of me they put out to the world.'

'What do they get out of that?'

'Press. Obviously. This revelation that maybe I wasn't as much of a victim as everyone decided I was.' Cam looks like he's waiting for me to get to the point. 'Do you understand?' I ask. I know he doesn't. He's not online in the way I am. He doesn't understand how ready people are to tear a fake victim apart.

'I don't get why it matters what they say about you,' he says. 'You and me and Jane will know it isn't true.'

'Sure, but—'

'And it's not like you're still trying to make it in the industry. I mean, it doesn't matter what this does for your career because you don't have one any more. To put it bluntly.'

He's right. But it still matters. I still care what the world thinks of me. It's a delicate thing right now, but it's swinging my way. People feel bad for me. They like me. I don't want to lose that. I don't want everyone to hate me again.

So I go back.

I meet them all in the hotel where Donna and I had our first lunch date. They're sat around the same table, all surprised to see me.

Rupert must have told them all I quit just for a fun reaction shot. Faye raises her glass to me and smiles.

'Look who it is,' says Roni. She seems genuinely pleased. 'She'll go down now and then but you can't take her out.'

I give her a quick hug. It's always nice to be in Roni's good books.

'Good for you,' she whispers into my ear, so soft that no mic could catch it. 'Keep them on their toes.'

I'm expecting warmth from Kendra – our most recent conversation was almost friendly, after all. Instead, she's frostier than ever, staring out of the window as I approach, giving me a tight smile when I sit down before letting her eyes move past me. She doesn't even offer a sardonic comment.

'This is strange,' I say, as I look around me. It's all I can ever think to say, when they put us in situations like this. I must be coming across as permanently baffled. 'Can we get food? I was never allowed to eat here. Continuity.'

'I think that still applies,' grins Faye.

'Shame. The stuff they put down in front of me always looked great.' Everyone laughs. It's probably the first hint of personality I've shown on camera in the entire special so far. I hope they leave it in.

'This is where Donna used to take you, right?' asks Roni.

'Yeah, she loved this place.' I keep my voice level. 'It's beautiful, isn't it?'

'It's gorgeous,' says Hannah. I wonder if Hannah has set herself a target number of words per scene. I wonder if she's meeting it.

'Faye,' comes Rupert's voice, 'ask if anyone's still in touch with Donna.'

Annoyance shows in Faye's face, only for a second, and then her professionalism takes over. It's just enough of a pause for me to wonder why he didn't give the question to Kendra – and to realise that it's because Kendra's answer is going to be important.

Faye clears her throat. 'Is anyone still in touch with Donna, by the way?'

Everyone shakes their heads. Everyone is watching Kendra.

'I am,' she says. 'A little.'

We wait. My heart is beating in my throat.

'I mean, I wasn't, but she reached out to me yesterday. Wanted to know how I was.' Her eyes land on me. 'I told her we were filming this. She was sad she wasn't a part of it.'

'I don't know why you'd ever reply to her,' says Faye, looking down at her lap.

'Well,' says Kendra. 'She had some interesting things to say.'

A beat. 'Like what?' asks Roni.

Kendra shakes her head. 'We aren't supposed to talk about Donna. Right, Belle?'

I'm trying to gather myself to formulate a response when Kendra looks straight over to Rupert and waves her arm.

'Right,' she says, 'can we have a break and actually eat something? I'm fucking starving.'

She doesn't get a red card, or even the threat of one. Rupert laughs and asks a runner to fetch some menus. I watch him go, absently. When he hands me one and I turn back to the table to read it, I see that Kendra is watching me. She holds her menu like it's a hand of cards.

Fred is in the doorway of the restaurant, smoking, technically outside but being an asshole about it. I slip out of my seat as everyone's ordering and approach him. He looks around as I walk up, like he's waiting for Rupert to come out of nowhere and side tackle me.

'You need to be straight with me,' I say.

'If you have a concern, talk to Rupert.'

'Rupe will tell me whatever he thinks I want to hear.'

He shrugs. Fred doesn't give a shit. He doesn't care enough to lie. 'Is she coming?'

He holds my stare, taking another drag of his cigarette. 'You know we couldn't swing that.'

'No, I don't know.'

'You know we'd love to get her. I mean, shit, that would make this whole thing ten times more interesting. We wouldn't have to pad it with fucking restaurant lunches and love-ins at your old dance studio.' He shrugs. 'It isn't an option. We'd never have got this thing off the ground if Donna was attached.'

'Why not?'

'You know why not. Network TV has some sense of decency.' He almost grins. 'Unfortunately.'

In the reflection of the window, I can see that Kendra is texting someone. Funny to think that in all our worst moments, throughout all our Tom and Jerry antics, I never really thought that she actually, truly hated me.

After lunch, we film an argument. We pick it up as if Kendra has just told us that she's still talking to Donna. Faye yells at her, standing up at the table to point her finger in Kendra's face. *'How could you be this callous to Belle?'*

Kendra yells back. There's laughter in it. When Roni rubs my back I produce real tears, hot and messy, inspiring fresh, derisive material in Kendra. We wrap it up with Kendra storming off, which doesn't really make sense but I think she's bored and wants the scene to end. I wipe my eyes as she lingers outside, unwilling to slink back in and make small talk.

'You've still got it!' says Rupert, slapping me on the shoulder. Another tear spills over. 'Gripping stuff, girls.'

Cars are called. Hannah and Roni are heading to the Soho studio to film interviews to camera, but Rupert tells me we can finish mine another day.

'We'll ease you back in,' he says. 'That was great stuff there.' I don't like it when Rupert is nice to me.

At Soho studio, says Howie. *Where are you?*

I ignore him. Inevitably, my phone goes again.

Anyone would think you were avoiding me.

'You okay?' asks Faye, who is watching my face as we stand on the pavement.

'Fine.' I drop my phone into my pocket. 'I'd rather walk to the tube. Would you?'

'Okay,' she says, even though she's visibly cold.

I think I love her best when I'm walking with her along the south bank of the river. Time all happens at once here. We could be twelve on our way to find lunch, or fifteen on our way back from an audition, or twenty-six and trying to find the words. We can step right over that decade-sized gap in our history. The thought catches me by surprise, but it shouldn't – I've known her fourteen years and loved her most of them. That's the only thing that has to be true.

She walks a little ahead of me for a while. We are silent. She keeps her head slightly turned to the right, watching the city on the other side of the river. Her hair blows back behind her, so light and delicate it's hard to tell where it stops and the air begins.

'I hate that restaurant,' she says. 'Everyone in there is in a business meeting, always. No one ever goes there just to enjoy themselves. You can tell when a place is like that.'

'Yeah, you can.'

'You can tell Fred and Rupert chose it. They like impersonal places.'

'Donna told me she chose it.'

Faye shakes her head. 'Say what you want about Donna,' she says, 'and I can, believe me, I can say lots of things, but she liked to be connected to people.'

She falls into step beside me.

'I saw your post,' she said. 'Cute picture.'

'Jane's printing it out for her wall.'

'An honour.' She slips her hand into mine. 'How's she doing, after her audition?'

'Good, actually. It didn't get under her skin. Or at least it didn't stay there very long.'

'Oh to be that age again,' laughs Faye.

'Tell me about it.'

'I can't get stuff out from under my skin. I haven't been able to, for a long time now. Everything that gets under there stays there. You know?'

If I loved her at twelve, I was too young to know what love was. If I loved her at fifteen, I was too isolated to know how to love anyone else. If I love her now, I don't really know who she's grown into well enough to love her. I've spent too long without her to love her in completion, to love this new map of her. All of this is true. I love her all the same.

We're at the entrance to the tube. She's going to go on a bit further to the bus stop, she says. She pushes her hair out of her face and blinks at me. Frank, and uncomplicated, with so many sharp things under her delicate skin. I don't know how to begin explaining to her how I feel. None of this has ever been simple.

'I'll see you tomorrow then,' she says.

When she hugs me, she lets go like it's easy. I watch her walk away and I'm furious with myself. I'm not fifteen any more. I know better than to ache after this.

My phone goes off.

Leaving Soho studio now. Drinks in Soho??

I stare at the message.

Don't you want to know what they asked me? he says, after a few seconds.

Where? I reply.

I meet him at the same Wetherspoons we all got caught in last time. He's ordered me a vodka coke when I arrive – as a joke, I think, because he laughs when he pushes it towards me.

'Still your drink?'

'Yes, because I'm still fourteen.' I take a sip anyway. I actually do like a vodka coke. He rumples his hair and grins at me, lopsided in his chair. He still has the mannerisms of a nineteen-year-old.

'I'm not staying long,' I say. I already feel an unpleasant pressure on my chest, the kind I always get when I think about Howie.

'Okay.' He shrugs.

'I have to get home and see my sister.'

'What's she like?'

I shake my head.

'You act like I'm going to go and offer her a flask.'

'Wouldn't put it past you.'

'Ouch.' He grins.

He tips back in his chair, smiling. Waiting.

'How was the interview?' I ask.

'Interesting.'

'Jesus, Howie, tell me.'

'They asked about my memories of you all as children.'

'That was it?'

'Obviously not.'

'Did they ask you about the finale?'

'Obviously.'

I put my face in my hands. He reaches over to shake my shoulder.

'What are you so worried about? We're ride and die, me and you.'

'So what did you say?'

'I told the truth,' he says. 'I told parts of the truth. I didn't lie, but I let them fill in the gaps.'

I breath out. 'Honestly?'

'Honestly.'

I nod, staring down at my drink. He really does care about me, in some strange way.

'Congrats,' I say.

'On what?'

'You got me here.'

'I know.' He applauds himself. 'A victory!'

'Just say your piece to me.'

'What piece?'

'I don't know. Whatever you've wanted to say to me that's made you so desperate to get me alone.'

'There's no piece.' He spreads his hands. 'Why don't you believe that I care about you and I miss you?'

I nearly do, for a minute. He looks so genuine.

'Please.'

'What do you think you were to me?'

There's a pause. I laugh and push my glass away from me.

'What?'

'I'm not answering that.'

'Why not?'

'Because it's a fucking trap.'

'Please,' he says, 'answer the question. What were you to me?'

He tilts his head at me. Then he pushes my drink back towards me, with one finger. I sigh and wrap both my hands around it.

'You called me your little sister, a few times,' I said. 'Actually, I think you called me your hot little sister.'

He grimaces. 'Real way with words I had back then, huh?'

'I don't know what I was. I was entertainment, maybe. Someone who made your job a little bit more interesting because I was a teenager who fucking hung on your every word. I don't know. I was an ego boost, I guess.'

He's shaking his head. 'Wrong. And a bit self-pitying.'

'I don't know, Howie. You tell me. Stop making it a game.'

'It's not a game. It makes me sad, genuinely, that that's what you think.' He places his chin on his clasped hands. 'Belle, I adored you. You were like family to me. I literally would have done anything for you.'

'I think we remember those days a bit differently.'

'Who helped you more than me, in the end?' I'm silent. 'See,' he says triumphantly.

Actually, vodka coke is too sweet. And it's sticky – you can feel it on your lips after every sip. It's tacky and doesn't come off even when you rub. You can feel it on your teeth too, and your tongue. It coats your throat as it slides down.

'You think I want something from you,' he says. 'I don't want anything from you.'

Everyone wants something from someone.

'Honestly,' he says, like he can tell what I'm thinking. 'All I want is this.'

I can give him that. I can sit here and talk with Howie. Because – and this is the crucial thing – Howie does adore me. I can see it in his eyes as he looks at me. He can't believe his luck. Even when I was a kid, when he didn't have to pay any mind to me, I never had to fight for his attention. I never had to doubt what he thought of me. Howie has loved me, always, exactly as I am.

And maybe it was too much, at times. Maybe he treated me as too adult. But that's no more than everyone else around me. If I can forgive my mum, I can forgive him too.

It's nice to be able to make someone feel like the luckiest person in the world, just by sitting in a Wetherspoons and hardly saying a word.

Howie is staying in a Travelodge in the city centre, near Liverpool Street. He fills the tube ride and the short walk with memories, stories from when we were younger. His favourite thing to talk about is the day that I walked into the production room, at twelve years old, and he handed me a sheet of production notes without me having to say a word.

'And your *face*,' he says, and laughs uproariously. It's funny when Howie tells it.

He has a bottle of vodka in the wardrobe of his room, like he's a teenager hiding it from his parents. He opens it, hands it to me and says, 'Go on, show me you've still got it.'

I take a healthy sip. The burn is intensely nostalgic. It eats away at the edges of those memories, those scenes from our strange friendship, and suddenly I find it all funny too.

'I used to have the most intense dreams about you,' he says, watching me from the bed. I sit in the upholstered chair and drink again. 'Still do, sometimes.'

'Dreams?'

'Us, doing this.'

I thought he meant a different kind of dream. He must catch it in my face because he laughs. 'And other things, sure. That happens, apparently, when you're close to people. Doesn't mean much.'

'I don't have those kinds of dreams,' I say.

'At all?'

'Ever.'

'Nothing to draw on?' He winks.

'Oh, shut up.'

'So you're not still—'

'No, Howie.'

He holds up his hands. 'Okay. Forgive me for asking.'

'You really think I wouldn't have? By twenty-six?'

'I don't know. You still give off a pretty virginal vibe.'

Something in my gut twists. 'Is that a compliment?'

'Just an observation,' grins Howie, hands behind his head. He gestures for me to throw him the bottle. I sit beside him instead, bringing it with me. 'Was it Faye?' he asks as I settle myself onto the pillow next to him.

'God, you're obsessed.'

'Was it?'

'No.'

'The two of you have never—'

'Me and Faye? No.'

'That's a shame,' he says.

'Is it?'

'So much wasted potential.'

I don't drink much any more. I'm not used to it. Everything's already feeling a little fuzzy. I take another sip. 'I don't think so. I'm not sure she even likes me that much.'

'Come off it,' he laughs. 'We both know that's not true.'

I don't like talking about Faye with Howie. 'How old do you think I was?'

'When you lost it?'

'If you had to guess.'

He considers. 'Seventeen.'

'Twenty-one.'

'No. Really?'

'I cried after.'

'It was that bad?'

'It wasn't bad. I just . . . I don't know. I don't know why I cried. It was just what it was.'

'And that's a bad thing?' he asks.

'I don't know. He was nice. We dated for a bit. I suppose I just thought it would be like, *finally, I'm an adult*. And I didn't feel like that.'

'Huh,' he says.

'The actual thing was underwhelming, as well. Like, sex causes so many problems and heartbreaks and criminal acts, sometimes, and when you get down to it, it's just sex. It really isn't anything at all.' He's laughing again. 'What?'

'Belle,' he says, 'have you ever had good sex?'

'No.' He raises his eyebrows. 'But I think good sex is a myth,' I say. 'Like the Yeti.'

'Like the Yeti?' he says, still laughing.

'Or like horoscopes. It's more fun to believe in horoscopes than not to believe in horoscopes, right?' I'm starting to sweat. That always happens when I get drunk. 'I mean, have you ever had good sex? Actual good sex?'

'Yes,' he says.

'Like, sex that was good beyond "Wow, I'm having sex with someone!" Like, an actual transcendent feeling. Like how art tells you sex is supposed to be.'

'Yes. I've had good sex.'

I roll onto my back. 'Maybe it's different for boys.'

'Maybe you're not having sex with the right people,' he says.

'Maybe.'

There's the weight of his hand on my chest. He places it in the centre, between my breasts, solid on my ribcage. 'Your heart's beating really fast,' he says.

I don't say anything. It slips further down, resting on my stomach now.

'You're so thin,' he says. 'I can feel your hipbones.'

'I've always been thin.'

'Do you eat enough?'

'Yes. I've always been thin.' I have always been thin, but I definitely haven't always eaten enough. You can't say that, though. You have to pretend you don't even think about your body.

'Other girls must hate you.'

Just do it, I think. The ache to be guided by someone else, to be wanted by them, is almost unbearable. My eyes are stinging. I remember why I used to do this, in my late teenage years and my early twenties. I need it again. It might as well be with Howie, who loves me, whatever else his crimes.

'I guess this is why you're kind of a loner. Other girls must just be intimidated by you.'

I nod. His hand slips down, down.

'But you and I have always understood each other,' he says. 'Haven't we?'

I turn my head. His face is very close to mine, large and dark in my vision like a blind spot. When he kisses me, it's dry and cracked, and occasionally painful, the bristles on his chin scratching my lower lip. I kiss him harder. He moves his hand and I make sounds that I think are the right sounds. He rolls me on top of him and I settle how I'm supposed to. He groans.

'Can I take this off?' he asks, tugging at my top. I nod. He pulls it over my head, and then he unclasps my bra and presses my breasts hard with both hands and groans again, eyes closed. I feel like I might throw up.

But I am everything he has ever wanted.

He rolls me onto my back. The lights are still turned all the way up and I can see every detail of his face.

'Is there a dimmer?' I whisper.

'No,' he says. 'I want to see you.'

After a while, after he has taken off all of my clothes and all of his and moved, shuddering, over me, his chest hair tickling my breasts, I turn around and put my face in the pillow. Now I am unseen. Into the cotton, I breathe.

'Oh god,' he moans, from somewhere behind me. 'I'm going to—'

I shift, just in time, which reminds him to pull out. Howie goes to get toilet paper from the bathroom to clean off the sheets as I sit there, the duvet pulled around me. He comes towards me and leans down to stroke my face. I smile at him.

'That was insane,' he says. 'I can't believe we finally did that.'

'I know.'

This is what sex is. It's not earth-shattering orgasms or needing someone pressed against you or inside you more than you've ever needed anything. The rest of the world is kidding themselves. Sex is being enough.

Season Four

When you're fourteen years old and you've just been to a rooftop bar in St Paul's to meet a group of adults who all think you're wonderful, and you're sat in the car with the most beautiful, luminous woman you know and she loves you like you're her own, like you've been sent to her, and the evening is warm and purple and you've drunk a cocktail that tasted like Strawberry Laces and was decorated with flowers, you don't feel like the villain. You don't think that all of that, all of those beautiful things, have added up to make anyone cry. You don't think that anyone hates you; you don't think that your phone is about to ring and bring it all crashing down.

When you're thirty-four and sat in the back of the car pressing the hand of the little girl beside you, ignoring texts and emails, turning your phone on silent, still tasting wine behind your teeth, do you know? Do you guess what you've set in motion?

Mum called me in the car on the way back from the bar. 'Did you go to the theatre?' she asked.

I looked at Donna. She held her hand out for the phone.

'Hi, Sofie,' she began.

'I want to talk to my daughter,' came Mum's voice.

'Is everything okay?'

'Donna, give the phone back to Belle.' Donna grimaced at me, then winked. 'Now,' said Mum.

I took it back, my palms sweaty. 'Mum, Donna set up this meeting—'

'Did you sign anything?'

'Not yet. I need you there for the next one.'

'Belle,' she said. 'Ruby is very hurt.' This was Roni's mum. 'Roni's hurt too. So are the rest of the girls, I imagine.'

I said nothing.

'I'll talk to you when you're home,' she said. The line went dead.

'It'll be okay,' said Donna when the car pulled up outside my flat. 'Just tell her how wonderful you were tonight. Don't tell her that I let you have a drink!'

'I won't, I promise.' I waved goodbye to her from the pavement. There was a feeling in my chest like something was chasing me. If I opened the door, it might jump out and grab me. But if I stood here, it would wind its way through the streets of London like a curse and curl itself tightly around my ankles.

She was in bed, a pile of tissues next to her. She didn't say anything when I first entered the room, gingerly – she only beckoned me towards her. 'How was it?' she asked.

'It was good. They want to sign me. It's the same label that Donna's on—'

'Naturally.'

'—and they think I could be really massive.'

'Do you want to be a singer?'

'Yes.'

'You don't like singing.'

'Yes, but it isn't about the singing, really. So much as the rest of it.' I liked the look of the rest of it. Popstars were shiny and desired. 'It's a great opportunity.'

She blew her nose and sat there for a few seconds with the tissue clutched in her hand. 'Belle,' she said, 'This is difficult for me. I mean, I don't know how much of this is your fault.' I said nothing. 'You're fourteen. I think that's old enough to take some accountability. I think you chose yourself over those girls tonight.'

'That's what this industry is.'

She pointed at me. 'But see, that's not you. Those aren't your words.'

'Donna's just trying to help me.'

She nodded, pulling another tissue out of the box and folding it in half. Then she said, 'I don't think we'll be coming back for Season Four.'

The room spun. 'What?'

'This isn't good for you,' she said. 'This environment, it's not the right kind of way for you to grow up. It's so much harder for me to help you.'

'You mean it's harder for you to control me.'

'Belle,' she said sharply.

'You're so *jealous* of Donna.'

'This isn't about that,' she said. 'This show is poison. These people are poison.'

'This is all I want to do with my life.' I was starting to cry. 'This is the only thing.'

'It won't be forever.'

'You're going to ruin my life.'

'We'll talk about it in the morning,' she said. 'We both need to sleep.'

'I'll emancipate myself. Like Donna did. I'll emancipate myself if you do this.'

'Belle, please. With what lawyers?'

'Donna has lawyers.'

She looked at me, and for a second I thought she was about to scream, or swear, or slap me. Then she started to cry. Her body in her striped pyjamas heaved. She put a hand over her face and cried into it like someone had died.

220

I threw myself at her. I clung to her as she shook. 'I'm sorry, I'm sorry, I'm sorry,' I repeated. She held onto me tightly. We cried together, fingers curled around each other and digging into flesh. Even at fourteen, I knew what I was feeling was a kind of madness. But leaving wasn't an option.

Mum knew that too, really. So we stayed.

She told me the truth about the finale the next day. She'd been smart enough to work it out, smarter than even Donna had been. When she told me I cried again.

'I don't want to be the villain. Kendra's supposed to be the villain.' Kendra knew that, I was pretty sure. She was comfortable in it.

'Well,' said Mum, 'people love a good villain, don't they?'

I knew that when the finale aired, when everyone saw me skipping out on Roni's opening night to start my music career, that would solidify it. It would be me and them. I texted Roni and Faye the same thing.

I'm so sorry. I didn't know Donna had set this up

Neither of them replied. I sent another message to Faye.

Call me please

I called her repeatedly. She didn't pick up. None of them spoke to me over the break. When we returned for Season Four, they greeted me like I was a stranger. They'd been on trips to visit each other, they'd seen shows together, but I hadn't been invited to any of them. They had decided that I wasn't one of them any more.

That was fine, I decided. If I was going to keep doing this, I needed to have a career at the end of it, or it had all been for nothing. My only job now was getting ahead and staying there.

On the first day of filming, Howie looked me up and down and asked, 'What are you now, fifteen?'

'Yep. Last week.'

'Looking pretty good for it.' He grinned.

Faye was watching me from across the room, her hands busy untwisting the straps of Hannah's leotard. I grinned back at Howie. At least someone still wanted something to do with me.

I had signed my record deal just before filming started. Donna gave me a small silver music note to add to my bracelet. It made me so anxious to look at, when she presented it to me, that I almost forgot to thank her. At the end of our first week back, Mum and I went to the studio to hear the debut single they had written for me. Execs met us at the door, shaking both our hands with enthusiasm. One of them was Tony, the man I had met at my first fancy party a couple of years ago.

'I'm so excited we're finally doing this,' he said, pumping my hand up and down.

We sat in a boardroom as someone plugged a memory stick into a laptop and pressed the space bar.

'This is just a demo,' said Tony. 'It'll be Belle's voice, naturally.'

The song was bad. It was radio pop about going on a night out and being the centre of everyone's attention and the only lyrics in the chorus were 'la la la'. I caught Mum's eye. She looked like she was trying not to laugh.

'We've got some other options,' said Tony. He played us two more songs of impressively similar ilk – I could have sworn the third one was the first one again, only slightly faster.

'Thoughts?' he asked.

'Belle's too young to do some of that stuff,' said Mum. 'Going out to clubs and drinking.'

'Think of it like she's playing a character,' said Tony. Nods from everyone else around the table. 'If we have her doing happy,

Disney-label stuff then she'll be looked at as a child pop star. We want her to be a legitimate pop star. We don't even want people thinking about her age.'

'Well, I have to think about her age. I'm her mother.'

'I appreciate that,' said Tony. 'Belle? Do you like the songs?'

'They're great,' I said. 'Really catchy.'

When we walked out of the door and turned the corner, I stopped and put my hand on the wall. I doubled over.

'Belle?' asked Mum, stopping beside me.

'I can't sing that.' I was welling up. My chest was tight. 'I can't sing about being the centre of attention. I can't sing about being the greatest.'

'It's fine,' she said. 'You don't have to. *Breathe*, Belle.'

'Everyone hates me enough already.'

'No they don't.'

'They do! This will make it worse. I—' I was breathing rapidly now. Mum held me tightly to her, rubbing my back as I breathed in and out.

'Wait there,' she said, when my breathing had slowed.

I watched her round the corner, out of sight. The drowning feeling was not quite gone and I didn't really compute what was going on, until Mum reappeared. She was out of breath. She seized my hand, tugging me along after her with such determination that I nearly tripped.

'Where did you go?' I panted.

'I sorted it.'

'What does that mean?'

'It means they're going to bring you in for a song-writing session and you are going to be involved in the process of writing something more suitable.'

I stopped. Her hand tugged insistently on my wrist. 'Did you tell them I didn't like the song?'

'I told them it wasn't suitable.'

'You can't do that.' I was beginning to work myself up again. 'That's unprofessional.'

'Belle, it's *fine*. I've fixed it. You don't have to stress.'

'You don't understand!' I shook her off. My fists were balled. 'No one will want to work with me if I'm difficult!'

'Listen to me.' She put her hands on my shoulders. 'You need to accept something right now. If we stay, if we keep doing this, then this doesn't mean I'm completely handing over the reins to you or to Donna. Sometimes I am going to step in, and I am going to do something to protect you. And you might not always like it, or you might not always agree with it, but you are going to let me do it because you are fifteen. Okay?'

I walked next to her in silence.

'Are you angry?' she asked.

I said nothing. I was angry, but it wasn't as simple as that. What I would never tell her, because I couldn't articulate it, is how strangely glad I was, sometimes, when she took these decisions away from me and into her own hands.

I hated song-writing sessions, but Mum was right – they were far better than the alternative. There was a lot of compromise involved, and sometimes I would play my demos for Mum at home and we would laugh until it hurt, but thankfully most of the songs the label were excited about didn't make me want to cry at the thought of singing them.

'This is so exciting!' said Donna when I brought three to play for her. 'Who knew you could write as well?'

I couldn't really. The team in the studio would ask me, 'Do you want to write a break-up song, Belle?' and I would mumble, 'Sure, that would be cool.' They would fire ideas past me and get me to sing random lines and occasionally ask for my opinion until it was time for me to go home. Every other part of what Donna and I did together made me feel talented and special. Music just made me feel thick.

Shortly after we returned, I booked a West End play called *Saturn's Return* alongside a well-known TV actress. Donna was elated.

'You *have* to do it.'

'Won't it be too much time off camera?' Between the play and the music stuff I was skipping more classes than ever. I hardly saw the other girls.

'I'm working something out,' she said.

She'd had a word with Tony. The cameras would now be coming to film me as I worked on my music, which was a horrifying prospect that saw me crying myself to sleep for three nights straight, quietly, so that Mum wouldn't hear and tell Donna I didn't want to do it. We stretched in the dance studio as Donna stood off to the side and explained the plan to Rupert and Fred.

'I'm not happy about this,' I heard Fred say.

'She's got to do both. It's the right thing for her.'

'Right, but you understand that our priority is the show. It's not the right thing for the show.'

'Don't worry about that,' she said.

'Don-na,' came Rupert's voice, liltingly exasperated.

'Don't worry about it,' she repeated. 'I've got it under control.'

I could tell that Kendra and Faye were both listening. I could see it in the stillness of their shoulders.

'Have you got something?' asked Rupert. His voice was quieter now. In the mirror, I saw Donna shrug slightly.

'Is it good?' asked Fred.

'I'll put it in an email later.'

'It's compelling, you think?'

'It's a slam dunk,' she said. 'Trust me.'

They had to listen to Donna, really. Without her, there was no show.

I loved *Saturn's Return*. The cast were all adults, and I was much more comfortable in a room full of adults than I was around people my own age. The rehearsals weren't as rigid and disciplined as musical theatre, meaning that there was plenty of time to explore, to develop our characters, stuff that made me feel like what I was doing was actually, legitimately art.

'This is what I want to do forever,' I would tell Mum after every rehearsal.

On set, the other girls were working on auditions for *Charlie and the Chocolate Factory*. The material that they were rehearsing felt silly and juvenile compared to what I was doing, although no one could deny that Kendra made a fantastic Veruca Salt. I wasn't on set regularly enough for me to commit to this storyline and so, instead, I became Donna's unofficial teaching assistant. I leant into the role. There was no reason not to. Everyone hated me anyway.

'I'm concerned,' Donna told them all one morning. 'None of you seem to be progressing. I look around this room and I feel as if Belle is the only one who still actually wants this.' I smiled. 'If no one books this job,' she said, 'then things will start to get a lot stricter around here.'

They barely looked at me any more. Even Faye still wasn't talking to me. When I walked into the dressing room to change, conversation would cease, or they would whisper to each other, which was worse. My schedule made it easier not to care. I hardly had time to miss them. I bounced between *Saturn's Return* rehearsals and filming and music at a dizzying pace. Sometimes I would get headaches that would last for over twenty-four hours, making it nearly impossible for me to sleep.

Donna gave me a collection of oils that I could diffuse at night or dab on my wrists. She gave me crystals to carry in my pockets to help with anxiety and stress toys to fiddle with. After a difficult day or a draining rehearsal, she taught me to sage the space I was in – my room, or a practice studio, or wherever it was – to get rid of negative energy. We would burn the sticks together and wave them in opposite corners, and then she would sit cross-legged on the floor with me and hold my hands whilst I breathed in and out.

'That's all bullshit,' said Howie when he found me.

Panic had become an unavoidable part of my life. It found me on set, in rehearsals, in the studio, in my bed. Sometimes it hit me out of nowhere, like a train; other times it stalked me slowly throughout the day, gathering over me as I was getting ready for bed and causing me to curl up on my carpet and sob. I didn't always know what I was crying about. Most of the time I wouldn't have been able to put words to it. It was just a thing that I did now, a feeling that I carried with me. It was one more ball to juggle.

Howie discovered me in the music room one day. Practising had devolved into crying on the piano stool, taking gasping, shuddering breaths.

'Hey, hey,' he said, sliding onto the stool next to me and hugging me to him. 'What's up?'

I couldn't get any words out. He sat with me for a while, until my breathing started to slow.

'Panic attack?' he asked.

'I don't know. Maybe.' I wasn't really sure what constituted a panic attack. In films, rooms swam and voices got echoey, and then everything went black. That wasn't how it was for me. It was just a feeling that came over me like I was being hunted.

'I've been there,' he said. 'Sucks. You want to smoke something?'

'I don't smoke.'

'I've got weed. It'll help, trust me. You've heard of CBD for anxiety?' I shook my head. 'It's good,' he said. 'Calms your mind down.'

'Okay.' I was willing to try anything.

The two of us hadn't hung out like this since the night Faye and I had kissed. I couldn't remember now why I had been so scared of him. He was just Howie. Skinny arms in black t-shirts, dark stubble on a pale chin. The wiry kind of muscle I liked and a smile that surfaced when I spoke back to him. Howie was familiar to me. And although he always wanted me around, he never wanted me to do anything but be there beside him, breathing the same air.

He opened the window and lit the joint, and we passed it between us. I coughed and he laughed. It made me lightheaded, but it also made me feel cool, and that was as good a remedy as any.

'I think I'm overworked,' I said.

'Are you going to slow down?'

'Fuck no. Can't.'

'Then burn through it, baby,' said Howie, and between us we smoked the entire thing. Mum was out on a date with her boyfriend, so I went home and ate half a lasagne on the sofa and watched *Pretty Woman*. I felt relaxed for the first time in weeks.

I knew that the *Charlie* audition was fake as soon as I was told by Rupert to come with and watch. We borrowed an off-West End theatre auditorium and the girls took it in turns to stand on stage and dance and sing. None of their hearts were in it. Hannah forgot her words halfway through her song and just waited through the rest of her second verse, bouncing a little on her heels with her hands clasped behind her until she found her way back to the chorus.

'Great job,' a casting director type told them afterwards. 'We'll let you know.'

'Thank you,' said Kendra. It was poisonous. She left with her dance bag unzipped, a crisp packet falling onto the carpet behind her as she pushed with both hands on the door. In the corridor, she nudged Faye and muttered, 'They won't let us know shit.' I trailed behind them.

The next day, before Donna entered the room, we were arranged in a line.

'None of you booked *Charlie,*' were her opening words to us. They were heavy. They fell accordingly. Beside me, Roni sighed.

Donna had five folders in her hands. Resumes. She flicked through them, tilted down, so we could see which girl's she was looking at. Her eyes ran down them, with an air of weariness.

'I think we'll need to stop auditioning for a while and go back to training, just to catch you all up to where you should be.'

'Are you serious?' exploded Kendra.

'What's wrong, Kendra?'

'That was a fake audition!' spat Kendra.

'The attitude in this room is appalling,' said Donna. She opened the next folder. My headshot beamed out from the page. I watched the edges of her mouth curl upwards as she read. She looked almost relieved. 'I can feel the bad energy,' she said. She waved her hand towards the other girls, without looking at them. 'We need to work on that.'

'This is insane,' said Kendra.

'So much jealousy directed towards the one student who is succeeding and excuses for every failure. It's all incredibly unprofessional.'

'Fake auditions are unprofessional.'

Donna's eye hit her. 'These conspiracy theories are another level, Kendra. Even for you. Go and get changed for dance.'

To my horror, Kendra looked like she was going to cry. Donna nodded at me, and I moved towards the doors, the other girls following. Just as we were disappearing into the corridor, I felt Kendra's hands on my back. She gave me a small shove.

'Stop,' boomed Donna.

We all froze.

'Come back here.'

Obediently, skittishly, we trotted back over to our line. There was a commotion on the other side of the room – Fred and Rupert attempting to prevent our mothers from entering. 'They're just about to go get changed,' came Rupert's voice. 'Class is about to start.'

'Kendra, what did you just do?'

Kendra blinked. 'I don't know.'

'I think you do.'

'I was telling Belle to hurry up—'

'How,' came Donna's booming voice, 'can you *ever* hope to have a career in the entertainment industry if a setback encourages you to physically assault your peers?'

'Okay, woah.' Laura, Kendra's mother, had pushed past Fred and was striding over to us. Laura never got involved. 'It was a small push,' she said. 'It was stupid. Kendra, apologise to Belle.'

'Sorry, Belle,' mumbled Kendra.

'Good. So let's put that behind us.'

'You don't tell me what to do!' yelled Donna.

Laura took a step back. It was almost a stumble.

'You have raised a brat! You are making her unemployable!'

'Donna—' said Mum, her hands raised.

'Stay out of this, Sofie.'

Kendra shook her head slightly, as if telling herself off. Down by her side, her fingernail dug into her thigh, picking at the skin.

Donna and Mum stared at each other.

'Girls,' said Donna, eventually, 'go and get changed.'

We made a break for the doors. Kendra sprung forward from her spot, but as she got close to me, she slowed, pulling back. They all moved around me like repelling magnets. When we got into the dressing room, Faye pulled Kendra in for a hug and she cried then, loudly and violently like I'd never imagined Kendra would cry. Roni and Hannah moved towards her, the four of them a dense knot, reaching for each other.

I stood in the doorway, my arms heavy.

Then Faye looked over. She held out her hand to me. 'Belle. Come here.'

I ran to them. I knew that they still hated me, but for a minute it didn't matter. The five of us clung to each other. We didn't know what else to do.

I wasn't getting much better at smoking. It made me feel sick and so I hadn't had much more than a few puffs after the first joint Howie had given me. But it did make me feel better to stand by the window with him and smell it and tell him everything I had to do that week and listen to him marvel at how I kept up with it all.

Sometimes we would talk about sex. It was usually me that brought it up because I liked hearing how he explained things as if they were all obvious and boring. 'You still haven't?' he would ask. I would shake my head and he would laugh at me. Once, when I was really out of my head, I told him that I wasn't even sure if I would know what to do.

'I can show you some stuff if you like,' he said. Then, at my face – 'Oh my god, Belle, not like that. Don't be disgusting. You're like my little sister.' He took a sip. 'My hot little sister. But still gross.'

'What did you mean then?'

'You know. Porn.'

I went home and discovered porn for myself. I didn't like it very much, but it was hard to stop watching it. I was captivated by the idea that what these people were doing was both a performance and the real thing. I wondered how they had sex in private, and whether they were like this, or completely unrecognisable, or whether they even did it at all.

I waited for him in the music room that evening, after Donna and Kendra's fight. After a while, my phone lit up.

Sorry, heading home. Tomorrow?

I sat on the floor with my head against the wall, my eyes closed, and breathed in and out.

'Belle?'

I started. Faye stood in the doorway in her leotard, hovering.

'Hey,' I scrambled to my feet.

'I was going to practise,' she said. 'Are you . . . Is everything okay?'

I shrugged. She took an uncertain step forward, and then another, and then she walked over and set her music on the piano.

'That was awful today,' she said, 'wasn't it?'

'Yeah, a bit.'

'She's so scary now,' said Faye.

'She isn't most of the time.'

'Not to you maybe.' She sat down at the piano. 'Do you mind if I practise?'

'If you don't mind me sitting here.'

'I don't mind,' she said.

I sat back down against the wall and listened to her. She was getting very good. Donna didn't think it was worth as much time as Faye was putting into it – 'It's not a very employable skill,' she said. 'I mean, what would you rather be? An actress, or a piano teacher?'

'Piano teacher,' Faye said to me later, with a laugh. I wasn't sure if it was a joke.

She lifted her head as she finished, looking for applause. I obliged her. 'Beautiful.'

'Isn't it?'

'Did you write it?'

'Of course not,' she said. 'I can't write things.'

'Have you tried?'

'Yes, lots. When I'm not sober, I think I can do it. But it's always shit.' She came to sit beside me. 'I'm sorry I've been ignoring you,' she said.

'It's okay.'

'Kendra made us all make a pact that we were done with you.'

'I figured.' She nodded. 'I kind of deserved it,' I said.

'No,' she said, 'this stuff is hard. If Donna loved me, I wouldn't ever want to upset her.'

'She does love you.'

'Okay,' said Faye.

She had a scab on her knee. She picked at it as we sat there in our matching leotards, sun slanting in from the window. She shivered.

'It's cold in here.'

'Oh,' I said, realising. 'The window.' I jumped up to close it.

'Why do you have that open? It's winter.'

'Oh, you know.'

When I looked back, her eyebrows were raised. 'I don't,' she said.

'Fresh air.'

'Mm.'

I laughed at her. 'You sound like my mum.'

'Are you smoking?'

'Or like my disapproving aunt.'

233

'Belle?'

'It's just weed,' I said.

'Where did you get it?'

'Howie.'

She rolled her eyes at me. 'I thought you guys might have been hanging out again. I think you're an idiot.'

'It helps.'

'Do you not remember what he's like?'

'He's just Howie.'

'He made us hide in the toilets.'

She was hugging her knees to her chest, the scab very red against the white and black of her. I watched her gnawing on her lip, not looking at me.

'Did it really freak you out?' I asked.

'It did when he was banging on the door.'

'I meant when he tried to make us kiss.'

'I didn't mind that so much,' she said. Someone else might have made it sound like a joke. Never Faye. 'Well,' she said, 'I did a little. I minded it like that. I didn't want us to kiss for him. Like he was watching a show.'

'Oh.'

'I guess . . .' she said and stopped. 'Do you like me?'

'You know I like you.'

'I know. But . . .' She swallowed. 'I've really missed talking to you.'

I had too, I realised. It had been hard to notice it, with my schedule, with Donna, with being stoned. If I'd had Faye, maybe it all would have felt easier. Maybe I wouldn't have needed to start hanging out with Howie again.

'I'm sorry,' I said.

'It isn't your fault.'

She still wasn't looking at me. One fingernail gently pried up the scab on her knee. I watched her reveal the smallest bead of blood.

'I did want to kiss you,' she said.

'Yeah?'

'Yeah. Just, I want to kiss you when no one's looking.'

I stared at the carpet, trying to formulate a response to this. It was a whole new kind of feeling. Terrifying, but not in the panicked too-much-at-once way I was used to. Terrified like anything could happen, and like that anything might be good.

'No one's looking,' I said.

She lifted my chin towards her like a question. And then she kissed me, delicately, wonderingly, like she was trying to figure out how to do it right.

Reunion special

It's not a rare thing, is it, to lie awake in the dark and take comfort in the steady breath of another person? And yet I've never felt it. I sometimes feel I'm not built to be known intimately. I don't think I would hold up upon close inspection. I want to know other people in great detail, to be able to predict every thought and choice and action. I don't want them to know me at all.

I lie listening to Howie's breathing. He falls asleep clutching the pillow, his face in it. I'm grateful that he hasn't reached for me, and it also makes me sad.

When I'm certain he's asleep, I slip out of the bed and stand naked for a few seconds by the edge of the bed like some unfriendly spirit. I wish I'd told him to put a condom on. Pharmacies are the worst places to get recognised in. Also, Howie has never been straightforward about his sexual history. Who knows who he's been with.

I gather my things. I move slowly and heavily, but not quietly. He's a heavy sleeper. Some things you just know about people without ever having to learn them. I still carry my shoes in my hand as I creep out the door though, because I think it's the done thing.

I call an Uber. I had a friend in my early twenties, Daisy. She was one of those girls who took pride in being the 'mum friend', even when all that meant was vaping when everyone else was doing ketamine. She taught me to leave a hair in every Uber I took at night, just in case something went wrong with the tracking. Jane saw me doing it once when she was too young to understand the implications. I told her it was for good luck. Now it sort of is. I drop the hair and make a wish to start over.

I don't know what to feel.

I didn't do ketamine beyond a couple of times. I rarely did coke – it made me feel far too alive. All I ever really did was drink and smoke with those girls. But I was never the mum friend. I never will be. No one will ever meet me and think, *here's a person I can depend on to get me home in one piece.*

Cameron is still awake when I get home. He's cleaning the kitchen, which he only does late at night if he's looking for an excuse to stay up and wait for me to get home. In the couple of years I spent going on nights out with Daisy and the others, he organised every cupboard in the house and I yelled at him for throwing out the napkin holders Mum had never got around to using.

'Hey,' he says, when I walk in.

'It smells like lemon in here.'

He points the surface cleaner at me. 'Want a sample?'

'Don't you dare.'

'Where were you?' he asks, moving the cloth over the already clean sideboard.

'Just out. With a friend.' The implication is clear and he drops the topic, but I can tell he's surprised. I don't discuss my sex life with Cameron, but I imagine the state of it over the last few years has been fairly obvious.

'How was filming?' he asks. I tilt my thumb upside down and blow a raspberry. 'That good?'

'Always is. Just have to soldier through.'

He says nothing, still moving the cloth over the sideboard.

'Faye called,' he says suddenly.

I blink. 'For me?'

'For Jane. She called to say well done on getting through the audition. I think she told her some of her own horror stories.' He looks up at the sound I make. 'Are you crying?'

'No,' I say, unconvincingly.

He walks over and puts his arms around me. 'Anything I should be worried about?'

'It's all just a lot.'

'Yeah,' he says, still hugging me.

I wonder how much of it he's guessed.

In the morning, I wake up and I see that Howie hasn't messaged. Then I block his number, before he gets a chance.

Rupert calls. 'Good news,' he says. Always a dangerous thing to hear from Rupert. 'You've got a day off.'

'Why?'

'Less of the suspicious tone.'

'You've spent all week telling me how badly I'm needed on set.'

'Well, today you're not.'

'Don't I need to do the rest of my interview to camera?'

'We'll review the footage and let you know,' he says.

'Right.' I suppose they already got what they wanted. I wait for him to tell me what it is that they don't want me for, but all he says is: 'You've been begging for time away from us all. Enjoy it.' The line goes dead.

I'm staring at my phone when Jane wanders into the room. 'I'm ready.'

'You'll need your hair up,' I say. 'Like for dance.'

'I'll be dancing?'

'Well, you might be. Come here, let me do it.'

This is what the money is for. The money is to make Jane happy. Right now, the thing that's going to make her happiest is enrolment in a weekend youth performing arts programme in Marylebone.

'You're sure?' asked Cameron when I told him my plan. 'You don't want to wait for her to grow a slightly thicker skin?'

'She can do it until she enjoys it, and if she doesn't enjoy it any more then we'll pull her out.' I hope it'll be that simple. I know it isn't always. But kids have to be able to try things that the grown-ups around them failed at. Otherwise, none of us will ever grow up.

We take the tube and I walk her to the door. Then, once she's run inside, I trace the route that Faye and I walked around Soho. It still stings that Rupert was the one who inspired that walk.

Faye meets me on her lunch. She's tied her hair back today and her clothes are neat and tailored, in neutral colours. She's not as colourful as she used to be. She used to wear mismatching gloves and crochet her own hats. I wonder who in her life – or outside of it – told her that she was trying too hard. I would never have told her that if we'd stayed by each other's sides. I would have applauded every time she put down her needles and held up a finished hat.

We sit in a fast-food restaurant from which The Savoy is visible. Jane is right – I never act as if I have money. Apparently, Faye doesn't either. Maybe she actually doesn't have any money, any more.

'Are you talking about Season Five?' I ask.

'Did Rupe tell you?'

'What else would it be?'

'True,' she says, picking at her fries. I'm not sure to ask how it's going, or if that's even the right question. 'It feels wrong,' she says.

'What does?'

'Just discussing it like this. It feels like the kind of thing we shouldn't be talking about. In some ways I think it would be better if you were on set for it, but then it would also be awful. There's no good way to do it, really.' It's not often that Faye's not sure what to say. She shrugs it off. 'I think it'll play well, though.'

'Yeah?'

'Yeah. There's quite a sensitive tone being struck so far. It's all just a lot of sympathy for you, obviously, especially since Kendra's not there.'

'What?'

'Kendra's off too,' says Faye. She frowns. 'I thought you'd be pleased.'

'Where is she?'

'I don't know. Family thing.'

'They let her off for a family thing?'

'Well, they can't physically force any of us to be on set, Belle. You've proven that.'

I sit back. 'Did they tell her not to come in?'

'I don't think so. I don't know why they would.' She's still frowning at me. 'What is it?'

'It's off.' I can't think of a single reason why Fred and Rupert would deliberately keep Kendra out of that scene. But Kendra ditching set for a vague family thing isn't real. It would never happen. I can feel it in my stomach.

Under the table, Faye places a tentative hand on my knee. 'I'm sorry. I shouldn't have brought it up. I just thought you'd rather know.'

'I would.'

She looks her phone. 'Shit, I've got to get back. I'll see you tomorrow.'

'When are you done?'

'I don't know. Five, maybe.'

'Will you have time after?'

'Are you going to wait?'

'I'll be in the area,' I say. 'I've got some stuff to do.'

I buy a book by Kafka and read the whole thing in a café. I wasn't a reader in my teenage years – I didn't really have time to be – but now I'll read anything. Reading feels like achieving something. It's the opposite of wasting time.

It's a short book, and when I finish it, I sit in the café window and watch the street. I see her coming quite a while before she spots me, and I get to watch how she is when she feels unobserved. It's something I've only had the chance to see a few times in my life. She walks like there are stories happening in her head.

When she sees me, she takes a hand out of her pocket to wave and then pushes it back in with a small shiver. It makes me think of when we were fourteen and I watched her tying her shoes wrong and giving a little huff, just to herself, and retying them faster like she had something to prove. It took me years to articulate the feeling that moment inspired in me, why it stuck with me long after we left the dressing room. It was the first time I had watched someone do something completely innocuous and boring and been in love with the action.

The bell jingles as she opens the door. 'This place is cute,' she says.

'I've drunk four of their coffees. I think I might be high.'

She laughs. 'Come on. Let's get you some fresh air.'

She's wearing a coat now and this feels more Faye, blue and plaid with a rainbow badge on the collar. When she loosens her hair she looks instantly younger. I think she regrets doing it, because now the wind has picked up and she keeps having to push it away from her mouth, but when I will her silently to leave it down, she does.

It's easier to talk to her when we're on the move. I stare ahead of me and say, 'Something happened to me last night.'

'Okay?'

'I wanted to talk about it with someone and you're kind of the only person I can talk about it with.'

'Is this about Howie?' asks Faye, her hands deep in her pockets so that her elbows lock. I must look surprised. She bumps her hip into mine. 'He's been trying to get close to you again, right?'

'How did you know?'

'He messaged me a few times. Asking me about you.'

'Fuck,' I say. 'I'm sorry.'

'Why? Not your fault.'

'I had sex with him.'

I wait for her reaction.

'Oh, Belle,' she says. It's in the same tone that you use when a dog chews off the back of your shoe.

'You don't seem surprised.'

'Well,' she said, 'I guess I thought it might happen. He always wanted to.'

'Yeah.'

'You didn't used to believe me, when I told you.'

'I know.'

'I guess it seemed like you always wanted to as well.'

'I was a kid,' I said.

'You were a teenager. You could have wanted to.' She corrects herself. 'I mean, don't get me wrong, I think he's awful. Truly. He makes my skin crawl. But teenage girls get crushes. I didn't judge you for wanting to.' I give her a look. 'Alright, I don't now.'

'Yes you do.'

'I don't understand it,' she says. 'At all. I won't pretend to. But I don't judge you.'

'I judge me,' I say.

She's quiet for a minute. '*Fuck,* Belle,' she says.

'What?'

'You really had sex with him? Really?'

'Sounds like judging to me.'

'I'm just worried,' she says, 'that's all.'

'If it helps, it was shit.'

'Why did you do it?'

'I thought it might make me feel better. I don't know why I thought that.'

She takes my hand. The light is beginning to fade. We walk past yellow shop windows and long lines of headlights. It rained earlier when I was sat in the café. The pavements are glossy with it. If I listen carefully, underneath the cars and the people and the music and the laughter, I can hear the damp step of Faye's shoes.

'Did your mum ever find out about all that stuff with Howie?' she asks.

'No,' I said. 'I never told her.' It's one of those things I wish I could talk through with her now. There's so many things like that. I sort of assumed that every story I never told her would eventually get back to her one day, when the time was right. Now they just sit heavy in me. 'Did you tell Alex?'

She nods. 'After you went to LA. She made me go to therapy.'

'Just because of Howie?' Are there parts I've forgotten?

'Not just because of him,' says Faye. 'But he used to really scare me. Even after he left.'

'Mum never liked him,' I say.

'Well,' says Faye, 'to be fair, I think your mum hated everyone on that set.' I can tell what's coming by the way she pauses. 'Can I ask? How did she . . .'

'Donna stabbed her.'

'What?!'

'I'm joking. Cancer.'

'You're a dick.'

'Like Mum would have lost that knife fight.'

She laughs, swinging our hands. 'True.'

I look down at our clasped hands. Both our fingers are cold and stiff, but she isn't letting go.

'Do you do this with everyone?' I ask.

'Do what?'

'Hold their hand.'

'Not everyone,' she says. 'People I love.'

'Do you love a lot of people?'

'Oh, lots and lots. Too many to count.'

She rubs her thumb along the side of my index finger. I want her to tell me that I'm special.

'You know,' she says, 'it's funny. In some ways I can't wait for this to all be over. But it's also sort of nice. There were good parts. I think I'd been forgetting that.'

'What were the good parts?'

'Well,' she says, using her other hand to reach diagonally across her face and push her hair behind her ear, 'we did learn a lot. And it was all so exciting when we were kids, getting those parts in plays and on TV shows. The first time I saw myself in that film I thought I was going to burst. I thought I was wonderful in it.'

'You were okay.'

'Please. Just because I was cast over you.'

'Donna told me they really wanted me. That probably wasn't true,' I realise suddenly. 'Oh, shit, I bet she was lying.'

Faye laughs. 'I bet she told you that every time you lost a part.'

'Not every time.' A worrying amount, though, looking back. 'She really did just invent her own truths, didn't she?'

'It's a wonder I grew up so well-adjusted.' I'm pleased when she laughs, but it also hurts my feelings. 'Go on,' I say. 'What else was good?'

'Oh,' she says, 'pizza on Fridays, until we all started dieting. All those games we used to play. Drinking with Howie—' I look at her incredulously. 'Awful, in hindsight,' she says, 'but I'd be lying if I said it didn't make me feel incredibly cool at the time.'

'What else?'

'Going to awards shows and seeing famous people. When Donna was in a good mood with us and we would go on daytrips. The money. And all the free things.'

'What else?'

'You know what else,' she says.

We've found our way to Marble Arch. Faye leads us over the road to the corner of Hyde Park. The evening is pale and smoky.

'I think about it a lot,' she says.

We've stopped just where the pavement turns into path. I watch her walk over the grass to rest her back against a tree, her hands pressed behind her, into the wood. She looks a little afraid of me. I stay where I am.

'Have you been in love?' she asks.

The question is so sudden that it frightens me. My mind goes blank. 'What?'

'I've been wanting to ask you. Have you, since we last saw each other?'

'Since this morning? Not that I can remember.'

'Oh, stop. Answer the question.'

'I dated a couple of guys,' I say. 'I had a boyfriend for a while when I was nineteen – I had this group of friends who were all in uni together and they introduced us at a house party. It lasted about six months.'

'Why did you break up?'

'We didn't really have anything in common. Also, at least three of my friends were sleeping with him.'

'Ah,' said Faye. 'That'll do it.'

'I cried, at the time.'

'Did you love him? Or any of the guys you dated?'

'No.'

'I was with a girl,' she says, 'for a while.'

'Really?' Whoever it was, I hate her.

'It was a couple of years ago now. I loved her, I think. We said it to each other. I don't any more.'

'What happened?'

She shrugs. 'I'm not sure I'm easy to love.'

'I think you are,' I say.

She doesn't reply, staring down at her feet, but through the gloom I see her smile.

'I think about how you left a lot too,' she says.

'Yeah, so do I.'

'I feel so guilty,' she says.

That's not what I'm expecting to hear. 'Why?'

'Well, I never reached out.'

'I didn't either.'

'Yes,' she said, 'but you were with *her*.' She looks up at me. 'I wish I hadn't blamed you. I guess that's what it is.'

I don't say anything. She's still staring at me through the dark, silvery hair pushed back behind her ears. She rests her head on the tree trunk and I watch her hair weave itself into the cracks in the bark.

'Why aren't we together?' she asks.

I still don't say anything.

'We wasted so much time. I wasted so much time being mad at you. I look back now and I don't understand it.'

I want to say something. I feel like I'm going to throw up. I don't know if it's a good or bad feeling. I'm shivering. She watches me for a second, and then she holds a hand out to me. The walk over the grass is in slow-motion. She shimmers in and out of existence, in the shadow of the tree.

Kissing her is stepping back onto the path and asking myself why I'd spent so long wandering, when the way ahead was always so clear.

Cameron is cleaning cutlery when I get home. He looks up when I enter and sees me, and smiles. It's a relieved smile. 'Better night?' he asks me.

'Why do you say that?'

'You look happy.'

'I am,' I say.

'Who's brought this on?'

'You know,' I say. He sets down the fork he's cleaning.

'I owe your mother ten quid,' he says.

I wait for her outside the Soho studio the next day with two coffees. I feel goofy, ungainly, larger than myself. I hope she likes the way I look today. My phone is still off, so I don't know if she messaged or called. It doesn't matter. Faye no longer assumes the worst of me.

But when I see her step out of her car and hurry down the pavement towards me, she looks frantic. She waves a hand as I make a motion for the door. I freeze.

An assistant appears. 'Belle!' she says. With a gentle but authoritative hand on my arm, she turns me away from Faye and towards the door. 'We're ready for you in here.'

'Belle,' calls Faye. I turn my head, but the door is already closing behind me and the assistant. I hear her start to run as I'm guided down the corridor.

'I know where it is,' I say. The other girls are already there. Roni and Hannah look nonplussed. Kendra's been briefed. I can see it in her self-satisfied smile. She's practically a producer at this point.

Faye bursts in. 'Are the cameras on?'

They're rolling, I realise. She clocks it quickly too and clams up, her mouth a flat line. Rupert hurries towards us but Faye has already grabbed me by the elbow and pulled me into the corner of the room. I stare down at her phone screen as she scrolls through messages and missed calls from a number she doesn't have saved.

Faye, I've been trying to get in touch with Belle. Are you with her?

Tell her to turn her phone on please.

This is urgent I promise. It's not about me and her.

At least tell her not to go to set this morning.

Faye, please get her to pick up. This is about Donna.

I stare at the last message, and then up at Faye. We lock eyes for just a minute before Fred grabs us each by the shoulder and pulls us apart. It's the first time he or Rupert have ever laid a hand on either of us. The force of it stuns me for a second.

'For fuck's sakes,' he growls. Then he steps back so that the cameras can move in. The other girls aren't watching us. Their attention is on the other entrance to the room, at which Rupert is making hurrying motions from a distance.

There it comes. The click of heels.

She's in a long mink coat. Her hair is bigger than ever, impossibly brassy, skin around her eyes and on her forehead impossibly taut. Her waist is still tiny. Her arms are still slender. She walks into the room with her arms spread, like she's preparing to hug us as a collective.

'I heard you all were having a reunion!' she calls.

We're paralysed. Only Kendra is smiling.

'God, what a gruelling flight that was. I only touched down about two hours ago. But I wasn't going to miss a party with my girls. I never would.'

She stops a few feet away from us, eyes dangerously bright.

'Who's ready to hear my side of the story?' she asks.

Season Four

Faye and I enjoyed the subterfuge. We left notes in each other's dance bags and stole moments in empty dressing rooms. When we stayed late to practise, we did it on days that we knew Howie wouldn't be around, when the studio would be entirely empty. I would go home glowing. We were tentative with each other, nervy, mostly spending our time just talking against the wall with our knees tucked up to our chests. We never went much further than kissing, although the first time we tested that boundary even a little I went home in such a golden daze that Mum demanded to know what I'd taken.

Life was still overwhelming, but it had pockets of sunshine that hadn't been there before. When I cried, when my chest felt heavy, I would call Faye and she would answer. Sometimes I would lie on the floor of the music room with my head in her lap and she would stroke my hair. We never spoke about what we had, never put a name to it. It felt a little like if we acknowledged this fledgling thing too boldly then we might lose it, so we just let it be.

'You've been happy lately,' said Donna, one night at her house. We were watching *The Sound of Music* and I'd been singing along in a range of different voices, which had her laughing her musical laugh. That laugh didn't thrill me as much as it once had. I had loved Donna intensely and adoringly, like one loved a deity. It felt as if that love had been diluted.

'Everything's going well,' I said.

She squeezed my knee. 'I'm glad you're feeling more capable of managing it. I know you've been struggling.'

I bit the skin around my thumb. She lowered my hand gently. 'I didn't say that I was struggling,' I said.

'You didn't have to,' she said. 'I noticed. But I've also noticed that you're doing better. I think it's wonderful that you've managed to pull yourself out of your funk like that. It's a quality you need in this industry.'

She was right, in a way. I was happier. But I wasn't necessarily doing better, I thought. I just had a little extra help.

Aside from Faye, I was hated. Donna had put a complete freeze on auditions for the other girls. Kendra, who had been on the cusp of a burgeoning TV career, was arguing with Donna almost daily. It had got to the point recently where Donna had lost her temper and thrown a Biro at Kendra, right at her face. She ducked, and it smacked hard into the wall where her head had been.

Kendra's head turned towards Laura, her mum. Laura rolled her eyes, but she didn't get out of her chair.

'She's going insane,' said Faye when she passed me in the corridor.

I looked back through the door of the studio. Donna was stood in a small huddle with Fred and Rupert, talking earnestly. When Fred said something, she nodded and then took her phone from her pocket and scrolled through her calendar, pointing things out to them. She looked sane enough to me.

Mum was spending the weekend in Cornwall with her boyfriend and I was at Donna's. Mum and Donna hardly interacted any more.

On set, they gave each other a wide berth. 'You can stay home alone now, if you want,' said Mum. 'You're old enough.' I told her I would rather be with Donna. I didn't want Donna's feelings to be hurt if she found out I'd chosen to stay away and, besides, I liked it at Donna's. In that house, as soon as I set foot through the door, everything revolved around me.

Saturn's Return had opened a few weeks prior. It was going to be a limited run, just three months. My name was very big on the posters, my photo blown up outside the theatre. People had gathered to see me at the stage door when I was in *Alice*, but now they bought personalised gifts and wrote cards to me as if we were old friends.

'You don't have to talk to them,' Donna said. She knew that generally I didn't like being approached in the street because it caught me off guard, which made me seem rude. Stories would surface about me on social media – *Belle Simon was SO MEAN when I recognised her! She didn't want to talk to me AT ALL.* When Donna introduced me to people at parties or mixers, with two hands on my shoulders and a reverent '*This* is my Belle,' I felt myself summoning energy I didn't have, beaming, talking in a voice higher than my own. Sometimes she would leave me for a while with whoever it was, a casting agent or a studio exec. I was always afraid that I would betray myself by some moment of flatness or weariness, that they would know I wasn't thrilled to be there and that, actually, I didn't like being the only teenager in a room full of adults, trying so hard to impress that I felt myself to be insufferable.

'She's a great kid,' one of them told Donna once, in front of me. 'Needs a little more sparkle, I think, but she's a great kid.' Donna was quiet with me for the rest of the evening. After that, it was important that none of them ever had cause to say that about me again.

But stage door was different because everyone there liked me. No matter how tired I was after a show, I would listen to their stories about how far they had travelled and what they had thought of my performance and I would feel loved. I had posted on social media asking that no one take photos or videos at stage door, and for the most part the rule was respected. It was nice to connect with people in moments that left no footprint.

I got the tube back to Donna's after a particularly long stage door meet and greet, wiped but content. She was waiting for me with stir-fry and a mini éclair each from our favourite patisserie, and when she saw me she took me in her arms like I was twelve again, practically lifting me off my feet.

'I'm *so sorry* about earlier,' she said.

I was still in my theatre daze, which was what Mum called the pleasant spaciness I experienced after a show. It took me some time to remember dance class that afternoon, the pen hurled at Kendra's head. I pulled away from her.

'You didn't throw it at me.'

'I shouldn't have thrown it at all. Or, rather, I wish I hadn't needed to.'

'Is something going on?' She looks at me, questioningly 'I saw you talking to Fred and Rupert,' I said. 'Is there a plan of some kind?'

'There's always a vague plan,' said Donna, gesturing for me to sit down on the sofa. 'You've been doing this long enough to be aware of that.' She passed me my bowl of stir-fry.

'I think I've been doing this long enough to be in on it.'

'I promise that I'll tell you,' she said, 'when the time is right.'

'Tell me now.' I put my bowl down. Donna's eyes followed it. 'That'll get cold.'

'I'm not a kid any more. I can handle knowing what's coming. Maybe if I know, I can even help. Move things in the right direction. You know I'm good on camera.'

'I do,' said Donna. 'Eat.'

'So, why not?'

'Belle, please. I made that for you.'

She waited. Slowly, I reached out and picked the bowl back up. Donna watched as I dug my fork in and took a bite.

'Good?' she asked.

'Yeah.'

'Good.'

'I don't understand why I can't know.'

'You're not a producer,' she said. 'You're a cast member.'

'Okay but fuck that.'

'Belle!' she reproved.

It was the first time I'd known her to use that booming, authoritative voice on me.

'You're not a producer either,' I mumbled.

'I'm an honorary one. It's my show. Please keep eating.'

I shovelled an excess of stir-fry into my mouth and then set the bowl down and sat back to chew, grumpily. Donna reached across to squeeze my knee.

'I always ask you to trust me.'

'Yes, you do.'

'I'm asking you again.'

She squeezed my knee again, harder this time.

'What we're making,' she said, 'is a kind of art. It's a combination of cinema and performance art and sociological documentary. It's a delicate thing, because we want our art to be sincere, and it only can be if the subjects are almost unaware of its processes.' She held a hand up, pre-empting my interruption. 'Now, I know you aren't unaware and you never have been, because you're a smart girl. But you are still unaffected and natural and genuine on camera, and if you always knew what was coming then that innocence would be lost.' She tapped my thigh. 'Everything hinges on that innocence.'

'Why?'

'If you believe, they believe.'

'Who believes what?'

'Everyone believes that this is, and has always been, your story.'

I think this is her giving me something. I can't quite piece it together. 'Mine?'

'Yours,' she says. 'Unequivocally. Yours.'

Faye and I lay on the floor of the music room with our noses almost touching. Howie was coming back at eight to lock up, he had told me, in case I wanted to smoke with him. I had told him I didn't.

'You're avoiding me,' he said. 'You just use me when you're feeling lonely, and then you chuck me out,' he said. I couldn't deny it. I tried to push the guilt down.

'Donna hates me,' said Faye.

'She doesn't.'

Faye rolled onto her back. She'd been told off that day for speeding up when she led the counts in dance, her 'One, two, three, four' getting less certain as we went until Donna asked me to take over. I'd felt bad for her, but also, she had sped up. There was a tendency amongst the girls these days to pretend that any criticism they received was unfair, and I couldn't entirely sympathise with it.

'Faye,' Donna had said, 'do you think you'll ever make it to the West End if you can't stay on the beat?'

'Not if I'm not allowed on any auditions,' Faye had replied. She'd been ordered out of the room.

'It's all for a reason,' I said now, watching her side profile.

'What reason? Humiliating us?'

'I don't know exactly. But she doesn't hate you.' I thought back to our conversation on Donna's sofa. 'It's art.'

'The show?' Faye wrinkled her nose.

'That's what she said.'

She rolled back over to face me. 'You guys talked about how things have been recently?'

'Just a little.'

'What did she tell you?'

'Not much. She never does.'

'Come on,' she groaned. 'You have your little sleepovers with her . . .' She'd never brought them up to me before. 'You must know some stuff.'

'If I did, then I'd tell you.'

'Kendra thinks you're in on everything. She thinks Donna tells you everything she tells Fred and Rupert.'

'I wish.'

'She doesn't tell you anything?'

'She goes on and on about protecting my innocence.'

'Ew,' said Faye, wrinkling her nose again.

'For the show. She wants the show to be good. If the show succeeds, we all succeed.'

I realised how false the words were as they were coming out of my mouth. Faye caught the change in my face. 'What?'

'What?'

'Did she say that?'

'Not in those words, exactly. I mean—' What had she said? 'She was talking about me specifically, but it's the same idea.'

'It's not,' said Faye. 'Sometimes I don't think she wants all of us to succeed. Just you.'

I turned this over in my head. As much as I didn't want to admit it, it sounded right. 'She said something weird, the other day.'

'What was it?'

'That this was my story.'

'Just yours?'

'I guess. I think – I think she was saying that they're doing this whole show for me.'

'So, she really doesn't care what happens to the rest of us.'

I reached out to touch her cheek. 'I care. I'll talk to her.'

Faye looked sceptical.

'I will.'

'You never try very hard.'

'That's not fair,' I said, even though I knew it was.

'I just want to feel like you're on my side.'

'I am. I promise.' I slid my hand into hers. 'I know I'm pretty shit at standing up to her. But I will try.'

'Okay,' said Faye. She rolled over, pinning me to the floor. She planted a kiss on my nose. 'You've got a nice nose,' she said. 'I can see why they wanted to make a show about you.'

'Shut up.' I went to push her off. Below us, the door slammed. Faye sat bolt upright.

'Is that Howie?'

'*Shit.*'

'Belle?' I heard him call.

We escaped out of the back door of the studio whilst he was tidying the green room. As we ran hand in hand towards the street, I looked back and, just for a second, I thought I saw his face in the window, watching us. Only for a second, and he was gone. No one saw her kiss me. No one saw her fingers reach for mine, holding on even as our arms stretched and our feet moved in opposite directions, until we absolutely had to let go.

'Faye,' said Donna when she walked into class the next day. 'Good to have you back.'

Faye nodded.

'Let's not be sullen.'

'Sorry.'

'Are you ready to be a professional?'

Faye nodded.

'Can you tell me using your words?'

'Yes.'

Donna directed an eye roll my way.

She was making them all learn a group routine that they were going to enter into a local competition – embarrassing, easy stuff, designed, I think, to make a point. As they rehearsed, I was stood with Donna at the front of the class, offering corrections when asked for them and demonstrations when prompted. The other girls barely looked me in the eye any more.

This was boring for me. I wondered if it would be boring for an audience, if that's why Rupert and Fred had been exchanging glances all season and muttering to each other behind Donna's back. There had been plenty of fights – more fights than ever, actually – but aside from me no one was really doing much. I was being followed to meetings, to recording sessions, to TV guest star slots. The other girls were sat in the studio, slowly boiling over.

But Donna was bringing it somewhere. That's what she would have assured them. They just had to trust her.

'Hannah,' she said.

I pressed pause on the CD player. Hannah stopped, right in front of Donna, her shoulders slightly hunched.

'Your leotard is too small.'

Hannah immediately looked to Faye. At twelve, she had still not inherited her sister or her mother's self-possession. Faye gave her the smallest of nods. 'It's my normal one,' said Hannah.

'Well, you're growing up now. You have to be conscious of changes to your body. Performers have to be aware of those things.'

The hunched shoulders made her look sullen. I willed her to pull herself up, straighten her neck. Smile, and nod, and promise she would fix it. She stood there.

'Alright,' said Donna. Another eye roll at me.

The dance resumed. Hannah's alignment was off. She was twisting unnaturally as she moved, trying to follow herself in the mirror. Into the glass behind her shifted two dark shapes. Fred and Rupert, in black t-shirts. Rupert was typing on his phone, but Fred was watching keenly, with an enthusiasm in his face that I hadn't seen in weeks.

'Stop,' said Donna. I pressed pause on the CD again. 'Come here, Hannah.'

Faye's eyes followed her sister as Hannah moved to the front of the class. Donna held two fingers in the air and made a swivelling motion. When Hannah didn't move she did it again, her mouth thin and impatient.

Slowly, Hannah turned so that her back was to Donna. Her eyes sought each of us out for help. Donna lowered her hand and placed her two fingers very lightly somewhere at the back of Hannah's thigh. She moved them up and down. Hannah's eyes opened wide, her chest rising rapidly.

My finger was still frozen on the pause button.

'Should a dancer's bum jiggle like that?' asked Donna.

Faye took a step forward to reach for her sister's hand, but Alex, their mum, was faster. She stood up from her chair, crossed the room, rapidly, pushed Hannah towards her sister – and went for Donna, hands reaching to pull at her hair.

The crew stepped in to restrain her. Donna emerged from the fray, blinking in what seemed like genuine shock as Alex was pulled back by two assistants, the other mothers coming forward to ease them off and pull Alex back to her seat.

'Don't EVER lay your hands on my twelve-year-old again!' she was screaming. Hannah stood with her hand in Faye's, slightly behind her. She wasn't crying.

'Your mother is insane,' Donna told Faye and Hannah.

'What gives you a right to comment on their bodies?'

'Alex. They work in entertainment.'

'She is *twelve*,' spat Alex. 'You *monster*.'

'Would you physically assault a teacher who gave your child a bad grade? I mean, *really*.'

Mum was slumped in her chair with her head in her hands. When she did look up, she looked near tears. She didn't go to Hannah, and she didn't stand up to yell with Alex. Her eyes were fixed on me.

Alex was still screaming. I had never seen her lose her cool like this. She sounded like Charlene. Donna flinched at the swear words, but other than that she stood there, making amused eye contact with me. I stared back at her. I had no idea what my face looked like. I only knew that they were both looking at me, Donna and Mum, and I didn't know what either of them wanted me to do.

'Done?' said Donna when Alex finally subsided.

Alex wiped away a tear. 'Why are you doing this?' she asked hoarsely.

Donna took in the frightened group of girls in front of her. Her lips pursed.

'I don't know any more,' she said.

They stood there, cowering away from her. Hands reaching out for each other. I sat by the CD player, back up against the wall and watched. In the mirror they looked like a painting, four girls in matching black leotards with their hair scraped back and their hands by their sides. None of them moving. Then Faye reached for Hannah's hand.

'I'm going to let you all go,' said Donna.

I think Faye realised first. Maybe it was just that it was her face I was watching. Either way, it was Kendra who broke the awful silence. 'What do you mean?'

'You're fired,' said Donna. 'All of you. I've done my best with this group, but the fact is, I think that you're all just very average little girls.'

Alex went to speak, but Donna held up a hand.

'There's nothing wrong with being average little girls,' she said. 'But it doesn't work for my purposes. You'll be released from your contracts. You can all go.' Her head snapped round. 'And, Belle, we're leaving. Tonight.'

She made a motion towards the door. I sat there, uncomprehending.

'Belle. Come on.'

I still didn't move. Her brow crinkled slightly, and her lips pinched. Then she walked over to me and lowered herself ungracefully to my level in a way I had never seen her do for any of us before.

Her hand reached out to cover her mic. Her hair, long and loose, fell over her shoulder. The other girls stood hidden behind it. She smiled at me, gently. There had never been more adoration in it.

'I know this is scary,' she whispered. 'I know what I must seem like to you right now. But the show wasn't going to continue as it was, and if it had stopped, we wouldn't have been able to keep your story going.'

I covered my own mic. 'I could still work.'

'You need this show. This show is what's making people want to work with you.'

'But I can't do it forever.'

'Not forever,' she said. 'But you need it right now.'

I chewed my lip. I tried to force back my tears.

'Leave the room with me right now,' she said, 'and I'll explain everything, I swear. It's all figured out.' She reached out and squeezed my knee. 'Belle, I'm not a monster.'

'I know.' I did know it, really. I knew it through everything. I felt the love every time she looked at me – deep, real, human love. The kind of love you can't fake.

'Don't listen to what that awful woman said.'

She moved slightly, so that I couldn't see the way the other girls were looking at me in the mirror. She leant in even closer.

'Look,' she said, and she took out her phone. 'I've already booked the flights.'

She held out the screen to me. I blinked at it, then looked back at her. Her face gave nothing away, at least not to the cameras, but it was as if she was whispering directly into my ear. *These are our tickets that I'm showing you. You have to act like these are our tickets.*

It wasn't our tickets. It was a picture of me and Faye. She was pressed against the wall around the back of the studio. I was leaning into her, our fingers intertwined. Our lips locked. I couldn't remember the kiss. Seeing it on the screen, it didn't even look like me. Donna gave me two seconds to take it in, and then she calmly slid the phone back into her pocket.

'Remember,' she whispered, barely louder than a breath, 'I've been on your side through it all. Every time you weren't quite right for the part, I still pushed you. Every time you turned up at my door, I looked after you. I never told. And I can still help you now. If you let me.'

I stared at her. I couldn't understand what to make of it, but I knew I was scared. And I knew that somehow, she was trying to warn me of something.

'I'll explain everything. I promise.'

'I don't—' My eyes flickered to the mirror, but I couldn't see Faye, just Donna's shoulder.

'I love you,' she said, still in a whisper, still with her hand covering her mic. They had to be able to hear her, though. 'Everything I'm doing is for you. Because you're special. If you don't come with me right now, it's all for nothing. If you do, then you're going to be big.'

She moved, ever so slightly, back into my direct line of sight. Pale-green eyes looked straight into me. She squeezed my knee again. She held out her hand.

'How big?' I whispered.

She smiled. 'The biggest thing in the world.'

I took her hand. She helped me up. In the mirror, I saw Fred and Rupert standing in Mum's way as she moved to follow us, her hands pushing into their chests. Kendra was laughing to herself, quietly and breathily through her nose, but the corners of her mouth were turned down. Donna opened the door.

And I wanted to take one last look back, like we were parting in a movie, and see Faye looking after me, and nod at her, and watch her nod back, and know in a sad sort of way that it was all going to be alright. I wanted to be able to tell her with my eyes, *This is for you. I don't know how, but this is for you.*

But when I glanced back at her face, I wished I hadn't. She looked at me like she didn't even know who I was.

Reunion special

Donna takes a step towards me. I inch back.

'Belle,' she says.

Faye stands between us.

'Well, really,' says Donna, 'this is all very overdramatic.'

'We're not doing this,' says Faye. 'Fred, Rupert, we're not doing this.'

'Red card,' says Rupert.

'Oh, *truly* go fuck yourself.'

'Sit down,' says Donna.

'This woman is a criminal. She should be behind bars.'

'Jesus, Faye,' says Kendra, 'way to believe the conspiracies.'

'Conspiracies? Are you kidding me?'

Hannah has come to stand beside me. She squeezes my hand. Roni has her phone to her ear, talking low to someone. She hangs up the call and clicks her fingers at us.

'Car's coming,' she says. 'So is my security. If anyone follows us then they should bear in mind *just* how good my security is.'

'How long?' asks Faye.

'They're round the corner.'

'Perfect.' She takes a step back, her eyes still on Donna. She finds my other hand. I'm stood between the sisters, clinging to them both. 'Let's go.'

'Hang on.' Rupert jumps into action and hurries after us, cameras be damned. 'Let's sit down and just work something out here. Does anyone want a drink? Some water? I'm sure we can figure this out between us—'

The door slams behind us. We walk down the corridor in silence, Faye and Hannah still clinging to each of my hands.

'Is this all of us?' asks Roni, still typing on her phone.

'Kendra's not here,' says Hannah.

'Fuck Kendra.' She waves to a SUV with tinted windows. *Like we're in a spy film,* I think, numbly. 'We're going to my place,' she says.

'I thought you lived in LA?'

'I've got a place here. Where do you think I was staying?'

'In a hotel. Like a peasant,' adds Faye, in response to Roni's look. In spite of myself, I let out a snort of laughter. It seems to remind them that I'm there. 'How are you feeling?' asks Faye as we strap ourselves in.

'I don't know,' I say honestly.

'It's not far,' says Roni. 'I've got drinks at mine. And stronger stuff, if you want it.'

'Right, because she should really be pinging right now.'

'Please, Faye.' Roni looks out of the window. 'Not all of us get by on cucumber water and making pots.'

Roni's place is in Kensington, obviously. It's a three-storey townhouse with a surprisingly modest exterior, at least for someone with a bank balance equivalent to the assets of a small nation. The inside is high-ceilinged and white, full of the expensive nothingness of the uber-rich. We seat ourselves on white leather sofas and watch as Roni fixes us drinks from the bar.

'Kendra would make a comment about not being able to get the help these days,' said Faye.

'When she's not here to make the comments, why do we have to hear them anyway?' Roni hands me a gin martini, which has never been my drink. I put it away in seconds. 'I'm furious at her,' she says.

'I think we all are.'

'It was one thing replying to that awful woman, let alone admitting it on camera. But inviting her to set?'

'Didn't Fred and Rupert invite her?'

'There's no way. They can't have been building up to this. It was so random. I thought it was Paget they were trying to get.' She's back at the bar, placing olives in the remaining martini glasses. 'I think Kendra brought the idea to them recently and Donna got on a plane as soon as everyone signed off. My lawyers will tell us the exact details.'

'Sure,' says Faye.

'What?'

'This isn't a legal thing. What would we be accusing them of?'

'We could sue for emotional damage.'

'Please.'

'You don't think a jury would sympathise with Belle?'

'Donna's never had a suit brought against her,' says Faye. 'I just don't think it would hold up that thirty seconds in a room with her traumatised any of us to the point of financial compensation.'

'We get restraining orders against her, then. At least one for Belle.'

'I don't think Belle wants to deal with all that litigation.' Faye glances at me. 'I assume that's why you've never tried before.'

I nod, once. Roni sits down beside me, lip jutting out. Under all her polish, she's still the same eleven-year-old girl with the same need for things to be fair. 'I just want to do *something*,' she says plaintively.

I take the second drink she hands me. 'This is something.'

'I know her career dried up,' she says, 'and I know her reputation went to shit, but it doesn't feel like enough. She humiliated all of us, individually. And the way she treated Belle was on another level.'

I feel Faye's hand between my shoulder blades.

'I'm sorry that we were so awful to you about it,' says Roni. 'The position you were in – I mean, she was bad to all of us, but she was worse to you. I wish I hadn't blamed you. We just didn't realise how scared you were. You never seemed it.'

There's a knock at the door downstairs. We look at Roni expectantly, but she only sits and waits. Below us, there are footsteps, then voices. Someone starts up the stairs.

'Do you actually have staff?' asks Faye, incredulous.

'Shut up.'

'You're so rich.'

'You're so northern.'

There's a knock on the door of the living room. Kendra stands in the doorway, in her TV top and comfy trousers, holding her coat. She gestures with her head towards an empty chair across from us.

Roni stands up. 'I should have told them not to let you in,' she says.

'Oh, please. Donna was right – you're all so overdramatic.' Kendra sits down. 'I suppose that's a symptom of growing up on TV.'

She's cold in a performative way, but when she shifts in her seat she's a little too quick and bouncy, like she's on a spring.

'Did you invite her?' I ask.

'I told her it was happening,' she said. 'She came.'

I nod. I'm trying to decide how to play this – anger, level-headed cool, watery-eyed shock – when I remember that there aren't any cameras in the room.

'How did you swing it with Rupert and Fred?' asks Roni, arms folded, still standing by the door.

'We're still not doing this.' Faye is looking around her. 'There must be a button you can press in a house like this, or a bell you can ring, or something . . .'

'Jesus, Faye,' says Kendra.

'I'm not having you in here.'

'I only told her it was happening,' says Kendra, 'I swear. Everything else is between her and Rupert and Fred.' She leans forward and slams her bag down on the table and suddenly she's not Kendra who always has a comment to make, or Kendra who always gets the last word. She just wants to be believed. 'Belle's lying,' she says.

Faye sits down beside me and takes my hand in both of hers. 'Shall we go? Do you want to go?'

'Jesus,' says Kendra again.

'Belle? We can go if you want.'

'It's fine,' I say. I'm rigid. It's an effort for her to bend my fingers around hers. Faye raises my hand to her mouth and kisses it, gently, like she's breathing warmth back into it.

There's a brief silence. Then Kendra says, 'Have you two ever grown past fifteen?'

'That's a shitty thing to say,' says Faye.

'Why?'

'You know why.' Faye is looking very quickly and cautiously between Kendra and me. 'It's a well-known fact that when . . . that abuse can . . .'

'Please,' says Kendra, her hands clasped, 'for the love of God can *someone* just get their words out?'

'We're being sensitive,' says Roni.

'You're pandering. She's a liar. You're playing into her hand.'

'Why are you saying that?' I half-whisper. My lips are dry. Faye clutches my sweaty hand tighter.

Kendra gestures to her phone, lying on the table. 'Because I've heard the other side of the story.'

I cover my face with my hands. I feel Hannah's arm go around my shoulders, her skinny form pressed against mine, as Faye and Roni talk over each other. Kendra tries to interject a few times – I can hear her, attempting the start of a word here and there – but Faye and Roni aren't having it. It's all I ever wanted, for the two of them to go to bat for me with this much passion. I can't enjoy it.

'You need to go,' says Roni, as Faye subsides, sitting down heavily on the sofa beside me again and slipping her hand back into mine.

'I just want you to listen to what she told me,' pleads Kendra.

'I don't give a shit what she said. Abusers lie. It's how they live with themselves. For fuck's sake, Kendra, you're supposed to be clever.'

'She's not an abuser!' says Kendra. 'Look, I agree, Donna is very far from a saint. But show me actual evidence of abuse.'

'The whole world saw the evidence! It was literally nationally televised!'

'And you're telling me that after everything, you still believe what you see on TV?'

Roni is quiet for a minute. Then she says – 'I don't need to. I lived it. We all did.'

'We all did? So Donna hurt you, did she? She hit you? Gave you bruises?'

'Emotional abuse still hurts.'

'I'm not like the rest of you,' says Kendra. 'I don't throw the word "abuse" around like it's nothing. You know what we lived? We lived tough love.'

Roni turns away from her, crossing the room to close the curtains. She stands in front of them, looking out at nothing, as Kendra carries on.

'We did! We lived the reality of being young girls in a brutal industry. We lived a life that made us stronger and we grew thicker skins and look at us now! Faye, I know you bowed out gracefully from it all but you can't tell me you aren't still enjoying the money and the sponsorships.' She gestures to the room that we're in, to the white leather sofas and the oak bar. 'Roni, you're A-list. You're where everyone dreams of being.'

'I got myself here,' says Roni, turning around with folded arms. 'No one did shit for me.'

'Your mum put you on that show, made you stick with it. Donna built you. She gave you a platform. So did Fred and Rupert.'

'My mum handed me over to abusers and refused to take my trauma seriously. Donna, Rupert and Fred destroyed my adolescence.'

'Right,' says Kendra. 'You sure look like someone whose adolescence was destroyed. Jesus, girls sleep on the streets at twelve. They get married off in some countries or sold into prostitution. And we're all crying about how we had to go on a TV show and be famous and make money?'

'We're not crying about it,' says Faye. She's trying to take my hand again, to peel it off my face.

'And if it was *that fucking terrible,* why come back? I get that we're not all making Roni's money, but none of us were starving. None of us actually needed this. None of us are victims.' There's a beat. 'Especially not her.'

I uncover my face to find her staring pointedly at me. Roni and Faye have followed her gaze.

'You know who is a victim?' she asks.

'That's too far,' says Faye.

'Donna really did build a career all by herself. She left home at fifteen and went to London and made something of herself. And then when the work started to dry up, she created the show with

270

Rupert and Fred and she built it all over again. Granted, sometimes she did it by being an utter cunt—'

'I can't believe we ever used to accuse Belle of being a suck-up,' says Roni.

'I just called her a cunt!'

'She's done a number on you. I don't know how you can't see it.'

Kendra bends down, her face patronisingly close to mine. 'Belle, did Donna hit you?'

'Leave her alone.' Faye pulls her upright.

'They all hung her out to dry,' says Kendra. 'Rupert, Fred. Belle. They threw her under the bus.'

'Well, of course she'd say that,' says Faye.

'It's true. Like, *actually* think about what you know for sure. Because you can't trust a word that Belle says. All she's done is lie about Donna, ever since she left.'

'That's not true,' I say.

They all look at me.

'You're twisting everything.' I can't stand the way Kendra starts smirking the minute I open my mouth. 'I haven't been lying!' She spreads her hands. 'You know how I can promise you that?'

'Go on.'

'Because I haven't said a thing! Not one word!' My fist hits the leather seat of the sofa. Beside me, Hannah jolts. 'I haven't given one interview, I haven't made one social media post – her name hasn't crossed my lips since the show ended. I haven't even made an insinuation. Nothing, absolutely nothing that anyone can point to and claim to be a lie. *Nothing.*'

Kendra spreads her hands. *Well,* her face says, *there you go.*

There's a pause.

'What?' manages Faye.

'Lying by omission,' says Kendra. 'Because she knows people will fill in the blanks.'

'No,' I say, 'that's not what I said—'

'It's what you've been doing. You know what everyone thinks, and as long as you just don't say anything, you know they'll go on thinking it.'

'It's not my fault what people think.'

'It is, because you started this. What you said on camera started this.'

'I was scared.'

'Did Donna hit you?'

'She was frightening me. I felt like she could—'

'But did she? Had she, ever?'

I want to bite back. The words aren't coming. I can feel Faye's eyes on me.

'Belle?'

'She did other things—' I start.

Kendra spreads her arms, triumphantly. Roni's hand goes to her mouth.

'Oh, god,' she says.

'Belle.' Faye squeezes my hand. 'It's fine. It's okay. Just tell us what actually happened.' I shake my head. 'You have to,' she says.

'Why?'

'Because we need to know.'

I shake my head again. There's so much I want to say to her, but the real story isn't simple to tell, especially not with everyone listening in. 'Can we talk alone?'

'Don't let her manipulate you,' says Kendra.

I ignore her, focused on Faye. 'I just want to talk to you alone.'

'Just promise me you didn't lie,' she says.

'It's – it's complicated.'

'But did Donna ever actually hurt you?'

'Yes,' I whisper.

'Physically?'

I swallow. 'I—'

'Belle?' asks Faye, gently.

I can't even cry.

'Shit,' says Faye. She sits back. I feel her hand slip out of mine. Beside me, Hannah is staring out of the window. Her shoulders are hunched up, her back arched so harshly it looks like it's hurting her. I wonder where she's imagining she is.

In my lap, my phone starts to ring.

'You can answer it,' says Kendra.

'I know I can.'

'You were just staring at it.'

In a daze, I pick it up. 'Belle,' comes Cameron's voice. 'Have you seen the pictures? At the airport?'

I haven't, but I can guess. 'She came to set.'

The others can hear him. Roni pulls the pictures up on her phone, shows them around the room. There's Donna, walking through the airport in white sweats and white trainers. Glowing like one of her own veneers. She wanted to be seen.

'Where are you?' asks Cameron.

'Kensington. At Roni's.'

'Get in a car and come home. Please.' His voice is shaky.

'I'll be there soon.' I hang up and start to gather myself. The other girls watch me from the various corners of the room into which they've retreated. They're shell-shocked. Only Kendra leans forward and watches me fiddle with the straps on my shoes, her hand balled up under her chin.

'Does he know? Your mum's guy?' She grimaces. 'Did she know? Did anyone aside from you and Donna actually know the real truth?'

I point my finger at her. I get very close to her face. She doesn't move, and her expression doesn't change, but I've known Kendra long enough to know when she's afraid.

'You don't know. You don't know *shit*. Okay?'

'Fucking sociopath,' she mutters as I leave the room. As the door closes behind me, I linger in the hallway for a second, waiting for Faye to defend me. She doesn't.

Outside on the pavement, I unblock Howie and call him. 'They know, Howie, they fucking know.'

'Woah, slow down. Who knows what?'

'They know that everyone got it wrong. They think I lied.'

'How?' asks Howie.

'Donna talked to Kendra. They all believe her.'

'Shit.'

'I just – I don't know what happens now. What do I do?' I'm starting to panic. 'This is going to be the big hook. Everyone, everywhere is going to watch the special. And I'm going to become, what, this fucking fake victim that everyone hates? I can't live a life where everyone hates me.'

'Breathe, Belle.'

'I can't do it, Howie. I can't.' I don't want to be hated again. 'They all think I lied,' I repeat. Maybe I did lie. I'm not used to thinking of myself as a liar, but maybe letting people draw their own conclusions is a form of lying. Maybe I deserve to be hated. 'I can't do it. I can't do it.'

'*Breathe*,' he says. 'Let me come over. I'll bring weed.'

'You're not coming to my parents' place.'

'Come to my hotel then. You ran out too quickly the other morning.'

'No.'

'Why not?'

'I'm dealing with shit, Howie.'

'Let's deal with it together.'

'This isn't something I fix by smoking weed with you. Don't you get that? This is serious.'

'No,' he says, suddenly irritated, 'it's not. This is not life or death shit, this is not "what if the law catches up with me" shit. This is TV shit. This is, "what if twelve-year-olds with social media accounts stop liking me?" None of this is real.'

'It's real to me.'

'You're so fucking whiny,' he says. 'You always have been. Always the poor-little-me stuff. Donna was right – you're a fucking princess.' His voice becomes high-pitched and snivelling. '*Please, save me, everyone's being mean.*'

I hate that Howie is the one making me sob.

'Yeah,' he says, 'there we go. You always want me there when you need someone but you're never there for me. You were never there for me when we were younger and you're not now.'

'Fuck you, Howie. I was a kid.' I hang up. It should feel good. There's a shout from somewhere above me. I look up.

A stream of something falls down through the air towards me and hits my eye. It splatters over my face, into my hair. It's sticky and red, and when I press my lips together and splutter it tastes sweet.

'You're a lying bitch,' calls Kendra. She slams the window.

A Cosmopolitan to the face. She really was made for reality TV.

The Uber driver either doesn't notice my appearance or doesn't care enough to ask. We drive in silence back to Bethnal Green as I get all the milage I can out of the single tissue in my purse. After a while I sit back and accept my sticky hair and cold, damp skin. At least it wasn't wine.

'What happened to you?' asks Cameron when he opens the door to me.

'Kendra.' I wash my face in the kitchen sink. He watches from the table. 'Where's Jane?' I ask, turning round.

'At a friend's house,' he says. 'The one with the awful mother.'

'Susanne?'

'That's the one.'

'Thank god for Susanne,' I say.

He pats the seat beside him. I sit down. The ends of my hair are sticky. I roll them between my fingers as Cameron waits, very quiet and still, beside me.

'They think I'm a liar,' I say.

'Why?'

I'm about to answer when my phone rings. I'm expecting Rupert. I'm hoping for Faye. Instead, the number is one I don't recognise.

'Don't answer it,' says Cameron, but I reach forward and click the green button. I put it on speaker. There's a crackly silence.

'Belle?' comes a voice. 'Are you there?'

'*Jesus*,' says Cameron, slumping in his chair, his hand on his head.

'Is this Belle Simon?'

There's another pause.

'I can hear someone.'

'It's me,' I say.

She breathes out and I realise that she's nervous. The unfamiliarity of a nervous Donna is staggering. I thought I knew her inside and out.

'Hi,' she says. 'Hello, Belle.'

'I'm here too,' says Cameron. I wave a hand at him, but he shakes his head.

'Who is that?'

'It's Cameron. Sofie's partner.'

'Hi, Cameron,' says Donna. 'I was so sorry to hear about your wife.' There's a hitch in her throat. 'Your mum, Belle. We had our differences, but I broke down, when I heard. I couldn't stop thinking about you. I couldn't bear that you were without a mother.'

I turn my head away, as if I don't want the voice on the phone to see me cry.

'If you don't have a good reason for calling then I'm going to hang up,' says Cameron.

'I do, I do,' she says quickly. 'I couldn't bear what happened today. That's never what I wanted.' Her voice is thick. 'I still care a great deal about you, Belle, even after everything that's happened. I never, ever want to be the person who upsets you like that.'

'Then leave,' says Cameron.

'There are things we have to talk about, the two of us. I can't live with it being like it is any longer.' She hurries forward. 'I know you won't want to do it on camera. And I'm keen to avoid that too, if we can. If you just give me what I want then I don't have to sit down in front of a camera at all.'

I turn back to look at Cameron, my eyes wide. He holds up a hand.

'Okay,' he says, 'so what exactly is it that you want?'

'To talk. Off camera, just me and Belle.'

'No,' he says.

'Don't you think it should be Belle's decision?'

'Belle's done with all of that,' he says. 'They can say what they like about her. She's not going back on that show, and she's sure as shit not having anything else to do with you.'

'I need to hear it from her.'

Silence. Donna's breathing crackles down the line.

'Belle—'

I reach out and end the call, quickly, like squashing a bug.

Season Five

She tugged me quickly down the corridor and out the door, into the cold afternoon. A camera followed us, running a little to keep up. I imagined the footage, shaky and frantic. My head was swimming.

'What's happening?' I asked.

She looked over her shoulder and then put her hands on my shoulders, grabbing me in motion. I stared into her face.

'That's your next storyline. Do you understand?'

'No.'

'Belle, please don't be slow. Does your mum know? About you and Faye?'

'No.'

'Do you want her to?'

'I—'

'Do you want anyone to know? Do you want the world to know? Do you want footage of you and Faye out there, doing stuff? Do you want the show to tell this whole story where the two of you are experimenting together? Do you want that for her?'

Her questions were hurting my head. I squeezed my eyes shut. 'No.'

She gave my shoulders a little shake, but it wasn't rough. It was kind. I felt her hands squeezing. 'I'm not trying to scare you,' she said. 'But we need to move. The flight leaves soon.'

I licked dry lips and tried to steady myself in her grasp. 'Where's my mum?'

There she was, bursting through the doors just as the car pulled up. It already had cameras in, I noticed. But no one had caught that brief conversation between the two of us on the grass. Donna was protecting us, me and Faye. She was protecting us both.

'What the fuck are you doing?' Mum yelled. 'Where are you going?' She strode over the pavement towards us.

'Sofie,' says Donna, like she was expecting her. She held open the car door. 'Get in. I'll explain everything on the way.'

'She's not going anywhere with you,' said Mum.

'Listen,' said Donna. 'You have to listen. I know this was—'

'You know this was awful. You hated it as much as we did. But we have to trust you. Right?'

They held each other's gaze for a minute.

'Get in the car, Belle,' said Mum.

I was sandwiched between her and Donna, my fingers twisting around themselves in my lap. 'I've been setting it all up,' said Donna as we drove away. 'I've got opportunities lined up for her in LA. Jobs she won't even have to audition for. Every single one of my contacts says they think she's going to be the biggest thing ever.'

'LA?'

'I've got a place out there. That's where we're going.'

'LA.' Mum gave me a dazed look. 'We can't go to LA.'

'Belle,' said Donna, 'when are you turning sixteen?'

'In six months,' I said.

'Okay,' she said. 'We could maybe do that. We could maybe put it all on ice for six months. Rupert and Fred won't like it, but we could.'

'She'll still be a minor,' said Mum.

'Sixteen is easier to work with,' said Donna. 'If we have to go down that road.' She leant across me to look Mum in the face. 'You don't understand, Sofie. All of this has always been about her.' She held up a single finger. 'I always wanted one girl. Five or six is a school. I never wanted to be a schoolteacher. One girl, I can really be someone to. I can make her something amazing.'

'So this was always the plan? Getting rid of the rest of them?'

'It was a negotiation,' said Donna. 'Fred and Rupert always preferred the group dynamic. But I've been guiding us here. I named the show after one child, not six. One real deal.'

'Jesus.' Mum put her head in her hands.

'This is what's best,' said Donna. She caught my eye. 'For everyone.'

I couldn't speak. But I made myself nod, up and down, mechanically, and she nodded back.

'Belle is coming to LA with me,' she said. 'Now, I don't know what I'll have to do to make that happen, but I know that it is happening. I have flights booked for us tonight, all three of us, and we're getting on them.' Mum said nothing. 'Sofie, look at it this way—'

'Stop talking,' said Mum.

Donna closed her mouth, stunned.

'I mean it. Don't say another word. I want you to drive us home.'

'But—'

'I want you to drive us home. You're going to wait in the car. Make conversation with the driver if you're bored. Belle and I are going to talk this through and we will come back to you with an answer when we are ready.'

Donna looked at her for a second. Then she nodded once, curtly, and folded her hands into her lap. Mum gave the address to the driver. As she leant forward to do so, I tried to catch Donna's eye, but she was staring forward at the headrest in front of her with unsettling focus.

Back at home, we left Donna in the car. Mum turned the key in the lock and then ushered us in. We sat at the kitchen table across from each other.

'Tell me what you want,' she said.

'I want LA.'

'You've just heard about it. It could be shit, Belle.'

'It won't be.'

'How do you know?'

'I trust her.'

She took my hand in both of hers and kissed it. She held it under her chin.

'Still?'

'Yes,' I said.

She nodded, staring down at the back of my hand. I didn't know how to start telling her how important this was. What was happening between Faye and I didn't feel like something I could articulate even to her, let alone the entire world.

And even beside that, I wanted this, I told myself. I wanted LA. I wanted everything Donna saw written in the stars for me.

'You know we have to go,' I said. 'I mean, moving, all the arguments, everything we've gone through . . . we sacrificed it all for this, didn't we? For a shot?'

'Yes,' she said, 'but we could walk away from the table now and it wouldn't feel like a sacrifice. You've got some success, and a platform. We have money. We have this place. It would feel like winning.'

'Not to me,' I said.

She was quiet for a minute. Then she said: 'What about what I want?'

'Well, what do you want?'

'I have someone here that I love, Belle.'

I had never heard her say that she loved him before. 'I haven't even met him.'

'That was your choice,' she said.

She got up to put the kettle on. She was facing away from me, stood at the kitchen counter, when she reached a hand up and took hold of the handle on the cabinet above her head, opening it wide. Then she slammed it, the force of the action springing it open and closed again, rattling the mugs inside. She slammed it again. I sat, staring down at the tablecloth.

'I never wanted this for you,' she said. 'This wasn't how it was supposed to be. We were supposed to stay on that farm, just the two of us, and have a good, normal life.'

'I don't want a normal life.'

'I do. God, Belle. I do.'

I was going to LA, I told myself. No matter what tantrums she threw, no matter what she said or did. Donna was waiting for me in that car outside, and I was going to pack and get in it. Because she was wrong. The game was only worth it if I played it all the way to the end.

'I think this industry is terrible,' she said. 'It makes me scared for you. The people around you make me scared for you. The way you are, the way it makes you act, makes me scared for you.'

'Please,' I said. 'Mum. I have to.'

She turned around, fingers curling over the edges of the sideboard behind her.

'I know,' she said.

She told me to wait upstairs while she went to talk to Donna. I watched from the window as the two of them got out of the car and walked a little way down the street, so as to be out of view of the camera. It swung around then, finding me, and I threw myself to the carpet and lay there, heart pounding.

I sat up when Mum came back into the house and kissed my forehead.

'You have a month,' she said. 'Then we go home.'

She took her time packing. 'Donna will wait,' she said. When we went downstairs, Donna was still there, half-asleep against the car window. The driver was playing Sudoku on his phone. I loaded my suitcase into the back of the car and shook her shoulder.

'Hm?' she said, blinking heavily, like a child.

'We're ready,' I said.

'That's wonderful,' she said. Her arms reached for me.

A production van met us at the airport. Rupert and Fred were going to follow us out, but we got to share our flight with a single camera operative who tailed us through the airport. He couldn't film us on the flight, but I could see him, sat a few seats in front of us. He had the chicken for dinner and watched *Terminator* and *There's Something About Mary*. I tried to remember his name. We had long since stopped collecting personal details about the crew.

Donna was in Business Class, but Mum and I sat in Economy together and slept on each other's shoulders. When the plane hovered over LA the next morning and the clouds cleared, I pressed my face against the window and stared down at sprawling freeways and dusty hills. Mum didn't like the descent. She gripped my hand tightly as the plane went down, down, the ground rushing closer, but the minute we touched the tarmac in LAX she let it go.

This was Season Five, but it didn't feel like TV any more. There was no break in which I rediscovered the distinction between the show and real life and mentally prepared myself to re-enter. I couldn't see the storylines that they were pulling together any more and I couldn't use Fred and Rupert's faces as a marker for whether or not I was getting things right. I didn't see them much these days.

Donna's summerhouse at the end of the garden had become the production room and they mostly kept to themselves. Occasionally, when I stood on the porch and looked over the long lawn towards the summerhouse, I would catch a glimpse of one of them in the window. Watching me back.

'No more forced drama,' sang Donna as she showed us around the house and introduced us to the new set up. 'No more scheming and lying and underhand tricks. This is what all three of us have wanted from the beginning. This is true documentary.'

'Too true,' said Mum. 'It's a fucking nature show.'

Over the first couple of days, we watched them prepare Donna's house. Every inch of it was rigged with cameras, from the living room to the kitchen to the garden. Only our bedrooms and bathrooms were safe. Even then, I only got undressed for the shower when I was already safely behind the frosted glass, like I was living at the gym.

We lived and worked and ate and talked, and they filmed. There must have been hundreds of hours of footage to comb through. I launched straight into a whirlwind of auditions. We would prepare at home, and then Donna – never Mum – would drive me to countless studios around LA to take meetings and read lines. I met my new music team and filmed a video for my single, which I hated because pretending to sing over my real, tinny voice in the background made me want to curl up and die.

But for the most part, life was better. I smiled around the house and sang for Donna on request. The three of us watched movies on the sofa and cooked meals together, and the few times I did see Rupert and Fred, their obvious annoyance at the state of things made it seem even more precious. They were no longer in control.

'They're not happy, are they?' Mum said to Donna, after a particularly terse encounter in the garden.

'They don't quite get it yet,' said Donna, 'but they will. This is a much better show.'

I got used to sleeping with the covers pulled right up over my head so that not an inch of me was showing. Every night before I slept, I texted Faye. Sometimes it was a long message, full of details about my day and jokes I hoped she'd be forced to acknowledge, and sometimes it was brief. Once it was just: *sorry.* She never replied.

At least I had Howie.

He arrived a week after I did with a bunch of other crew members and found me in the garden, sat by the pool with my feet dangling in the water, learning my sides. When he grabbed my shoulders I shrieked, and hit back, and we both ended up in the pool. My sides were drenched. Howie helped me to dry them out with a hairdryer in my bedroom.

'Damn,' he said, looking around. 'Donna put you up in the nice room, huh?'

'They're all nice,' I said, which was true. Donna's house, as she told me proudly, had been featured in *Architectural Digest*.

Howie wasn't around as much – his job now seemed to entail running over the whole of LA rather than just the Southbank – but since I rarely left the house except for auditions we saw a lot of each other. He would slip into my room regularly so that we could hang out away from the cameras.

'Who would have thought?' he said, more than once. 'Me spending so much time in Belle Simon's bedroom.'

I didn't find Howie attractive like I once had. I didn't even particularly like him, as time went on. He was always a bit too much and where his jokes had once flattered me, now they made me uncomfortable. But I was always around adults, these days. At least Howie didn't feel like an adult.

'I don't like him,' Mum said one day, after she caught us chatting in my room.

'You don't like any of them.'

'No,' she said, 'I don't.'

She moved slowly through the house, around the garden, off and onto the sofa. At dinner, when Donna ran through the next day's schedule with us, Mum would sit and move her mouth slowly like she was chewing the cud, twisting her watch on her wrist. Sometimes, late at night, she would slip into my bedroom and climb into bed with me. She would curl her arms around me and hold me close to her. When I woke up in the morning, she was always gone.

Donna was the one who reminded me to practise my lines. Donna controlled what food came into the house and laid out clothes for me on audition days. She planned my school schedule and laid out my sleep regime. Sometimes I would look over at Mum to see if she was going to object. She did now and then, at the beginning. One evening I watched out of the window as she stormed down to the bottom of the lawn and in through the door of the summerhouse. She returned with her mouth in a flat line. She rarely inserted herself after that.

But she stepped in over Lucy.

'Absolutely not,' she said, when the sides came in. She refused to let me read them.

Lucy was a teenage prostitute on a show called *Young Delicacy* and she had a six-episode arc that ended in her violent murder at the hands of a client. They were offering it to me with no audition required. Donna insisted that the role was career-making.

'It's provocative. It provokes a reaction, Sofie.'

'Yes, that's the definition of provocative.'

'Fred and Rupert think she should do it.'

'Huh,' said Mum. 'I wonder why they think that?'

286

Howie snuck me the slides so that I could read them under my covers with my phone torch. I adored Lucy. It wasn't just that she was straight-talking and world-wise – she was *sexy*. She was supposed to be fourteen, a year younger than I was, and yet she was cooler than I had ever felt myself to be. If I played her, at least a little of her cool surely had to rub off on me.

Donna set up a phone call between Mum and the director, who assured her that the safeguarding measures on set would be 'top notch, far above industry standard'. We said yes. It was only afterwards that Donna told us she would be an executive producer.

'I didn't want to sway you either way,' she said, when Mum (quite loudly) expressed her annoyance. 'I wanted Belle to want the part simply because she connected with it.'

'I don't particularly want Belle to connect with an underage sex worker.'

'Well,' said Donna, 'she'll have to now.'

'You have to let me,' I told Mum.

'I don't have to let you do anything,' she said. 'I'm your mum. I get to decide.'

Two weeks later, Donna drove me to set early in the morning. The sun was only just beginning to rise, but LA was already up. As Donna said, LA was one of very few places in the world where you'd hit traffic at 5am.

'Do you feel ready?' she asked.

I squared my shoulders. 'Yes.'

She tilted my chin towards her. 'Be provocative,' she said.

I'd had a fitting the day before and revelled in my wardrobe – skimpy camisole dresses, tiny denim shorts. There were even a couple of nightgowns that could definitely pass as lingerie. I was elated. I had never worn lingerie before.

'Oh dear.' Donna had laughed as I paraded before her and the wardrobe team. 'Let's hope your Mum never watches this.'

They dressed me for my first scene in one of those nightgowns, red and black lace with cups that pushed my chest up so that I couldn't stop staring at myself in the mirror. My hair was let loose and I gritted my teeth as grease was applied and tangles created. Mascara was rubbed under my eyes and lipstick smeared just past the edges of my lips. I looked edgy, damaged, completely unsheltered.

'Oh, *amazing*,' said the director, Doug, when I was brought out to him. He was a jovial, round-faced man in his forties who shook my hand when we met and said, 'We're going to have lots of fun, aren't we?' as if this was a Nickelodeon show.

My first scene was easy. We were filming in an old hotel that Doug jokingly called 'Lucy's office'. I had to pose seductively in a doorway as a man in his thirties walked towards me and disappeared with me into the room. I then had to lie on the bed and let him kiss my neck, whilst staring at the camera with empty eyes.

'No lines, but a whole lot of face and body,' said Doug. 'You ready?'

The actor I was working with wasn't very good-looking, I thought, as he came towards me with a creepy sort of glee. I didn't love the feeling of his hands on my shoulders as he pushed me down onto the bed. Was he supposed to push me? I couldn't remember exactly what it had said in the script.

'Cut!' called Doug. He gave way to the intimacy coordinator, who talked us through the neck kissing. I didn't like it very much. The actor's beard was scratchy. In between takes, he would sit up and look at the director or the intimacy coordinator as if I wasn't there. His name was Peter, and he'd been in some Jane Austen film that Mum had liked. She'd said he was fit, but I couldn't see it.

We filmed the kissing a few times before Doug was happy. 'Great stuff, Belle,' he said. 'You can really do that haunted, lost soul thing brilliantly.' He laughed. 'Almost concerningly well!' I laughed with him. 'Let's get in the doorway again,' he said. 'I have a few ideas.'

We went back out into the corridor. I stood in the doorway with my hands reaching up to hold it on either side of me. The action made the nightgown rise up my legs. I moved them closer together.

'Okay,' said Doug, 'that's great, Belle. Keep going.' Peter was pulled aside so that they could get a close-up of me batting my eyelids in the doorway. 'A bit poutier, if you can,' he said. 'Hey, can you move your strap?'

I took hold of the strap of my nightgown.

'Yeah, that's it. Just wiggle that down your shoulder a bit, if you can. Only if you're comfortable. Like you're playing a game with him. Like, "Hey, I'm gonna take this off! Just kidding!"' He mimed it for me, pouting his lips and wiggling his shoulders. I broke character to laugh. 'That's great,' he said. 'With that same kind of childish energy you've got there. That really works.'

I went to copy him, to shimmy the strap slightly down my shoulder with a grin and a giggle. Donna nodded, clapping her hands together silently and whispering something to Doug, a wide smile on her face. I watched, delighted – and then the silk strap slipped out of my grasp. The cup of the nightgown slid down. I grabbed at it, horrified, pulling it back up.

Doug broke the silence with a cough. 'That was great, Belle. Really great stuff.'

We took a break for lunch. I sought out Donna at craft services. She was reaching for an apple when I appeared by her side, silent and mortified. She took one look at me and laughed, tossing the fruit to me.

'Eat something.'

'I'm not meant to, yet.' We had just started me on an intermittent fasting schedule, after I'd gone to Donna and told her that I didn't feel like I had the same body as the other girls in LA. She'd told me not to worry and asked if I felt comfortable skipping breakfast. Now I only ate between 2 p.m. and 8 p.m. every day. We were being disciplined. Donna said it was good practice to be disciplined about food. These were habits that would set me up for life.

She checked her watch. 'Ah, right. God, you're good. I was nowhere near as good about food at your age. Are you okay?'

'I feel sick.'

'Oh, honey.' She hugged me to her. 'It's *fine*. You got a little too into character out there, is all.'

'That's not funny,' I moaned.

'It's a little funny.' She tickled under my chin. I pushed her off. 'Come on,' she said, sharply. 'Be a grown-up about it. No one wants a brat on set.'

She waited. 'Sorry,' I said.

'It's fine.' She hugged me to her again, her arm rubbing my shoulder. People were looking. 'We'll get it expunged, of course,' she said. 'No one will ever see the footage.'

'Are you sure?'

'If it ever gets out, I'll ruin the names of every single person in this room. I can end their careers in this town.'

I relaxed. 'Okay.'

When I resumed position in the doorway and they started to switch up the lighting around me, I tried to let the weight off my chest and smile, and beckon, and giggle. Doug said those were my best takes yet.

Mum wasn't in the living room waiting for me when we got home. She wasn't sat out on the patio or lying in her bed reading. I searched the house for her, my panic mounting. The two of us never went exploring in LA. We were supposed to tell Donna before we went and did anything, so that a decision could be made about whether or not it should be filmed.

Donna was waiting for me at the bottom of the stairs. 'Any luck?' she asked.

I shook my head, but just as I did so we heard the rattle of the gate opening, and then the front door. Mum walked in, a little out of breath and sweaty.

'Sofie!' exclaimed Donna, a hand on her chest in a show of relief.

'You're back,' said Mum. She didn't sound pleased.

'Where have you been?' Donna asked.

'The shop.' She held up the plastic bag in her hand.

'Did you walk?'

'Obviously,' said Mum, crisply. She was still annoyed that no one was willing to source her a car.

'You don't walk places in LA,' laughed Donna. 'Honestly, Sofie, we need to get you adjusted to the lifestyle.'

Mum didn't laugh. She headed straight for the stairs, breezing past me as if she couldn't see me.

'What did you need?' asked Donna. 'I could have put it on the list for you.'

'It was urgent,' said Mum.

'Well, what was it?'

She didn't answer. When she was safely upstairs, we heard the click of the lock on her bathroom door.

I sat on the floor of her bedroom outside her bathroom door and counted the seconds in my head. Inside the bathroom, her phone timer went off. There was silence.

She didn't look surprised to see me when she opened the door. Still in silence, she sat down on the floor next to me. She held out the stick.

'I don't want to touch that,' I said.

'Just look at it.'

I did. It didn't quite register. She rested her head against the wall.

'We have to go back,' she said.

'You're not even showing yet.'

'I don't want to start my medical care out here. I want Cameron to be at every doctor's appointment with me. I can't cut him out of all of it.'

'I've never even met him,' I said.

'I know.'

'And now you're having a baby with him.'

'I know.'

'And you're going to leave and the two of you are going to move out of London and live in a little house with the stupid baby . . .' She didn't react. 'Stupid baby,' I repeated again, petulantly.

'Yes,' she said. 'Stupid baby.'

I tried to imagine her being someone else's mother.

'This TV thing you're doing,' she said. 'The one you started filming today. Is it the most important thing in the world?'

'It's not just that. I've got my music—'

'Your music which you love so much.'

'—and I'm in talks for that film, and I'm going to do my first late-night show soon, and we're still filming this season . . .'

'Is it the most important thing in the world?' she asked. 'All of this?' I hesitated. 'Be honest,' she said.

'Yes.'

She nodded.

'It's just – this stuff, it makes it all worth it.'

'I know,' she said. She pulled me closer to her. I put my head in her lap. 'My love, I know.'

I couldn't relax into her. I stayed stiff, my eyes wide open. 'You're going to force me to come home.'

'I'm not going to force you,' she said. I sat up, to look her in the face. 'Belle,' she said. 'Come on. You're fifteen.'

'Donna—'

'Donna got emancipated at fifteen. So you've told me. Do you want to get emancipated?'

She said it almost teasingly. 'No,' I said. She waved a hand like, *there you go.* 'But I will. If I have to.'

Her face didn't change, but her hands, holding the stick, shook. 'No, you won't.'

'Donna can help me.'

'So you've told me. But you won't. Because you and I love each other.'

I hugged my knees to my chest. 'I do love you,' I said.

'I know.'

'But I'd still do it.'

I didn't look at her.

'Why?' she asked, and her voice was very far away.

She knew why. Because this was the most important thing in the world.

So she let me stay. Three weeks later, when she was packed up and booked on a flight back to London, she and Donna signed the papers at the dining room table, in front of Donna's lawyer. For as long as I was in LA, Donna was my legal guardian. And Mum was free to go.

'Remember,' she said to me, 'this doesn't mean that she is your parent. If you want to say no to something, you call me, and I will yell at her until she backs down.'

'Okay.'

'And you can come home whenever,' she said. 'You can decide you want to be home, and a day later you will be.' It wasn't really true, but I knew that she needed to believe it.

We didn't go with her to the airport. The filming schedule didn't allow it. I climbed onto the patch of roof outside my bedroom window and ignored the lens pointing up at me from the driveway as I sat and watched the orange of her suitcase through the car boot window, moving steadily away from me, fainter and further, until the road ran out.

Reunion special

Faye needs time, she says. She's confused about her feelings and about my actions and she wants some space to figure it all out. *Just give me a couple of days*, she writes. None of the other girls reply. Even Rupert doesn't try to contact me. I sit on my bed with my knees tucked up under the duvet and feel my stomach turn over on itself, repeatedly, until the knotting is something I'm almost used to.

The only one who reaches out to me is Donna. I block the number she called me on originally, but it doesn't matter. Now that she knows how to reach me she calls all the time, on such a range of devices I begin to wonder if she's buying burners just to ask me to talk. I stop answering calls that I don't recognise. She texts me pleadingly, sometimes angrily. She tells me that she loves me and that I'm an evil little liar for ruining her life the way I have. She begs for a conversation. *Just the two of us. No cameras.* She says I owe her that much. *After everything.*

Howie calls. 'I didn't think you'd pick up,' he says.

'Well, I did.'

'Did you see her?'

'Yeah. I didn't talk to her though.'

'Good,' he says. 'You shouldn't. She's a piece of work, that woman, I swear.'

Maybe this is what ties me to Howie. He's always known everything, and he hates Donna anyway.

'I'm going back to LA,' he says. 'I'd like to see you. Can I see you?'

'You can see me. You can't *see* me.'

'I'll take it,' he says.

We meet in a park not far from me. He's early. I'm late, because I know I can be, and I don't respond to any of his texts asking where I am. I've never really had any power over Howie, but feeling like I do, sometimes, has always given me a rush.

He's in a t-shirt and a denim jacket, and fingerless gloves. He must be freezing. I keep looking over at him and catching him shivering. He always stops when he thinks I can see.

'It's weird to be leaving,' he says.

'I'm glad you're going.'

'That's hurtful.'

'I will miss you,' I say. 'I don't want to, but I will.'

'I'm on a roller coaster here, Belle.'

He was the only person who understood me, at one point in my life. The only person I felt I could depend on. But he shouldn't have been. Howie is not a good person. Howie might not even see me as a person at all.

I still want to say goodbye.

'Maybe I'll move back to London one day,' he says.

'Stay in LA,' I say. 'It suits you I think.' What I want to say is that LA feels like the kind of place where people like Howie never really have to grow up.

'You're not in LA, though, Belle.'

'Howie.'

'I love you,' he says. 'I've loved you since I was seventeen.'

'Howie . . .' I want to say, *how old was I when you were seventeen*? I want to ask him to do the maths. But he knows. He answers the question before I've asked it.

'It doesn't matter,' he says. 'I still love you now, so how could it matter?'

'It does,' I say. 'It matters.'

I don't hug him goodbye when he leaves. I sit on the bench and watch him walk away, and I kick my legs, and I wonder if this time I'm actually rid of him.

I pick Jane up from school that afternoon and the two of us take the tube to her acting class. She has a big poster about natural selection under her arm, on the back of which she's written in capital letters: MRS HORBURY IS A HOMOPHOBIC DICK.

'She doesn't like *Rent*,' she explained, when she saw me looking at it.

'You can't call someone a homophobic dick for not liking *Rent*.' Apparently, going by Jane's look, you can when you're in Year Seven.

Jane's acting class are doing some accent work. She gives me her best Russian and French on the tube, as well as a northern accent that she's apparently modelling after Faye. 'Her voice is so nice,' she says. None of them are good. Her Russian is especially terrible and has me begging her to stop because people on the Piccadilly line are looking.

I think Cameron is right, and Jane is a little bit spoilt. She's a little bit cocky sometimes, and a little obnoxious. But she's such a light. She's the one thing, sometimes, that makes me feel as if the world still needs me in it. For that, she deserves everything.

Outside the entrance, she hands her blazer and poster to me and waves goodbye. I watch her ponytail swinging as she runs through the doors.

'Excuse me,' says a voice behind me.

It's a man probably around Cameron's age. He's very close to me and very breathy, with a grin that's slightly too wide.

'Is that your daughter?'

'Why?' I ask, alarmed.

'I wondered if you might have had a secret child that none of us knew about.'

I'm already moving away, smiling politely but firmly. He follows me.

'Is she your little sister, then?'

'I'm sorry,' I say. 'I don't really want to talk right now.'

'Please give me a minute,' he says, grabbing my arm. I freeze. 'I'm a massive fan. I loved you in *Young Delicacy*.'

I forced myself to maintain a smile. 'That was a long time ago.'

'You were wonderful.'

'Please let go of me,' I say.

He ignores me, reaching into his pocket. He pulls out his phone. 'Can I show you my lock screen?' It's a grainy image that makes my stomach drop instantly. I haven't seen it in a long time. 'How about that?' he grins at me.

I want to scream. 'I'm fifteen there,' is all I can manage.

'Really?' he squints at the screen. I wrench my arm free and hurry off, hoping he won't follow. I head for a crowd that I can lose him in. When I look behind me, I see him heading into the tube station. The relief is powerful, but short-lived. He saw Jane's face.

I can't help it. I call Faye.

'Is everything okay?' she asks when she answers the phone. She sounds tired.

'I'm-I'm sorry, I know I shouldn't be calling, but—' I'm struggling to breathe. 'I just met a man who has that picture of me from when I was fifteen, the one that leaked from that horrible show—'

'Belle, I'm sorry,' she says, 'that sounds awful, but do you have anyone else you can talk to about this right now? Please? Can you call Cameron?'

'He saw Jane,' I say. 'And he showed me this picture, and I'm a kid in it, and it was like he didn't even understand what I was saying—'

'Belle,' says Faye, 'please. I'm really sorry. I just don't think I can be there for you right now.'

'No, you don't understand . . .' I'm losing her. 'I'm sorry,' I say. I'm crying. 'Please, can we just talk? I can make you understand.'

'What do you mean, make me understand?'

'I can explain myself, if you just let me talk.'

'Belle,' she says. She sounds tired. 'Please, call Cameron. Get home and look after yourself, okay?'

'Okay. Sorry.'

The line goes dead. I put my hand over my mouth and breathe rapidly through my nose. *Fuck.* I haven't panicked like this in years. I'm in the tube station now, almost on autopilot, but for the first time in my life I can't work out what train to get on. I stare at the tube map, and then at my phone. I stumble onto the Central line and collapse into a seat. I put my head in my hands and sob.

Then someone sits down beside me.

'Belle?'

I recognise the voice. I don't know where from. But there's something instantly comforting in it, and a memory that makes me sad.

I look up.

'Hey,' she says. 'Do you need help?'

Paget wears her hair curly now. She used to straighten it when she was a teenager, but now she lets it dry naturally and she bundles it up on her head and collects the curls in a silk tie. She likes long skirts and the colour blue, and she makes her own earrings. She shows them to me, laid out on the table, as the kettle boils.

She's still tall and still skinny, but her angles are soft. She moves gently and fluidly, skirt moving around her ankles, earrings jangling. Her face is bare and she has the faintest, tiniest laugh lines around her eyes. She makes fantastic tea.

'I have a whole collection,' she says, holding the cupboard door open for me to show me rows of pretty tins and boxes. 'Mainly fruity ones. I love a fruity tea.'

She's an art teacher at a girl's grammar school near Crystal Palace. That's where she lives, in a little flat over a barbershop. It's not big, but it's very beautiful. The sun hits the kitchen table and lights up the wall behind like a spotlight. She's filled it with plants. A copper watering can sits on top of her microwave. On the wall there is a picture of Paget as a little girl, with her arms around Charlene's neck.

'I'm still close with my mum,' she tells me. 'She comes to visit all the time.'

'How is she?'

'Better,' she says. 'It was rough for her, for a while. She got really down after the show aired. But she's on the right antidepressants now, which helps a lot, and she's happier. She feels better about herself.'

I keep asking her questions. I ask her if the girls in her school recognise her, if they make jokes.

'They do,' she says, 'but not often. It's always big news when I get a new class and then within a week it's forgotten. Sometimes I catch them watching clips. It's good for me, though. It forces me to find the humour in it all.'

I nod, like I would have any idea where to begin doing that. I ask her if she lives alone. 'Yes,' she says. 'I love it.'

'Do you get lonely?'

'I never get lonely,' she says. 'It's a gift I have. I love my own company.' She sets my tea down in front of me. 'In summary,' she says, 'life is good.' I take a sip. 'You look surprised,' she grins.

'You just weren't so good, last time I saw you.'

'I was sixteen,' she says. 'Things are different now.'

'We were awful to you.'

'No. You were kids.'

It really is very good tea. She clinks her mug against mine and goes to get the biscuit tin. Even that astonishes me. I wonder how many years it will take me to get to a point in my life where I keep a biscuit tin full, just in case.

'Here you go,' she says. 'They're lemony. Do you like lemon?'

I nod. I have four. She keeps offering the tin to me, until eventually I have to tell her to put it away. 'I'll just keep eating and eating.'

'Do it,' she says. 'No judgement here.' She laughs. 'You still look shell-shocked.'

'I can't believe I ran into you like that.' I honestly expected to never see Paget again.

'It's not that big a city, really,' she says. 'I find that, the more I live in it.'

She has a cat now. It's a sleepy, golden-white thing that sits and washes its face on the sideboard as Paget pushes the biscuits back into the cupboard. She tickles it under the chin and I swear it smiles, whiskers rising. I watch her like I'm watching a play.

'You're happy,' I say, 'aren't you?'

'Yes, on balance.'

'I don't think any of the rest of us are.'

'Well,' she says, 'I was luckier than the rest of you. I got out first.'

'Do you get recognised?'

'A bit. Less so now, with the hair.' She gestures to her curls. 'More since the reunion news. Strangers stop me in the street and ask if I'm going to be in it. The kids at school wouldn't shut up about it for a week.'

'I'm sorry. That must have sucked.'

'I don't mind so much,' she says. She stirs her tea. 'I couldn't believe it when I saw you on the tube.'

'I couldn't believe it when I heard your voice.'

'It's so strange, knowing something of each other beyond the show.' She takes a sip. 'But nice,' she says.

I want to ask her how she did it, all of this. I don't know where to begin.

'Do you ever watch it?'

'No. I've seen bits, but I don't ever sit down and watch an episode.'

'Would you?'

'Maybe. One day.'

'Have you spoken to Donna, or any of the others?'

'No. Rupert called me recently, about the reunion. I said no.'

'And he just accepted that?'

'I guess. I never heard from him again.'

'You didn't want the money?'

'Of course I did,' she says.

'Then why didn't you do it?'

'Because,' she says, 'I don't want to give anyone more of a reason to talk about me. I would like everyone to just forget who I am. It's better that way.'

She asks why I was crying on the tube. I tell her – not just the encounter with the man outside Jane's acting class, but everything. The reunion, and Faye, and Howie, and Donna. The fact that I wasn't hit. The perfect victim I turned out not to be.

'And now they're not talking to you?' she asks. 'The others?'

302

'No. They think I'm a liar.'

'I don't think you're a liar,' she says.

'You don't?'

'No.' She tilts her head at me. 'Do you think you are?'

The words take a long time to come. 'Sometimes I do.'

'What you said on camera – well, I watched it. Everyone did. And you shouted it, in a panic. You just wanted her away from you. You were fifteen. You haven't stood by it. You haven't spoken on it.'

'But I think I sort of have been . . . pretending,' I say slowly. 'I think I've been carrying myself like a traumatised person. Like someone who had something really awful happen to them. I think I even pretend it to myself.'

'I think I do too,' says Paget.

'Really?'

'Yeah. And I used to feel guilty about it because, really, what happened to me? A woman was mean to me on TV. That's not life-altering.' She dips her biscuit in her mug. 'But, see, I have this therapist, and she's helped me a lot with that. I don't treat it like a tick box exercise any more, you know?'

'But you never actually pretended. You haven't tricked everyone.'

'Did you trick everyone? Or did the show trick everyone?'

'I never spoke up. I never told the truth.'

'So? The way I see it, you don't owe anyone anything.' She finishes her tea. 'The way you grew up is allowed to have left a mark on you,' she says. 'You don't have to meet everyone's individual trauma yardsticks. You feel how you feel. It affects you how it affects you. If it takes a toll on you then it takes a fucking toll on you. No one else's opinion can change that, as much as they might try.'

I want to cry. I never realised how long I'd been waiting to be told that.

'But you also have to be brave,' she says. 'It sucks, but you do. You can't hide from all of this stuff forever.'

'But what does that actually mean? Like, what are you actually telling me to do?'

'Get closure,' she says, 'I suppose. You seem stuck. If you don't mind me saying.'

'I don't mind. But I don't think I know what closure looks like.'

'Unfortunately, I think it looks different for everyone.'

I look down into my mug.

'Sorry,' she says. 'I'm not sure this advice is particularly helpful.'

'Do you think I should talk to Donna?'

'Is there a part of you that wants to?' she asks. 'Do you have things you want to say to her?'

It takes me a long time to answer. 'I think so,' I say, eventually.

'You'll just have to work out if it's something you need to do or not.'

'The thing is,' I say. 'I don't even know what I need. As in, I don't know how much of it comes from me.'

'How so?'

'She made me feel like I needed her. Like what she thought of me was everything. So, do I want to see her because I want to get things off my chest? Or is it because I want to please her, still?'

'I see what you mean.'

'So, if I see her, I'm playing into her hand. But if I don't, and it turns out to be something I want, then it's like I'm holding myself back because I'm scared of letting her in my head again. And I just feel – well.'

'Stuck.'

'Exactly.'

'Then you should see her,' says Paget.

'You think?'

'You feel stuck. And you don't like feeling stuck.'

'Yes.'

'Maybe means you have to make a move. If your options are leaving things as they are, or seeing her, then maybe you need to see her. So that you don't stay stuck.'

We used to think she was immature. We used to say that she seemed younger than us. But she's been growing, since she left. None of us have grown. We're all exactly what we were a decade ago. Paget is the only one who got any of it right, in the end.

'How did you do this?' I ask her, finally.

She knows what I mean. 'Well,' she says. 'I cried a lot. And I felt sorry for myself. And then I thought maybe, after everything, I deserved to take myself someplace nice.'

That's the best way to describe it, her little flat in Crystal Palace with the plants and the sunlight and the copper watering can. It's someplace nice.

I meet Cameron in the bookshop as he's closing up and tell him all about it.

'I see what she's saying,' he says.

'You do?'

'Yeah. Obviously, my instinct is to tell you to never talk to that awful woman again.'

'But?'

'But that's because I'm scared,' he says.

'I'm scared too. I don't know if that's a good enough reason to not do it.' I sit on the counter as he does inventory. 'I think about her all the time,' I say. 'When I get dressed, I wonder what she'd think of my outfit. I imagine running into her in the street. When good things happen to me, I want to tell her.' Cameron leans on his elbows and smiles at me, sadly. 'I want to let her go,' I say.

'Do you think this will help with that?'

'Maybe. Maybe it will help me to stop feeling like I did something wrong, by never speaking up. Or maybe it will help me to forgive her. Or,' I add, 'maybe it'll make it all worse. But I think I'd rather know, either way.'

'Do you want me to be here, when you call?' he asks.

'I think I'll go for a walk.'

I wander a little way down the road, past the florists, to stand by the red post box. I lean on it as I unblock her number. My finger hovers over the button.

I feel twelve, and fifteen, and a hundred years old.

She answers the phone with my name, eager and uncertain.

'Hi,' I say.

'You called. I'm so glad you called.'

I'm shaking.

'Why did you call?' she asks when I don't speak.

'I'll meet you.'

'Oh,' she says, with a sigh so relieved that I feel it in my chest, 'Belle, that's *wonderful*.'

'No cameras. No mics. I'll walk out otherwise.'

'I swear. Send me the address, wherever works best for you. I'll make time tomorrow.'

I've said all I wanted to say. I can't say anything to her that I haven't prepared.

'I can't wait to see you,' she says, softly.

After I hang up, I stand between the post box and the florist's and close my eyes. I hope this is the right thing. I hope that this will move me forward through the swampy, marshy grey, through the heaviness, to whatever waits on the other side. I hope I will end up someplace nice.

Season Five

Within a week of Mum leaving, Donna had taken away my phone. She said it was making me ill, which might have been true. Word had leaked onto social media about my move to LA. Kendra had been posting videos online answering questions about the incident, the scene where Donna fired the entire cast, and it was safe to say that I wasn't coming across well. If people found me grating before, now they hated me.

'Everyone thinks I'm a terrible person,' I sobbed into Donna's shoulder on the sofa.

'No they don't,' she says. 'Don't listen to people online. Everyone loves you, everywhere we go.'

She was right, in a way. Directors and casting agents thought I was wonderful. Music execs couldn't get enough of me. At the parties and mixers Donna took me to, people would come up to me and say, 'Oh, you're Belle Simon! You're just fantastic!' We were cramming as many jobs as we could into my schedule because the work just didn't stop coming. I couldn't understand why so many people still wanted to book me when sometimes it felt as if I didn't have a single fan left in the world.

After I cried to her on the sofa, Donna told me that she was taking my phone for the sake of my mental health. 'It's awful for young girls to be stuck to their phones,' she said. 'It completely warps their body image and sense of self.'

'But I need to be able to talk to people.'

'You can still have it back to call your mum every Sunday,' she said. 'But who else do you talk to, really?' She was right. I let her take it.

We wrapped *Young Delicacy*, and I breathed a sigh of relief. I was ready to say goodbye to Lucy. It had been a gruelling shoot. I would come home with bruises on my wrists from being pinned to beds by adult actors. Donna told me that I should speak up, that this kind of thing would happen if I just gritted my teeth and bore it. But I didn't because I always wanted to say yes.

The day after we wrapped, Donna sat with me at the table and helped me compose a social media post about what an honour the whole experience had been. I posted behind the scenes photos of the two of us, and even one of me in my scandalous nightgown from the first day of shooting.

'Your mum is going to kill me,' groaned Donna, but she let me.

As a wrap gift, she took me to get my first tattoo, which I'd been begging for. I thought I might get a star on my wrist, but when the tattoo artist asked what we wanted she put an arm around my waist and said, 'We're going to get each other's initials.' I have always had a low pain tolerance. I tried to keep my face still, as the tattoo artist inked a delicate 'DM' on the side of my finger, because I wanted to look brave in front of the cameras.

'Fillers next?' I asked her as we compared ink.

'Oh, stop it.' She swatted at my ears. I'd become obsessed with the idea of fillers after a casting director had told me that I would look better with fuller cheeks and lips. I came home and pushed my cheeks up, trying to see if he was right. If he was, Donna had said, then it was easily corrected, but I was still a little young.

He'd booked me anyway, though. It was my first lead in a feature film, and it was a musical, which was daunting but made Donna incredibly excited. Filming was starting in a few months. I hadn't told Mum yet. I didn't know what it meant about going home. Home felt a little like a dream in those days. When I spoke to Mum on the phone on Sunday evenings and I heard Cameron bustling around in the background, they sounded like a radio show. But I hung onto it, the idea that all of this had to end at some point. That there would be a time at which I would rest.

Because I didn't have my phone, I didn't know about the leak until Donna told me. She sat me down and said, 'Belle, something's happened and I'd rather you heard about it from me.'

'Okay.' I thought she was going to say that I'd lost the film role.

'You know your first day on set for *Young Delicacy*?' she asked. 'When you had the wardrobe incident?'

My chest seized.

'I don't know how,' she said, 'or who, and *trust* me, I will find out, but . . .'

It wasn't the clip itself, but a photo taken on a phone, showing a paused video on a computer screen. The image was grainy, but you could see that my nightgown had slipped down. It looked as if I was deliberately exposing myself.

'Obviously,' said Donna, 'the police have been alerted and my people are busy scrubbing this from the internet. But you're a smart girl and you know that nothing on the internet is gone for ever. And now, people think that I put you, a minor, in a position where you had to get topless for a role.'

'Can't you just tell people that isn't true?'

She seemed annoyed. I couldn't stand it when Donna was annoyed.

'I can,' she said, 'obviously, and I have, but people seem to have a more general issue with you playing Lucy. Because people would apparently like to pretend that teenage prostitution does not exist and as such should never be depicted on television.' She rolled her eyes. 'It's not your fault,' she said, 'and no one's cross with you, but let's not have any more wardrobe malfunctions in future. This is ruining the reputation of a very good show before it's even been released.'

'I'm sorry.'

'You don't have to apologise,' she said. She still sounded annoyed. 'Your mother's been calling me all day, so you should probably speak to her.'

I couldn't face talking to Mum. I laid my phone down on the carpet beside me in my room and cried into my hands. I felt dirty. I didn't know how to bear the fact that the whole world had seen me exposed like that.

Donna found me about half an hour later. She came into my room and sat down next to me, wiping the tears from my cheeks.

'Oh, honey,' she said. 'I'm sorry if I was harsh.'

'It's okay.'

'It's awful. I'm mad at myself, really, that I put you in that position. I don't want people thinking you're that kind of girl.' She sighed. 'Why people have such a hard time separating the art from the artist I'll never know.'

'Has everyone seen the picture?'

'Not everyone. We're going to make it very hard to find. I'm sure a lot of people will never see it.'

'Okay.' My breathing was steadier now.

'It's all going to be okay,' she said. She stroked my hair.

She made me pancakes the next morning, breaking both the no sugar rule and the eating before 2 p.m. rule. 'Guess what?' she said. 'I've cleared your entire day.'

'Really?'

'Yes, because this is your treat day. You've worked so hard lately and with all this mess you deserve to be spoilt. So, guess what we're going to do?'

'What?'

She tapped her cheeks, then her lips. I jumped out of my chair to hug her, nearly bowling her over. She laughed.

'Happy?'

'Very!'

'Good.'

'I thought you said I was too young?'

'I know people,' she said.

She brought me to a salon in West Hollywood, where the very over-enthusiastic receptionist said, 'Belle Simon! You are just GORGEOUS in person!' and showed me to a big white chair. I nearly rethought everything when she brought out a long silver needle but Donna squeezed my hand, and I remembered that this procedure had been recommended to me by a very important person in Hollywood. This was for my career. It was smart.

The bruising was alarming. 'It'll go down in a few days,' said the technician, as I touched my puffy cheeks and lips. 'It's going to settle down beautifully, just you see. And we can do some more in a few months if you like.'

'No boobs until you're eighteen though,' said Donna, with a wink. I'd never even thought about getting a boob job.

In the car on the way home, I stared at myself in my phone camera for so long that Donna took it back from me. 'This is going away again,' she said, waving the phone. 'I don't want you becoming more Wicked Queen than Snow White.'

'Is this what it's supposed to look like?'

'No,' said Donna, 'it's still swollen. Didn't you listen to the woman?'

'Yes, but . . .'

'Are you not happy?' she asked.

My face looked alien. When we got home, I couldn't stop staring at it in the hallway mirror, touching it gently.

'Leave it alone,' said Donna, pulling me away. 'Are you crying?'

'No.' I hurriedly wiped my cheeks.

'Belle, you're being filmed.' No one would ever dare red card Donna.

'I know.'

'So why are you crying?' She was louder now. I was frozen. 'Belle?'

'It doesn't look how I thought it would look.'

'Oh, for fuck's sake.' She bent down close to me, blocking the view of the camera operative behind her. 'Be an adult,' she said. 'Can you do that?'

'I want to get it dissolved. They can do that, right?'

'Just let it go down, and then see how you feel about it.'

'I don't like it.' I was crying hard now. 'It's not my face any more.'

'So you've decided to lash out at me? To try and make me look bad, like this whole thing wasn't your idea?' I said nothing, still crying.

'Whatever,' she said. 'You're being a child.' She stood up, and then, as she moved away from me, she pushed the cameraman stood in her path so that his camera smacked into the wall, hard. I jolted.

'Get out of my way,' snapped Donna, stalking off.

'The lens is broken,' said the cameraman, not to me or Donna, but to the sound guy beside him.

'Take it out of Belle's pay!' called Donna. She slammed her bedroom door.

She was all sweetness and light when she came back down for dinner. She handed me an ice pack for my face and said, 'Honey, it's okay if you really hate it. We can get it dissolved. Just give it a few days.'

'Thanks.' I took the ice pack. I could tell we were supposed to pretend like nothing had happened.

'She's insane,' said Howie when he snuck up to my bedroom later. 'Like, I genuinely think she might be crazy.'

'She was just upset.' Inside, I wondered if he might be right. I'd always thought that Donna was the way she was sometimes for the sake of TV, that she chose to turn it off and on, but maybe this was just what she was like.

I asked her the next day if she thought I could take a trip home, before shooting started for the film.

'Oh, not for a while, I'm afraid,' she said. 'I just booked you a guest judging slot on *Small Voice Big Moment*.' This was a children's singing contest that Mum and I used to watch back in the Cotswolds and make fun of, because it was so unbearably twee.

I told Mum on the phone that I didn't have a gap in my schedule. Our communication was becoming more and more irregular. I hadn't told her that Donna was controlling my phone time – I worried it would make her angry – so she blamed me. She was furious that it took me so long to call her after the photo leak, and nearly frantic with worry.

'Just come home,' she'd pleaded with me, 'at least for a bit.'

'I've got this guest judging slot,' I told her now, 'and then I'm singing in a few places, and then I've got to start preparing for the film . . .'

'So Donna said no?'

'Well, it was both of us. It just isn't possible at the moment. Sorry,' I added.

She was silent for a few seconds. 'Belle,' she said, 'every day I fight the urge to come and take you away from that place.'

The morning of the day that *Young Delicacy* dropped, Donna decorated the living room with silver and gold balloons and bought tiny cupcakes with pictures of me on them. It was a still from the show – me posing in the doorway, arms raised to grip either side of the frame. She was arranging them when she looked up and saw me, and then she scooped me up in her arms and spun me around. I laughed.

'You're going to be a star,' she sang.

'I'm going to be sick.'

'This is your year,' she said, gripping my hands. 'The sky is the limit.'

She handed me a cupcake. Food before 2 p.m. *and* that food was cake? She was happy to the point of being delirious. I took it and stared down at my figure in the doorway.

'Try it,' said Donna, so I obediently took a bite. I wasn't often hungry these days. 'Okay,' she said, 'so we can celebrate for exactly forty-five more minutes and then we need to get you over to *Small Voice*. Feeling critical?'

'They're kids,' I said, taking another smile bite.

'So?'

'So, I probably shouldn't be critical.'

'I think we want your image to be nice, but tough. But fair. But hard to impress.'

'They'll be little, won't they?'

'It's ages seven to thirteen, so they're not babies. They should be able to cope with a little friendly criticism. You were in that age bracket when you first auditioned for me and look at you now. Skin as thick as anything.'

'Right,' I said.

I had a phone interview in the car as we drove to *Small Voice Big Moment*. I dodged questions about whether I'd felt safe on the set of *Young Delicacy* and talked about how wonderful Doug's direction had been, and how honoured I was that I got to tell Lucy's story. Donna nodded along beside me.

'Do you feel this was appropriate subject matter for someone your age?' asked the reporter.

'Well,' I said, 'in some ways, no. But that's the brutal reality of it. For lots of girls out there, they don't get to stop when the director calls "cut".' This was a line Donna and I had rehearsed together. It went down very well.

'Nicely done,' said Donna, after the interviewer had thanked me and hung up. 'I swear, if people try to crap all over your moment I'm going to be so pissed. What's wrong? Are you feeling carsick?'

'No,' I mumbled.

She pinched my cheeks. 'Big day. I get that you're nervous.'

I wasn't nervous to do *Small Voice Big Moment*. I was barely even thinking about it. I usually tried so hard to be sweet and chatty in the make-up chair, so that people would only ever have good stories to tell about me, but I was struggling to maintain conversation and after a while the hair and make-up people lapsed into silence. 9 p.m. loomed. As soon as I was done telling young children whether or not they could sing, the whole country was going to watch me have sex with an adult man. I felt sick.

Donna pulled me aside, as crew members bustled past. 'What's up with you?'

'Nothing.'

'This is live TV.' We had the slot before the *Young Delicacy* premier. Donna hadn't stopped talking about how exciting it was that viewers would be getting two and half consecutive hours of me. 'You're going to need to be dazzling,' she said.

'I know.'

'So why are you so flat? What's the issue?'

I whispered it. She leant in closer.

'What?'

'I don't want the show to come out.'

She started back as if I'd spat a swear word in her face. 'What do you mean?'

'I don't want Mum to see it. And everyone I know back home. I don't want them to see me like that.'

Donna sighed. 'How many times do I have to explain that your breasts are not going to end up on TV?' Her eyes fell on something just past my shoulder. She straightened up. 'Don't say anything else.'

We were wearing our mics. I was so used to having mine clipped to the front of whatever I was wearing that I barely noticed. Fred had somehow wrangled access for a handheld camera and himself backstage. I turned and saw him, standing a little way off next to the camera operative. Watching.

Donna covered her mic with her hand. She leant in close.

'I don't know what the fuck is going on with you lately,' she said. 'Get it together.' She straightened up, and then she smiled at me, dazzlingly. I blinked. 'It's going to be wonderful,' she said. 'Truly. There's nothing in the world to worry about.'

I opened my mouth.

'Nothing at all,' she said, before I'd even had a chance to speak. 'Okay?'

The stage was horrendously bright. I sat in my seat and squinted at it. Somewhere in the left of my vision, someone was counting down with their fingers. The audience murmured and shifted behind me. The host stood on stage, blurry, his finger pressed to his ear.

The crew member lifted a hand, disappearing into the wings. The audience went wild with a suddenness that made me jump.

'Welcome to *Small Voice Big Moment*!' the host boomed. He was a moderately successful radio presenter who I'd been interviewed by before. He'd asked if I had a boyfriend and then told me he bet I had lots of options. The audience roared intermittently at his opening monologue. I didn't take in a word. I hoped my face was doing what it was supposed to.

'Belle Simon!'

Shit. I found the camera – thank God for rehearsals – and waved into it almost frantically. I kept beaming.

'This is going to be a close quarter finals . . .'

There was a little girl waiting in the wings, a producer's hand on her shoulder. She only looked four or five years younger than me. She shuffled her feet in their shiny red shoes and breathed out with round, puffed-up cheeks. The producer's hand tightened its grip on her small shoulder.

On her other side, a woman with shiny black hair crouched down next to her. She was talking very fast, using her hands a lot but holding them very close to her chest. The girl was nodding. Her eyes were round. I watched as the woman with black hair rubbed her back and gave it a very soft slap.

Another round of applause behind me, aggressive and far too close. The girl's face changed, wide eyes crinkling as she pushed her cheeks up and grinned a wide, toothy grin, her small nose scrunching. She stepped out onto the stage. I watched her walk in slow-motion to her mark, shiny red shoe in front of shiny red shoe. She gripped the mic between her two hands.

We must have looked endless to her. Rows and rows of people stretching upwards and outwards, forever.

Her face fell. It crumpled, horribly, like it was folding in on itself. My heart squeezed with a force that hurt me. *No, no, no. Smile. Please smile.*

She was looking at me.

'Belle?' Someone's hand was on my back. It was the model turned actress beside me. 'What's wrong?' she asked, in a thick French accent.

I was clutching my chest. I only realised it when I felt the material of my dress between my fingers. They were wet. The audience behind me was deathly quiet. Had I been shot?

No, I realised. I was just crying.

Fred took me home. He put me in the back of his car next to the camera operative and drove in silence back along the freeway. LA was lit up in a hundred different colours. It was too bright. I could still hear the audience roaring in the theatre.

I gulped once, tears thick in my throat.

'You're okay,' he said, without turning round.

'I'm sorry.'

'Why? Not my show.'

They weren't filming me, I realised. Donna had taken the car with the cameras in.

'Is she cross?'

'Donna? Pretty mad, yeah.'

'Shit.' I put my head in my hands.

'But she brought it on herself,' he said. 'Thinks she's a producer.'

The quiet violence in his voice ceased my crying. I was too afraid to make a sound.

She wasn't home. They left me in the living room, just me and a camera operative who blended into the background like a pot plant.

'Friendly advice?' said Fred, as he left to return to the summerhouse. 'Don't turn the TV on, while you wait. Just sit there.'

'Okay,' I said. I couldn't make sense of this. I listened, anyway. I was scared not to.

After a while her car pulled into the drive. I heard the car door slam and the click of her heels on the concrete. She was on the phone. I couldn't hear what she was saying, but I could tell that she was using her phone voice. I wondered if it was my mum.

She opened the door and took in the scene. Me, sitting on the sofa with my knees tucked up to my chest. The camera waiting. She ended the call.

'Well,' she said, 'you're off the film.'

'What?'

'The musical. You're out.'

The news didn't feel like anything. She could have been telling me we were out of cereal. 'Why?'

'Why?' she asked. Her voice was cutting. 'Because you just had a breakdown two fucking minutes into a live TV appearance. Like a fucking damaged child star.'

'Oh.'

'Oh?'

'I'm sorry,' I whispered.

'Do you understand how that made you look? Actually—' She was yelling now. 'Do you understand how that made me look?' She strode over to me, kicking off her heels. She grabbed my wrist and pulled me off the sofa, so that I was standing, facing her. 'You turned yourself into a fucking cliché and the whole world just saw it! You will *literally* never work again with the shit you just pulled!'

'I'm sorry.' I was starting to cry again. My chest hurt from the effort of it.

'Do you even want this any more? Belle?'

'No,' I whispered.

'No?'

'I don't think so. No.'

I pulled away from her and walked blindly, the room tipping. I headed for the kitchen. She followed me, always just over my shoulder. The click of her heels coming steadily after me.

'So that's it? You're just throwing in the towel?'

My hand hit the kitchen wall, pushed off of it. I moved into the dining room. She was still following me. Nothing around me looked familiar. I couldn't work out where to go. This wasn't my home.

'You're an ungrateful brat!' she yelled. 'You think people just get to play at this shit? You think this is some game you can pick up and put down?'

Back in the hallway now. There was a camera there, suddenly, walking backwards with its lens pointed in my face. I headed straight for it. There was nowhere else to go.

'I did everything for you! I gave up my fucking life for you! And for what? What have you even achieved? You played a fucking whore on one TV show and that's how you want the world to remember you?'

We were in the living room again. We must have been walking around the ground floor in circles. My phone was on the mantlepiece, tucked behind the bowl of fruit that never went mouldy and that no one ever reached for. The camera gave way to me, following my side profile. In the mirror over the mantle I saw my face, small and white, Donna blurry in the doorway behind me and moving ever closer. I picked up the phone. It wasn't a conscious action. Nothing around me made sense any more. I just wanted my mum.

Someone tore the phone out of my hand with a force that sent me staggering backwards a few paces. Now my back was to the wall. She stood in front of me. Two cameras now – one side on, one looking me directly in the face. I hadn't even seen the other one arrive. She waved the phone at me. Her hair was pinned at one side and she wore a long blue skirt, gentle where it hit her ankles, unforgiving at her waist. Every breath forced her ribcage upwards uncomfortably high. She stood barefoot on the carpet and held the phone in her hand, the two of us smiling out at me from the lock screen.

'Who are you calling?' she asked.

'No one.'

'*Belle.*' She looked at me with true exasperation in her face. 'Why are you lying?'

'I don't know.'

'And why are you crying now?'

'I don't know.'

'Why are you looking at me like that?'

'I don't know. I'm sorry. I don't—'

'Stop it!' she yelled. 'Stop fucking crying!'

'I'm sorry.'

'Stop fucking apologising.'

'I want to go home,' I sobbed. 'I want to go home.'

'Why are you saying that?'

'This isn't right. You're *hurting* me.'

'I'm what?'

I held out my wrist, the same wrist she'd used to pull me up from the sofa. The bruises from *Young Delicacy* were faintly green now, but still there. 'You're hurting me,' I bleated. 'You're hurting me.'

She glanced to her side, suddenly calmer. 'Let's go talk about this off camera.'

'No!'

'Belle—' She took hold of my wrist again. I wrenched it away from her.

'Stop it.'

'Come on. Calm down.' I could feel her hands on my shoulders, moving me towards to the corridor. 'Let's talk about this off camera.'

'You're hurting me,' I sobbed, even though she wasn't. They were the only words I could find. 'You're— She's—'

I looked around for an ally, anyone, and found the lens. The endless, all-seeing black of it. Rings of white. A small dot of blue. I headed into it. I was swallowed by it. I could hear myself speaking.

'She's hurting me. She's going to hurt me. She's—'

Donna's hand went over my mouth. I prised it off.

'DO SOMETHING!' I screamed at the camera. 'DO SOMETHING!'

And then someone else's hand was in mine. Someone whispered in my ear, '*Come on.*' As Donna reached for me, her mouth open in surprise, someone else was tugging me away from her. I fell further backwards from her, pulled through the door into my bedroom, and then again into my bathroom. Small dots of light hit the tiles. I was still in my sparkly dress.

'Lock the door,' came a voice. I did. 'Belle? You with me?'

It was Howie. I was locked in a room with him. I backed up instantly, my hands on the doorknob.

'Hey,' he said, holding out a hand like he was trying to calm a horse. 'Hey. It's okay. It's just me.'

'What's going on?'

He held up a finger. There was a thump on the door, and then another. 'Belle?' came her voice. 'Belle, come out.' It was controlled, but I could hear the anger in it. I held my breath. 'For fuck's sake,' she muttered. The footsteps retreated, turning down the corridor towards her room. She slammed her bedroom door so hard that the whole house rattled.

'Breathe,' said Howie. I tried, taking shuddering breaths. 'Breathe.'

I couldn't even begin to process what had just happened. I sat on the toilet seat and wrapped my arms around myself. 'Fuck,' I was repeating. 'Fuck. Fuck.'

'Listen to me.' Howie crouched down in front of me. 'Shall we just leave?'

'What?'

'Do you want the two of us to just leave? Go? We can, you know. We can just get on a train or a plane somewhere and run away. She won't find us.'

I stared at him. I couldn't understand what he was asking me to do.

'This is fucked up,' he said. 'Every other person around you is treating you in the most fucked-up way. I don't understand how you can't see it. I mean, that fucking mirror shattered, and we're all watching from the shed, and you know what Rupe did? He did this.' He held up a finger. His face went blank. *Wait,* it said. He came to life again and his fingers found mine. 'I don't want it to be true,' he said, 'honestly, but I feel like I'm the only person left who actually cares about you.'

'My mum,' I managed.

'She left you.'

I wanted to tell him that it had been the right thing at the time. I couldn't remember why either of us had thought that.

'Let's go,' he said.

Things were starting to become real again. I was re-entering my body. I couldn't believe what I'd said downstairs. No wonder Donna was mad at me. She was right – she'd put so much on the line for me and I'd just run it all down. 'I can't,' I said. 'She'll calm down, and then she'll be fine.' He gave me a sceptical look. 'She always is.'

'You don't get it,' he said.

'What don't I get?'

'She's always wanted you all to herself. It's fucked, Belle.'

'She loves me,' I said. 'I'm like her kid, I guess, in a way.' He shook his head. How could I say it? I wanted her to want me. Even this, even tonight, this was love. It was passion, investment in me. It was evidence that I was the culmination of all her hopes and dreams. I was adored.

'I need to show you something,' said Howie.

It was a production tablet. He'd grabbed it as he ran out of the summerhouse. He unlocked it and held it out to me.

It was Rupert's inbox. I looked up at him. 'How did you get into this?'

'Please, he leaves himself logged in everywhere. I've seen Facebook messages from his girlfriend. Look at this.'

He typed in the search box: *Belle and Faye.* I stared at the words as they appeared. Howie pulled up an email. RE: Belle and Faye. Fred's reply to something, cc-ing Rupert. Addressed to Donna.

> *I'd rather pursue this, I think, keep it a group thing, but I get LA is your ideal scenario. We can keep this on ice for now and if things get stale in LA we go ahead with this, maybe fly F out? Does that work?*

I scrolled up, Donna had replied:

> *Okay, that's fine. We'll work with that for now if LA is still Scenario A. Doubt it'll get boring.*

I looked up at Howie, reading over my shoulder. 'Scroll down,' he said. 'Look at her first email.'

It was dated mid-Season Four. *Hey,* it read.

> *Become aware of something happening with Belle and Faye, think they're experimenting a bit together. Neither of them has said anything to me, probably embarrassed. Wondering if someone could keep an eye out, get a photo or a video just to be certain before we decide how to move forward?*
>
> *Thanks,*
> *D x*

Rupert replied:

Donna,

One of our guys caught this (attached). Thanks for the tip. Think this could be fantastic for S5. Fred, thoughts?

It's the photo she showed me, and a video of us kissing. I clicked off it quickly, aware of Howie watching me.

Can't use this footage legally I don't think, they're minors, Fred had replied. *It's a bit too sexy. But can def look into it for storyline.*

Then Donna's tone changed. She wasn't sure about the ethics of it, she said, and she pitched them LA instead, the two of us out here together. An explosive Season Four finale where the entire cast gets let go. *I mean, come on,* she wrote. *Wouldn't you watch that?*

Howie took the tablet back from me. I gave it up easily. *It's a bit too sexy* was echoing around my brain. I realised that I was shaking.

'She showed me that picture,' I said. 'She told me they were going to use that storyline if I didn't go with her.'

'Of course she did,' said Howie. 'Do you get it now? You aren't just her surrogate bonus daughter. You are the husband, kids and fucking family dog she never had.' He held me by the shoulders and shook me slightly, so that the tears slid out of my eyes sideways. 'Get the fuck out.'

Donna had taught me how to speak so that people thought I was wonderful. She had taught me to prioritise work over everything, and to be both stronger than my competitors and more pliable. She had taught me to tread carefully, to never say something that might make me seem difficult or in any way unwilling. She had taught me to smoke.

She had also taught me to drive.

My wallet was in her bedside table. Packing a suitcase would have been too risky. I took only my passport and my toothbrush. The keys to her car, which was sometimes driven by her driver and sometimes by Donna herself, were left in the bowl by the door. Her purse was abandoned next to it. I opened her wallet and took out all the notes I saw – I didn't count it, but I guessed it was over a thousand dollars. I slipped quickly out of the door, but not before placing my bracelet with its many charms – the music note, the heart for *Alice*, the planet for *Saturn's Return*, the champagne bottle she'd given me just after we moved to LA – gently down beside the bowl of keys.

Howie was waiting for me. He was in one of his black t-shirts, counting a wad of dollars quickly, licking his index finger as he flicked through. He looked up when he heard me.

'Ready?' he said.

'Whose money is that?'

'Mine,' he said. 'Now.' And then he grinned.

'Put it back.' I brushed past him.

'You need money for a plane ticket, Belle.'

'I know that. I'm not stupid.'

'I know damn well that you don't have any cash, and I also know that Donna has your card.'

'I've sorted it. Put the money back.'

'So it's fine when you take some?'

'I need it.'

'Right.' He jogged after me. 'Look, I don't have time to put it back. We've got to get going.'

'I'm going alone.'

'You can't drive.'

'I can.'

'You're fifteen.'

326

'I can drive. I'm going alone.' I was stood beside the car, keys in my hand. I didn't unlock it, even though by now I knew they'd probably seen me on the cameras. I was scared he'd get in if I did.

He stood beside the door. His arms fell limply by his sides, the wad of cash still clutched in his hand. One single green note fluttered down onto the driveway.

He looked dismal, standing there. He looked like the last familiar thing. He was Howie, and in some ways, I did love him. But he'd known about the videos. He'd probably watched them himself. I couldn't stop picturing him doing it, hunkered over the tablet, playing them over and over again.

'Why didn't you tell me?' I asked him.

He knew what I was talking about. 'I don't know.'

'It would have been so easy to just tell me. Then we could have been more careful. If you cared about me, you would have told me.'

'I do care about you.'

Not as much as he cared about knowing and keeping it close to his chest. Like it gave him some edge over me. Like he got to look at me even when I didn't want him to.

'I saved you,' he said.

I took a step backwards, as a test. He stayed where he was. I took another, and then I was running. I threw myself into the driver's seat and slammed the door. I turned the key. I hit the pedal.

As I pulled backwards out of the drive, someone came running out of the front door. I looked away from the wing mirror and straight in front of me, expecting to see Fred or Rupert, or a frantic assistant, or a camera. I wasn't sure if they wanted to stop me or if they just wanted a good shot.

I didn't think it would be her. She was in her dressing gown and bare feet, her hair pulled back. There was make-up under her eyes, like she'd been in the middle of wiping it off. I had never seen her so dishevelled, not in all the times I had stayed over in her house.

We locked eyes through the windshield. Just for a second, we were both still.

Then she started to run again, pelting forward with her arms spread as if she was preparing to throw herself onto the bonnet of the car. I pulled out onto the road before she could reach me. The image of her, white and open-armed, stayed printed on the windshield for just a second. Before I turned out of sight, I caught a glimpse of her in the wing mirror. She was still running.

There were no black SUVs speeding down the road to take me back. There was only the night, and the quiet, and the LA traffic. I willed the cars ahead of me to move. I trembled at every turning. About five minutes from my destination I ran a red light, and a cacophony of beeps and honks sounded around me. Gasping through my tears, I gripped the steering wheel tighter and kept going.

When I pulled into the LAX carpark, I didn't waste time trying to stay within the lines but stopped as soon as I was close enough to read the adverts near the entrance. If anyone yelled at me, I was too far gone to hear them. I scrambled out of the driver's seat and almost fell onto the tarmac. I didn't close the door. I ran towards the airport entrance with the toothbrush and passport and money in my jacket pocket, the car door still open behind me. I don't know why I left it like that. Maybe, even in the middle of it all, I remembered the cameras. Maybe I knew what a great last shot that would make.

Reunion special

She was in a movie called *Just Enough* when she was about my age, back when she wore her hair parted at the side and she'd just got her boobs done for the first time. There was a scene where she went up to a man in the restaurant he owned and begged him for a second chance. It went like this:

DONNA: I think we deserve it.

MAN: What?

DONNA: All of it. The house and the kids and the family dog . . . the whole picket fence picture. All of it.

MAN: You think you deserve it.

DONNA: No. Both of us.

MAN: You're still only talking about what you want.

DONNA follows MAN through the restaurant as he straightens cutlery.

DONNA: Well, I do think I deserve it.

MAN smirks.

DONNA: I do. I think I deserve the world. Don't you think I deserve that?

MAN: Sure. But I don't have to give it to you.

He did, though, at the end of the film. The final shot was the two of them stood in front of their white picket fence, kissing. Critics called it 'so sweet it should only be consumed in small doses, if at all'.

We'd watched *Just Enough* together, me and Mum, in the hotel in Trafalgar Square, a couple of nights before Season One began filming. Donna's eyes, the way her lower lip quivered, the way she strode after the man through the tables and pushed chairs out of her way . . . No wonder she got her picket fence in the end.

When she walks into the bookshop, her hands in grey mittens, her hair pushed behind her ears, she has the same look on her face. I stay behind the till.

'Hello,' says Cameron, from where he is stood by the bookshelves.

Donna says nothing. She looks at him for a second, and then back at me, over the till. I keep both my hands pressed on the surface of the counter.

Cameron pulls up a chair for Donna and one for me. Neither of us moves.

'I'll be in the stockroom,' he says. As he moves past, he lays a hand on my shoulder.

Donna waits for me. I begin cashing up. The clash of coins is louder than it usually is. I count slowly, under my breath. She watches. I write down the numbers. She stands there.

When it's all done, when there's nothing else to occupy myself with, I make a move towards one of the chairs. Donna takes off from her spot like she's on a spring. She walks in a semicircle around the ladder that Cameron has left propped up against the shelves and sits down opposite me, hands clasped in her lap. I look at her, and I realise she doesn't know where to begin. Or she's acting.

'You grew out your hair,' she says.

I want her to say something that doesn't make this sound like a scene from a film.

'Take off your coat.'

'I'm cold,' she says.

'There're pegs by the door. You can hang it up there.'

A small smile crosses her face. 'Do you think I'm wearing a wire?'

'There's no way they've sent you here with nothing. I'm not stupid.' She shakes her head. 'Take it off,' I say. 'Then I'll talk to you.'

A moment's more hesitation. Then she crosses the room and hangs her coat up by the door. She sits back down in the chair. When she pushes her hair behind her ears, I see that she never got her tattoo removed, like I did – it's still there, although slightly faded. What a ridiculous decision that was of hers, to get *BS* inked on her forever. I wonder why she never corrected it.

'Better?'

She looks younger than I thought she would. I don't mean because of the surgery and the make-up and whatever stylist she's working with these days. She just looks only twenty years older than me – which is what she is and what she always has been. I never put it together in my head that she was younger than Mum.

'This place is beautiful,' she says.

'Yeah, it is.'

'Do you read a lot?' she asks. I nod. 'You never used to.'

'I got into it.'

'Do you have a favourite?'

'Not really. I like Dickens a lot.'

'Well,' she says, 'aren't we fancy? I never thought I would hear that come out of your mouth. Why Dickens?'

'He just writes good stories.'

'Not too old and dusty for you, then? I always think of Dickens novels as being old and dusty. And having yellow pages.'

'I like yellow pages,' I said. 'And I like reading old things.'

'Why?'

'It's nice to know that people have always been more or less the same.'

'I understand that. It's why I like classic cinema.'

'You've told me that before.'

'I have,' she says.

Her hand reaches out to the bookcase beside her. She pulls out a book. *Ballet Shoes*, by Noel Streatfield. 'Have you read this?' I shake my head. 'You should. It's about little girls at dancing school.' She smiles, waving it at me.

'I know.'

'Like you,' she says.

I don't say anything. She slips it back onto the shelf.

'So,' she says. 'That was the famous Cameron. He's not how I imagined him.'

'No?'

'No. But he's nice?'

'He's very nice.'

'Come on,' she says. 'You have to actually talk to me, if this is going to work.'

'What do you want me to say?'

'I don't know. Tell me things. Let's just chat, a bit.' I look back at her helplessly. 'You know,' she says, 'a lot of people in my life told me I shouldn't do this.' Her finger trails along the spines of the books beside her. 'Kendra was very against it.' Her eyes dart quickly to my face, and then away again. 'But I felt it was only fair to give you a chance.'

'To give *me* a chance?'

'Yes,' she says, suddenly reinvigorated. 'I wanted to give you a chance to explain yourself. The way you've been behaving—' She shakes her head. 'Well, it's not the girl that I knew. I mean, it's malicious, Belle, truly. You were never a cruel girl.'

'I haven't done anything. I've said quite literally *nothing* about you.'

'Well,' she says, 'exactly.'

I shrug at her. My arms are folded.

'I blame the editing more than you,' she says. 'Rupert and Fred knew what they were doing. They hated me, by the end. Thought I ruined the good thing they had going.'

'Yeah, that was obvious.'

She waves a hand. 'Exactly. Even you could see it. So they chopped together all those things in the most awful way. The role on that TV show, with that gown incident, some stupid comment I made about a boob job, other things, mostly jokes, but all cut up like that I suppose they looked pretty damning.'

'How was that my fault?'

'That wasn't,' she said. 'It wasn't. But then you left. We have a fight – which happens, Belle, people fight – and they film me losing my temper—'

'You did more than that,' I said.

She looks at me with real softness then, like she's actually sorry. 'Maybe. But I did less than they implied. Than you've all implied since.'

'I haven't implied anything. I've said nothing.'

'They film me guiding you upstairs – to calm you down, those were my intentions, not that they showed that, and then the next thing they get is you running down the stairs with your passport and stealing my car and weaving down the freeway and running away from an open vehicle like you've got the Devil after you. I mean . . .'

Her voice is thick.

'And all those quotes you gave, when you were younger. All the stuff they pulled up where you talked about how the two of us had sleepovers all the time, all the horrible things they insinuated . . .'

They'd really run with those. It was stuff from teen magazines and small online blogs, interviews I'd given when I wasn't really anyone, where I'd just gushed about Donna and how close we were and how I had my own bedroom at her house and how she used to let me dress in her clothes . . .

'All it would have taken,' she says, 'is one quote. Just one statement to the press, putting an end to the speculation.'

'Mum and I said we would never talk about it all again.'

'Bullshit,' she says. 'You're doing a fucking reunion special.'

'It's good money. And they've said I won't have to talk about – that.'

'Convenient,' she says. Her voice is rising slightly. 'Just admit it, Belle. It was personal.' She still sounds like she's going to burst into tears, but when she looks up at me again, her eyes are dry. 'I need to hear you say it.'

'Okay,' I say. 'It was personal.'

She puts her head in her hands. Her shoulders shake.

'Stop it,' I say. I'm surprised by how sharp my voice comes out. I can tell by the way she jumps that she is, too. Her head stays in her hands. 'I still never lied about you.'

Her head snaps up again. Still no tears. 'You just said nothing. Kept your hands clean. I bet you were thrilled when you knew that's what they were saying.'

'That's not true.'

'You were, though,' she says.

'Donna,' I say. 'There's a lot I could have said. It could have been much worse than silence.'

'Like what?'

'People don't know you kept my phone away from me.'

'That was to protect you. People online were so cruel.'

'I was fifteen. I missed my mum. I needed to be able to contact her whenever, not just on Sunday nights. And the emails, Donna.'

She looks blankly at me. 'Emails?'

'Your emails to Fred and Rupert.' She has to know I saw them. 'About – about Faye and I.'

'I protected you in those emails.'

'You were the one that told them.'

'They would have found out anyway. I made sure they didn't use it, just like I promised.' She can see I'm not convinced. Her voice wobbles. 'I don't understand what I did to you that was so terrible. I loved you so much, Belle. I gave you everything. And when you walked away, I was hurt. I mean, it really hurt me. But I understood.'

I know she's lying. She has never understood.

'But I never expected this. I kept waiting for you to speak up, thinking, she's sulking right now but she'll snap out of it and she'll set all of this straight. But you let everyone go on thinking that I'd done something terrible to you, that I'd physically hurt you, that I was some kind of monster—'

'I didn't let anyone think anything,' I say. 'It wasn't me saying those things. Anyway, you did hurt me. You hurt me over and over.'

'I got you jobs you wanted. I got you fillers you asked for. I taught you how to have the body you aspired to have.' She sounds out of breath. 'Belle, I always took my cues from you. I would never have pushed you into anything you didn't want.'

'I was a child,' I say. 'I didn't know what I wanted. I just knew that I wanted to be loved.'

'And I did love you,' she says. 'Vastly. I loved you vastly.'

Despite it all, I do believe her.

'And then you ruined me,' she says, in a suddenly different tone. 'You ruined my reputation, my career—'

'Fred and Rupert never spoke out either.'

'They didn't know for sure what happened.'

'They did,' I say. 'They do.' I'm sure of it. Fred and Rupert have always known.

'Even if that's true,' she says, 'they aren't you.'

She looks at me, then, and there's something real in her expression.

'My Belle,' she says. She reaches forward to touch my knee. 'Were you always pretending? Did you really never love me at all?'

I can't bear the way she's looking at me. Like no parent should ever look at their child. 'I did,' I say. 'Of course I loved you.'

But Donna was never my mum.

She squeezes my knee. I sit rigid, with the distinct feeling that something is closing in on me. 'One quote,' she says. 'One state-ment. That's all it would take.'

She doesn't say it, but the implication hangs between us. *Don't you owe me that much?* But I don't. That's the point, the one Mum and Cameron and I fixed on between us when we sat at the kitchen table staring down at the headlines on my phone, all those years ago. I don't owe her anything. I don't owe any of them shit.

She sees the change in my expression. She pulls back and her face twists. Sickness spreading through my chest and into my stom-ach. Violent, lurching heartbeats in my throat. I want to crawl behind the counter and hide. I can't make myself move.

'You're a fucking monster,' she said. 'You're a spoilt fucking industry brat. You'd be nothing if it wasn't for me.'

She's entertainment. That's all she knows how to be. She's either the simpering heroine or the monster in the cupboard.

The sun has slowly lowered itself so that it sits right in the pocket of sky caught in the glass window over the door. Gold spills over the carpet and up my legs, stopping at my chest. Dust dances. Clouds move. Somewhere behind me, in the storeroom, pages rustle.

I am nothing. She failed.

Two days after I turned sixteen, Jane was born. She was three weeks premature. Cameron was taking down decorations in our central London flat when Mum's waters broke. It landed on the carpet just as Cameron's foot came down on a gold balloon, and he looked over at her in complete shock.

'Are you doing a bit?' he asked.

'*How* would I be doing a *fucking* bit—'

And so Jane's entry into the world began.

We called a car to take us to the hospital. She was coming fast. I sat beside Mum and rubbed her back helplessly as she curled up on all fours and made hooting sounds. Cameron kept trying to make conversation with the driver.

'Madness, isn't it, what women have to go through?'

'Leave the poor man alone!' yelled Mum.

She was born after only a couple of hours of labour. I took all night, according to Mum, but Jane was impatient. She was very small, but insistent. It took me by surprise, the definite way in which she grabbed my finger, like she knew what she was doing. I looked down at her, her rosy, wrinkled face with eyes that didn't look capable of opening, let alone perceiving a world unique to her. I thought, *this feels like a scene from a TV show.*

We tell her this story as we sit in the garden on our camping chairs. 'And then she looked down,' says Jane, ruefully, 'at this small baby in her arms, and she said, "I'm going to give her a grandma name".'

337

Cameron laughs. I take her hand.

'She called you Jane,' I said, 'because it isn't the name of a princess, but of a real, sensible, capable woman. And that is who she hoped you would become.'

After Jane goes to bed, Cameron says, 'I always thought she was named after Jane Austen.'

'Well, that too.'

We've got the kind of flat, rectangular garden I always wanted as a kid. Jane has a trampoline down the end of it. I bought it for her for her second birthday, as soon as she was old enough to jump. It's old now, and there's always leaves on it. Cameron's started talking about selling it, but even if it isn't safe to use any more, I still like looking at it.

There's a part of the story that I left out. I don't want to tell Jane how scared I was that I would hate her. But her eyes weren't even open yet when I held her. If Mum had left me behind for this creased unfurling of a small person, in a way, I understood. When Jane opened her eyes, I also wanted her to see something worth looking at.

I don't tell Jane this, but I do tell Cameron. He listens quietly.

'Are you ever angry with her?' he asks. 'Your mum?'

'For leaving me with Donna?'

'For any of it.'

I nod. I'm not sure if he's seen me in the half-darkness until he says, 'I am too, sometimes.'

'Really?'

'Because I imagine Jane in four years' time, and I think about how young you seemed when I met you, and I wonder why she let you call the shots so much. Why she didn't just tell you "no" and pull you off that show and make sure you never spoke to Donna again.'

'It wasn't that simple,' I say.

'Then why do you get angry?'

'Sometimes I think it should have been.' I watch another leaf land on the surface of the trampoline. 'She didn't want me to hate her for making me give it all up.'

'Would you have hated her?'

'Probably, for a while. But I wish she'd cared less about being hated. I wish she'd followed her gut regardless.'

'I hope I'll be able to do that with Jane,' says Cameron.

I hope so too, I think. But it's hard. I know I would never want Jane to hate me.

My phone rings. I pull it out of my pocket and stare down at the screen and then up at Cameron. He smiles. 'I think you'd better take that.'

I walk into the kitchen before I answer, leaving Cameron sat in the garden. 'Hello?'

'Belle?' says Faye.

'Hi.'

'Kendra said . . .' There's a pause. '*Did* you?'

'Yeah. I did.'

'Was it . . . awful?'

'It was okay,' I said. I don't know if I can say I'm glad I did it. I haven't worked that out yet.

She's quiet for a bit. I wait, cautious. I don't want to say anything that'll make her hang up.

'Why did you do it?' she asks simply.

'It's hard to explain.'

'Try me.'

'I didn't do it on purpose. I just – I said it, because I wanted her to leave me alone and I wanted someone to make her leave me alone. And then I ran. I felt like I'd been out there with her forever. I was so tired. Honestly, I didn't even think about how it would look. I just wanted to get away. But then the episode aired, and people were talking about it online, and then the think pieces started, and it all just got away from me so quickly.'

'I see that,' she says. 'I do. But what were you running from? What made you need to get away?'

There's no easy answer. It was the parties, and the meetings, and the people who told me I was wonderful to my face but said God knows what as soon as the door swung shut behind me. It was Donna watching over me as I sat at the kitchen table and went through the motions of doing schoolwork, as I lay on Lucy's bed on *Young Delicacy* and acted over the shoulder of an adult man whose body was pressed onto mine. It was the sudden frost that would invade her expression, the fear of not knowing what would happen if the rules weren't obeyed. It was the fillers, the fasting, that fucking photograph. It was crying on live TV. It was being all alone. It was missing my mum.

But the moment of ignition, those first sparks under my wheels – that I can pinpoint. That's where I can start.

'It was because of you,' I say. 'I left because of you.'

I never asked you what it was like, she texts me later that night. *The flight home from LA.*

Terrifying. I felt like she was on the plane.

What did your mum say when she answered the door?

She just said oh.

Oh?

Then she hugged me for like a year.

340

What did Cameron say?

He said nice to meet you.

She sends a laughing face in response.

'I wish I'd saved you,' Mum had told me, a few days after Jane was born, both of us too tired to be anything but frank. 'I wish I had been the one to come and take you away.'

'You were pregnant.'

'I know,' she said, 'but I still wish I had.'

I wished she had too. When she got sick, Jane's small mouth faltering around the word 'hospital', always dropping the 's' and the 'l' to make it 'hop-it-a', I wished it more than ever. It was hard to see her grow small and fragile before her time and know that I wouldn't remember her as a hero who would always be there, but as someone else I had loved with a frustrating caution and expected to have to learn how to do without.

That's not how I think of her now. Now, when I think about Mum, I don't even really think about the show or LA or Donna. I just think about our farm, and our strange sloping garden, and all the years we spent being everything to each other.

Anyway, she did save me. She gave me Cameron and Jane. She left me with somewhere to fall.

'What happened after that?' Faye asks me the next day when I meet her on Columbia Road. 'When you were home? What was it like with your mum?'

'It was okay,' I say. 'It was a bit weird, at first. She cried a lot, partly because she was pregnant. And I was kind of quiet. I was nervous around Cameron and I just clammed up in conversations about the baby. Didn't want to hear it.' I rub my thumb over my fingers, to warm them. 'I still felt guilty.'

'For staying in LA?'

'No,' I say. 'For leaving Donna.'

'Oh, Belle,' she says.

I think she might take my hand, for a minute, but she doesn't. 'What fixed it?' she asks.

'Nothing, really. Time, a bit. And Jane, a big bit. We understood each other more, with Jane, because it was like we were both raising her. Especially after Mum got diagnosed. But it was a strange kind of understanding.'

'Strange how?'

'I got to know Jane and Cameron. I understood why she'd chosen them.' I can feel her watching me. I keep my gaze on our shoes, walking in time. 'It still made me sad.'

I'm still waiting for her to hold my hand. I'd thought it would be more of a revelation, what I'd told her on the phone last night, but she took the news very quietly.

'And then what?' she asks.

'Real life.'

'More specifically?'

'You first.'

'I went back to school.'

'Did you really?'

'It was okay,' she says. 'It was nice, for a bit. I left when I was sixteen.'

She never tried to do music, she says. She worked in shops and cafes, not for the money necessarily but just for something to do. Sometimes she sang at open mic nights. It was hard to do it in London, she says. She kept thinking that Donna or Fred or Rupert would be there. So she went back up north. She wrote poetry. She painted. She learnt to make pottery. She tried to find something that would make her happy.

I tell her that I've never done anything. I've never even tried.

'What do you want to do?' she says.

'I don't know,' I say. 'Something normal.'

We've had a snow warning. It's a stinging kind of cold, the kind that leaves its handprints on your cheeks. Half the dogs that we pass on our way are wearing little jackets. That's what I'd like to do, I think. I'd like to get a dog and dress it up in a little jacket.

'You've got time to work it out,' she says. 'The luxury of money.'

'Maybe I just want to work in the bookshop for ever.'

'Well, that's okay.'

'Is it?'

She looks at me sideways, blowing on her fingers.

'The nice thing is,' she says, 'You don't actually have to be anything. You can work in a bookshop and take your sister to dance class and fall in love and drink wine in the street and watch the same film three times in one week, and it doesn't have to be depressing or boring or like you're not going anywhere, because you don't have to go somewhere, you know?'

'I want to go into my thirties having achieved something.'

'Stay happy,' she says. 'That's an achievement.'

We pass another dog. It's a very small, very fluffy dog in a tartan coat, and when it sees us, it pulls at its lead a little to get us. Faye kneels down and offers her hand to it. She straightens up. She smiles.

'I really like that one,' she says.

I watch her, smiling about the dog she likes, and the ache to move towards her is overpowering. She looks up at me. Suddenly she's standing, and her arms go around my neck, and I hug her tightly.

For a moment, everything is very quiet.

'I'm going back to Manchester in a week,' she says when we pull apart.

'Will the special be done by then?'

'Apparently.' We walk in silence for a few seconds. 'I was thinking maybe you could come visit,' she says. 'If you wanted to.'

'Oh.'

'You don't have to.'

'You still . . . You still want to do this.'

She stops in front of me, head tilted in her knitted hat.

'Belle,' she says. She takes my hand.

After a second, after we've started walking again, she says, 'This is awfully regressive of us.'

'Is it?'

'The two of us, back at the same shit. Some would say it's a sign we never aged past fifteen.'

'That's very much not the sexiest thing you've ever said to me.'

She laughs. 'Sorry, I didn't realise we were being sexy.'

'I'm trying to,' I say.

'Be sexy?'

'Grow up, I mean. Or grow past. Or whatever term I'll likely learn in therapy.'

'You're going to go back to therapy, then?'

'Maybe. Donna always swore by it. Not that that's an advertisement, thinking about it.'

She smiles, sadly. 'How was it?'

I tell her, as we wander along the street. She holds my hand and tries to understand with an effort that I can feel in every press of my fingers.

'What was the last thing she said to you?' she asks. 'Before she walked out?'

'She said that she hated me. Then she said that she was going to call me.'

'Jesus. What did you say?'

'Suck my dick.'

'Did you actually?'

'No. I said, "Bye, Donna".'

'I sort of wish you'd said the other thing.'

I smile. 'So do I.'

Hannah has a photo of all of us on her mantlepiece. It's from about midway through Season One. She's on Faye's shoulders, clinging onto Paget's hand to keep from falling. Kendra and I have our arms around each other. Roni is pulling a face. I stand in front of the mantlepiece as Hannah finds seats for Faye and I and try to remember that day. It must have been before *Alice* because my hair hasn't been cut yet.

'Cute, isn't it?' says Hannah softly as she passes me.

We're up there amongst her family. Near the back, but up there all the same.

Roni is in the kitchen, helping Hannah make tea. I wasn't expecting Kendra to show up but she's there. She doesn't look happy about it. She's sat off to the side on the window seat, arranging and rearranging the cushions. I take a seat on the sofa, feeling small. Her eyes meet mine, briefly, before she rolls them and looks away.

'Belle.' I look up. Roni is standing over me, holding out a cup of tea. 'Here.' Her face is kind. I take the cup, and she sits down across from me, beside Hannah. Faye takes a seat next to me on the sofa. Kendra stays where she is at the window, a little further off.

'So,' says Faye. 'Who's first?'

I open my mouth, but Roni cuts me off. 'Hannah. At 7 a.m. We're staggered after her.'

'I think we all need to say the same thing,' says Faye.

'I agree.'

'I'm not going to lie,' says Kendra, staring out of the window.

'No one's asking you to.' Faye sees my confusion. 'What's wrong?'

'What are you all talking about?'

'We have interviews to camera tomorrow. You're not on the call sheet. I guess we can assume they're going to ask about the finale.'

I still can't put it together. 'I just – I want to explain. You can all say whatever you want, but—'

'Belle.' Roni leans forward. 'Faye already told us everything.'

My mind goes blank. I wait for her to elaborate. Eventually, I ask— 'Everything?'

'The photograph. All the other stuff in LA. She filled us in. It's okay.'

I'd thought I was coming here to make my case. I'd thought they were hearing me out.

'Alright,' says Faye, as I blink back tears, 'what are we going to say?'

'I'm not going to lie,' repeats Kendra from her window seat. She has her feet up on one of Roni's side tables.

'Are you just here to say that?' asks Faye. Kendra shrugs. 'Why did you come?'

'I just don't think it's really enough. She's still been lying for years. She still made it seem like Donna was this monster. I mean, how do you know it wasn't all a play to stop Rupe and Fred from outing you both? It would have been worse if they'd found out on their own, wouldn't it? I mean, at least this way she stayed in control of the situation.'

'Oh, fuck's sake.' Roni presses a finger to her forehead. 'Kendra . . .'

'Yes, okay, she never outright lied, but it doesn't really matter, does it? She knew what everyone thought. Just because someone does something bad doesn't mean they deserve to have everyone think they committed an actual crime. Because that's what everyone thinks. And nothing Donna did was ever illegal.'

'Do you hear yourself?'

'And, like,' pressed Kendra, talking very fast, 'it would have been one thing if she'd actually leaked the picture, wouldn't it? I mean, that would have been unforgiveable. But she didn't, did she? She actually did protect you, like she said. And just because it was uncomfortable at times . . .'

'Why are you fighting her corner?' asks Faye. 'She never fought yours.'

'She did.'

'Really? When?'

Kendra is quiet for a second. 'I'm not as keen to hate her as you all are,' she says. 'I don't think it's so black and white.'

She takes her feet off the side table, curls her legs up underneath her on the window seat. She's back to staring out of the window, down at the passing cars. She seems skinnier now than she even did at fourteen, although I don't know if that's true, or if it's just the way she's sitting there with hunched shoulders, bony and pale, red hair pushed behind one ear.

'Kendra,' I say. She still doesn't look at me. Someone honks on the street below her. 'She cut you out of the *Brighton Street* audition. Didn't want them picking you over me.'

'Definitely comparable to hitting a child,' says Kendra. Then she turns. 'Did she really?'

'She told me like I should be pleased.'

'Were you?'

'A little.'

We share a smirk.

'She did it to all of you, at different points,' I say. 'She wouldn't put Roni up for anything that wasn't marked "ethnic". She tried to keep Faye away from jobs that involved singing.'

'Okay,' says Kendra, 'that's all true, but you realise, don't you, that none of that amounts to an actual crime?'

'You know there were worse things.'

'Yes, I know. She was fucked up now and then, especially towards the end. But she was trying to prepare us for careers in a pretty fucked-up industry.'

'It's not just her. It's all of it. Remember the stories we used to find online? The pictures people would doctor? That time we got rushed in the shopping centre? Hannah basically didn't go outside for months.'

'Yes,' says Kendra, 'that stuff was tough, but it didn't mess us up.'

'It messed me up a bit,' says Hannah.

She's sat on one side of the sofa, beside Roni. There's a cushion against her chest. She takes a big breath, as if the effort of the sentence is draining.

Kendra and I look at her. We look at each other.

'She never hit me,' I say.

'I know that.'

'But didn't she do enough else? I just want to be understood. And all of that stuff, it's too messy. It's too hard to explain.'

'Bullshit,' says Kendra. 'You liked that everyone though it was worse.'

'What's worse? Do I owe anyone worse? It was still all fucked up, even if no one ever hit me.' I take a breath. 'Look, I can be honest.'

'Do it, then.'

'I mean, I can be honest when I say that it's been nice. Having this thing, this concrete, traumatic by anyone's standards thing that I can hang it all on, I guess. That makes it all . . . valid.' I say the last word almost as a question. It sounds like such therapy speak. 'Or real. Or worthy of sympathy. It makes it neat. And sure, maybe the picture people have isn't entirely accurate. But they're on my side.

And I think I deserve that. I don't want to be hated. I know there were things I could have done better. I know that.' My eyes find the photo on the mantlepiece. 'But we were so young.'

'So you lied for sympathy,' says Kendra.

Faye puts her hand over her eyes, leans her elbow on the footstool. 'It's like you're not even trying to understand.'

But she is. I can see it in Kendra's face as she looks at me, that small, almost imperceivable give.

'If this comes out,' I say, 'everyone will call me a liar. They won't see the grey in it all. I'll have lied. That's all it'll be. You're right, what you said. People see everything so black and white.'

'You're no better,' says Kendra. 'You just remember it all as terrible.'

'I don't.' She raises her eyebrows at me. 'Seriously. There were lots of good parts. I think I'm lucky, on balance. I didn't used to believe that, but the more life I live and people I meet, the more it seems stupid not to. But I just—' I swallow. 'I don't think all the bad stuff should come to nothing. I gave a lot away. I just want some of it to be on my terms.'

'I think you're spoilt,' says Kendra.

'Okay. I'm sure lots of people think that. They could be right.' She smirks again, face turned to the window. 'Aren't there parts of it all that stick with you?'

'Of course there are,' she says.

She was so confident, at thirteen. It wasn't performative like it is now. It was hilariously innocent, the way she would parrot lines from cool girls in TV shows and establish herself as leader of any group she found herself in. She was always determined to be stronger than all of it, to be too smart to suffer and too clued in to ever let her mind rule her reality. It must have been horrifying, when she realised that she couldn't keep it all at bay forever. That she was now one of those girls who looked at herself in the mirror and sighed.

Roni thought the world should be fair, and Hannah thought it should be gentle, and Faye thought it should be honest. It isn't any of those things. All children learn that. Jane will learn that too. But she will learn it by degrees, and when she does she will run and bury her face in my shoulder, and then she will walk back out into it with one hand in mine and another in Cameron's, and no one will be judging her steps. At twelve or thirteen or fourteen, she will not be the sworn enemy or sole life-affirming force of strangers around the world. She will not be the sexual fantasy of men decades older than herself before she has started to bleed. She will not be expected to grow up faster than her body does, or to stay younger than her mind is. She will be allowed to fail with no one watching.

And the love that she experiences from the people who tell her what they hope for her will not be conditional. When we dream for her, we will do it tenderly. There will be no ego in it, or at least as little as we can manage. She will never have to wonder if she is enough for us.

'Why did you reply to Donna, when she messaged?' I ask Kendra.

She shrugs. 'I don't know.'

'Was it because you wanted to believe her?'

She's quiet. The red hair lying across her shoulders rises and falls.

'I'm not asking you to lie for me. I'm just asking you to understand me.'

When she looks at me again, her face half-lit and still, I know that she does.

There's a sequence in *The Real Deal: Ten Years On,* in the third episode, that Cameron cried when he watched. Cameron doesn't often cry, but when he sat in front of the TV with his hands on his cheeks, I saw tears falling through his fingers.

It goes like this: each of the girls sits in turn in front of the cameras. They tuck their hair behind their ears. They smooth down their clothes. A voice off camera asks them each the same question.

'Was Donna Mayfair ever physically abusive towards any of her students?'

'No comment,' they say.

Hannah says it quietly. Roni speaks clearly, her face set. Kendra tilts her head. The edges of her lips curl up. They don't cut away from her immediately, so you get a few seconds to take it in – that very small, very deliberate smile.

In Faye's take, if you watch very carefully, you can see the exact fraction of the second when her eyes slide past the interviewer, straight into the lens.

ACKNOWLEDGEMENTS

I've spent about half an hour trying to figure out a good and original way to begin these acknowledgements, and it turns out there isn't one, so I might as well dive straight in.

Thank you to the entire team at Lake Union who have made the process of publishing my first book so wonderful. To my editor, Victoria Oundjian – your enthusiasm and excitement about Belle's story made the editing process incredibly enjoyable, against the odds. Thanks also to Celine Kelly, for her considered comments and for pushing me to be better, and to Nicky Lovick and Frances Moloney. The process of putting a book out in the world is a long and complicated one, and more goes on behind the scenes than I'm likely even aware of, so to anyone else who has had a hand in *The Real Deal* to any degree – thank you.

To my incredible agent, Silvia Molteni – thank you for taking on a very inexperienced but very enthusiastic young writer and giving her time and space to figure out who she wanted to be as an author. Your guidance, patience and advocacy throughout this whole process has been invaluable. I can't tell you how much I've appreciated it.

To my earliest readers: Paul Shellard, Guy Moss, Ella Devlin, Dianne Devlin and Catherine Horden. Thank you for the encouragement and honesty. This book would have been worth writing even if you were the only people who ever read it.

To every teacher and educator I have ever had – thank you. I couldn't mean it more. An extra special thanks to Trevor Allinson and Edward Derbyshire of Pates' Grammar School and Caroline Lea of Warwick University, for making me feel as if I could really do it.

To my parents, who were a little unsure when their daughter chose to do a degree in Creative Writing but hid it very well, thanks for all of it. Especially the exam years. You're both saints. A huge thank you as well to all my family and friends who've been there throughout it all – you know who you are.

I didn't know where to start with these acknowledgements, but I knew where to finish. Thank you to Paul, who fell in love with my writing first, and who kept me both fed and sane throughout the entire process of bringing this book into the world. And thank you to Ella and Joe. I might still have started telling stories, had you never existed, but I would have gotten a lot less practice, and it would have been a lot less fun. I love you.

ABOUT THE AUTHOR

Photo 2023 © Caitlin Devlin

Caitlin Devlin studied English and Creative Writing at Warwick University before graduating to work in music and theatre journalism. As a teenager, she started writing novels as Christmas presents for her younger sister and brother. Since then, her work has been recognised by competitions such as the Iggy & Litro Young Writers' prize, the Flash 500 short story competition and the Exeter Writers short story competition. She is also a performed playwright. She currently lives in London with her partner and spends all her money at cafes.

Follow the Author on Amazon

If you enjoyed this book, follow Caitlin Devlin on Amazon to be notified when the author releases a new book!
To do this, please follow these instructions:

Desktop:

1) Search for the author's name on Amazon or in the Amazon App.
2) Click on the author's name to arrive on their Amazon page.
3) Click the 'Follow' button.

Mobile and Tablet:

1) Search for the author's name on Amazon or in the Amazon App.
2) Click on one of the author's books.
3) Click on the author's name to arrive on their Amazon page.
4) Click the 'Follow' button.

Kindle eReader and Kindle App:

If you enjoyed this book on a Kindle eReader or in the Kindle App, you will find the author 'Follow' button after the last page.